W9-CHO-109

Praise for
There's Something about Sweetie

"Hilarious . . . focuses on the brilliant qualities
that make us ourselves." —*TODAY*

"Adorable, joyous." —*BUZZFEED*

"A love story that fans of *When Dimple Met Rishi*
will adore." —*BUSTLE*

"Anytime your soul needs a hug, pick up
a Sandhya Menon novel." —*BOOK RIOT*

★ "Hits all the right notes." —*BOOKLIST*, starred review

"There's something about the way Sandhya Menon writes love stories.
I'm head-over-heels for this charming, funny, romantic, life-affirming
book." —Becky Albertalli, *New York Times* bestselling author of
Simon Vs. the Homo Sapiens Agenda and *Leah on the Offbeat*

"A thoroughly delightful romance featuring a spirited,
confident, and lovable heroine and an unexpectedly dashing
romantic hero. Add to your must-read shelves!"
—Melissa de la Cruz, *New York Times* bestselling
author of *Alex & Eliza* and *Love & War*

"There's something irresistible about Sandhya Menon's novels—
the romances are sweet and winning, the humor is cheerful
and sly, and the families are warm and complicated."
—Stephanie Perkins, bestselling author of *Anna and the French Kiss*
and *There's Someone Inside Your House*

"An entertaining romance." —*KIRKUS REVIEWS*

"Swoon-prone readers will wish the Patel boys
came in six-packs." —*BCCB*

Also by
Sandhya Menon

When Dimple Met Rishi

From Twinkle, with Love

10 Things I Hate about Pinky

Of Curse and Kisses

Sandhya Menon

There's Something about Sweetie

SIMON PULSE

New York   London   Toronto   Sydney   New Delhi

This one's for Jen

This book is a work of fiction. Any references to historical events, real people,
or real places are used fictitiously. Other names, characters, places, and events are
products of the author's imagination, and any resemblance to actual events
or places or persons, living or dead, is entirely coincidental.

SIMON PULSE

An imprint of Simon & Schuster Children's Publishing Division

1230 Avenue of the Americas, New York, New York 10020

This Simon Pulse paperback edition May 2020

Text copyright © 2019 by Sandhya Kutty Falls

Cover photographs copyright © 2019 by Jacob Pritchard

Also available in a Simon Pulse hardcover edition.

All rights reserved, including the right of reproduction in whole or in part in any form.

SIMON PULSE and colophon are registered trademarks of Simon & Schuster, Inc.

For information about special discounts for bulk purchases, please contact Simon & Schuster

Special Sales at 1-866-506-1949 or business@simonandschuster.com.

The Simon & Schuster Speakers Bureau can bring authors to your live event.

For more information or to book an event, contact the Simon & Schuster Speakers Bureau

at 1-866-248-3049 or visit our website at www.simonspeakers.com.

Cover designed by Sarah Creech

Interior designed by Mike Rosamilia

The text of this book was set in Adobe Garamond Pro.

Manufactured in the United States of America

2 4 6 8 10 9 7 5 3 1

The Library of Congress has cataloged the hardcover as follows:

Names: Menon, Sandhya, author.

Title: There's something about Sweetie / by Sandhya Menon.

Other titles: There is something about Sweetie

Description: First Simon Pulse hardcover edition. | New York : Simon Pulse, 2019. |

Companion to: When Dimple met Rishi. | Summary: Told in two voices, disappointed-in-love

Ashish Patel and self-proclaimed fat athlete Sweetie Nair begin to find

their true selves while dating under contract.

Identifiers: LCCN 2019004082 | ISBN 9781534416789 (hc)

Subjects: | CYAC: Dating (Social customs)—Fiction. | East Indian Americans—

Fiction. | Family life—Fiction. | Overweight persons—Fiction. | High schools—Fiction. |

Schools—Fiction.

Classification: LCC PZ7.1.M473 2019 | DDC [Fic]—dc23

LC record available at https://lccn.loc.gov/2019004082

ISBN 978-1-5344-1679-6 (pbk)

ISBN 978-1-5344-1680-2 (eBook)

Author's Note

I feel incredibly privileged to share Sweetie's story with you. For so many authors, stories rattle around in our heads for years before they ever make it on the page, and I am no different. In fact, I wasn't even sure if I would ever tell a story like Sweetie's—while I was living my life as a fat woman of color, I never thought beyond my immediate experience, my immediate pain.

Fast forward a few years, and I began reading more and more about the body positivity movement. Body positivity simply means taking pleasure in the body you're in, whatever that body happens to look like. Within the body positivity movement, "fat" is not a bad word like it tends to be in casual, everyday conversations. "Fat" is simply the opposite of "thin," and as such, carries no other moral connotations.

I remember reading voraciously every single article I could find about celebrating your body for what it is. Although at the time of this writing I am a thin person, at various points in my life I have been fat. Nothing has surprised or hurt me more than how differently people treated me depending on what I looked like on the outside.

When I first got the idea for a story about a fat athlete, I knew I had to make her South Asian. Growing up in an Indian household, the messaging I got every day was, "Unless you're thin, you're a failure as a woman." This was especially baffling considering my family was full of fat, beautiful, talented women. But I digress.

I wanted to write honest conversations between a fat Indian-American teen and her mother. I wanted to put the same messaging I—and so many others—got onto the page, and I wanted to have this strong, beautiful main character refute it on the page. I knew Sweetie would be the perfect person to take on this toxic, harmful messaging in her own sweet, gentle way.

If the word "fat" makes you cringe, I hope you'll stop and examine why that is. What do you think when you see the word "thin"? My guess is nothing, or at least, nothing bad. So then, is there anything inherently wrong with being fat? Or have we just been conditioned to see the words "worthless" or "lazy" or "bad" instead of "fat"?

I realize that for some readers, the word "fat" has been weaponized so many times against them that they'll never be okay using it to describe themselves. I completely respect that. My hope when telling this story is to encourage some long overdue discussions about what it means to move through the world when you don't look like a *Vogue* model. I hope you'll join me.

CHAPTER 1

Ashish

List of totally overrated things:

1. Love
2. Girls
3. Love (yeah, again)

Ashish Patel wasn't sure why people ever fell in love. What was the point, really? So you could feel like a total chump when you went to her dorm room only to find she'd gone out with some other dude? So you could watch your mojo completely vanish as you became some soggy, washed-out version of your former (extremely dashing) self? Screw that.

Slamming his locker shut, he turned around to see Pinky Kumar leaning against the locker next to his, sketchbook in hand, one purple eyebrow up (as usual; she'd probably been born like that, all skeptical).

"What?" he snapped, adjusting his backpack with way more force than necessary.

"Oh." Pinky blew a bubble with her gum and then continued chewing. She'd drawn all over her black jeans with a silver marker. Her parents would probably be pissed; no matter how often Pinky messed up her clothes for her "artistic statements," their corporate lawyer selves could never get on board. So yeah, they'd be pissed. But not as pissed as when they saw she hadn't thrown out that *Pro-Choice IS Pro-Life* T-shirt they thought was so "vulgar." "Still IMS-ing, I see."

Asking about IMS—Irritable Male Syndrome—was Pinky's common refrain when Ashish was grumpy. According to her, it was about time people began blaming cis *men's* emotionality on their hormones for a change. "I am not . . ." Ashish blew out a breath and began stalking down the hallway, and Pinky fell easily in next to him. She was tall—almost five feet eight—and could match him pace for pace, which was really annoying sometimes. Like right then, when he wanted to get away.

"So why do you look all cloudy?"

"I don't look—what does that even mean?" Ashish tried to keep his voice mellow, but even he could hear the thread of irritation running through it.

"Celia texted you?"

Ashish opened his mouth to argue but then, sighing, reached into his pocket for his cell phone and passed it to Pinky. What was the point? She could read him like an open book. It wouldn't be long before Oliver and Elijah, his two other best friends, found out too. Might as well get it over with. "I don't care, though," he said in his carefully-practiced-last-night *I am so over Celia, in fact Celia who?* voice.

"Mm-hmm."

Ashish didn't lean over to read the text with Pinky; he didn't need to. The words were burned into his freaking retinas.

I'm sorry, Ashish, but I wanted you to find out from me. It's too hard . . . I

2

can't keep driving myself crazy thinking about you. Thad and I made it official tonight.

Ashish had had to read the text about twenty-two times before it finally sank in that (a) Celia was truly going out with someone named *Thad*, (b) she'd been the one to move on first, and (c) Ashish's first real relationship had been a spectacular bust.

Ashish had been irrationally optimistic that he'd get to the moving-on stage first. He'd had to suffer the indignity of being dumped; the universe had to hand him the consolation prize of dating someone new before Celia did, right? Instead the universe decided to blast out a cute little song called "Ashish Is a Loser and Everyone Should Know It." Well, screw the universe. Screw it all the way to the Milky Way. He was Ash-freaking-shish. He was debonair. He was brilliant.

Okay, so he hadn't had a date in three months. So his basketball game was suffering a bit. His mojo wasn't *gone*, though. It was just . . . on hiatus. Kicking up its shoes on the table, snoozing. Taking a little trip to Hawaii or something. For frick's sake, even his über-nerdy, Boy Scout–level goody-two-shoes older brother, Rishi, now had a serious girlfriend.

Pinky handed the phone back to him. "So what?"

He glared at her as they rounded the corner to the cafeteria. Oliver, Elijah, he, and Pinky had eaten breakfast together before school started every morning since freshman year. Now that they were juniors, it wasn't even a tradition anymore—it was just a habit. "Easy for you to say, *Priyanka*. You're not the one who's in serious danger of damaging your playa rep."

"It's *Pinky*," she said, glaring at him like her eyes were blades that could slice and dice. "Only my grandma calls me Priyanka."

Ashish felt a prickle of guilt. He was being petty; he knew she hated to be called Priyanka. "My bad," he mumbled.

Pinky waved a hand. "I'm going to let that go because you're obviously having a bad day. But seriously. Just date someone else. Come on." She pushed him with her shoulder and scanned the other students at the lunch tables. "Oh, look. There's Dana Patterson. You've had the hots for her forever. Go ask her out, right now."

"No." Ashish pushed back, but not hard enough to knock Pinky over, though he seriously did consider it. His palms felt tingly, like they might be on the verge of sweating. At the thought of talking to a hot girl. What the hell was happening to him? "I—I don't want to ask her out, okay? It's just—it's weird to ask girls out in the cafeteria."

Pinky snorted. "Really? That's the excuse you're gonna go with?" They got in line for breakfast burritos.

"What's weird?" a familiar male voice said from behind them.

Ashish turned to see Oliver and Elijah, his two other partners in crime since middle school, saunter up to join him and Pinky. Oliver was the taller of the two, but Elijah had the muscles that just about everybody in school swooned over. They were both black, but Oliver was paler than Ashish, while Elijah was a shade or two darker than Pinky.

The four of them had been Richmond Academy's "Fantastic Four" since seventh grade, when they'd coincidentally—some might say fatefully—all concocted the same harebrained excuse about why they hadn't done their book reports on *The Scarlet Pimpernel*. Apparently, Mrs. Kiplinger, their English teacher, found it hard to believe that all four of their mothers' water had broken on the same exact day. The excuse was totally ridiculous, considering Mrs. K.

4

found out they were lying with a quick phone call to each of their moms. Despite (or maybe because of) their shared lack of finesse in executing subterfuge, they became instant best friends in detention.

Pinky answered before he could. "Ashish suddenly thinks it's weird to ask girls out in the cafeteria." She smiled at him spitefully and he rolled his eyes.

"Since when?" Elijah said. "You ask girls out in the greeting card section at Walmart. What's the difference?"

They'd laugh until they choked on their own spit if he told them he was nervous. "Nothing."

Oliver, the more empathetic of his best friends, put his arm around Ashish. "Aww. Tell Ollie what the problem is."

He didn't have to say anything, though. Pinky filled them in on Celia's latest text.

"I don't get it," Elijah said, frowning. "You were already broken up, right? Ever since you went to her dorm and found out she was out with that guy Thad. So what's the big deal?"

"The big deal," Ashish said, annoyed that his friends really didn't get it, "is that I thought this whole thing with *Thad* was supposed to be temporary. She said it wasn't serious. She was just . . . bored or experimenting in college or whatever. We were still texting. There was still the possibility that we might . . ." He stopped abruptly, feeling more like an idealistic loser than ever. He'd really thought they might get back together at some point, hadn't he? God. He wasn't the basketball-playing Romeo/*GQ* model he'd thought himself to be at all; he was a freaking Teletubby. And he was now seventeen. One year away from being an official, card-carrying adult. Why couldn't he keep a girlfriend?

Oliver, sensing his embarrassment, pulled Ashish closer. "I'm telling you, Ash, you gotta just get back up on the horse again. Just do it. Celia's doing it."

"Yeah, man," Elijah added. "It doesn't even have to be a particularly nice horse. Any old mare will do."

Pinky glared at him. "Nice."

Elijah made a *What?* face, and Oliver shook his head and sighed. Pinky turned to Ashish. "Look, if you're afraid, I can do it for you. I know Dana . . . sort of." She took a half step in Dana's direction.

Ashish grabbed her shoulder. "I'm not *afraid*, for crap's sake."

"Then do it," Pinky said, crossing her arms. "Right now. You won't have a better opportunity." Ashish darted a longing glance at the burritos, and she added, "I'll save your place in line."

Ashish adjusted his backpack and surreptitiously wiped his definitely damp palms on his shorts. "Fine. You jerks." And then he walked over to where Dana sat with the other cheerleaders, dressed in a crop top and amazingly tight jeans. She'd probably end up in the principal's office over that outfit before the day ended, but that was the cool thing about Dana: She just never gave up.

She looked up as Ashish approached, her face breaking into a smile. Tucking a strand of short blond hair behind one ear, she slid over on the bench. "Ash! Come sit with us."

Dana had been pretty openly flirty with him at the last few basketball games, even given that he'd been a ball-fumbling shadow of his former shining-captain-of-the-team self. Ashish knew she'd say yes if he asked her. He *should* ask her. Pinky, Oliver, and Elijah were right: The only way forward was through. He needed to get this first-date-after-Celia thing out of the way. Jeez, it had been three months. It was way past about time.

"Thanks," Ashish said, sitting. He smiled at her friends Rebecca and Courtney. And then stopped. His smile faded. What was he doing here? His heart was so not into this, it was on another continent entirely. Ashish suddenly felt like a total jackass.

Dana put one hand on his. "Hey, are you okay?" Her blue eyes were soft and open, concerned. Her friends leaned in too.

"Fine," Ashish mumbled automatically. Then, as if his mouth had been charmed by an evil, sadistic magician, he found himself adding, "Actually, no, I'm not. I got dumped three months ago and last night I found out that she's making it official with a guy whose parents actually looked at his red, scrunched-up newborn face and said, 'You know what? This miniature human looks like a Thad Thibodeaux.' *Thad Thibodeaux.* I met Thad once at a party, you know. For some reason known only to him, he likes to punctuate every sentence with a thumbs-up sign. And she chose *him*. Over me. So what does that say about me, exactly? I'm lower on the dating ladder than 'Thumbs' Thad Thibodeaux.

"Oh, and let's not forget that the reason Richmond's spring basketball league has won any games these past few weeks hasn't been because of me. It's been *in spite* of me. I've been performing the same function as that chandelier in the student lounge that doesn't work. I look pretty but I'm essentially useless. I'd have been more useful serving Gatorade than taking up space on the court. I'm seventeen, and I'm already past my prime."

Whoooooaaaa. Ashish snapped his flapping mouth shut.

Had he seriously, literally just said all that to Damn-Fine Dana and her friends? Ashish thought he should be more embarrassed, but could he really fall any lower? See exhibit A: playing like a JV basketball newb when he was supposed to be the prodigy captain. Or appendix B: being dumped for Thumbs-Up Thad. He'd already scraped the bottom of the barrel. No, scratch that. He hadn't just scraped it, he was now curled up on its moldy bottom and preparing to take a very long, very soothing nap. Ashish Patel was beyond humiliation.

But Dana didn't move away with a nervous laugh like he expected. She took her hand off his and wrapped her arms around him instead. "Oh, you poor baby," she crooned, kind of rocking him. Ashish only vaguely noticed her boobs pressed up against his arm. *Meh, boobs*, he thought, and then: *Oh my God, what has Celia done to me?*

"Breakups are the worst," Rebecca added, reaching over the table to pat his arm. The beads on her braids clicked together. "I'm sorry."

"It's totally her loss, Ash," Courtney said, tossing her curly red hair. "You're a hottie."

"Absolutely," Dana said, letting go of him to take his chin in her hand. "You're gorgeous."

Ashish smiled faintly and ran a hand through his hair. "Yeah, I know. But thanks. I just feel really . . . off."

"Totally normal," Dana said, leaning over to kiss his cheek. "But when you're ready to get some revenge, you just let me know, okay?"

Oh God. The pity in her eyes. He was a charity case. He was a storm-soaked puppy. Ashish sat up straighter and forced a laugh, which came out hollow and fake. "Ah, I'm fine. Really. And I need to get back to my friends."

With deliberate swagger, he pushed himself off the cafeteria bench and, throwing the best approximation of what Richmond Academy girls called the Ash Smolder their way, sauntered back to his friends.

"So apparently, I was wrong," Ashish said to them, smiling jauntily for Dana's benefit, just in case she was still looking at him. "I *can* sink lower. I've broken through the bottom of the barrel to the quicksand below."

"Dude, what're you talking about?" Elijah said.

Oliver grinned. "She kissed you, my man. On the cheek, but still. That's progress."

"Yeah, it was totally disgusting to watch, but I'm happy for you," Pinky said, stepping up to grab her burrito. "Really."

"Believe me, it's not what it looked like," Ashish said, feeling bad about bursting their optimistic little bubbles.

Once they all had their food, they sat at their usual table by the big window that overlooked the organic garden.

"So what happened?" Pinky said, tearing off a big bite of her burrito. "You were supposed to ask her out."

"I tried," Ashish said. A concrete wall of hot shame slammed into him as he recalled saying the words "past my prime" to three incredibly hot girls. What the hell? "I ended up telling her about Celia breaking up with me instead." He said the rest quickly and quietly, needing to get it off his chest but also hoping the others wouldn't hear. "And I might also have moaned about how much I suck at basketball and compared myself to a broken chandelier."

Elijah groaned, but Oliver silenced him with a glare.

Ashish took an aggressively nonchalant bite of his sausage burrito, to show he didn't care that he'd just embarrassed himself in front of three of the school's cutest girls. A guy had to retain *some* self-respect, even if it was all bullshit.

The burrito was Richmond Academy's specialty spicy cardboard flavor. Awesome. "Wait." Pinky gave him a funny look. "Were you in love with Celia or something?"

Ashish looked slowly around the table at them all. "Uh. Yeah. And she didn't feel the same way at all, so now I'm just some high school man-baby she can laugh about." Oops. He hadn't meant to say that last part. Talk about super-not-cool.

Everyone was staring at him in silence, their eyes wide. Shocked that Ashish Patel, player extraordinaire, had been in *love*. And that he was now completely wrecked as a result. The pity on their faces was the freaking cherry on top of everything, a special prize, just in case he wasn't feeling like enough of a loser already.

Pushing his tray back, Ashish stood. "You know what? I . . . I'm going home." And then he walked right out of the cafeteria, not even turning around when he heard his best friends call his name.

Sweetie

Sweetie held the shampoo bottle up to her mouth. It helped her get into the right headspace. In here she wasn't just Sweetie, she was Sizzling Sweetie, Sexy Shower-Singing Sorceress. She liked alliteration, what could she say?

"R-E-S-P-E-C-T!" she belted out.

"Find out what it means to me!" Kayla, Suki, and Izzy shouted back.

"R-E-S-P-E-C-T!" Sweetie sang again.

"Gimme those Jujubes!" Izzy sang, at the same time that Kayla sang, "Open sesame!" and Suki sang, "Mayfair, pretty puh-lease!"

They stopped suddenly, and then Kayla said, "Jujubes? Are you kidding me, Izzy?"

"Oh, like 'Open sesame' is any better?" Suki retorted from her shower stall.

"What about 'Mayfair'?" Izzy said. "That doesn't even make sense!"

"Guys, guys," Sweetie called. "It's 'Take care, TCB.'"

"What?" the three girls chorused back.

"What does that even mean?" Suki said.

"Nothing, that's what," Kayla said. "If you ask me . . ."

Sweetie knew the argument could go on forever, so she just launched into the "Sock it to me" stanza. The others fell quiet, listening.

This was how they were, their postpractice showers. The other girls on the team didn't even say anything; they enjoyed it when Sweetie began to sing.

She shimmied in the shower, her round, robust voice echoing across the tile like a symphony of clear bells, bouncing off the glinting silver faucet and showerhead. When she was done, she bowed her head, letting the water rush over her, her arms held up high and triumphant.

There was thunderous applause, just like every other time. Sweetie closed her eyes and smiled, enjoying this one moment when she felt supremely confident and unquestionably beautiful.

Then as the last of the applause faded, she sighed, turned off the shower, and reached for her towel.

Out by her locker, Sweetie dried off and climbed into her clothes quickly. She didn't even know why she was moving quickly. . . .

It wasn't like Kayla, Suki, and Izzy would judge her. But Amma's voice echoed in her head: *Cover your legs and your arms. Until you lose weight, you shouldn't wear sleeveless tops and shorts.* If her mother felt that strongly about a sleeveless shirt, she could imagine what she'd say about Sweetie being naked in the girls' locker room.

"You slayed it, as usual!" Kayla called from her locker. Her deep-brown skin was flawless, her abdomen toned and her legs shapely. She didn't rush to put on her clothes.

"Thanks. You weren't so bad yourself." Sweetie smiled, trying to shake off her thoughts. She'd kicked butt on the track today, beating her own best time on the 1600 meter run. She should be feeling nothing but happiness. *My body is strong and does everything I want it to do*, she told herself, repeating the mantra she'd always chanted silently after one of Amma's "motivational" talks. *I'm the fastest runner at Piedmont High School, and the second-fastest high school student in the state of California.*

It was true, too. Sweetie could leave anyone in the dust. There was a reason the local paper had called her the Piedmont Road Runner recently (but it had been a mistake to read the comments on the online article—those were full of people who couldn't stop asking variants of the asinine question, How does she lug all of that around the track?). Coach was always telling her she could get a scholarship to pretty much any college if she kept it up.

"Hoo, check this out!" Suki called from her locker. She'd thrown on a skirt and a top and was sitting on the bench, bent over her cell phone as usual, her straight black hair all wet.

They gathered around her. It was a picture of a handsome guy in a basketball jersey on the sports page of the *Times of Atherton*, the local paper.

"Ashish Patel at last weekend's game," Izzy said, leaning in. Her pale cheeks were flushed from the hot shower. "Yum-eeee."

"I heard he led Richmond to another victory," Kayla said. "He's their golden goose. Coach Stevens wants to poach him."

"Good luck with that," Izzy scoffed. "His dad's the CEO of Global Comm. His kind of money would never go to a school like Piedmont."

Sweetie laughed. "We're not a hovel. But yeah, we're definitely not the Ivy League incubator that Richmond is either." She crossed her arms, frowning a little as she looked at Ashish's picture. "Is it just me or does he look kinda sad to you guys?"

Kayla, Izzy, and Suki just looked at her blankly.

"What would he have to be sad about?" Kayla said. "The boy's got everything."

Maybe on paper, Sweetie thought.

"Why? Is your Sweetie Sense going off?" Suki said, laughing.

Sweetie felt her cheeks get warm. She'd always been perceptive, prone to listening to her intuition about people. But Suki thought it was a bunch of crap, that Sweetie just believed what she wanted to believe. Who knew, maybe Suki was correct.

"Yeah, you guys are probably right." Slinging her bag over her shoulder, Sweetie said, "Hey, want to get some breakfast before class?"

Suki put her phone away, and her friends all stood, laughing and talking about how Coach had seemed even more stressed out today than usual, chewing viciously on a wad of gum. Then she'd yelled at Andrea for not giving 110 percent and had almost choked on it.

Sweetie kept one ear on the conversation, but her mind kept drifting back to the picture of Ashish Patel at his basketball game. What did a boy like that have to be sad about? Sweetie gave herself a mental shake. *Come on, what do you care? It's not like you'll ever find out.*

CHAPTER 2

Ashish

Ditching school was a nonevent, as always. Ashish had made a digital copy freshman year of the one legit pass he'd gotten to go off-campus, and he'd been printing it out and reusing it ever since. Updating their passes to stave off delinquents like Ash obviously wasn't high on Richmond's priority list.

Ashish parked the Jeep in his circular driveway and trudged up the marble stairs into the house.

The moment Ma saw him, she rushed up and put her hand on his forehead. *"Kya hua? Sardi hai, beta? Bukhar hai? Bolo na, kya hua?"*

Ashish tried not to cringe away at the litany of questions about his health. Usually he let her think he was sick when he ditched, but today he just didn't have the energy. "No, Ma, I don't have a cold or a fever. I'm just . . ." They walked together through the foyer into the large den. Ashish took his favorite chair and Ma sat next to him on the ottoman. He leaned his head back and closed his eyes, sighing as she ran her fingers through his hair. "Girl trouble, Ma. Girl trouble."

Her fingers stilled for just a moment before she began combing again. It was no secret that Ma, especially, intensely disagreed with Ashish's *badmashi,* or "mischief," as she called it. Pappa tended to look the other way, chalking Ashish's medley of girlfriends up to his youth, or as he liked to say, Ashish's *javaani.* Recently, though, he'd looked pretty annoyed at all the texts Ashish was sending Celia, as if he thought even *javaani* should have some kind of limit.

Ashish thought both Ma and Pappa had been secretly relieved when the texts stopped, maybe taking it as a sign of their younger son hopefully becoming more mature and seeing the error of his ways. Ha. As if. That would be Rishi, Ashish's older brother and golden child. Ashish would always be the black sheep, the dark horse, the coal sack to Rishi's freaking diamonds—

"*Celia ke sath kuch hua?*"

"*Haan.* She broke up with me for good." He gave her a moment to wipe the smile he knew was there off her face before he rolled his head to look at her. "It really sucks, Ma. I thought we were serious. Like, I thought that at some point she'd get tired of being without me and come back. I mean, seriously, how could any girl not want *this*?" He made a vague gesture at his person. This was more information than he'd ever shared about his love life with her, but Ma's outward appearance belied any internal screaming that might be going on.

"Dude. Celia dumped you?"

Both Ashish and Ma looked up, and then Ashish groaned. Great. "Samir," he said, straightening and glaring at the Indian boy in front of him. "What sewer did you crawl out of?"

Ma slapped his knee and got up. "Don't be rude to Samir. I invited him and Deepika auntie over."

"That's right." Samir grinned and sauntered over, then lounged on the couch like it belonged to him. Well, he'd been over often enough that it sorta did.

Samir and Ashish had been frenemies since they were eight years old and Samir's family moved into the nearby estate. Rishi, of course, got along with him just fine. But what annoyed Ashish about Samir was his self-assurance. The guy didn't play sports and was homeschooled (the only Indian kid Ashish knew who was). As if that weren't enough, he was completely smothered by his overbearing mother, whose only fear was that something bad would befall her only child. Deepika auntie told anyone who'd listen that her little miracle was born with a caul on his face, which apparently was a bad omen and required constant attention to ward off lurking evil. (Ashish had looked up what a caul was online. . . . Big mistake. Talk about lifelong nightmares.) Still, in spite of everything, Samir thought he was a gift to everyone.

Rishi always joked that Ashish's and Samir's egos couldn't coexist even in the mansion they lived in, and maybe that was true. All Ashish knew was that Samir was not the person he'd want knowing his deepest, darkest secrets, and now he did anyway.

"Ashish!" Deepika auntie said, walking through the door. "Why aren't you in school?"

Ashish opened his mouth, but nothing came out. Even his ability to think on his feet—previously one of his best qualities—was shaken. Damn.

"He had a fever at school, so I let him come home," Ma said, winking at him when no one was looking. Ashish pretended not to see, just to salvage the tatters of his own ego. He didn't need rescuing, and especially not from Ma.

"'Fever.' Riiiight. Tell me what really happened, man," Samir said as Deepika auntie and Ma headed off to the kitchen, probably to get chai and snacks. "Last I heard, you couldn't stop bragging about your college girl and how hot she was."

Samir, of course, wasn't allowed to date. Deepika auntie said girls couldn't be trusted not to break her beautiful son's fragile heart, so when he was old enough (say, around forty-five or so), she'd find him a suitable girl. Even Rishi and his perfect Stanford-attending girlfriend Dimple's happy story wasn't enough to change her mind.

"We've been broken up for three months. It's, like, not big a deal at all," Ashish said, picking up a decorative glass ball from the bowl on the table and tossing it from hand to hand. He was doing it to show Samir how little he cared about the breakup, but he also wished Ma would stay in the kitchen, because she might just kill him if she saw him. She was weirdly attached to her knickknacks.

Samir clucked his tongue. "It's true what Mummy says, I guess. Girls can't be trusted."

"Whatever, man," Ashish said, feeling the heft of the glass orb in his palm. "I don't even know anymore."

"So, I mean, what's the big deal? Just find another girl."

Ashish laughed. "Oh, yeah. Because it's that easy. Dude, you've never even had a girlfriend, so, you know. Maybe STFU on this one."

Samir's cheeks flushed and he looked away. Ashish felt a little—a *very* little—bad for pouring salt in his wound. "So what?" Samir muttered. "I've seen you go through this a lot."

"Fair enough," Ashish said, because Samir really did have a point there. "I guess I don't know. . . . Something's off, man." Then, making sure to put on an extra-nonchalant tone, he added, "I'll figure it out, though. I always do."

"Unless . . . maybe . . ." Samir glanced at him and then quickly away. "Nah."

"Nah what? Unless what?" Ashish felt a prickle of curiosity. Samir never swallowed his opinions. It was one of the most annoying things about him.

"It's just . . ." Samir shrugged one shoulder. "Your parents did a pretty good job with Rishi, right? Setting him up?"

Ashish raised an eyebrow. "Yeah . . . ?"

"So, I mean, they could set you up too."

Ashish stared at Samir for a full twenty seconds before he burst out laughing. "Dude, are you serious? My *parents*? They'd probably pick someone, like, totally . . ." Shuddering, he paused, trying to think of an appropriate comparison. "Okay. Imagine the most delicious BLT you've ever had."

"Okay, easy. The one from that deli on Rivers."

"Yeah, amazeballs, right? Now imagine if they took out the bacon, lettuce, and tomatoes. Oh, and that spicy sauce they put in there."

Samir's smiling face sagged. "So . . . just two slices of bread?"

"Exactly. That, but in girl form. No, thank you."

Samir shook his head. "But that's not what Dimple is. You said she's, like, the perfect yin to Rishi's yang."

"Yeah, and it'd be totally different for me. My parents are constantly trying to rein me in. They'll just get me the most boring girl in the world, hoping she can tame me or something." He sighed and then, as he heard Ma and Deepika auntie walking toward the living room, added in a rush, "Oh, and don't tell my mom about the BLT thing." The whole Patel family was supposed to be vegetarian. Ha. As if Ashish would ever give up bacon. What would life even be without it?

"So, what are you two talking about?" Deepika auntie asked as Ma set a snack-and-chai-bedecked tray down on the coffee table.

"Gir—" Samir began before Ashish cut him off with: "School stuff."

They exchanged a glance; Ashish tried to make his extra withering. Samir was the kind of boy who'd share any old thought with his mom if he wasn't prepped in advance. The guy had no filter. Whereas Ashish, now, *he* was a connoisseur of secrets.

"Basketball *kaisa chal rahaa hai*, Ashish?" Deepika auntie asked, taking a sip of her tea. "I saw your photo in the paper."

"The season's going really well, auntie," Ashish said. "We're on track to go to state."

"Very good," she said, smiling at Ashish and his mom.

"I think I'd like to play basketball on a school team," Samir said sort of wistfully.

"You play at the country club," Deepika auntie said.

"Not the same," Samir muttered, but Ashish didn't think his mom heard him.

"You could do your senior year at Richmond," Ashish said, taking a cookie.

Samir opened his mouth to reply, but his mom cut him off with her laughter. "No, no," she said. "Richmond is very nice for you, Ashish, but Samir likes to study at home with me. *Na, beta?*"

"*Haan*, Mummy," Samir said, but his eyes were sort of bleak.

"Dude, you wanna go shoot some hoops outside?" Being around

Deepika auntie sometimes made Ashish feel like *he* couldn't breathe. He couldn't even imagine what Samir felt like.

"Sure."

They headed outside to the full-size basketball court Pappa had installed on their property freshman year, when it became clear basketball was going to be a serious thing for Ashish.

Ashish got a ball out of the ball holder in the corner and began to dribble. "So . . . you know you can just tell your mom you want to play at Richmond." They'd had this conversation many times. Ashish knew it wasn't apt to suddenly change Samir's mind, but he couldn't help it. Samir, as annoying as he was, was still one of his oldest friends.

"Nah, man. You know I can't."

Yeah, Ashish knew. Samir's mom had been diagnosed with breast cancer seven years ago. She'd beaten it twice, but it had come back. She was now in remission again, but her overprotectiveness had started when she was first diagnosed and Samir was very young. Now that he was older, he felt too guilty to say anything. They'd never talked about it openly, but Ashish had read between the lines. "Yeah, but . . . still. Dude, it's obvious you're not happy with the current situation."

"Are you gonna flap your gums at me or are we gonna play?"

Ashish narrowed his eyes. "Fine."

They played some one-on-one for about thirty minutes straight, and then Ashish tossed the ball to the side and shook the sweat from his head in a spray that doused Samir.

"Okay, seriously disgusting!" Samir grabbed a towel and a water bottle from the cart on the side that the groundskeeper restocked twice a day. They walked over to the bench to sit together in the shade of an old oak tree after Ashish had done the same.

Samir checked his watch. "We only played for thirty minutes. That's a record low."

Squeezing some water from the bottle into his mouth, Ashish shrugged, trying not to let show how much that bothered him. He used to love basketball. No, he used to *live* basketball. And now it was just like . . . an orange sphere that you slam into the ground over and over? What was the point?

"Don't you have a game this weekend? You should probably practice a little more."

"We're playing Osroff. I don't think it's going to require more than fifty percent of what I can give."

"If you do say so yourself."

Ashish shrugged, staring off into the distance at the swimming pool enclosure. "I know my strengths." Then, glancing sideways at Samir: "At least I *have* strengths."

"Pssh. You're just jealous of my baby-faced beauty."

"I'd rather have a rippling, masculine physique than baby-faced beauty," Ashish said. It was their usual way of ribbing each other, but this time it felt flat. Even his teasing mojo was gone. Damn Celia. She'd taken all his best skills.

"You're like some cardboard-cutout version of yourself, bro," Samir said, frowning. "I mean, I don't even care, but seriously. If you don't want to repel people more than you already do with your relentless body odor, you should probably do something about that."

Ashish focused on drinking his water. He could feel Samir staring at the side of his face.

"Damn."

"What?"

"I didn't know you were in love with her."

Ashish didn't say anything. There was nothing to say.

Later, when Samir and Deepika auntie were on their way out the door, Samir turned to Ashish and said, "Think about it."

"About what?"

"Asking your parents." Ashish stared at him blankly, and Samir leaned in. "You know. About setting you up."

Ashish rolled his eyes. "Are we back to that again?"

"What's the alternative? You zombie-shuffle your way through the rest of the year? Does that really sound fun to you?"

Ashish opened his mouth to answer, but nothing came out. To be honest, this mojoless feeling was the literal worst thing he'd ever felt. His entire world felt off-kilter, like he couldn't quite get his balance. It sucked.

Samir punched him on the arm. "Didn't think so." Then he turned and left.

Ashish walked back inside and headed upstairs to his room after telling Ma he had homework to do. Asking his parents to set him up was such a Rishi thing to do. *Ashish* found his own way around girls. He was *born* winking at the cute doctor who delivered him. He didn't need help.

Then he thought about this morning with Dana Patterson and felt a vague cringing inside that he knew would be full-on, cheeks-burning, armpits-sweating humiliation if he didn't wall it off immediately, which he did. He'd done his fair share of being both the breaker-upper and the breaker-uppee, but at no point had he or the girl in question ever felt bad about it. All his relationships had been window dressing, just a way to pass the time for both him and his girlfriends. Until Celia, of course. And that had turned out so well.

Groaning, Ashish lay back on his bed and covered his face with a pillow. He knew the truth; he just didn't want to face it. Maybe he hadn't ever needed help before. But he was all kinds of messed up at the moment, and he probably could use a little help. Or even more than a little. Maybe dating was like basketball. If the play wasn't working, it was time to try something new.

Still, asking his *parents*? That was totally outlandish and completely off the table, right? Ashish took the pillow off his face and stared at the ceiling. Yep. Completely off the table.

CHAPTER 3

Sweetie

Sweetie felt a heavy, sinking weight as her car edged closer to home. Her foot eased off the gas pedal automatically, and she turned up Kesha's "This Is Me," a favorite that always made her feel just a tad stronger. She pulled into the garage just as the song faded. Putting a smile on her face for her mother, Sweetie walked into the house.

Amma looked up from the stove, where she'd been stirring something that smelled like a heaven made out of cardamom, coconuts, and sugar. Amma didn't have a full-time job, but she did keep the Indian stores and bakeries within a fifty-mile radius stocked with her delicious sweets. She could be a serious businesswoman if she chose; she just didn't choose. Her full-time occupation, she always said, was being Sweetie's mother. (But her love of baking had obviously bled into the naming of her only child.)

"Hello, *mol*!"

"That smells so good, Amma." Sweetie walked over and dipped a finger into the pot and then stuck it immediately into her mouth before it could burn her. "Mmmm."

Amma swatted her arm. "No sweets for you."

Sweetie sighed. "Amma . . ."

"Go in the backyard."

"Can I at least have a minute to get a snack?" At Amma's arched eyebrow, she raced to add, "An apple."

"No. No snack. First you run, then you can eat." Amma brandished her spatula at Sweetie, and sighing, Sweetie made her way out into the yard.

The utter indignity of having to run laps around her backyard every day after school had not faded at all over the past three years. This had been going on ever since freshman year, when Amma decided there was a link between Sweetie's size and her activity level. The fact that Sweetie was on the track team meant almost nothing; Amma was convinced that Sweetie somehow slacked off during practice. Of course, Amma weighed about ninety-five pounds soaking wet, which might have something to do with her sincere belief that if only her daughter tried a little bit harder, she could be just as thin. The fact that Sweetie was built like Achchan and the rest of his family was totally lost on Amma.

The weird thing was, Sweetie thought as she ran, Amma wasn't happy with her own appearance either. She frequently pinched the skin on her hips and complained that it was too fat or that she was gaining weight in her "old age." If she ate more than a tiny serving at dinner, Amma moaned about how she'd have to eat only *kanji* the next day, this really disgusting, tasteless rice gruel she made Sweetie eat when she had a stomach bug. But Amma didn't seem to notice the contradiction in her own actions and words. She was adamant that Sweetie would magically gain happiness when she lost weight.

After the requisite ten laps, Sweetie came in and grabbed an apple from the fruit bowl. "I bested my time on the sixteen-hundred-meter run, Amma. And it's the best time on the team, too."

Amma, who was now scraping the mixture onto a pan, smiled at her. "Wonderful, *mol*. Now just imagine how much faster you'll go once you lose weight."

Sweetie froze on the way to biting into her apple. Her brain reacted in the perfect way: *But I'm already beating my own time and everyone else's*, it said. *Like, there's literally no one faster than me.*

But no matter how confident she felt in her own skills as a kick-ass athlete, all of that confidence evaporated under her mother's gaze.

"Everyone knows," Amma continued in the silence. "Thinner is healthier."

Sweetie bit into the apple, swallowing all the things she wanted to say: How she'd legit downloaded research papers off university websites about how what you saw on the scale did not necessarily correspond to what was going on internally. How this entire freaking "We're afraid for your *health*" angle was perpetuated by a society too afraid and too shallow to recognize a person's worth in any other way besides their dress size but too "polite" to always say it in those words.

What would it feel like, to just let loose? To finally tell her mother how she felt? Sweetie imagined it would feel like the sweetest, freshest breath of a spring breeze, but she really wouldn't know. The words always shriveled up before she could expose them to light and air.

"I'm going to the farmers' market this weekend," Amma said, washing her hands at the sink. "You want to come?"

Sweetie cleared her throat and finally broke her silence. "Sure." She always helped Amma run her baked-goodies stand at the farmers' market. Amma and a few of her Indian auntie friends all had booths for various things, and while the pretext was that it was good for a bit of pocket money, it was really more of a social networking (aka gossiping) opportunity for them all. Sweetie liked sitting in the sunshine, letting their rapid-fire accented English wash over her. "By the way, Amma, what do you know about Ashish Patel's family? You know, the basketball star at Richmond?"

Amma looked at her over her glasses as she took off her apron and sat at the table with a cup of chai. Sweetie went to sit by her with an apple and a chai of her own. "Why?"

Sweetie shrugged. "Just . . . I saw a picture of him in the paper. And I wondered if you knew the family."

"They're very prominent. Kartik Patel is the CEO of Global Comm, and their first son, Rishi, is supposed to be matched with a good girl at Stanford, Dimple Shah. I don't know much about the younger boy, but he seems to be on track to get into a good university. He's very handsome, Tina auntie says."

Of course she did. Tina auntie had a rating system of the prettiest desi girls and handsomest desi boys in her head at all times. She was like a walking Indian version of *People* magazine. Needless to say, Sweetie did not rank anywhere on her list. In fact, she was probably on some anti-list of some kind, knowing Tina auntie. "Top Ten Fat Feminist Desi Girls to Keep Your Boys Away from Before They Go Over to the Dark Side" or "Five Girls Whose Bodies Do Not Match Their Pretty Faces—BEWARE." To Tina auntie, Sweetie's fatness was both outrageous and personally offensive.

Amma turned around the magazine she was reading. "You can wear this for your birthday party, *mol*." It was a voluminous, somewhat shapeless *salwar kameez* made of thick silver brocade fabric. Sweetie was pretty sure she'd seen the mother of a celebrity wear it in one of Tina auntie's Bollywood gossip magazines.

"Um, yeah, I guess I could. . . ." Setting her apple down, Sweetie grabbed a catalog from the stack in the center of the table. Her sweaty palms stuck to the pages as she flipped through it, her movements feeling artificial and weird. Surely Amma could tell something was up? Wiping her palms on her shirt, Sweetie took a few surreptitious deep breaths. *Come on, Sweetie*, she told herself. *What would Aretha Franklin do?* She'd toss the catalog to Amma and demand some R-E-S-P-E-C-T, that's what. Sweetie flipped to the dog-eared page in the catalog and stared at the picture for a good ten seconds, psyching herself up. "Actually, Amma . . ." Her voice came out a squeak. Dang it. She cleared her throat and tried again. "I was, um, kind of thinking maybe something like this instead?" She slid the catalog over, her eyes on the page and nowhere near her mother's.

Amma took the catalog and studied the page, her face giving away nothing. Sweetie could see the outfit through her eyes: It was an Anarkali suit. The top was made of the most gorgeous emerald-green georgette fabric—long and flowy and mid-shin-length—and would expose just a bit of the pale-gold leg-hugging pants underneath. But the style of the top was what had caught Sweetie's eye and heart. It was a halter cut, and her upper back would be bare. Best of all? They made it in plus sizes.

Sweetie knew Amma wasn't opposed to halter-cut clothes like

some other Indian parents. Last Diwali, when Tina auntie's daughter, Sheena, had shown up in one, she had actually complimented her. Of course, Sheena was a size two. And therein lay the rub.

"It's really cute," Sweetie rushed to put in when Amma continued to study the picture in silence. The sound of her thundering heart almost drowned out her words. "And I think that color would look really good with my eyes. You know how you say they're light brown until I wear something green and then they look green? Plus, it comes prestitched, so you wouldn't have to take it to—"

"*Mati*. That's enough. You can't wear that." Amma put the catalog in the stack without looking at Sweetie.

"But . . ."

"No. People will laugh."

Sweetie swallowed the lump in her throat. Of course Amma was embarrassed. Why wouldn't she be? Sweetie was no size two, and apparently to her, that meant Sweetie was shameful, something to be hidden. Sweetie felt the bitter burn of hurt. "So?" she found herself saying. "Who cares?"

Amma looked up sharply. "Me. I care. You would too."

Sweetie stared at her, feeling that old pressing, weighing sense of disappointment. "Right. Okay, then. I won't wear that. I wouldn't want you and Achchan to be embarrassed by me." She got up.

"Sweetie, it's not . . . That is, I'm not worried about . . . ," Amma said, but when Sweetie waited, she stopped and shook her head. "Nothing. There's nothing to say."

Sweetie nodded and turned to go to her room. "Big surprise," she said under her breath, her eyes glinting with tears.

Ashish

"Chef really outdid himself this time," Pappa said, leaning back and belching quietly. "That *kulfi* was out of this world. Never tasted anything that came close to . . ." Then, seeing Ma's expression, he added hastily, "Of course, it's nothing compared to yours, Sunita!"

Ma laughed easily. "It's okay, Kartikji. After twenty years of marriage, I suppose I can take a little competition. Plus, if Chef frees up my evenings and I don't have to cook, then I'm a happy woman!"

She turned to smile at Ashish, and he returned it just a moment too late. Her smile faded. *"Thik ho, beta?"*

"I'm fine," Ashish replied. Then, forcing himself to take a bite of his dessert: "Yeah, this *kulfi*'s great, Pappa."

There was silence around the table, punctuated only by Ashish's spoon scraping against the small clay pot, or *matka*, the Indian ice cream had been served in. Ashish glanced up at both his parents; they were watching him with concern. Pappa's bushy eyebrows were pulled so low, Ashish could barely see his eyes. Jeez. As much of a pain in the butt as Rishi was, at least he'd been another person for them to pay attention to. Since Rishi left for college, it felt like 149 percent of their attention was always laser-focused on him.

Ma darted Pappa a knowing glance. Why did parents think their kids never saw that stuff? Ashish could practically touch the thought bubble she was transmitting at him: *TALK TO YOUR SON.*

"What's this, *beta*?" Pappa asked. "Ma tells me you're having some . . . problems? *Ladki vaali* problems?"

Oh God. The fact that Pappa had just said "problems of the girl variety" did not bode well. He was probably gearing up for a relationship talk. Pappa would just tell him again that this was his youth, aka *javaani*, talking, and in due time he'd find Ashish the perfect Indian girl just like he had for Rishi. To not take any of this seriously. To just live life. As if the pain Ashish was feeling were only as serious as a stomach upset, nothing that a cold glass of *jal-jeera* wouldn't fix. (Which, okay, the cumin drink was delicious, but it smelled like farts and no one ever talked about that. Anyway.)

"You know, Ashish, you're young. And in our *javaani* we must all make certain mistakes. Don't be so serious, *beta*!" As if on cue, Pappa laughed heartily. Ashish was pretty sure he'd laughed in exactly the same spot during the last relationship talk. Did he have a script stashed somewhere? "When the time comes, Ma and I will make that decision for you. And then you'll see the difference!" He and Ma smiled at each other.

Ashish glared at them from over the top of his *matka kulfi*. So smug. Oh, so smug. "Oh yeah? What difference is that?"

Pappa raised his eyebrows in a *Really? Are you serious?* way and then began to count off on his fingers. "Crystal. Heather. Yvette. Gretchen. And Celia." Then, holding up his other hand, he raised his index finger. "Dimple. See the difference?"

Ma cleared her throat and glared at Pappa. "What Pappa means to say, *beta*," she said in that gentle way of hers, "is that we have years and years of life experience that you don't have. So of course you're going to make mistakes. And be . . . hasty, hmm? It's no wonder you feel like this."

Ashish knew she was trying to help. But it just rubbed him the wrong way. They kept saying what a mistake this was. They kept implying he was just some silly kid, whereas they, in their infinite wisdom, would never make the same mistake he did. Like, the instant they thought of a girl for him, Cupid himself would descend from the clouds and rope Ashish and the girl into an everlasting bond. "So you're saying you'd never make a mistake? Whatever girl you found would be the perfect one, no question?"

"Of course that's what I'm saying!" Pappa said just as Ma said, "Not exactly in those terms, but . . ."

They smiled at each other and shrugged, like, *Well, if you want to put it like that, we won't stop you. . . .*

Ashish pushed his *matka kulfi* aside. Samir's voice began to echo in his ears. Something else, probably his survival instinct, told him not to listen to it. *Walk away, Ash, man,* it said. *Walk away while you still can. Before you make a gigantic mistake.* But Ashish was in no mood to listen. He just wanted to prove Ma and Pappa wrong. "Okay, then. Do it."

Ma and Pappa sat back and looked at him. "Do what?" Pappa asked.

"Set me up with a girl you think would be good for me. Rishi wasn't much older than me when you set him up with Dimple."

"Yes, but he was out of high school," Ma said. "Now is the time to focus on studies and basketball—"

"Ma, I never focus on studies, and basketball is going to be a part of my life through college, too." Ashish shrugged. "Unless you want me to ask Dana Patterson, the cheerleader, out." Like he could even do that in his current demojoed state. But they didn't know that.

Ma's eyes widened and she looked at Pappa, making frantic hand motions that, Ashish supposed, he wasn't meant to see.

"So you're saying you'll . . . date someone we pick for you," Pappa said. "I want to make sure."

"Yes, exactly. And I know I'm too young for this to be an arranged marriage or whatever, but it's the same thing with Rishi, right? I mean, he and Dimple probably won't get married till she's done with grad school at least. But *if* the girl and I don't get along, you have to both promise to never give me another relationship talk again. For as long as any of us are alive."

Ma and Pappa looked at each other across the table and then at him. They were both smiling. "Okay," Ma said, her voice bubbling with excitement. "But you are going to lose, *beta*."

Pappa nodded seriously. "You are going down to downtown," he said in his thick Indian accent, and Ashish couldn't help but laugh.

CHAPTER 4

Ashish

"Hand me the pink. I want pink because this poster's going to be really pink," Pinky said, reaching over Elijah for the paint.

"Say 'pink' again," he said, handing it over.

"Pink," she said automatically, beginning to paint in the lettering on her poster. Her hair was up in a multicolored pile on her head, and tendrils of green and purple and blue blew lightly in the breeze.

Ashish squinted down at the poster. They were all sprawled in the garden portion of the backyard, sheltered by a grove of trees. "So what's this protest for again?"

"They're developing that section of Bennington Park where Bennington Lake runs. Their plan is to drain the lake." She looked up at them, brown eyes wide in outrage. Her nose ring winked in the sunlight.

They all stared back at her, completely blank.

"So?" Elijah said finally.

"Um, it's where beavers live? Not to mention all the other wildlife they're totally gonna murder just to build another playground or whatever. It's unconscionable." She went back to stabbing the poster with her paintbrush.

"Right, right, unconscionable," Ashish said, itching the back of his neck. To think he'd actually wanted to go out with Pinky at one point in his life. Thankfully, they'd both realized, before it could happen, that they were too much like brother and sister for that to ever work, but jeez. He'd dodged a bullet. She'd probably make him sign a petition every time they hooked up or something. Her zeal was actually kind of hilarious because her parents were both the most buttoned-up, conservative people he'd ever seen. Seriously. They made Rishi, the rule-following traditionalist, look like a commune-living hippie.

Elijah and Oliver looked at each other, shrugged, and went back to helping her paint her THIS IS NATURE'S PLAYGROUND, NOT YOURS!!!! sign. Oliver had drawn an angry beaver family in the corner. (Ashish hadn't known beavers could be made to look angry. Oliver had gotten really creative.) They were all used to Pinky's ways. In kindergarten she'd organized a sit-in as a way to get more story time. It had worked until snack time rolled around and most of the kids lost interest.

"So what are you disaffected youth up to today?" Pinky said. Taking a moment to pause in her painting to glare at each of them, she added, "Since you're all too busy to come to the protest with me."

"E. and I are celebrating our two-year, two-month anniversary," Oliver said, and he and Elijah leaned over the poster to kiss.

"Don't smudge the beaver!" Pinky yelled, pushing them apart.

"That sounds so dirty," Ashish said.

Oliver raised an eyebrow at him. "Or you just haven't been with a girl in forever."

"Love is for losers," Ashish said. "Uh, no offense."

"On that note," a female voice said behind them, "Ashish *beta*, may I speak with you?"

Ashish spun around to see Ma dressed in a light silk top and pants, her sunglasses pushed up on her head. He smiled, his heart softening. Something about his mother radiated gentleness and kindness, and in spite of himself, he responded to it. Not in the devout-son way Rishi did, but still. "Of course, Ma."

"Hi, Mrs. P.!" Pinky called, not looking up. "You don't want to go protest at Bennington, do you?"

"Not today, *beta*," Ma said. "But if you stop by the kitchen before you go, Chef can send you off with a picnic basket." She'd always had a soft spot for Pinky.

"Wow, thanks, Mrs. P.," Pinky said, smiling up at her.

"And for you boys on your date, too," she said, beaming all maternally at Oliver and Elijah. "I couldn't help but hearing—congratulations!" Ma thought they made the cutest couple.

"Thank you!" Oliver and Elijah chorused.

She walked off a few paces and Ashish followed her, realizing that if she'd heard Oliver and Elijah, she'd also heard his beaver comment. His cheeks flushed. Ashish was a rebel, but he wasn't shameless. He didn't want his parents to know his mind was in the gutter 98.9 percent of the time. It was a fun gutter, but still. This was *Ma*.

Ma turned around and—thankfully—didn't mention any beavers. "Now, I wanted to tell you, when I set you up with this girl, I don't want any mischief. This is Pappa's and my reputation, not just yours, Ashish. Not to mention Sweetie Nair's reputation in the desi community. Vidya and Soman Nair don't want to deal with that."

He stared at her for a moment, not understanding. "Wait, wait." He took in her high heels, her red lipstick, her going-out bag that cost over $10,000 (he'd seen the receipt on the counter when she bought it early that year). "Are you on your way to talk to her parents *right now*?"

Ma laughed. "Of course not!"

Ashish relaxed. "Oh, okay, because I—"

"I'm just going to talk to her mother. And if it goes well, *then* Pappa and I will go talk to both parents."

Ashish's smile did a slow fade. He knew because he felt it melting off his face. "Um, what now?"

"Her mother sells baked sweets at the farmers' markets every week! In fact, we've bought some sweets of hers before at the Indian market on Pearson. You really liked the *gulab jamun*, as I recall." She paused. "Or was that Rishi?"

"Ma, please, focus."

She looked at him again but didn't seem particularly concerned by the panic he was sure was in his eyes.

"You're doing it today? I thought I had some time before you and Pappa went off on some kind of matchmaking rampage."

Ma took his chin in her hands. She had to practically climb a ladder to do it, but she managed. The heels helped. *"Beta, pareshaan kyon ho rahe ho?"*

Ashish sighed. "I'm worried because you're running off to do this thing and I sort of just said what I said on a whim. I mean, it wasn't even really my idea. Samir was the one who thought I should ask you and Pappa for advice, and then I did it out of pique, and now . . ." He took a breath. "It's all happening way too fast."

Ma squeezed his arm. "So you want me to wait?"

38

"Yes."

"For what?"

He looked at her. Huh. What was he waiting for, exactly? Yeah, he'd lost his mojo. But was it magically going to just return the longer he waited? Was he somehow just going to start playing basketball with energy and enthusiasm again like a flip had been switched? Was he suddenly going to twirl Dana Patterson into his arms and ask her out? Ha. To be honest, the only reason he wanted to wait was because he was . . . scared.

He was scared of what it meant that the only girl he'd ever truly loved had dumped him without a second thought. He was terrified that he was seventeen, had been in nearly a dozen relationships, and yet no one had completely given her heart to him. He was starting to believe he might be romantically unlovable on some deep, fundamental level. The thought made him physically shaky.

Oh, dear God. He, Ashish Patel, had somehow turned into a giant wuss.

Ma's voice jolted him out of his abyss of horror. "You're going to date a girl sometime, correct?"

He nodded, still not quite able to find his voice.

"So why not date a girl Pappa and I choose for you? Why not see how this plan works out? What do you have to lose?"

He looked into Ma's steady, calm, kind gaze and realized he really had nothing to lose. And if he wanted to fight that whole demojoed, unlovable, wuss thing, this was his chance. "Okay." He straightened his shoulders. "You're right."

Ma chuckled as she hitched her purse on her shoulder and turned around. "I'm always right, *beta*. When will you learn?"

Sweetie

Ugh. Why was it so hot in freaking April? Stupid climate change. Sweetie fanned herself with the stack of flyers that advertised Amma's business. All she needed was for Tina auntie to see her sweating like a pig. That was another bullet point on Tina's auntie's hit list: girls who sweat. Apparently, Tina auntie and Sheena only got "dewy," which was much more feminine and alluring than the salt baths Sweetie usually took. Of course, Sheena didn't do anything more athletic than lounge on a pool float, which might explain that.

"Customers!" Amma said, sitting up straighter and putting her magazine away.

Sweetie put her stack of flyers neatly on the card table and arranged the jars and boxes of sweets. She'd added little bud vases today with sprigs of baby's breath from their own garden, which Amma had really loved. Maybe next time she'd buy some burlap and tie the boxes with those for a vintagey look.

"Hello!" Amma said to the young white couple in their midthirties—a woman with a soft, slightly rounded face and a man who looked like he spent his weekends biking and drinking that awful green sludgy drink beloved by health nuts everywhere—who'd stopped by to look at the sweets. "Would you like a sample?"

"I'd love one! My husband and I are total Indian food fanatics," the woman said, reaching for a *peda*. She popped it into her mouth and immediately closed her eyes. "Oh my God, this is so good!" She elbowed her husband. "Try one, Daniel."

He laughed and took one reluctantly. "Oh, man. I'm going to be working this off all weekend, but okay." He had pretty much the same reaction as his wife, just about swooning over Amma's baking, which didn't surprise Sweetie one bit. "So, so good."

"So? Should we get a box?" the woman said, already reaching for the biggest one.

"Definitely." The man, Daniel, beamed at Sweetie and then at Amma. "Your daughter looks like she enjoys your baking, which is just about the biggest compliment any chef can get, am I right?" His wife laughed.

Sweetie froze. She didn't dare look at Amma, who was similarly unmoving beside her. The man continued to beam obliviously at them, super proud of what he imagined, Sweetie was sure, was a fantastic compliment. This was the worst: when people tried to be helpful or kind or nice in some way but just ended up making her feel awful. Just like the horrendous "such a pretty face" compliment, which implied that if only Sweetie could stop being such a cow, other people could enjoy her beauty more. This guy thought mentioning Sweetie's size was a compliment to Amma's baking, but . . . no. All it did was call attention to the fact that he thought it was okay to comment on Sweetie's body because she was fat, and that she'd obviously gotten that way by stuffing herself full of sweets.

"Okay, just one box?" Amma asked, breaking the horrible spell.

"For now," the woman said, laughing. "I'm sure we'll be back for more, though."

When they were gone, Sweetie sat back down, still refusing to look at Amma. "Where's Tina auntie?"

Amma paused slightly at the topic change before responding. "She and Sheena wanted to look at the stalls. Sheena's planning on a retro prom outfit, and she wanted to get the perfect necklace."

At least there was that. Tina and Sheena (ew, even saying their rhyming names in her head annoyed Sweetie) would've totally relished the moment that had just transpired. To be honest, someone was always commenting on Sweetie's body in some way, so there was always an opportunity for them to gloat and feel superior. Sweetie counted her victories when she could.

"That man is stupid, Sweetie," Amma said. Sweetie glanced at her, but Amma was busy rearranging the boxes, her small frame swathed in a bright-blue *salwar kameez*. Her hair was in a loose ponytail that fell all the way down her back.

"Yeah, but he's saying what everyone's thinking. Every single person who walks by this stall probably thinks I should stop eating your sweets. So I guess they're all stupid."

Amma turned to her, her eyes bright. "They *are* all stupid. People are stupid and thoughtless. That's why I want you to lose weight. So you don't have to deal with those remarks."

Sweetie shook her head, her brain ready with what she would say if only she were a little braver, a little less scared of letting Amma hear her true voice. *That's the thing, Amma. I don't want to change just to keep other people quiet. I don't think I can change and just suddenly look like you, but that's not even the point. The point is I don't want to. I like who I am. I just wish you could see that.*

"Hello!"

They spun around to see a fashionable Indian woman about Amma's age, dressed in a very expensive-looking silk outfit. Her Gucci sunglasses shaded her eyes for a moment, but she pushed them up on her head and smiled. Her dark-honey-colored eyes reminded Sweetie of warm, rainy summer days somehow. They were full of a cozy comfort.

"Hello," Amma said, nodding. "Would you like a sample?"

"I'd love one!" The woman reached over and grabbed a *kaju burfi*. "Mmm, so good! You know, we buy your sweets every month from the Indian market. And, of course, for Diwali!" Smiling, she brushed off her hands and pressed them together. "*Namaste*, Vidya. I'm Sunita Patel. I don't know if you remember me, but we met at a birthday party for a mutual friend last year—Tina Subramanian?"

"Oh, yes, of course." Amma pressed her palms together too, as did Sweetie. "*Namaskaram*. This is my daughter, Sweetie."

Sweetie smiled. "Hello, auntie."

"Sweetie." Sunita auntie regarded her warmly. "You go to Piedmont, no? I've seen your picture in the papers for your excellent running records. And of course, your parents couldn't stop talking about you at the party last year."

"Thank you, auntie," Sweetie said. *Please don't ask how I manage to run, please don't ask how I manage to run, please don't ask how I—*

"So." Sunita auntie looked over their table. "I will take . . . all of this."

They stared at her and then glanced at each other and then looked back at her. "All of it? Are you sure?" Amma asked.

Sunita auntie chuckled. "Believe me, I have a teenage son at home and another one who visits frequently."

As Amma made change for Sunita auntie's $500 (seriously, who carried that much cash around?), Sunita auntie said, "So, now that I've selfishly taken all your delicious treats, what will you two do?"

"Oh, maybe go home and start cooking some lunch!" Amma said, laughing. "You know how it is with teenagers. You have to cook early or they start moaning and groaning!"

Sweetie glared at Amma—she didn't think she moaned and groaned *that* much—but Amma didn't seem to notice.

Sunita auntie obliged with a laugh, but somehow Sweetie got the idea she didn't spend much time bent over a hot stove. "Well, if you're up to it," she said, "I'd love to take you both out for lunch to Taj. My treat!"

"Oh." Amma looked at Sweetie all happily, her eyebrows raised. Taj was one of those famous Indian restaurants where celebrities went to eat and every meal required middle-class families to mortgage their houses beforehand. Sweetie could tell Amma was besotted with Sunita auntie already, just like she was besotted with Tina auntie because of her "glamorous" ways. Sweetie had known Sunita auntie for only about two seconds, but she thought Sunita auntie was the much more glamorous and classy one of the two. "That would be so nice! Let me ask Tina if she wants to come."

Drat. Sweetie sighed surreptitiously. She had been looking forward to enjoying a meal at Taj, and now she'd probably have to listen to snickers and passive-aggressive comments the entire time instead. Eating was so fraught when you were fat: If you ate something unhealthy, thin people would say it was no wonder you were fat. But if you ate something healthy, they'd roll their eyes, laugh, and say, "Yeah, right."

After they packed up their stall, Amma and Sweetie made their way to the parking lot. Amma texted Tina auntie, who said she'd meet them there. The sun was full-on out now, blazing with a viciousness that made Sweetie want to fall to her knees and beg for mercy, but Sunita auntie seemed to be of the dewy persuasion. As they approached a large, shiny pearl-colored SUV with tinted windows, a man in a driver's uniform leaped out and rushed over to them.

"I'll take your packages, madam," he said, taking all of the plastic bags from Sunita auntie's hands.

"Thank you, Rajat," she said. Turning back to them, she asked, "Would you both like to ride in my car?"

"No, we'll follow you. We have to put our things away in the car anyway," Amma said, glancing at Sweetie. Sweetie could see the fangirling going on there. Amma was from a very poor family, and the slightest show of wealth had her completely starstruck. Which was weird because they were pretty well off too—Achchan was an engineer. But for some reason Amma didn't seem to see that.

"Sunitaaaa!" The high-pitched voice came from behind them. All three of them swung around to see Tina auntie power walking with Sheena in tow.

She was wearing skinny jeans and a black halter top, while Sheena was dressed in the exact same thing, except that her top was hot pink. She rushed over and grabbed Sunita auntie in a bear hug, which was kind of hilarious to watch because she was much shorter. "How are you, darling?"

Sunita auntie smiled sweetly, but Sweetie thought she could see the strain in it. Rajat, the driver, was stone faced as he climbed back into the driver's seat, having deposited Sunita auntie's bags in the trunk, but the corner of his mouth twitched. Sunita auntie stepped a half step back. "Hello, Tina. I'm well; how are you?" Her gaze flickered over to Sheena, who was looking down at her phone. "Hello, Sheena." Sheena flashed a smile and then went back to her phone.

"So, we're going to Taj!" Tina auntie said. She smiled very briefly at Amma and Sweetie before turning back around to Sunita auntie. "I went there on opening night, you know! It was packed with celebrities! I saw Will Smith and Jada, and they just looked so happy! I got the same thing as them—the lamb vindaloo. It was spicy. I hope you came prepared!" She trilled a laugh that nearly punctured Sweetie's eardrums.

Sunita auntie gestured to Amma and Sweetie, moving her body so they were suddenly part of the conversational circle again. She did it with a practiced gracefulness, so it wasn't completely evident she was doing it unless you were really watching. "I hope you both like it. The chef is supposed to be world class."

"I'm sure we will," Sweetie said politely. She already liked Sunita auntie. She was classy and glossy while simultaneously being approachable and momlike somehow.

Tina auntie and Sheena just about muscled their way into Sunita auntie's car, so Sweetie and Amma headed over to their sedan.

"So!" Amma said, just as the engine turned over. She looked at Sweetie. "You know who that is? Kartik Patel's wife."

When Sweetie looked at her blankly, Amma clucked her tongue. "The CEO of Global Comm?"

"Oh," Sweetie said. "Ashish Patel's parents?" Oh, right. Sunita auntie had introduced herself as Sunita Patel. "Well, that explains the chauffeured car and buying five hundred dollars' worth of sweets, I guess."

"And the invitation to Taj." Amma smiled. "But Sunita is very down-to-earth, you know. Very modest. I spent quite some time talking to her at Tina's birthday party. We have the same values for raising our children."

"Cool," Sweetie said absently. Ashish Patel's sad eyes flashed in her memory again. So apparently, in addition to lots of money and the adoration of hundreds of basketball fans across the state, he also had a really sweet mom. What was the hairline crack in his perfect life?

CHAPTER 5

Sweetie

Taj was just as opulent and pretentious as Sweetie was expecting, but it was still really fun to be in an environment like this one, so different from anywhere she usually went. There were models roaming around—beautiful, pin-thin people with peacocks on delicate leashes, iridescent feathers trailing behind them. Sweetie wondered what happened when the peacocks pooped. Or maybe they'd been trained not to do that somehow. Maybe they saved all their unsightly activities for after hours.

She saw the Indian maître d' (a brown Ashton Kutcher) take in her and Amma's not-quite-Taj-level attire with a slightly disdainful sneer. Then he saw that they were with Sunita auntie, and his entire face changed. He went from looking like a man who'd bitten into moldy bread to someone who'd just been visited by the lottery fairy. "Mrs. Patel!" he said, clasping his hands together.

"Hello, John," she said. "I don't have a reservation, I'm afraid, but—"

"That's not a problem at all, Mrs. Patel! You know we always have a spot for you. I will show you to your favorite table." With a smile, he led them toward a table upstairs, with a bird's-eye view of the entire restaurant. To either side, windows showcased the beauty of the impeccably kept rose gardens.

When they were all situated with their gold-foil menus in their hands, Tina auntie spoke up. "What's the occasion, Sunita? Why are we here today?"

Sunita auntie's glance passed over Sweetie, as if she was weighing something. And then she smiled breezily. "No real occasion. I was in the neighborhood and remembered you'd said Vidya is at the farmers' market on Saturdays. We were sorely in need of some sweets."

"Oh, well, good thing we were at the farmers' market too! Sheena was finding some jewelry for the prom, you know." She elbowed Sheena, who was still on her phone. "Sheena *beta*, you don't have a date to the prom yet, do you?"

Sheena looked up from her phone. "Well, I was going to see if . . ."

Tina auntie smoothed a lock of her hair off her forehead and she stopped talking. "It's so hard to find a good boy to go with, even as friends. These American boys just want one thing."

"Um, I'm American too," Sweetie said. "And so is Sheena. We were born here."

Tina auntie waved her hand. "Oh, you know what I mean, Sweetie."

"Not really," she mumbled under her breath, before going back to studying the menu. Ooh, they had lamb biryani. But then there was the shrimp korma, which was probably equally delicious. Oh, and she'd read on Zagat on the way over that the paneer makhani was a must. Dang.

"Sweetie's birthday—" Amma began in the silence, but Tina auntie cut her off.

"So is Ashish going to his prom, Sunita?" She was smiling so wide, Sweetie was afraid to look directly at her whitened teeth. And jeez, the lady had no game. It was so obvious she wanted Sheena to hook up with Ashish, it was almost like some sitcom situation.

Sunita auntie held up a finger. "I think Vidya was about to tell us something," she said, and she sounded so much like a teacher telling off an overzealous kindergartner with no manners that Sweetie almost choked on her water.

Amma smiled gratefully. "Oh, yes. Sweetie's birthday party is coming up in four weeks. We've been trying to find her an outfit."

"I already know what I want," Sweetie mumbled. She wished she were just a bit braver so she could say it loudly.

"So what kind of outfit are you thinking of?" Sunita auntie asked, leaning forward. "Something Indian or something Western?"

"An Anarkali suit, I think," Sweetie said. She noticed Tina auntie fidgeting, eager to bring the conversation back around to Sheena and Ashish. "I always like Indian clothes for special occasions."

"That's nice," Sunita auntie said. "I wish Ashish wouldn't be so opposed to wearing a kurta every now and again."

"Yes, but the Indian outfits for girls nowadays are becoming so risqué!" Amma said, shaking her head. Sweetie tried not to roll her eyes. "Halter tops and exposed backs . . ."

"Nothing wrong with halters!" Tina auntie laughed, wiggling her shoulders to show off her own halter top. "But of course, one has to have the body for it, no?" Smiling snidely, she took a sip of her water.

Sweetie felt her face get hot. Here it was, the beginning of Tina auntie's efforts to show, once again, how amazing she and her offspring were and how damaged Sweetie—and by proxy, Amma—was. Sunita auntie opened her mouth to say something right when their waitress, a college-aged Indian woman, approached.

"Hello!" she said, smiling brightly. "My name is Lakshmi, and I'll be taking care of you today. Would anyone like some lassi?" She looked at Sweetie.

The yogurt drink was one of Sweetie's favorites. "Yes, please," she said. "I'll have a mango lassi."

Tina auntie made a noise. "Not for me or Sheena," she said. "Lassi is one of the fattiest drinks you can get. We'll stick with water."

"I'll have a *jal-jeera*," Amma said quietly when it was her turn, and Sweetie's heart sank. She'd never, ever stood up to Tina auntie for her. Not once.

"I think I'll have a *namkeen* lassi," Sunita auntie said. She smiled at Sweetie. "After all, what's the point of coming to Taj and not trying their famous lassi?"

Sweetie smiled weakly. She got what Sunita auntie was trying to do. It just . . . didn't really help. She didn't want people making snide remarks at her, but she wasn't a charity case either. Why couldn't people just leave her alone? She picked up her menu and began to study it as if it were the most important thing in the world.

After they'd all ordered—Tina auntie helpfully telling Sweetie the dal had the least calories—Sunita auntie pulled her phone from her bag and looked at it. "Oh! Tina, do you remember that sideboard you saw in the dining room and asked about? Well, my furniture person says he just got another one in stock from France now, but he's afraid there's another customer who's *very* interested." She tapped out something and then made a face. "Mm. He says he can't hold it because she wants to buy it on the spot, but if you can get down there in the next thirty minutes, he'll give it to you as a favor to me."

"Oh, I really need that sideboard," Tina auntie said, looking genuinely distressed. "But all this food we've ordered . . . and I don't want to leave you!" She looked at Sunita auntie a little desperately.

"Oh, don't worry," Sunita auntie said. "I'll be sure to pack the food up and donate it to the homeless shelter on the way home. And I won't be alone—I have Vidya and Sweetie to keep me company, after all."

Tina auntie glanced at the two of them dubiously. "Yes . . . of course." As if making up her mind, she nodded and grabbed her purse. "Come on, Sheena! Let's go. Thank you for the heads-up, Sunita."

"Of course," Sunita auntie said, smiling sweetly. "Rajat can drive you there and then straight to your house so you can get it all set up."

"Really?" Tina auntie grinned, looking pleased. "But won't you need the car?"

Sunita auntie waved a hand. The golden ring set with pearls sparkled. "Oh, don't worry about it. I'm sure he can be back in plenty of time to pick me up."

"Great. Thank you again, Sunita!"

Tina auntie and Sheena tip-tapped out of the restaurant, Tina auntie's eyes laser focused, her expression hungry.

Sunita auntie took an audibly deep breath once it was just them. "I admire Tina's passion, but . . . sometimes she can be a little intense."

"Oh, she's not so bad," Amma said loyally. But why? Why was she so loyal to someone who was such a total douche?

Sweetie grinned. "Did you really get a text about the sideboard?"

Sunita auntie laughed. "No. But I did text Ishmael to tell him she was coming. Hopefully, he'll have something else to please her."

Sweetie relaxed. This act of kindness didn't feel like charity. She got the feeling that Sunita auntie genuinely didn't like Tina auntie too much, and the thought cheered her. The waitress arrived with their food, and Sweetie dug in with gusto. "Mm." She closed her eyes. "Those Zagat reviews don't lie. This is heaven."

Amma gave her an embarrassed smile. It was Amma's opinion that Sweetie should never talk about food. "If you act like you don't like it, then people will assume you have thyroid problems, *mol*," she often said. Because thyroid problems were sympathetic, but being fat was not. Fatness made you the enemy of the people.

"Isn't it delicious?" Sunita auntie said. "I've never had such good *aloo mattar*." Dabbing her mouth with a napkin, she said, "You know, my oldest son, Rishi, loves *aloo mattar*." She smiled a little wistfully. "None of us like it as much as he does, so we hardly ever eat it anymore now that he's away at SFSU."

"How often do you get to see him?" Sweetie asked.

"Once a month or so. He tries to divide his time between us and Dimple, but of course, Dimple usually wins." She said it without bitterness, with a fond sparkle in her eye.

"And how are things? With him and Dimple?" Amma asked.

"Absolutely great," Sunita auntie said. "I would like them to get married after Dimple finishes graduate school, but Rishi tells me I must not ever bring it up. Apparently, she's of the more modern mind-set and would prefer not to think of marriage until her thirties." She sighed.

"Kids nowadays have their own ideas about how things should be," Amma said, and Sweetie could almost hear the *tsk*ing.

"Oh, yes. Ashish is completely different from Rishi. He's very . . . modern. Very Americanized." Her gaze darted to Sweetie. "Have you run into him at any of your games, Sweetie?"

She shook her head. "No, but some of my friends have. So I know of him. I saw his picture in the paper recently. Oh, and congratulations! I hear he has a really good shot at playing basketball in college."

"Yes, yes, he's very athletic, just like you," Sunita auntie said. "Everything on that front is going well. But . . . I really wish he would find an Indian girl to date. These other girls just break his heart,"

Amma looked a little embarrassed. She wasn't opposed to Sweetie dating, but that wasn't a problem she'd ever had to worry about, and Sweetie got the feeling that both she and Achchan were happy that things were that way. "Oh, perhaps when he's in college . . ."

"Yes, that's what I thought, but then it occurred to me: If he's already like this with our moderating influence, can you imagine what he'll be like in college? He seems to think that if he dates an Indian girl, we'll be breathing down his neck the entire time. But I keep telling him, it's not like we expect him to get married at seventeen! Maybe dating Sweetie will show him we can restrain ourselves." She smiled at Sweetie.

Amma laughed, a nervous, high-pitched sort of thing. "Yes, yes, maybe you're right. Of course, we wouldn't know about such matters."

Sunita auntie's careful gaze slid from Sweetie to Amma. "Sweetie's not allowed to date? I was under the impression that you and your husband—Soman, isn't it?—were not opposed to it."

The waitress came by to check on them, and there was a slightly awkward shift as they all reassured her that their food was, in fact, as delicious as they'd expected. When she was gone, Amma said, "Well. This was absolutely delightful, Sunita! Thank you so much for inviting us. But now, I think, we must go." She smiled a fake smile that looked like someone had just suggested she eat a bag of hair but she wasn't sure how to refuse politely. "Soman is returning from his business trip in an hour."

"But I thought Achchan was gone till tomo—"

"He called. His flight changed." Amma glared at her. "Come on." She reached for her purse, but Sunita auntie waved her off.

"Oh, no, please, this was my treat." After pausing, she asked delicately, "I hope I haven't offended . . . ?"

"No, please, don't worry; we are just in a hurry. Nothing to do with you. Thank you very much for the lunch." Amma kept smiling that rictus fake smile as she and Sweetie got up and made their way outside, leaving a somber-looking Sunita auntie behind.

"Amma, what—" Sweetie began as soon as they were out in the parking lot.

"Nothing." Amma walked briskly to their car. She could move at a pretty good clip for someone who was totally unathletic in every other way, and Sweetie sped up too.

"Is Achchan really coming home today?"

"No."

They got in and buckled up, Amma already backing out before Sweetie was fully finished. "Then why did you—"

"I have my reasons, Sweetie." That tone meant, *Don't ask me any more questions, because you're not getting any answers.*

Sweetie sighed. "Is it because it's Ashish Patel? Do you not approve of him?"

Amma said nothing. Her eyes were glued to the mostly empty highway as if it were that old Malayalam movie *Kilukkam*, which featured Amma's lifelong crush, Mohanlal.

Sweetie tried a different tack. She could actually kind of see herself dating him. That picture of his that Suki had shown them . . . that kind-of sadness in his eyes . . . how athletic he was . . . She had a feeling Ashish Patel might be an interesting guy. And, to be honest, if their parents were setting them up, it was a lot less scary than her approaching a guy she liked. Which she'd never done. Because what was the point? She saw the way guys at her school looked at her. At first it had just been disdain and mockery because of her weight. And then, as she beat record after record, it was respect. *Platonic* respect. The kind of platonic respect that made them laugh when anyone even suggested that they might take her to the prom, as Izzy had suggested to Brett Perkins once. Sweetie had been sitting across the cafeteria, but she'd heard him say something along the lines of, "Aw, man, I love Sweetie like a sister. Or actually, like a brother. She's just not the kind of girl you take to the prom, you know? I mean, I don't even really think of her as a girl." That had been a year ago, but you didn't forget that stuff easily.

"I thought you and Achchan would be happy—an Indian boy for my first date. Plus, if his parents are setting it up, you know he's going to be on his best behavior. Not to mention he's from a good family." Sweetie personally didn't give a crap what kind of family he was from, but she knew it was important to Amma and Achchan. She was totally cheating, but whatever. Amma wasn't sharing everything with her, and she was going to get to the bottom of it.

Amma darted a glance at her and then focused back on the road. "No, Sweetie."

No, Sweetie. There really wasn't much else to say about it, was there?

Sweetie slumped in her seat and rested her head against the window, watching the world go by.

CHAPTER 6

Ashish

Ashish sat on the terrace in the gloom of dusk, watching the sun set in the distance. He was alone again. It was Saturday evening, and he was alone. *Hello, Loser Territory, may I please plant my flag here? I think I am your new king.* He took a dejected swig of his Coke. Pinky had hooked up with some guy at the protest. She'd taken a picture with Mr. Hippie White Boy Dreads and texted it to him with devil horns drawn on her own head. Ugh. Ashish didn't want to know what she had planned. Oliver and Elijah were on their romantic date. And here he was on the terrace, sipping a Coke, watching the sunset. By himself. Even his parents were off doing more interesting things. He was like some forty-five-year-old dude, minus the wife and kids. This had happened more often than he cared to admit over the past three months, ever since he and Celia had broken up. And now that there was zero hope for reconciliation thanks to some douche with over-zealous thumbs, Ashish supposed this was what he could expect for the foreseeable future. "Depressing" didn't even begin to cover it.

The sound of tires crunching on gravel had him looking down over the thick, ornate railing. Ma's car had pulled up, and Rajat got out to open her door. He brought her many bags of shopping to the door. Ashish turned and walked downstairs, feeling just the slightest tingle of anticipation in spite of himself. *Do not get excited*, he reminded himself. *This is a girl your* parents *want you to go out with.* But still. Didn't it beat sitting on the terrace by himself Saturday night after Saturday night? At least going out on a date with her would be something to *do*.

Ma had set her bags down in the den and was pulling out her cell phone when she looked up and saw him enter. "*Beta*," she said, a warm smile on her face. She walked across the room and kissed him on the forehead. (He bent down to make it easier.) "Where's Pappa?"

"He's at that golf and dinner thing, remember? With the Apple people?"

"Oh, yes." She slapped her forehead with an open hand. "I'm sorry you were alone. I thought Pappa would be here to keep you company."

Ashish scoffed. "Ma, please. I'm not a kid anymore; I don't need you guys at home with me." Even though it had sucked to be alone. "So, um . . . how was your day?" He tried to say it nonchalantly, but his voice got all squeaky at the end. Dang it.

Ma sighed and shook her head. "It did not go as planned. Vidya Nair was strangely opposed."

Ashish felt his face fall, and then rallied by putting on his usual nonchalant expression. So what? He didn't care at all. Sweetie Nair was probably some awful Goody Two-shoes much more suited for Rishi than him.

Ma reached out and squeezed his arm. "*Fikr mat karo, beta.* I will get to the bottom of it."

"I'm not *worried*," Ashish said, making his voice extra scoffy for her benefit. "I knew it wasn't going to work." The thought of endless Saturday nights spooling out before him made him feel a little physically ill, so he injected even more bravado into his voice. "I'm just glad we can put this silly idea of yours to rest."

It was a monument to Ma's patience that she didn't remind him that the idea had been his. Her eyes, soft and kind, told him she knew exactly what he was thinking. "Well, I'm still going to find out what happened. Because *I'm* curious," she added when he opened his mouth to object. "I know you don't care."

She dialed a number on her phone and sat on the chaise lounge. Ashish sat on the couch across from her and picked up one of Pappa's tech magazines. He held the magazine up so the bridge of his nose was covered, but kept his eyes on Ma over the top.

"Hello, Vidya?" she asked. "*Haan*, this is Sunita Patel. I wanted to make sure you and Sweetie got home safely this afternoon." She listened for a minute. "Oh, yes, yes, Rajat came and picked me up not long after you left. No problems at all." Another pause, and then Ma laughed. "I am sure they'll be very excited to eat all of these *mithai* over the next few weeks! And of course we will be coming back for more!" A pause. "Did Sweetie's father arrive safely?"

Ashish flipped a page just to keep up appearances. Jeez. Was she ever going to get to the point?

"Oh, yes, flights are so unreliable nowadays. Mm-hmm, yes." Another long pause while she listened. Then the money question: "Vidya, I must ask your forgiveness if I somehow crossed a line today. I did not mean to offend you or Sweetie with my talk of dating." A pause. "I see. I was wondering if it was Ashish's history of dating other girls . . . ?" She glanced at Ashish and winked at him, though he could tell she really was uncomfortable asking the question. He felt a slight twinge of guilt. Ma really didn't deserve as much girl grief as he gave her. She frowned. "But, Vidya, that does not bother me, and I know it won't bother Ashish—" She listened. "No, I'm sure it's not—" Then she sighed. "Okay. Yes, I understand. She's your daughter, after all. Yes, please do. We must do lunch again soon. Bye."

Disconnecting the call, Ma looked at him. "Well, I know the truth now, at least."

Ashish sat up and put the magazine down. "Which is what?"

"How do you kids say it?" Ma thought for a moment. "Oh, *haan*. It's not you; it's her."

Sweetie

Sweetie stood at the doorway, listening. She didn't snoop on phone calls usually; she knew it wasn't cool. But the way Amma had just totally shut down the whole Ashish thing today and refused to provide an explanation, she knew there had to be more to the story. They'd been finishing up dinner when the call came through. Sweetie had seen *Patel* on the caller ID on Amma's cell, and the way Amma had jumped up and run off to her bedroom, it didn't take a rocket scientist to figure out the truth. It was Ashish's mom calling.

They'd mostly been talking about inconsequential things, but when Amma's tone turned darker and her volume quieter, Sweetie knew to lean in and hold her breath.

"No, no," Amma said. "After all, boys will be boys. But you see, Sunita, your son is . . . athletic. He's handsome. He's . . . thin. And Sweetie is, well, she is working on losing weight. But as you noticed, it hasn't happened yet. And at the present time, they are simply not well matched."

Sweetie felt her vision tunneling. So it had nothing to do with Ashish Patel at all? Amma had refused, had left Taj in such a hurry, because she was just that embarrassed of her fat daughter? Sweetie turned away as she heard Amma say, "I am happy to hear it does not matter to you or Ashish. But I cannot allow them to date, Sunita, I'm sorry. Sweetie is simply not at Ashish's level right now."

She ran down the hall to her bedroom and shut the door quietly, one hand over her mouth. Her breath came in sharp gasps; there was an intense pain in her stomach, and she thought for one whole minute that she'd puke. But then the minute passed. On wobbly legs Sweetie walked to her bed and sank down onto it. Her face flashed hot and cold. Her own mother. Her own mother was *that* ashamed of Sweetie's looks. She thought Sweetie was an abomination.

Sweetie had always known, obviously, that Amma was ashamed of her. The refusal to let her wear things that exposed even the slightest bit of skin, making her run in the backyard after school every day, tempering every compliment about Sweetie's athletic accomplishments with "Well, yeah, but if you lost the weight . . ."—all of that was a pretty obvious freaking message. But this? To think that Sweetie was actually less than that Ashish guy simply because she was fat and he wasn't? Sweetie grabbed her pillow, pushed it against her face, and screamed.

It was so unfair. She pulled the pillow off her hot, sweaty face and swiped angrily at her tears. Enough. If Amma was that ashamed of her, well, whatever. She just couldn't think of it right now. Sweetie walked across the room to her closet and pulled her rolling craft cart out. It was made out of three bright-green plastic bins stacked one on top of the other and held all the stuff she needed to make her anger go away: ribbons, buttons, dried flowers in small plastic packets, boxes of every kind. Sweetie was officially in charge of Heera Moti Baked Goods, Amma's business.

She pulled out one of the boxes she'd been working on and looked at the embossed letters of the company name Amma had chosen: Heera Moti. It literally meant "diamond pearl" in Hindi, but the general meaning was "jewels" or "gems." Though her parents were from Kerala, which was in southern India, and didn't speak too much Hindi (they spoke Malayalam instead), Amma had thought it would appeal more to their customer base to have a Hindi name.

Ironic, Sweetie thought, that *moti* could mean "pearl" or it could mean "fat." It just depended on how you pronounced the *t* sound. She pulled out a length of burlap and wrapped it around the box. If she added just a touch of dry lavender with some raffia, it might look—

There was a soft knocking at her door. Sweetie looked up and sighed. "Come in." Amma never knocked unless she figured Sweetie was mad at her for something.

Amma peeked in, a smile on her face. "Sweetie *mol*. What are you doing?"

Not trusting her voice, Sweetie held up the box silently and then went back to putting the lavender on.

Amma came in and sat next to her on the floor. "That's a nice look. Did you see it on Pinterest?"

Yes, Amma. Let's talk about Pinterest instead of anything real. "No. I saw some wedding centerpieces in that magazine you have, and it gave me ideas." Sweetie attached the raffia and squinted at the box. It was missing . . . something.

"Mm." Amma sat silently, watching Sweetie paw through the plastic bin on the bottom. "Ashish's mother called."

Sweetie's hands stilled for a moment, but then she forced herself to keep going. "Oh. What did she say?" Her voice sounded robotic, but it was either that or tearful anger, and she'd settle for robotic, thanks.

"She asked if she had made me angry and that's why I refused, but I told her no."

Sweetie pulled out a pack of high-quality stick-on cubic zirconias and then discarded it. No, that wasn't it either. "Right." Her hands tightened around the gems, but she kept her tone neutral. "You know, you haven't told *me* why you refused yet."

"Yes, I know. Sweetie . . . you might have noticed. There are certain differences between you and Ashish."

Sweetie picked up a packet of small purple bows, then threw it back in the bin and kept rummaging. "Really? Like what? I mean, he's Indian, I'm Indian. He's an athlete, I'm an athlete. We both live in Atherton. Oh, do you mean because he's Gujarati and we're Malayali?" She saw Amma shift uncomfortably in her peripheral vision and felt a tiny glow of satisfaction. Good. Let *her* be the uncomfortable one for a change.

"*Mol* . . . you still have to lose some weight. No?"

Sweetie's hands shook as she set the box in her lap and looked at Amma for the first time since she'd come into her room. "So?"

"Ashish is . . . he's thin. If you date him, people will laugh at you. I don't want people to make fun of you." Amma's lips were a thin brown line.

Sweetie stared at her mother, her mouth filling with words that she knew she'd never say. Why did Amma assume people would laugh? And if they did laugh, why should Sweetie care? What gave them the right to dictate what she could and couldn't do? Come to think of it, what gave *Amma* the right? But she knew what Amma would say to that last question: *I am your mother, and that gives me all the right.* The space between a desi mom and her kids was a lot smaller than the one between some other moms and their kids.

"When you lose weight, *mol*, you will be a suitable match for him."

Sweetie knew in her heart that she was good enough for Ashish just as she was. But why couldn't her own mother see that? "I'm . . . I'm sorry you're so ashamed of me," she said quietly. "But I'm not ashamed of myself." Her eyes burned with tears.

Amma shook her head and stood up. "I am not ashamed. I am just saying that you could do better. Make yourself healthier. Why is that so bad?"

Because! I'm like this now! Sweetie wanted to say. *Why are you always saying you'll like future me,* thin *me, better? Why can't you just like me how I am?* Instead she turned back to her arts and crafts, away from her mother.

Amma took a deep breath. "One day you will see that what I'm doing, I'm doing because I am your mother and this is what good mothers do." She paused, and when she spoke, she sounded farther away, like she was on her way out. "I am going to Tina auntie's Mary Kay party. Priscilla Ashford, my friend from the California Business-women's Society, is also coming, so I told her she could drop the baby here for you to babysit him tonight. They'll be here in thirty minutes."

"Fine." Sweetie looked down at the box in her lap as Amma closed the door. Inspiration hit, and she reached over to the top bin and pulled out a sheet of stickers. Very carefully she smoothed a pale-purple heart onto the corner of the box. That's what it had been missing this entire time—love.

CHAPTER 7

Sweetie

"Feetie!" Henry hurtled his three-year-old body into her with the force of a tiny hurricane capable of great damage.

"Hey there, little man." Sweetie picked him up and blew a raspberry into his belly, which made him screech like a little banshee.

Priscilla, his mom, a tiny redhead, watched with a fond smile on her face. "Thank you, Sweetie," she said. "Giving up your Saturday night for us."

Sweetie laughed. "That's okay, I didn't really have any plans tonight. All my friends are going to this concert in San Francisco, and Amma didn't want me to go."

"Oh, I agree with your mother," Priscilla said. "Those rock concerts can be scary." She shuddered theatrically, and Sweetie laughed. Priscilla was an accountant, and the idea of wearing bright colors during the weekday scared her.

"Any problems, just call my cell phone," Amma said, not fully meeting Sweetie's eye.

"Okay." Sweetie put Henry on her shoulders and began to gallop around as he chortled. "We'll be fine! Have fun!"

After about twenty minutes she pulled him off and set him down. "So, now what should we do?"

"Chocwate!" Henry yelled, putting his tiny fists in the air.

"Ah, I don't know about that. . . ." Sweetie put her hands on her hips. "What would Mommy say if I gave you chocolate at this hour?"

"Yes, Feetie! Good job!" Henry yelled, his fists still victoriously in the air, adorable belly poking out from under his *Weekend Forecast: Movies with a Chance of Pizza* T-shirt.

Sweetie laughed. "All right, who am I kidding? You have me wrapped around those little fingers. Come on."

She got him a mini Kit Kat bar out of the pantry. "So now what?" she asked. "Wanna play some Chutes and Ladders? Candy Land?"

"*Yo Gabba Gabba*!" Henry yelled, holding the Kit Kat bar high above his head this time.

"Not surprised, young Hank," Sweetie said, taking his hand as they made their way back into the living room. "But you might want to consider expanding your palate one of these days." Henry shot her a look. "Only if you want," she said, holding up her hands in surrender. She turned the show on for him and he settled into the couch, his eyes already glazed. She opened the Kit Kat and handed it to him.

Sweetie sat next to him and watched for about ten minutes before her phone buzzed. It was a text from Kayla, Izzy, and Suki, a picture of the three of them at the concert. Sweetie could barely make out their faces in the dark, but they looked like they were having a blast. She tapped in a SO JELLY and then sighed. She wasn't even a big fan of Piggy's Death Rattle, but she would've liked to go anyway, just to do something different for once. Something unsanctioned by Amma. Not that Henry wasn't great. She watched him, all zoinked out, and smiled a little. He was a cutie. But she was almost seventeen. She wanted to do something . . . rebellious. Something for herself, something to prove that Amma was wrong.

She felt a tug of hurt and anger as she recalled their last conversation. Amma thought Ashish was too good for Sweetie. She was afraid the very sight of her fat daughter with a thin boy would cause people to throw rotten tomatoes at her and shriek with cruel laughter. What the actual . . . ? Sweetie knew people could be cruel; she'd been dealing with it her whole life. But she was finally getting to the point, thanks to the team and her body, where she felt like she was so much more than the size label sewed into her pants. It was still hard—it would always be hard. But she had found a modicum of peace within herself that Amma was somehow bent on taking away.

Sweetie pulled up the article on her phone, the one featuring Ashish Patel that Kayla, Suki, and Izzy had been looking at yesterday. There he was, soulful brown eyes the same color as his mother's, staring back at her. His muscles bulged; his stance was cocky and confident. His sweaty hair hung low on his forehead. Why was this boy automatically better than her? Why did Amma assume Sweetie didn't have as much to give as he did? Especially considering Sunita auntie had apparently told her that Sweetie's weight didn't matter to her or Ashish?

On impulse, she texted Kayla.

Trey from Richmond is there too right?

Yeah why

Can you ask him for Ashish Patel's cell number

Sweetie pursed her lips and waited for the inevitable onslaught.

What???? Why????

I'll explain tomorrow promise

K you better it's 6505550108

Thanks bb

Sweetie sat back. She glanced at Henry, but he was still entranced by all the psychedelic *Yo Gabba Gabba* magic. She had eighteen minutes before the show was over and this window of opportunity (and her cojones . . . er, her *ovarios*) vanished. She pulled up a new text message to Ashish's number.

Hi this is Sweetie Nair

Should she clarify? What if he had no idea who she was? But surely Sunita auntie would've told him who she was. . . .

Hi

She stared at the message: *Hi*. What did that mean? Did he know who she was? Was he playing it cool until he could figure it out?

Our moms had lunch together yesterday

Yeah I know

She stared at his messages, frowning slightly. Why was he being so cryptic? Ugh, but she wasn't exactly giving him anything to go on either, and she was the one who'd texted him. *Just tell him what you want, Sweetie.* Which brought up an interesting point: What *did* she want?

Meet me at the Piedmont track tomorrow at 9 am, she typed in before she could even think about it. And bring your running shoes

My what

Running shoes

K running shoes 9 am Piedmont got it. Are you gonna tell me why or ?

Not really

K see you then

Sweetie set the phone down, smiling.

Ashish

If there was one thing Ashish loved, it was a girl of mystery. Sweetie Nair, he'd erroneously thought, would be a Goody Two-shoes, full-bottle-of-coconut-oil-in-the-hair, devout Indian daughter. Basically a female version of Rishi, his perfect older brother. But this? Texting him (who knows how she'd even gotten his number) behind their parents' backs? Asking to meet him alone at the school on a Sunday? Okay, so the running shoes thing was weird. But whatever. The important thing was that maybe Sweetie Nair was just as much of a dark horse as he was.

The thought had him hopping up to take a shower. After he'd lathered and rinsed multiple times, Ashish put some gel in his hair for good measure (and for the first time since the breakup). He debated what he should wear, but ultimately decided on his looks-handsome-but-not-like-he's-trying-too-hard outfit of a simple red T-shirt and gym shorts. He laced up his tennis shoes and was heading out when Ma said, *"Kahaan ja rahe ho is vakt?"*

Dang. Busted. He spun around slowly. "Oh, just to Oliver's. Shoot some hoops."

Ma glanced at the clock on the wall. "At eight forty-five on a Sunday morning?"

She had a point. Ashish had been known to ask her if she was trying to "off him" when she woke him up before noon on the weekends. "Uh, yeah. It's just . . . you know, I couldn't sleep. And so I just texted him and . . ." He trailed off as Ma stepped closer, her nostrils flaring.

"Are you wearing cologne? And gel in your hair?"

"Um . . . kind of?"

She raised one eyebrow, crossed her arms, and waited.

"Ma . . ."

"Ashish. Just tell me the truth. Are you meeting a girl there? One of your cheerleaders?"

Ashish sighed. At least he wouldn't have to lie. "No, I'm not meeting a cheerleader or any one of those other girls you and Pappa don't like, okay?"

She studied his face and then nodded. "Okay. Do you want some breakfast before you go?"

"Ah, no, that's okay, Ma. Thanks." He was actually too nervous to eat, he realized. Weird, considering he had no idea what Sweetie even looked like, beyond the fact that her mother apparently thought she weighed too much. After that phone call, he hadn't even bothered to ask Ma for a picture.

He could pull her up on his phone, he knew. She was probably on some social media website—and hadn't Ma mentioned she'd been in the local paper recently for some sport or another? But Ashish decided to wait anyway. He wanted to see her in person for the first time, this girl who'd already defied his expectations.

The track at Piedmont was large, though not quite as luxurious as the ones (yeah, plural) at Richmond. Ashish parked behind the chain-link fence surrounding it and hopped out of the open side of his Wrangler. The day was cool and dry, and the wind ruffled his gelled and coiffed hair. He felt a slight flutter in his belly; the first such feeling he'd felt in forever. *And I don't even know this girl*, he thought. He did know she wasn't afraid to take control, though, and that he really, really liked.

She wasn't there yet. He walked past the fence onto the track and looked around. It was empty this time of day. His phone beeped, and Ashish fished it out.

Ready to race?

He spun around and saw her. She'd just gotten out of her car and was walking toward him in track pants and a long-sleeved T-shirt. Her hair didn't look doused in coconut oil. Even at this distance, he could see the sun sparkling off its shiny black waves. She had it up in a high ponytail, and it bounced slightly with every step she took. As she got closer, he noticed other details too.

Her skin was smooth, the creamy color of that moonstone bracelet he'd bought Ma for Mother's Day last year, a shade or two lighter than his own. Her stride was confident, her full hips swaying with every step. She smiled.

Ashish blinked. So she wasn't the kind of girl you saw in *Sports Illustrated*. She wasn't the kind of girl he or any of his friends had ever dated. But even he, in his demojoed state of mind, could see that there was something about her. Something magnetic, something that had him closing the gap between them even though he'd told himself he was going to play it cool, dammit.

"Hi," he said, telling himself not to gaze too long into her hazel eyes and then doing it anyway. He held out a hand. "I'm Ashish."

She took it. Hers was soft and small, and he felt his grip automatically loosen. "Sweetie." Squinting in the sun, she looked up at him. Wow, she was as tiny as Ma. "You ready to race?"

Right. She'd said that in her text, too, hadn't she? "Race. As in . . . ?" He looked around the track.

"Yep. Come on. We're gonna do a four-hundred-meter dash."

Ashish looked at her, frowning. "Uh . . ."

"That's one full lap around the track." She began to walk toward the starting line, and he hurried to follow.

"Okay, but . . . why are we doing this again?"

She looked at him seriously. "To get it out of the way."

Ashish waited, but there didn't seem to be more forthcoming. "Get what—"

"You'll see," she said, taking her place. She gestured to the marker on the adjacent lane where he should stand. "Okay, when I say 'go,' that's when we start running. Ready?"

He opened his mouth to ask again but then shut it, nodded, and turned around. He copied her stance, butt in the air, hands on the ground.

"One, two, three—GO!"

CHAPTER 8

Ashish

Ashish took off like a rocket. He was just wondering if he should slow down, give the girl a chance, when her shadow encroached on him. He barely had time to look over his shoulder before she was zooming past him, the look on her face telling him she was in Balltopia. Or, in her case, Tracktopia.

Balltopia was a term Ashish, Oliver, and Elijah had come up with to describe that feeling of pure adrenaline, pure bliss, that came with really kicking butt on the court. You were so in the zone, you needed a different zip code. Nothing could shake Ashish out of Balltopia when he was in it. He hadn't been there for a couple of months, thanks to Celia, but that was another matter.

He almost wanted to stop and stare at Sweetie. He wanted to drool over her total Tracktopia face. He wanted to get back to Balltopia so badly, but in the past three months he'd only been able to graze around the circumference.

Ashish kept running, beginning to take in different things about her. The way her legs ate up the track easily. Her arms were bent loosely by her sides, her breathing was perfectly paced, her gorgeous, high ponytail swung and bounced. She was power. She was grace. She was beauty.

She was totally kicking his ass.

Ashish rallied and made a gallant effort, but he could see there was no point. There was no way he could beat her now. Winning was a huge part of Ashish's identity—he was unapologetically competitive. But even so, watching her mercilessly crush him on the track didn't hurt his ego at all. Weirdly enough, as he closed in on the finish line, he was smiling.

Sweetie was already there, smiling too, hands on her hips. Tendrils of hair were plastered across her sweaty forehead and neck; little drops of sweat beaded along the bridge of her delicate nose. Ashish found this detail almost painfully cute, and he had to rearrange his facial features to look chagrined. "Oh, man," he said. "What, did you pop caffeine pills with a Red Bull chaser for breakfast?"

She laughed. "Nope. I just wanted to show you."

"Show me what?" He remembered how she'd said she wanted to get something out of the way, and frowned at her as sweat dripped into his eyes. Stepping away, he shook like a dog.

"Good idea," she said like she was impressed. Then she followed suit. He watched the sweat arc off her in the sunlight, like crystal drops of rain. He tried not to notice other parts of her anatomy that were outlined rather nicely now that her shirt was wet with sweat. When she was done, she cocked her head. "I wanted to show you I'm not lazy, unhealthy, or any of the myriad other things people tend to assume. Or someone who's only on the track team because her parents know someone important. I'm really *good*."

Ashish nodded, sensing she wasn't done yet.

"And before you ask, I can run because I practice. My weight has nothing to do with my overall health. I kick pretty much everyone's butts at Piedmont, guys and girls alike."

"I can totally believe that," Ashish said seriously. "Are you gonna run in college?"

"That's the plan," she said, looking at him funny.

"Awesome. I'm gonna play ball in college."

She nodded, still with that funny look on her face. Finally she said, "Do you have any questions for me about my weight and track?"

Ashish thought about it, then shrugged. "No. Why should I? You're clearly ridiculously talented."

Sweetie smiled. It was like a ray of light piercing the clouds; Ashish felt his dormant heart spark just a bit. Her teeth were straight and just the right size, like a neat row of Chiclets. No, not Chiclets. Tic Tacs. White Tic Tacs. Nah, that wasn't it either. Damn, he really needed to get his compliments together if he was going to win her over with the trademark (and now hibernating, apparently) Ashish Patel charm.

"But I do have another question, though," he said.

"Okay."

"Why'd you ask me to come here and do this? Besides wanting to show me up as the clearly inferior runner, I mean." He grinned to show he didn't take it personally. If he was going to be beaten by anyone at an athletic event, he'd much prefer it to be someone as kick-ass as Sweetie.

They began to walk to the bleachers together. When the breeze blew, Ashish caught a whiff of her—even sweating, she smelled soft and sweet, like caramel laced with something heady and girly. He inched a little closer so his arm brushed hers, and she tucked a piece of hair behind her ear, like she was a little flustered. He found himself hoping she really was.

As they sat, close together, Sweetie answered his question. "I asked you here because I heard my mom talking to yours. About how . . ." She looked down at her feet and then back at him. The way her jaw was set, Ashish knew she was trying to be brave as she said the rest. But he heard the slight wobble in her voice and had to fight the urge to put an arm around her. *Totally not creepy at all, Ash. You just met the girl.* "About how I'm too fat to date you."

Ashish winced at the word. "Hey, don't call yourself that."

Sweetie looked at him frankly. "Why not? It doesn't bother me." She paused, considering her next words. "What does hurt is that my own mom thinks it's a reason I couldn't date someone like you. But the word itself? Doesn't bother me."

"Really?"

She shrugged. "Sure. I mean, the word 'fat' isn't inherently bad or gross. It's people who've made it that way. 'Fat' is just the opposite of 'thin,' and no one flinches at that one. So, to me, 'fat' is just another word that describes me, like 'brown' or 'girl' or 'athlete.'"

Ashish closed his mouth, put away all the responses he had lined up, and thought carefully about what she'd said. Why *was* "fat" such a bad word in most people's minds, anyhow? Studying Sweetie, he got an inkling that there were many things she'd had to deal with all her life that he'd never given a second thought to. "You're totally right," he said slowly.

"Yeah, I mean, obviously people can hurl it at me—and *have* hurled it at me—as an insult. But when I use it, it's not an insult. It's almost a way to take it back and reclaim it, if that makes sense."

Ashish nodded. "It actually does."

"Good. So . . . back to your question." The words seemed to flow out of her in a gush. "The reason I texted you last night is I heard your mom say my weight didn't bother her—or you. So, now that you've seen me and my body doing what it does best"—here Ashish had to force his mind out of the gutter—"I wanted to ask you if it was true, what your mom said. That my weight doesn't bother you. Or do you subscribe more to my mom's train of thought, that a fat girl and a thin boy will only be cause for mockery?"

Ashish looked at her, a little taken aback. She'd obviously given this a lot of thought. And to just put it out there like that without knowing him at all was . . . really brave. He'd never met a girl quite like Sweetie, and no lie, he was really, really intrigued. Ashish thought of a million charming things he could say in response. *Just more of you to love* or *Supermodel-thin just ain't my thing.* But in the end he settled for the simple truth. "I think you're beautiful. And I don't mean on the inside, though I'm sure that's true too. When you run . . . I see power and passion. I see focus and dedication. I see someone who isn't afraid to break people's expectations. And to me, that's way more attractive than the number on your weighing scale." He paused and then continued in a rush. "Okay, and also I think you're really just straight-up pretty. I want to lay it all out there in the open, and it's all one hundred percent true."

Sweetie studied him in silence. He wondered what she saw in his eyes. After a moment she graced him with a tiny smile. "I believe you."

"Great. So . . . is this your way of asking me out?" He jutted his chin toward the track in front of them. "Dueling me and making me lose?"

She narrowed her eyes at him. "If that were true, that would mean dating me is the loser's punishment."

He froze. "That's totally not what I meant at all—"

She laughed, a delightful sound like a bell pealing in a temple. "I'm kidding. But . . . yeah. I mean, I know my mom doesn't want us to date, but . . ." Shrugging, she tugged on her ponytail. "You ever get the feeling you just want to say 'screw it' and do whatever the heck you want once in a while?"

Ashish laughed, a little hysterically. "You've basically described my life and why my dad had an ulcer two years ago." More calmly, he added, "Actually, recently I've been more willing to let my parents take the lead. Hence my mom ambushing you and your mom."

Sweetie smiled. "She didn't ambush us. Your mom's lovely." After a pause she said, "So what happened, then? To curb your rebellious ways?" She asked it in a joking manner, but Ashish couldn't quite bring himself to return her smile.

"Ah, nothing I want to bother you with. But yes." He looked at her. "Let's do it."

She beamed. "Really? You're on board to go behind our parents' backs and everything?"

He took her small, warm hand in his and smiled. "Absolutely."

She stared at him and his breath caught. Suddenly her hand seemed to be made of electricity, arcing across his skin. There was an interesting beat between them.

Her phone trilled.

She jumped back and pulled it out of her pocket. "Sorry. It's Amma. Achchan's coming back from a business trip today, and I've got to go get ready. . . ."

Ashish ignored the disappointed thud of his heart. "Sure, no worries. But can I call you later?"

Putting her phone away, she smiled up at him. Then she squeezed his bare arm, sending a wave of something warm rolling through him. "Yeah. I'd like that."

So, Ashish thought as he watched her walk away, this weekend had turned out a little bit different than he'd expected it to. He had a feeling he wouldn't be sipping a Coke despondently on his balcony tonight. Ashish sat there at the track, whistling to himself, long after Sweetie was gone.

Sweetie

Sweetie drove back to her house, a smile on her face the entire time. That had gone way better than she'd even hoped. Seeing how kind Sunita auntie was and then hearing that she and Ashish apparently didn't have the same hang-ups about her weight as Amma did, she'd thought he deserved a chance. And she hadn't been wrong.

She turned up the Hindi love song "Bol do na zara" and sang at the top of her voice. Okay, this had been their first meeting. But there was something about Ashish Patel. Something completely and utterly compelling. It wasn't just his physique, though it had been hard to keep her eyes off those ridiculous biceps and broad shoulders. It was something about him . . . Behind the cocky smile and the easy laugh, there was something vulnerable and almost sad. Definitely something lonely, especially when she'd asked about what had curbed his rebellious ways. Whatever had happened, it had made him softer and sweeter, someone she wanted to get to know better.

She already couldn't wait for him to call her. Where would they go on their first official date? And was she really keeping this from Amma and Achchan? She felt a thread of guilt wrap around her brain, but it was immediately broken by excited anticipation. This was for *her*. This was to show herself that what she knew in her heart—that she was beautiful and worthy—was absolutely true. Sweetie laughed. Her first real act of rebellion at nearly seventeen years old. It was about dang time.

Achchan came home just as Sweetie was done with her shower and dressed in a nice *salwar kameez*.

"*Molu kutty!*" he said when he saw her, wrapping her up in a hug that smelled like airport. Achchan was wide enough that his arms actually wrapped all the way around Sweetie, which made her feel almost small. It was a nice break from being around Amma, who was about the size of a Hobbit (but with hairless feet) and made her feel like a giant troll in comparison. "How's my favorite child?"

Sweetie laughed as they walked, arm in arm, to the living room. "I'm your only child, Achcha. And I'm fine. How was the flight?"

He groaned. He'd been gone only a week, but he always said leaving them was the hardest thing about his job. "Please, let's not talk about that. How was practice on Friday? Did you beat your old time?"

Sweetie grinned. "I did. By a whole two seconds."

"*Adipoli!*"

They high-fived, Achchan's face pink with unadulterated glee.

Looking at his round, almost cherubic face, thick black mustache streaked with gray, and his big, soft belly, Sweetie felt a tug of affection. Achchan had always accepted her without question. It was like she was more his child than Amma's. They had the same heart, just cleaved in two.

"What else did you do this weekend?" Achchan asked, just as Amma walked in and smiled at him.

He gave her a peck on the cheek and grinned warmly back. This was about as demonstrative as they got with each other in Sweetie's presence, but Sweetie supposed it must be different when they were alone together. Her being alive was evidence of that, right?

Ew. Maybe it was better not to think about that.

"We went to the farmers' market. Sold all of our sweets."

"*Excellent!*" Achchan boomed. "Now you must expand your empire, Vidya."

Amma just laughed and rolled her eyes.

"You must have had a lot of customers to sell all of them, no?" Achchan asked, getting a glass of water.

Amma glanced at Sweetie before looking away. "No, no, it was just one lady. She was a big fan."

"Oh! Very nice." Achchan gulped down his water. "It doesn't surprise me, you know, Vidya. Your sweets are out of this world."

Sweetie felt a sinking in her stomach. Amma really wasn't going to tell Achchan about their encounter with Sunita auntie. Sweetie knew exactly what Amma would say if she were confronted: What was the point of bothering Achchan with something that was never coming to pass? Sweetie felt an electric bolt of anger. Amma thought she could control everything about Sweetie's life—who she went out with, what she wore, what Achchan knew. But she couldn't control Sweetie's heart. She couldn't control Ashish.

"Shall we go get some lunch at It's All Greek to Me?" Achchan asked when he was finished with his water. It was their ritual; anytime Achchan returned from a business trip, they'd go to this Greek restaurant and eat gyros.

"Sure," Sweetie said, and then, as Achchan grabbed his car keys, she added, "Do you both mind if I drive this time?"

This was unprecedented. Sweetie never, ever drove when her parents were accompanying her. She watched Achchan's mouth pop open slightly. She saw Amma's face go from suspicion to annoyance and back.

"Why?" Amma asked finally.

"Because I want to?" She coughed and tried again, getting rid of the question mark this time. "I want to." Sweetie's heart hammered against her chest; she'd never been so assertive in her entire life.

Amma opened her mouth to say something, when Achchan quieted her with a hand on her shoulder. "It's all right, Vidya. Let her drive. After all, she'll be driving us around a lot in our old age! Might as well start practicing now!" He began guffawing at what he thought was his razor-sharp wit. Amma acquiesced with a slight nod of her head.

Sweetie grinned on her way out the door. Man, it felt good to get her way, to say what she felt. Maybe she could ask for more stuff. Maybe this was how it would begin, her transformation from Sweetie the Softie to Sweetie the Sassy: one statement at a time. *Watch out, world. I'm coming.*

CHAPTER 9

Ashish

Ashish was humming as he walked in the front door. And not anything manly; he was humming "Love You like a Love Song" by
Selena Gomez. God, if the guys on the team heard him, he wouldn't
hear the end of it.

He crossed the foyer, nodding and grinning at Myrna, their housekeeper, who raised her bushy blond eyebrows at him in surprise. As he
entered the living room, he decided he'd take a shower and then go see
what Oliver and Elijah were up to. And, of course, he'd very casually
drop the good news: that he was finally back on that horse they'd been
urging him to rope and saddle. Also that he just happened to have
hopped back onto the horse with the best track athlete at Piedmont,
who also happened to be sporty and absolutely gorgeo—

Ashish stopped short. His parents were sitting on the couch in the
living room. They'd drawn the drapes to make the room darker and
had then turned on one lone light in the corner. They were staring
at him completely seriously.

"Uh, hello," he said, licking his lips. Jeez. What was with the
Godfather impression?

"Ashish, *idhar aao*. Come sit, *beta*." Ma patted the chair next to her.

Uh-oh. Pappa continued to stare at him, eyes narrowed, jaw set. That was never good. That was his boardroom someone's-gonna-get-fired face. He'd seen it once when he was a kid and Pappa had to take him in to work because Ma was sick. He'd never forgotten it. It was . . . make-your-butt-cheeks-clench formidable.

Ashish sat. He wanted to ask a million questions, but instinct told him to wait them out. Let them give him what *they* had, and then he'd see what to share with them. It was a careful game of cat and mouse he'd honed over the years.

"Ashish . . . *kahaan thay tum*? Where were you this morning?" Pappa's voice was low, almost just a growl. Ma put a warning hand on his knee, but he ignored it and kept glaring at Ashish.

"I . . . told you." Ashish looked at Ma, though he didn't like lying to her again. But this time it wasn't just about him. It was about Sweetie, too. "I was at, um, Elijah's."

Ma looked at him, her expression soft and hurt. "You told me you were at Oliver's."

"Th-that's what I meant," Ashish said quickly. "Elijah was there too."

"Really." Pappa leaned closer. "Do you want to change your story?"

"Don't cross-examine him, Kartik," Ma said gently. Then, looking at Ashish: "Oliver and Elijah came by, looking for you."

Dang it. Busted. He kept his face neutral.

"So, let me ask you again: Where were you, Ashish?" Pappa said, leaning back against the couch. He really would make a great don if he ever wanted a career change. Get out of the tech and business game, get into the breaking-kneecaps market.

"Look, I don't know what's up with the Indian Inquisition thing you've got going on here," Ashish said, crossing his arms. "But you're not getting anything out of me."

Ma looked from Ashish to Pappa and then back again. "*Hai bhagwan*, you're both so much like each other, it's scary sometimes." Sighing, she said, "Ashish, nobody's trying to interrogate you. We just want to know the truth. Were you with Celia?"

Ashish stared at them. "What? No!"

Ma held up her hands. "We're not judging, *beta*. But when I saw you all dressed up . . . I just had a feeling. And then you lied to us, so . . . *Beta*, she's broken your heart. Is it really worth the pain?"

Oh great. Now his parents thought he was a loser who'd go back to some girl who'd treated him like dirt and left him a zombie with no game. Ashish ran a hand through his hair and put his elbows on his knees before looking at his parents again. "Look, Ma, Pappa . . . I wasn't with Celia. I promise."

Ma's face relaxed, though Pappa's remained thunderous.

Ashish hesitated. He'd told Sweetie he was willing to go behind their parents' backs, and he didn't want to renege on that. But he also couldn't keep lying when he was being interrogated like this. Don't ask, don't tell was a different matter. "The truth is, though, that I did lie to you. And I'm sorry. I was with Sweetie Nair." He took pains to pronounce her last name correctly—so it rhymed with "buyer," not "hair"—because he didn't want to give his parents another reason to jump on him.

He watched as Pappa's face melted from pure thunder to vague confusion and back to murderous rage. Ma froze into a mask of neutrality. It was actually kind of comical.

"Sweetie Nair?" Ma asked. "What were you doing with her?"

"Sweetie Nair! Whose mother said she wanted nothing to do with the idea of you two dating? What were you thinking, Ashish!" Pappa roared. Turning to Ma, he said, "What do you think he was doing? Probably up to hanky-panky just like with those other girls! Are you trying to ruin her life?"

Ashish looked at them in disbelief. "Okay, wow. Can we all just calm down and tone down the Bollywood theatrics? Thanks for the vote of confidence, by the way, Pappa. I wasn't ruining her life with 'hanky-panky.'" He did the air quotes a little savagely, stabbing the air with his fingers. "If you must know, we were . . . running."

The confusion was back, on both Ma's and Pappa's faces this time. "Running?" they said together. "Is that some kind of slang for 'hanky-panky'?" Pappa added in irritation.

"Will you stop with the hank—okay, look." Ashish took a breath to flush away his annoyance. "Sweetie Nair texted me last night. She heard you and her mom talking, Ma, and she also heard you say that her weight was a stupid reason for her mom to say she couldn't date me." He held up a hand when Ma opened her mouth to protest. "I know you didn't say it in those exact words, but that was the gist of it and Sweetie heard that part. So she wanted to talk to me in person. And . . ." He shrugged. "She isn't a skinny supermodel, so she wanted me to see that she isn't lazy or whatever the stereotypes are for fat people." He had to force himself to say the word neutrally, like she had. "And the truth is, she impressed the heck out of me. She totally kicked my a—butt on the track. She's really nice, too, and smart. And so . . . we both decided that we do want to date."

"Oh ho! So you both decided?" Pappa said, his face getting pinker and pinker with each word. "Without asking your parents?"

"Ashish, Sweetie's parents don't know. It's not right for you to do this behind their backs." Ma's voice was soft, pleading.

"No, you know what isn't right? For her mom to decide that she isn't good enough to date me because of the size of the clothing she wears. Okay? Sweetie is thoughtful, intelligent, passionate, *and* beautiful. If you want me to stop dating girls like I have in the past, then you really couldn't do better."

"*Bilkul nahin!* I forbid it!" Pappa thundered.

But Ma was looking at Ashish thoughtfully. Putting a hand on Pappa's arm, she said, "Ashish, could you please step out for just a moment and give us some privacy? I'll call you back in a minute."

He looked from her face—she definitely had something cooking under that mask of neutrality—to Pappa's apoplectic one, then shrugged and stood. "Okay."

Ashish crossed the vast living room into the adjacent dining room. There was no door between the rooms, just a huge archway, but he was far enough from Ma and Pappa that he couldn't hear what they were saying. Well, *most* of what they were saying.

Occasionally phrases would leak through (mostly because Pappa seemed to be shouting them and Ma seemed to be raising her voice to match his tone).

". . . not appropriate!" Pappa.

". . . first time he's . . . nice girl . . ." Ma.

". . . nky-panky!" Pappa.

". . . our chance . . . he's got a reputation . . . good family . . . convince them somehow, eventually . . ." Ma.

". . . guidelines. No negotiations!" Pappa.

"Fine."

"Ashish? Ashish?" Ma again.

Silence.

Ashish sat up. Oh, she wasn't talking to Pappa anymore; she was actually trying to get his attention. He crossed the dining room quickly and went back to the chair in the living room. His parents were both staring at him in still silence, like two mannequins with moving eyes. "Back to the creepy, are we?"

Pappa raised his eyebrows. *"Kya?"*

"Nothing," Ashish mumbled.

Ma spoke first. "Ashish, we have decided, after much deliberation, that we will allow you to date Sweetie."

"And you won't tell her parents?"

"We won't." Ma held up a finger when he smiled. "But not because we think it's the correct thing to do. Rather . . . well, we think this will be good for you. You have always resisted learning about your culture, maybe because Pappa and I have pushed you too hard and you think everything we say is 'uncool.' But somehow Sweetie's family has managed to raise a daughter who is respectful and knowledgeable about hers. Maybe being with her will rub off on you, hmm? Besides, *beta*, I'm afraid you'll develop a reputation in the Indian community for being a rebel and feeling like you're better than Indian girls. Pappa and I have been worried about it, and we feel this will help change that perception."

Ashish laughed. "So this is like a PR campaign for my brand?"

Pappa glared at him. "It is not a laughing matter, Ashish. It is not

90

just your reputation, but your entire family's. Think of Rishi and Dimple. Do you want the focus to be on your wayward ways when it comes time for them to announce their engagement? For us to plan their wedding?"

Ashish sighed. And there it was: It always came back to Rishi, the golden child. "No, of course not."

Pappa nodded briskly. "Good."

"We'll tell her parents in due time," Ma said. "But until then . . ."

"We have some conditions you must follow if you want to date this girl."

Ashish froze. "Um . . . what kind of conditions, exactly?"

"You can only go on dates that are sanctioned by Ma and me," Pappa said, a smug smile on his face.

Ashish blinked. "Wait, what? *You guys* are going to tell me where to take Sweetie?"

"Yes. Four dates. You must go on all of those or the deal's off." Ma raised one eyebrow. "It's your choice."

Ashish huffed a laugh. "You know I could just go behind your backs and date her, right? I mean, I have a car and so does she."

Ma picked up her phone off the side table. "I can call her mother right now and tell her what you two have been planning. I have a feeling Sweetie won't be going anywhere after that."

Ashish shook his head slowly. "When did you two become such criminal masterminds?"

Pappa laughed, obviously pleased with this assessment of his character.

"We're not trying to control you, Ashish," Ma said. "We just want what's best for everyone in this situation."

"Yes, and assigning your dates will cut down on the funny business."

A frightening thought occurred to Ashish. "Wait. Where are you going to be sending us that you feel we won't be able to, uh, get into trouble?"

"We will refine the list," Pappa said, steepling his fingers, "but for the first date we are both agreed that it should definitely be the mandir."

Ashish looked from one parental face to the other, hoping that one of them would crack a smile to show that they were yanking his chain. But they just stared at him. He rubbed his face and tried to collect himself. "Are you serious? You want me to take her to the *temple* for our first date?"

"Why not?" Pappa said. "It is an auspicious place, full of good omens."

Ashish looked at Ma pleadingly, in a last-ditch attempt to salvage this thing. "Come on, Ma. Do you really think this is a good idea, or did Pappa bully you into it?"

Ma laughed. "Pappa does not bully me into anything, Ashish. Do not take my quieter nature as weakness. The mandir was my idea. And don't worry, we'll have three other equally well-suited places for you to take Sweetie."

"That's our deal; take it or leave it," Pappa said.

"And if I don't take it, you'll tell Sweetie's parents."

"Correct." Ma shrugged. "At least this way when we do tell them, we can say we kept a guiding hand on you two and made sure nothing untoward happened."

"So, do you accept the terms?" Pappa asked. "Can we close the deal?"

Sighing, Ashish closed his eyes. "Yes. We can close the deal."

"Excellent!" Ma said, smiling. "Then you better ask Sweetie to meet you here so we can give her the good news."

"And so I can meet her, of course," Pappa added jovially.

"Can't wait," Ashish mumbled, pulling out his phone.

CHAPTER 10

Sweetie

"Next month is someone's seventeenth birthday," Achchan said, stuffing an entire square of baklava into his mouth. Sweetie had two of the honey-covered sweets on her own plate as well, much to Amma's distress. "What should we have at the party? Magician? Petting zoo?"

Sweetie laughed and tried not to roll her eyes. "Achcha, I'm not eight."

"Okay, then, you tell me what you want and we will get it! What do the cool kids like nowadays?"

Sweetie ate a piece of baklava. "Well, I don't know about the cool kids, but I thought one of those giant chocolate fountains would be cool. I've always wanted to try one, and it'll keep the little kids happy too."

"Not a good idea," Amma said, folding her hands on the restaurant table.

"*Alle?*" Achchan asked. "Why isn't it a good idea? I've heard they're not too expensive."

"I don't think Amma's talking about the cost," Sweetie said quietly, though her hands shook under the table. Suddenly she was getting very, very tired of Amma's irrational fixation with her weight. Maybe it was that single act of rebellion, going to see Ashish Patel and deciding to date him behind her back, but it was like something bright and volatile was beginning to spark inside of her. "She's talking about my weight."

Achchan cleared his throat. "Vidya . . . it's her birthday. She'll be having birthday cake, after all."

"*Athey.* All the more reason she doesn't need a chocolate fountain also."

So now it was what she was wearing to the party *and* what she could eat there. What else might Amma want to sanction? How much air she could breathe? What words she could say, being a fat person? Maybe she shouldn't even talk about food. You know, just in case people thought she was some kind of glutton. In case she embarrassed Amma again. She could feel the pressure of the words behind her teeth, building and building until she was sure she'd scream. "Bathroom," she said instead, pushing out of the booth and speed walking to the ladies' room, leaving two confused parents behind.

Her eyes were hot with tears, and she tried to blink them back as best she could. Luckily, the bathroom was empty. Closing herself in a stall, Sweetie pulled out her phone and dialed.

"Hello, Sweetie?"

Just hearing Anjali Chechi's voice put her more at ease. "Hey. Are you busy?"

"Never too busy for you. What's up, little sis?"

Sweetie grinned. Anjali Chechi was her older cousin: a successful surgeon, married to an equally successful video game developer, and . . . fat. She was Achchan's oldest brother's child, and she got on

Amma's nerves more than anything. Because how dare she be happy, successful, *and* fat? Amma especially didn't like how Sweetie felt more comfortable in her own skin after talking to Anjali Chechi on the phone or after one of her visits. Amma'd once told Sweetie that Anjali Chechi would encourage her to remain unhealthy. Amma was of the opinion that surrounding Sweetie with Bollywood gossip magazines and fashion catalogs would inspire her to lose weight. But with Anjali Chechi, Sweetie could just be herself. She was constantly being forced to think of herself as the before picture, but when she spoke to her cousin, she saw that the after picture could include her just as she was right now. She didn't need to lose weight to become the success story Amma so desperately wanted her to be.

"Nothing; just having an *awesome* time at lunch with Amma and Achchan, though."

Anjali Chechi could obviously hear the sarcasm and hurt in her voice. She sucked in a breath. "Uh-oh. Lay it on me."

"It's not even worth getting into. It's just more of the same, you know? You can't wear that because it exposes too much of your fat skin. You can't have a chocolate fountain on your birthday because you need to lose weight. You can't date a thin boy because you're too ugly for him."

"Whoa, whoa. What's this about a boy? What boy?"

"His name is Ashish Patel. He's Richmond Academy's big basketball star, and his mom wanted me to date him, but Amma thinks we're mismatched and people will laugh at us."

She heard a male voice in the background that belonged to Jason, Anjali Chechi's husband (she'd married a white man—another reason Amma would never understand her). Anjali Chechi said "Ashish

Patel" away from the phone, her voice muffled. Returning to the conversation with Sweetie, she added, "Hold on. Jason's Googling the dude." A pause. "Oh, wow. He's seriously gorgeous!"

Sweetie felt herself get warm. "Uh, yeah, he is. And according to Amma, that puts him out of my league in an another-stratosphere sense."

"That is *ridiculous*," Anjali Chechi said, her voice loud with endearing vehemence. "You are a beautiful person, and I'm not talking about that 'on the inside' crap!"

Sweetie grinned. "Yeah, that's exactly what Ashish said."

There was a pause as Anjali Chechi processed this. "Wait. What do you mean that's what Ashish said?"

"I met up with him without telling Amma. Or Achchan, actually, but he was away on a business trip anyway. I, um, sort of challenged him to a race."

Anjali Chechi guffawed. "Niiiiice. And? How'd it go?"

"Really well. He's, uh, really nice. I mean, I won, naturally, but he was cool with it—not like a lot of guys. And he genuinely didn't seem to have a problem with my weight, either." She felt her cheeks grow warm at the memory of him calling her pretty.

"Oh? Do I detect a hint of first-loveness?"

Sweetie giggled. "Stop it. Anyway, I guess the plan is to keep dating without telling Amma and Achchan."

"Mm. And how do you feel about that?"

Sweetie thought about it. "Surprisingly okay. I feel like I'm ready to do things that Amma deems totally unsuitable for me and make up my own mind about them, you know? I mean, I know people really are cruel and stupid about fat people and I don't have to tell you that. Like that kid last year who said Amma should've made a business selling vegetables for my sake. And she was totally serious, too."

Anjali Chechi blew out a noisy breath. "Ignorant jerk."

"Yeah. But there's also a part of me that loves myself in spite of all that anyway? And I want to give Self-Love Sweetie some airtime. See what she thinks about dating a hot jock. You know?"

"I totally get it, sister. And I support you one hundred percent. You know my parents didn't know I was dating Jason until he practically proposed."

"Yeah, I remember. They wanted you to marry another Indian doctor." Sweetie chuckled.

"Yeah, and I got the whitest, most liberal, hair-dyeing, Hawaiian-shirt-wearing dork I could find." She laughed. "Jason says he did me a favor."

"He did!" Jason Chettan was one of Sweetie's favorite people, after Anjali Chechi and her parents.

"He totally did, true," Anjali Chechi says. "So we'll be there for your birthday party next month. Anything in particular you'd like for a present?"

Sweetie opened her mouth to say their presence would be present enough, but then she closed it, an idea beginning to take root. If she really was going to do more of what *she* wanted, to find out how *she* felt about things, then . . . "Actually, yeah. There is something you could get me." And she proceeded to tell Anjali Chechi exactly what that was.

Ashish texted on the drive home. Sweetie had relegated herself to the backseat after what Amma said in the restaurant, and the environment in the car was prickly and still and weird. She wasn't even sure her parents knew what the matter was, and if they were curious, they weren't asking.

Achchan would make these random comments, just interject them into the silence. Like, "Oh! Bob's Air-Conditioning!" because he'd literally seen a billboard and wanted to talk about it since that was better than what was going on in the car. Sweetie would've laughed if she hadn't been so pissed off.

Her phone buzzed and Sweetie pulled it out.

What are you doing later today

Her heart got all fluttery, like it was made out of feathers instead of muscle.

Nothing much why

Can you come over to my place

Huh. She didn't know about that. Was this a *Come over to my place—wink, wink—so we can make out* thing? OMG. She so wasn't ready for that. Her heart sank. Had Ashish just said all that nice stuff because he thought she was easy? It was one of her big fears. What if she found a good guy who she believed liked her for her, only to find out that he just wanted sex? The idea had terrified her ever since she overheard two guys at school say fat girls were "an easy lay" because they were so desperate for love.

Why, she typed with shaking hands.

We got busted. My mom and dad want to meet you

As she stared at the screen, horrified, he added, Sorry L.

Are they gonna tell my parents?

No, don't think so. They've got another nefarious plan though ugh

She relaxed a bit. Okay, so Ashish didn't want sex and her parents weren't going to find out, apparently. If his parents just wanted to lay into her, that was okay. She could take that. And obviously she'd ask Ashish if he still wanted to keep dating, because the Sassy Sweetie Project was now underway. But what if his parents forbade it too, and he decided he didn't want to go against their wishes? Ack. She needed to stop obsessing and just go with it. See what happened. Be chill.

K be there at 5?

Sounds good. He texted her his address—of course it was in the ritziest part of Atherton—and then she put her phone away, her heart thudding as she looked at the backs of her parents' heads. All of this sabotage, and they had no idea. It simultaneously thrilled her and made her uneasy. It would be so much easier if she didn't have to lie. If Amma would just understand her, and if Achchan would just stand up for her more. Oh well. This was what it was, and she had to make the best of it. That was all there was.

Ashish

Ashish paced the floor of his bedroom. It looked out over the driveway, so he'd see when Sweetie pulled up. God, what must she think of him? Their first meeting and he'd already managed to get busted and had shamelessly spilled his guts to Ma and Pappa. Well, at least that was one career down the tubes: spy. He could just strike that off his list right now.

The weird thing was that he was willing to try their ridiculous plan of going on the four dates they picked (like some kind of weird tourism/dating agency mash-up) if Sweetie was. If it was a choice between not seeing her again and adhering to their plan, well . . . If he was being honest with himself, Ma and Pappa had done a really good job picking someone who, at least on the surface, had stuff in common with him. He'd felt an instantaneous click, which had thrown him for a loop.

Of course, now the only *click* he'd hear might be the sound of Sweetie closing the door behind her after she heard what his parents had in store for them.

Her little brown sedan pulled into the circular drive, and Ashish stopped pacing. He watched as she got out, patted her long ponytail, and took a deep breath before beginning the walk up to the house. She was beautiful, even unsure and nervous. Ashish turned and ran down the stairs to meet her.

He yanked the front door open before she could ring the doorbell. "Hi." Just seeing her on his front porch—those big, soft eyes that reminded him of a doe's, that thick black hair, that athletic hoodie and pants—made him smile.

He realized he'd taken the smiling past the point of normal only when she frowned a little and said, "Are you okay?"

He put the smile away. "Oh, yeah, totally. Come on in."

She followed him in silently.

"So . . . thanks for coming," he said as he led the way to the study, where Pappa and Ma waited like hungry lions. Well, he was a gladiator. He'd protect Sweetie from them.

"Um, sure. I'm not clear on what they want from me, though. Are they going to yell at me or something?"

Ashish tossed her a sympathetic grimace. "It's a lot worse than that, unfortunately." They were at the door to the study. "Just, uh, whatever you want to do, I'll support you. I really hope you'll say yes, but I'll totally get it if you want to say no."

Her face was a mask of confusion. "Ashish, I'm lost."

Ashish sighed and pushed open the door. "You're not the only one."

CHAPTER 11

Ashish

Pappa and Ma sat in identical leather armchairs. Pappa gave them a tight-lipped smile, but Ma got up and enveloped Sweetie in a hug.

"It's so nice to see you, Sweetie. This is my husband, Kartik." She smiled. "Thank you for coming over."

"No problem, auntie."

Ashish gestured to the couch, and he and Sweetie sat. She kept twisting her fingers around, he noticed. He wanted to hold her hand, just to make her feel better.

"Sweetie, I know you must be wondering why we've asked you to come over today, so we'll explain right away." Ma glanced at Pappa, who nodded. "The thing is, we don't think it's right for you and Ashish to sneak around behind your parents' backs."

Sweetie straightened a little, but she didn't say anything. The finger twisting intensified.

"We are your parents," Pappa put in, staring at Ashish. "And lying to us doesn't get you anywhere." He looked over at Sweetie. "You're an Indian girl. This isn't how your parents raised you to behave."

"Pappa," Ashish said, resisting the urge to roll his eyes. "Sweetie wasn't the only one who lied. And her being a girl has nothing to do with anything."

Ma held up a hand, probably because she could sense an argument with no winners brewing. "Be that as it may, this behavior is very disappointing."

"I understand," Sweetie said. "I don't necessarily agree with everything you've said, but I understand. It won't happen again. I'm sorry." She made a motion to stand, and Ashish watched in alarm.

"Wait, *beti*," Ma said kindly. "We're not finished. The thing is, we know you're a very good girl. And you must have had a reason for doing what you did. We don't want to know those reasons; I'm sure they're private. But we also don't want to lose the opportunity for Ashish to date someone like you. So, Ashish's Pappa and I have come up with a plan. If you and Ashish agree to it, we'll keep the secret from your parents, for a little while."

Sweetie glanced at Ashish, and he raised his eyebrows at her in a *Yeah, I know they're super bizarre* way. "What . . . what plan?" Sweetie asked finally, looking around at them all.

Ma filled her in on the whole four-date thing. There was silence as Sweetie processed it, all three of them trying not to stare at her while totally staring at her. God, she must think they were all so weird. Ashish wouldn't judge her if she bolted out the door right now. In fact, he might judge her if she *didn't*.

She took a deep breath. "So . . . what you're saying is that I can date Ashish, but only if we go to the specific places you want us to go for our dates. Like . . . the temple."

"Correct." Ma nodded.

"It's our only offer," Pappa said, and Ma swatted him.

"*Kya offer-shoffer*, Kartik," she said. "This is not some software you're selling." Turning to Sweetie, she said gently, "We know this must seem odd, Sweetie. But we only want to make sure nothing happens that we'd be ashamed to tell your parents about. And this is the only way we know how to do that."

Sweetie stared out the window for the longest moment in the history of mankind and womankind. Then she looked back at Ma and Pappa. "O-okay. I guess I agree to your conditions." She darted a look at Ashish that was half panic, half confusion. He had a feeling she'd agreed only because she was being put on the spot. Aaahhh. Cringe, cringe, cringiest of cringes.

Rallying himself, he said, "Good. Then we're both on the same page." He could always talk to her later. Get her to see that he wasn't as much of a crackpot as his parents might have led her to believe.

They'd had a real connection this morning. He just had to remind her of that. His hand inched next to hers on the sofa. Obviously holding hands in front of Ma and Pappa would be out of the question. But if even the sides of their pinkies touched, Ashish could maybe convey that he was on her side, that he saw how bizarre this was too. But when he was less than a millimeter away, Pappa cleared his throat and stood, causing Ashish to jerk his hand away like it had been burned or something.

"I have something for you two," Pappa said, handing them each a sheet of paper from his desk.

Frowning, Ashish glanced down at his.

MEMORANDUM OF AGREEMENT

This Memorandum of Agreement is entered into by Kartik and Sunita Patel (hereafter referred to as PARENTS) and Ashish Patel and Sweetie Nair (hereafter referred to as CHILDREN) on April 7, 2019, in the city of Atherton, California.

Ashish looked up, one eyebrow raised. "You seriously drafted up a legal contract, Pappa?" He glanced at Sweetie, who was reading it with a wondrous look on her face. "You're going to scare her away."

"Sweetie's not scared of making things official! Are you, Sweetie?" Pappa boomed.

Sweetie chuckled, but it was a dry, withered sound, as if she were considering just jumping out of the window and running to her car. "Um . . . no, not . . . not really."

"Read, read!" Pappa ordered. He pointed with his pen toward the bottom of the document, where there was a numbered list.

Jeez, he could be bossy. Ashish scanned the list.

1. **Pavan Mandir.** Both CHILDREN shall have their first date at Pavan Mandir, located at 12 Oliphant Drive. The date shall commence next Saturday, April 13, to begin no later than 9:30 a.m. and terminate no later than 3:00 p.m.

2. **Holi Festival of the Indian Association of Atherton.** Both CHILDREN shall have their second date at Oakley Field, where the Indian Association of Atherton will be hosting the

annual Holi Festival on Saturday, April 20. Both CHILDREN must take part in the festivities. The festival will be from 9:00 a.m. until 12:00 p.m., after which the CHILDREN may go to lunch at a restaurant of their choosing.

3. **Gita Kaki.** Both CHILDREN shall visit the home of Ashish Patel's Gita Kaki (paternal great-aunt) in Palo Alto, California, on Saturday, April 27. They shall drive up in Ashish's Jeep and arrive promptly at 11:00 a.m. The visit shall terminate no earlier than 2:00 p.m.

4. **Free choice.** The CHILDREN shall make their own choice for this date, to be held on Saturday, May 4, with consent from both PARENTS.

Ashish looked up at Pappa, careful to keep his gaze away from Sweetie. He had no idea what she was thinking right now. She had to be internally screaming just as much as he was, though. "Gita Kaki?"

Pappa frowned. "Eh? What about Gita Kaki?"

"More like Gita Kooky. Wasn't she the one whose neighbors got a restraining order because she attacked their yappy dog?" Ashish said, fighting to keep his voice level.

Ma looked aghast. Darting her gaze between him and Sweetie, she said, "That was all blown out of proportion, Ashish." She laughed. "She was only being friendly! They misunderstood."

"If I remember correctly," Ashish said, "she ripped the poor dog's sweater off and screeched 'Banshee!' at it over and over again, until they called the police."

"The dog was very obnoxious," Pappa said. "Its owners had been fined for noise disturbance many, many times before! And it had bitten people too! Your Gita Kaki can hardly be blamed."

Ashish looked from him to Ma, who was nodding in eager agreement. "So. This is your idea of getting back at us."

He expected Pappa to get mad and tell him it didn't matter if Ashish liked it or not, this was the deal and he had to stick with it. And if he didn't like these punishment-dates, he shouldn't have been sneaking around.

But Pappa actually looked perplexed. Glancing at Ma, he shrugged, like *Kya? What is our son talking about now?*

Ma looked at Ashish. "*Beta*, Pappa and I put a lot of thought into these date choices. We wanted them to be fun but also culturally immersive. Do you . . . do you not see it that way?" She looked from him to Sweetie, her gentle face anxious.

Oh God. They actually thought these were *good* dates. They weren't trying to punish him or Sweetie. Before he could open his mouth or even think of a response, Sweetie was speaking.

"Auntie, uncle, these are all really thoughtful date ideas. I really think Ashish and I will have fun and learn a lot." She nudged him discreetly with her elbow.

"Uh, yeah, totally," Ashish said after a beat. "So fun. And . . . educational."

Ma and Pappa relaxed, both of them smiling. "Yes, correct!" Pappa said. "And see? We gave you a free choice for number four."

"I did actually have a request for that one already," Sweetie said a little nervously. "If Ashish is okay with it too, of course."

He raised his eyebrows, curious. "Sure. What do you have?"

"Well, May fourth is actually my seventeenth birthday party," Sweetie said. "It'd be nice if Ashish could come. . . . That way when we do tell them, after three of the dates are done, it won't be a total surprise. And he can meet them and I know they'll warm to him." She squirmed a little, as if she was embarrassed to be saying all that.

Ashish was secretly delighted. Meeting her parents in this context didn't signal anything super serious, obviously. But the fact that she did want him to meant she thought they'd be impressed by him. Heh. Heh, heh, heh. *You still got it, Ash.*

"Of course he can go, if it won't be an imposition on your parents," Ma said.

"It won't be," Sweetie replied. "They told me I could invite a few friends."

"Then it's decided!" Pappa rubbed his hands together, something Ashish knew for a fact he did when he'd closed a big business deal. The thought annoyed him; it meant Pappa thought he'd won. And he so hadn't. "Your first date will be Saturday."

"Okay." Ashish hopped up. "I'll walk Sweetie to the door."

"There's no need for her to rush off," Ma said. "Be a good host, Ashish. See if she wants a tour. She might enjoy the basketball court."

"Just don't take her up to your room," Pappa said suddenly. "I don't want any hank—"

"Okay, let's go," Ashish said loudly, drowning him out. He gently pulled on Sweetie's elbow and she stood too, still looking pretty stunned at everything that had transpired. Could you blame the girl?

"Bye, Sweetie," Ma said, waving.

"Bye-bye," Pappa added.

"See you later, auntie. Uncle, it was nice meeting you."

As the door closed, Ashish heard Pappa say in what he thought was a quiet voice but might as well have been an elephant trumpeting, "That's a nice girl! She won't stand for any hanky-panky."

Oh God, Ashish thought. *Kill me now.*

Sweetie

They walked out of the vast study into the equally vast hallway and then crossed into a vaster . . . Sweetie didn't even know what this was. A second living room? A den? It had a humongous fireplace in the corner, and the ceilings were about twenty feet high. Their footsteps echoed slightly as they walked.

So Ashish Patel lived in a mansion. It didn't even surprise her. The way he held himself, the confidence with which he spoke, all of that signaled someone who hadn't been denied much, if anything. Whatever doors his handsome face and rugged body didn't open, she was sure his wealth did. But he wasn't unbearably arrogant, Sweetie decided, watching him rub the back of his neck nervously. He was just cocky. And, somehow, that didn't annoy her. Yet. After what she'd just witnessed, she wasn't completely sure about her and Ashish Patel after all. His parents—especially his dad—seemed intense.

"So . . ." Ashish looked at her, his hand still resting on the back of his neck, the other in the pocket of his shorts. "How much do you want to run away right now? I totally won't judge you if you do."

Sweetie tried to laugh, but it came out high pitched and wheezing. "Um, a little bit. The thing is . . . your parents are—"

"Aliens in human meat-suits? Believe me, I've had that thought many a time, but I'm pretty sure they're just a little strange."

Sweetie did laugh this time. "No. I was going to say I think they really, really love you. And yes, their date idea is a little . . . out there. But I just don't get it. Why are they agreeing to this? They obviously think it's a bad idea to be doing this without my parents' consent."

"Oh, that's, um, because of me." Ashish gestured to the window. "Do you want to take a walk around the gardens?"

Sweetie shrugged, curious to hear what he had to say. "Sure."

CHAPTER 12

Sweetie

Ashish led the way out into the hallway and then out of the French doors. As they wound their way into a gigantic, rose-scented garden full of whispering trees and neatly trimmed grass that would've looked at home on *Downton Abbey*, he said, "Okay. So the reason my parents still want us to date is because they're apparently afraid I'll get this reputation of being incompatible with Indian girls. They're afraid that it'll follow me around and when it's time for me to get married to an Indian girl—because who else would I marry, right?— her family won't want me." He rolled his eyes. "I know, it's ridiculous. I'm seventeen. But that's just how my parents are. They live in fear of their black sheep of a son dying a lonely old man someday."

"Well, yeah, it is kind of silly. And you could definitely marry a non-Indian girl. One of the happiest couples I know is my cousin Anjali and her husband, who's a white American guy." Sweetie glanced at him. "But, um . . . why are they so worried you'd get that reputation of not being compatible with Indian girls?"

He rubbed a hand along his jawline and cleared his throat. "Probably because I've, uh, never dated one."

"Never?" It didn't take a relationship genius to see that someone like Ashish had probably had a ton of girlfriends. And not one of them had been Indian? "Why not?"

He stuck his hands in his pockets as he and Sweetie wound toward a pond in the center of the garden. The sunlight sparkled on its surface. "I don't know. . . . I guess I just didn't like the idea of Ma and Pappa following me around, wondering if it was something serious. And I knew if I dated non-Indian girls, they'd just pretend like I was single, because to them, I could never be serious about someone who didn't share my culture. Anyway, I just want to have fun, you know? I'm not like my brother, Rishi. He already has this girlfriend he knows he's going to marry, and he's still in college. So it suited me just fine that my parents never bothered with any of my non-Indian girlfriends. Even when I was serious with them."

His eyes got this distant, guarded look, the honey hardening to stone. "Who were you . . . serious with?" She was immediately embarrassed, sure she was turning bright pink. Sweetie had no idea why she'd asked that, and not just asked, but asked with a jealous edge to her voice. Urrggh. *Way to be chill, Nair.*

Ashish looked away, as if he was looking at the pond. But Sweetie had a feeling he was trying to collect his thoughts. Whoever the girl was, she must've been really important to him. She tried not to let herself be bothered by the thought. She barely knew Ashish Patel, even if they had shared that little spark at their first meeting earlier today.

"No one," Ashish said, his voice quiet. "No one at all."

They looped around the pond, Sweetie's tennis shoes squishing in the mud a bit.

"If you don't want to date, I'll totally understand," Ashish said finally. A bird warbled above their heads, perched in the big oak tree. "I know it's a lot. My parents' list and the agreement, my reputation . . ."

Sweetie thought about it. Dating Ashish didn't have to be a big thing. It wasn't like Sweetie was looking for a future groom—she was under no illusion that every boy you dated had to be your true love or anything. This was about proving to herself that boys like Ashish Patel could and did find girls like her datable. That was all. Which meant that his parents and that ridiculous memorandum changed nothing. She looked at him. "You know, I think it'll be fine. We should do it." Oh no. That totally sounded like she was saying they should have sex. Feeling her cheeks glow incandescent, Sweetie added quickly, "Uh, their four-date thing, I mean."

Ashish didn't seem to think anything was amiss; he just looked genuinely surprised. "Really?"

Sweetie smiled. "Really. Besides, I think your dad would take me to court if I broke the agreement."

"Wow." Grinning, he stuck a hand through his hair, leaving it all mussed. He would very easily look at home on the cover of *Esquire* or something. Sweetie tried not to let the thought intimidate her. "That's impressive, not gonna lie. I thought we'd freaked you out."

"Well, you did, a little." Sweetie laughed, pulling her mind back into the conversation. "But I don't scare that easily."

Ashish smiled at her, big and bright, and her heart went *thud*. "I'm really glad."

Sweetie pulled out her cell phone. "Um, I should go before my mom starts calling."

"Okay. I'll walk you to your car."

Their hands brushed lightly as they walked, and Sweetie found her breath quickening. Seriously? She'd thought she was less shallow than that. But she couldn't deny it; she found Ashish Patel incredibly, incredibly attractive. It occurred to her that now that they were going to be dating, there would be a real first kiss. And . . . maybe even more. She gulped a little. Ashish Patel might have dated thousands of girls. But the truth was, Sweetie Nair had never dated a single boy. The only time she'd been kissed was when she was seven, and Toby Stinton said he wanted to give her "boy cooties" so her face would "fall off."

"By the way," Ashish said, turning to her in the middle of the drive. She looked up at him, trying to quell her insecure flurry of thoughts. He stepped closer, his eyes smoldering in the setting sun. "I, uh, had a good time this morning. Hanging out with you, I mean."

"Oh." She gulped, her pulse quickening. "Me too." Her eyelids fluttered almost without conscious thought. Flirting! She was flirting! At least . . . she thought she was.

Ashish took her hand, a half smile on his face. Sweetie tried to keep her breathing nice and easy and normal. Passing out was not an option. NOT AN OPTION. "Good. You know, contractual mandates aside, I'm really looking forward to getting to know you better."

She gulped again. She'd be full of air if she didn't watch out. "M-me too." Acckkk. Couldn't she think of anything else to say?

Smiling, Ashish let her hand go as they walked over to her car. He held the door open for her. As she got in and smiled up at him, she thought, *I am so astonishingly unprepared for this.*

He must've seen something flash across her face—panic?— because he leaned down, his brow furrowed in concern. "You okay?"

"Totally." Her voice came out a squeak, but she forced herself to keep smiling. Oh heck. How many times had Ashish Patel kissed girls? How many times had he had sex?

"Okay." He straightened and, smiling, tucked a lock of hair behind her ear. Her traitorous heart juddered in her chest. "I'll see you later?"

"Me too!" she said, laughing a little hysterically. "Next weekend! Bye!"

He stood waving at her as she made her way down the drive. Oh, no. Oh, no, no, no. Why hadn't she thought this through? Why hadn't she *fully* considered what it might mean to date Ashish Patel? Had she really believed all Ashish Patel had ever done was hold hands with girls? What if he was so experienced with new sexual techniques that she didn't even know what he was talking about? What if he made a move next weekend, on their very first date, because he was so used to all his millions of experienced girlfriends throwing themselves at him? Sweetie knew she couldn't back out now, not without totally hurting his feelings. Besides, she still wanted to date someone like Ashish Patel. She couldn't just flee in fear, not now that she was Sweetie the Sassy Rebel. She'd totally lose face. To herself, but still. That was the most important.

Sweetie groaned. She had the feeling she'd just agreed to something way, way above her pay grade. And now there was no way to go but forward.

Sweetie was all jumpy at school the next day. *Five more days*, her mind kept saying. *Five more days until you find out what a first date with a boy like Ashish really means.* The thing was, it wasn't all negative jumpiness. Part of her was . . . thrilled, almost aching, to find out what it would mean to feel Ashish's big (hot—the boy was like his own mini nuclear reactor) hand loosely clasped around hers. To kiss him on those full lips for the first time. To hear him whisper her name under the stars. To find out why, exactly, his eyes always seemed just a little sad, even when he laughed. But there was a part of her that was worried it would all unravel. That she'd find out he was really shallow, that all he wanted was an "easy lay," like those other awful jerks had said. There was a part of her that was terrified to get hurt, to find out that Amma had been right all these years.

"Heyyy, whatcha doing?" Someone grabbed her around the shoulders and Sweetie shrieked. Kayla raised an eyebrow. "Jeez. Someone's on edge today. I know it's not about that chemistry test you're gonna ace."

Sweetie took a deep, shuddering breath. "Oh, sorry. I was just . . . thinking."

"I can see that," Kayla said, adjusting her bright-green backpack. "Maybe a different kind of chemistry on your mind?" She laughed. "What's going on? Did you text Ashish?"

Oh, right. Sweetie had actually forgotten that it was Kayla who'd given her his number Saturday night. It felt like forever ago. "I did."

"Uh-huh . . . and I'm guessing the shrieking had something to do with that?"

"Yeah. It's, uh, a long story, actually. I'll fill you guys in at lunch." Lunch and track practice were the only times all four of them got to hang out anymore at school. Junior year wasn't all it was cracked up to be. "But how was the concert?"

"It was fabulous!" Kayla singsonged, and then launched into a minute-by-minute rundown of everything that had transpired Saturday night. Sweetie was glad for the chance to put aside her own thoughts and doubts for a few minutes.

The rest of the morning passed in a sort of fog. Sweetie managed to focus on her chemistry test—Kayla was right; she aced it—and then her brain turned back to Ashish and the Four Dates. They were watching a video in English lit. She looked around to make sure no one was watching her, then pulled the memorandum out of her backpack (she couldn't just leave it at home, where Amma might see it). Smoothing it out on her notebook, she read it again. The temple. That's where they were headed Saturday. But what the heck would they *do* there? What kind of a date was that? Sweetie wasn't opposed to going to the temple. She went during the major religious holidays with her parents. It was a restful kind of place, with the bells and the smells of incense and the *pujari* chanting the prayers, the feel of the cool stone floor under her bare feet.

But still . . . it was a *temple*. A place of worship. She couldn't think of a less romantic date than that. And maybe that was the point. Maybe Ashish's dad was so concerned with . . . what had he called it? Oh, right, "hanky-panky." Maybe he wanted somewhere that would essentially be environmental birth control. Sweetie sighed. That was still better than the alternative—accepting Amma's opinion that someone like her should just stay inside, fully clothed, until she was thin. Besides, not having to worry about Ashish's experience as a sexpert was kind of a gigantic relief.

Kayla, Suki, Izzy, and Sweetie sat at a picnic table at lunch, their backpacks on the grass at their feet. A light breeze ruffled Sweetie's hair, and the sun was like a balm. She turned her face to it and closed her eyes.

There was complete silence at the table. Not normal. She opened one eye to see all three of her best friends staring at her. "What?"

"So? Are you gonna tell us why you wanted Ashish Patel's number?" Suki asked.

"I texted you yesterday," Izzy said, looking a little hurt. "You never responded."

"Oh, yeah, sorry." Sweetie took a deep breath. "Sort of a lot happened over the weekend and I just needed time to process, you know?"

"Hello?" Kayla's eyebrows were up in her hairline. "That's what we're here for."

Arrrgh. The guilt. Sweetie folded her arms on the table and put her head down. "I know. I'm sorry."

She felt Izzy's hand on her back. "What's going on?"

Sweetie sat up again but kept her eyes on the faded wood grain of the table. "So, um. I guess I'm kind of dating Ashish now."

"You *what*?" they all said together.

Sweetie looked up at their thunderstruck faces and couldn't help but smile. "Wow." Sniffing, she continued. "Yeah. Um . . . it was this big thing, and I don't think you guys want the nitty-gritty, but—"

"Um, I think I speak for all of us when I say we want the nittiest of the gritty," Suki said. The others nodded.

Sweetie looked from one face to the other. She'd never kept anything from them. But this? She felt a little weird telling them not just about how Amma had said she was too fat to date Ashish, but the fact that she and Ashish were going along with his parents' plan at all. Other people tended not to understand that. Even Suki. She listened to her parents and considered their opinions more than the kids whose parents had been born in America, but she was still allowed more freedoms than Sweetie. Although, it would be nice to have someone to talk about all this stuff to besides Anjali Chechi, who, let's face it, had her own life to worry about.

"Okay. I'll tell you." And she did, detail by detail, starting from the time Ashish's mom came up to Amma's stall at the farmers' market.

CHAPTER 13

Sweetie

When she was finished, there was complete silence.

"Oh . . . my . . . frakking . . . God," Kayla said finally. Her brown eyes sparkled in the sun. "You're going out with Ashish freaking Patel. I'm so frakking jealous." Kayla always said "frakking" a lot when she was in the throes of emotion, because her parents cut her allowance when she cursed.

Suki put her hand on Sweetie's. "I'm really glad you didn't let your mom decide who you're good enough for," she said seriously. "It really sucks that she tried to do that."

Sweetie felt a lump in her throat and swallowed. She just nodded; she couldn't say anything else.

Izzy came over and enveloped her in a hug that smelled like sweet fruit, Izzy's signature perfume. Then, sitting back, she grinned, her braces glinting in the sunlight. "This is amazing. Like . . . whoa. How do you feel? I mean, he's your first-ever boyfriend."

Sweetie laughed. "I really don't know how to feel. I mean, on the one hand, it's great that he's so cool and we just instantly clicked. On the other hand, his parents and the list of dates, oh my gosh. On the other, other hand, his experience."

"So you have three hands now?" Suki said, snorting, but Sweetie ignored her.

"Eh?" Kayla asked. "You lost me. What experience?"

"You know!" Sweetie waved her hands around in a vague gesture. Her friends continued to stare blankly. "His *experience?*" she said more quietly. "Like, with girls?"

"Oh, you mean sex!" Suki said in a completely normal, completely *loud* tone of voice.

Sweetie looked around. "Shh! I don't want the whole world to know, okay?" Kayla, Suki, and Izzy looked unperturbed. "Guys! I've never even kissed a boy."

"Now, that's not true," Izzy said, laughing. "What about Toby Stinton?"

Sweetie glared at her, and her smile faded. "That is not helping."

"This is the kind of thing you figure out together," Kayla said, putting her arm around Sweetie. "Ashish and you."

"Yeah, except he's already kissed, like, a billion girls," Sweetie mumbled. "He's probably going to think I'm a total freak."

"He is not," Suki said. "I promise he's not going to be thinking of his experience or your lack of it or anything else when you're together. Trust me. He's just going to be totally focused on you and how he gets to kiss you."

Sweetie sighed. She wished she could be half as confident as the other girls that things were not going to go humiliatingly wrong and blow up in her face. "Okay, thanks. But I kinda just want to change the subject now. So, how was the concert?"

After a pause, during which they apparently decided she really did want to stop talking about it, Suki said, "It was fabulous. But we really missed you."

"I missed you guys too. I saw your pictures on Insta, and oh my gosh. So jelly."

Izzy grinned. "Also, Kayla had an amazing idea."

"Oh yeah?" Sweetie looked at her. "What?"

Kayla straddled the bench so she could face Sweetie, the zippers on her gold shirt clinking together. "Okay, so you know how we're always saying we wish we could get better track jerseys for the girls' team, and the school's always saying they don't have any money?"

"Pfft. More like the money they have is going toward the guys' football team," Suki grumbled.

Sweetie rolled her eyes. "Yeah. We all know that's true."

Kayla nodded. "Exactly. Well, I thought maybe we could take matters into our own hands. It just came to me, watching Piggy's Death Rattle on the stage and how many people came out to just spend a night doing something different, you know? Like, how many people did we meet who had never even listened to their music but just wanted something fun to do on a Saturday night?" she asked Izzy and Suki.

"About ten," Izzy said.

"At *least* ten," Suki added.

"Right." Kayla turned back to Sweetie, who still didn't get what the big idea was. "So my plan was this: What if the four of us host a band night at Roast Me, that coffeehouse on Eighth Street? We could get the local high school bands to come out and play for exposure. If we charge, like, five dollars a head, we'd easily get the money we need for our jerseys."

"But would Roast Me really agree to it? A bunch of high school bands playing there?"

Kayla grinned. "They already have."

Sweetie stared at her. "What?"

"Yeah, I know someone who knows someone whose dad owns the place. And he was totally on board to let us have the place. More food and drink sales for him, plus his daughter's in a band too, so we just had to agree to let her band play."

Sweetie shook her head, completely in awe. "Kayla, how the heck do you do it?"

Kayla laughed. "Black-girl magic."

"Not gonna argue with that," Sweetie said. "So when should we do this band night thingy?"

"We were thinking a few weeks from now," Kayla said.

"That should give us enough time to get everything together and let people know about it." Suki popped her grape in her mouth and looked at Izzy. "So should we tell her now?"

"Tell me what?" Sweetie asked, cocking her head. She didn't like the look on her friends' faces.

"Um, so we're not just getting *other* bands to play at Roast Me . . . ," Izzy said, gnawing on her thumbnail.

"We want to play a set too." Suki took a breath. "Andwewantyou-tobetheleadsinger," she added in a rush.

Sweetie stared at her. *We want you to be the lead singer.* "Guys . . . no. I . . . no. I can't sing in front of a bunch of people." Just thinking about it made her hands damp and her armpits itch.

"Why not?" Izzy whined, turning the word "not" into stretchy, elongated taffy. "Come on, Sweetie, you have a beautiful voice!"

"We're all going to be up there with you, if that's what you're worried about," Kayla said. "I'll be on the guitar, Suki's gonna play the drums, and Izzy's going to be backup vocals."

"It's not that." Sweetie took a bite of her *dosha* and chewed morosely. She hated feeling this way. But it just . . . She couldn't help it. "I can't go in front of all those people onstage."

"You're not shy when you're running in front of all those people," Suki said, frowning. "And newspaper sports reporters."

Sweetie looked around at her friends' kind, loving faces. No matter how much they loved her, no matter how much they tried, they just couldn't understand. They were all extremely thin, conventionally attractive people. Everyone always told them how gorgeous they were, how fit, how toned.

Whereas Sweetie . . . Sweetie had been the butt of more fat jokes than she cared to remember. Her own mother had told her, from when she was in elementary school, that her number one aim in life was for Sweetie to lose weight. Everywhere she looked, Sweetie saw the markers of success as thinness, youth, and wealth. In that order. Movies never had fat heroines. Catalogs didn't regularly stock clothes for people her size.

Izzy, Suki, and Kayla never had to answer questions about how they could run so fast, because they were thin. No one ever assumed Sweetie could run. Quite the opposite, in fact. She had to prove herself worthy every single second of every single day, over and over and over again. It was exhausting. Why the heck would she want to spend her weeknight, her own time off, up onstage so people could make fun of her? So they could judge her and ridicule her, just because she was fat?

"Running's different," she said finally. She didn't say running was her lifeline. That she needed it more than she needed to not be judged. It was who she was. "I've been doing it so long that I can tune everyone out. But I couldn't do the same thing with singing." After a pause she pushed on. "You guys can't understand what it feels like to be . . ." She sighed. "To be fat and have to put yourself out there. There are a million things I'm always worried about, even just agreeing to go out on a few dates with Ashish. Will he be repulsed when he puts his arms around me and feels back rolls? What's he going to think when I order food in the restaurant? And then being up onstage? What if someone sneaks alcohol into Roast Me? Do you know how mean drunk people can be to girls who look like me? They won't be listening to me. They'll be *looking* at me, indignant that I felt I had any right to go up onstage in front of them all. I'm going to be like a target up there, just waiting to be hit."

Izzy shook her head. "I have those feelings too, Sweetie. I'm not fat, but I constantly feel self-conscious of my body. My hips are too big and my arms aren't toned enough. A lot of people—especially women—have those feelings."

"Damn patriarchy," Suki said darkly. "Holding women up to higher standards."

Sweetie smiled a little. "I appreciate you guys saying that. And I know you feel the pain of having to live up to beauty standards. But . . ." She looked around at them, not sure how to put it.

"But it's not the same," Kayla said quietly.

"No. It's not. When I walk down the road, people immediately make judgments about me based on my body size. That doesn't happen to you guys, no matter how self-conscious you might be about your bodies. You're still thin, and you get to exist in spaces without constantly being found wanting."

Her friends were all quiet for a moment, and Sweetie wondered if she'd offended them. She'd never quite put it like that before. She'd never had the courage to.

"I'm sorry it's so hard for you," Izzy said finally. "Because you're one of the coolest people I know."

"And the most kick-ass," Suki agreed.

"When you go out on your dates or up onstage," Kayla said, holding Sweetie's eye, "just know that you have three people in your corner. No matter what else happens, *we* will always accept you as you are."

Sweetie blinked and looked away. "Thanks, guys. I know," she said, her voice hoarse. "But I'm not sure if I can do the whole song thing. I'm sorry."

"I'm gonna give you time to think about it," Kayla said, holding up her hand when Sweetie tried to argue. "I know, I know, you won't change your mind. But do you really want those people to dictate what you do, Sweetie? I know what it's like to be prejudged based on physical appearance, okay? Believe me, I'm a black girl. And I also know you have what it takes to tell those people to shut the hell up." She smiled. "Just think about it. We don't start practice until next Monday, anyway. So you have some time."

Sweetie ripped off another piece of *dosha*. "You're so stubborn."

Kayla leaned over and kissed Sweetie on the cheek. "That's why you love me."

Ashish

"That's *her*?" Pinky asked, looking at Sweetie's picture on Ashish's phone. He'd been a total creeper and pulled a picture from her Insta profile (they followed each other now, a fact that made Ashish unreasonably happy).

He glared at her. "Yeah. Why?" He looked at Oliver and Elijah across the cafeteria table. They were both uncharacteristically silent. "You got something to say?"

Elijah just shook his head, but Oliver ventured timidly, "Um . . . she's just a little different from the other girls you've dated."

Pinky snorted. "Different? More like she's another species entirely from *Supermodelicus conceitedum*."

"Celia wasn't conceited," Ashish replied, purposely missing the point. He scrolled through Sweetie's posts to see if she'd posted anything else since yesterday. He wanted to hang out with her again, he realized. Which was weird because they'd barely spent any time together. It was like some dormant part of him began to blink to life in her presence or something.

"No, she just stomped on your heart and used the pieces for confetti at her I-have-a-new-boyfriend party," Elijah retorted. "Whereas this girl looks like she's never even *had* a boyfriend."

Ashish looked up from his phone, his temper flaring. "What, because she isn't thin?" he asked, his voice dangerously low.

Elijah shrugged, rolling those annoyingly gigantic traps Ash would've killed for, and Oliver didn't meet his eye. "You can't blame us for saying it," Elijah said finally. "Not with your track record."

"So maybe I haven't ever dated someone like Sweetie before," he said. "But that doesn't mean I don't—or can't—find her attractive. Or that other dudes haven't found her pretty and cool enough to go out with her. Come on, guys. Let's not make judgments about who we can or can't date. Do I really need to be telling *you* that?"

Elijah bristled, but before he could say anything, Oliver spoke up. "He has a point," he said to Elijah. "For what it's worth, I don't think you *shouldn't* date Sweetie. I was just . . . surprised."

"Do you really find her attractive?" Elijah said in a disbelieving tone that Ashish really didn't like.

"Yes, Elijah. I find her hair, her curves, the powerful way she runs around the track and the fact that she can totally kick my ass very attractive. She's gentle and insightful and kind, and I fight that hella hot too. Got a problem with any of that?"

"Whoa," Elijah said, raising his eyebrows. "You're not playing."

"No, I'm not. And I'd like to propose something: From now on, none of us ever judges someone else based on their physical appearance. Deal?"

Elijah held his gaze and, after a moment, nodded. "Deal. Sorry, man. I wasn't trying to hurt you."

"I'm sorry too," Oliver said, wrapping his skinny arms around himself.

"Thanks," Ashish said to the two of them, relaxing a little.

"But look," Pinky said from beside him. "I definitely don't think you should judge a person by their size, you know that. For me, it's more just . . . she looks so innocent and . . . and *sweet*, Ash. Like she thinks the world literally runs on rainbows and unicorn farts."

"Mm," Elijah said, licking orange Cheetos dust off his fingers. "I'm pretty sure you're going to get bored and break the poor girl's heart. Besides, you have to admit . . . you've been sort of shallow about choosing girls. And from what you just said, personality-wise, Sweetie isn't at all the type of girl you'd have dated before Celia."

Oliver nibbled on his thumb and nodded. He seemed the most nervous about this conversation, his gray eyes big and guileless. If Ashish knew him at all, and he did, he probably just didn't want to hurt his feelings. "What's this about, Ash? Why are you agreeing to do your parents' whole four-date thing? I thought their idea of the perfect girl and your idea were diametrically opposed."

Ashish sighed and put his phone away. Trust Oliver to get to the crux of the matter. The boy would make a kick-ass shrink some-day. "I don't know. I guess . . . I've tried my way for a long time. And what has it gotten me? Some conventionally hot girls, sure, but life should be about more than just who you're gonna do on Saturday night, right? It was different with Celia, but we all know what a spectacular success that turned out to be. So I just figured, you know, I'm gonna see what my parents have to say. Samir gave me the idea, to be honest. It seemed totally idiotic at first, but then they went on and on about how they could find me a good girl when the time was right, and they just seemed so confident. . . ." He trailed off and took a swig of his milk. He felt three pairs of eyes on him, waiting. "And then I met her. She's sweet—you guys are right—but she's also a killer athlete and intelligent and, I don't know, just seems like such a good person at the core. Like there won't be drama and angst and all that stuff there was with Celia. And I think right now . . ." He took a breath and ran a hand along his jaw. "Right now I think I need that."

Pinky scooted closer to him on the bench and put her arm around his waist. "Then we'll support you."

"Absolutely," Elijah said.

"We only want what's best for you, Ash," Oliver said, smiling a little. "We love you."

"Love you guys too," Ashish mumbled, feeling just a tiny bit stupid for saying it out loud. Especially to Elijah and Pinky, the least demonstrative people in the world. But when he looked around at their faces, all he saw was understanding and affection, the kind that came from a decade-long friendship mulled in secrets that had been shared in tree houses and late-night high jinks never to be repeated to parental units. The kind that felt like home. Ashish felt his shoulders relax for the first time in months.

Samir was waiting for him on the basketball court when he got home with Pinky, Oliver, and Elijah in tow. He saw him as he got out of the Jeep, so he tossed his backpack back in and they all walked over. "Yo."

Samir turned around and spun the ball on his finger. "Hey, man. Hey, Oliver, Elijah." He paused. "Um, hey, Pinky."

Pinky grunted something in response. There was no love lost between those two—Pinky called Samir "that spoiled homeschooled infant," and Samir called her "that pretentious, parrot-haired freak" (rubbing Pinky's face in the infamous lime-green-hair phase she'd gone through). After their earsplitting argument at the formal holiday party Ma and Pappa had thrown last year, Ashish had made a huge effort to keep them apart.

"Man, I wish you'd texted me. We're headed over to Roast Me in a minute."

Samir slapped his forehead. "Oh, right, it's Monday. I totally forgot it's your study night."

"Yeah, but if you come by tomorrow, we can shoot some—"

"Why don't you come?" Oliver cut in. "I mean, it's not like we *actually* study anyway." He laughed and looked at Ashish, totally missing the death glare he was giving him. Had Oliver forgotten what had happened just a few months ago at the party? If Pinky and Samir had both been dudes on the basketball team instead of the people they were, he was sure they'd have ended up in a fistfight, smashing the punch bowl and making kindling of furniture, like in the movies.

"Really?" Samir said, tossing the ball to the side. "You don't mind?"

"Not at all," Oliver said, smiling. He looked around at everyone else when they were silent. "Right, guys?"

"Fine by me," Elijah said, just as oblivious as Oliver.

"Right," Ashish said after a pause. He smiled at Samir. "I just need to pick up my calculus textbook and then we can go."

"Why do you need to do that if you don't actually study?" Samir asked as they began to walk to the house.

"Um, because it's all about impressions?" Pinky said in a way that suggested any moron should know that. "If the parents think we're actually getting work done, they won't care if we're out late on a school night. Duh."

"Sorry I asked," Samir mumbled, sounding genuinely chided.

Ashish tossed him a look. Huh. He would've expected a much more spirited response.

CHAPTER 14

Ashish

Once Ashish grabbed his book, they piled back into the Jeep and drove to Roast Me.

Samir followed in his car, and Ashish felt a little bad for him, always excluded from the group. It was tough, though. Samir spent his days at his house, while Ashish, Elijah, Oliver, and Pinky were together for eight hours a day every day at school and most weekends, too. Even when they did all hang out, it just wasn't the same. Something always seemed off.

Like last summer when they'd all gone to Ashish's parents' mountain cabin and Samir had left early, right in the middle of a basketball game they were all playing. He said it was because he didn't want his mom to worry, but they all knew the truth: Samir didn't belong, and it was painfully obvious. Ashish wasn't sure why Samir kept trying. Maybe because they were neighbors and Samir didn't really have any other friends? Which was sad, Ashish guessed, in a way. Mostly annoying, though, because it made things awkward.

They got their usual table at the back of Roast Me, with a couch and an armchair. They had to add a chair for Samir, which Pinky didn't look too happy about, but thankfully she didn't say anything Pinky-like and snarky.

There was a silence as they all settled in, and then Samir said, "I like your shirt."

Everyone's heads swiveled to him. He was talking to Pinky, who was wearing a T-shirt she'd distressed and embellished herself. It said *Nevertheless, She F*cking Persisted* on the front in glitter letters, and on the back, *You Can Bet Your Ass She Did*. Pinky loved wearing what her parents called "provocative" shirts. She said it expressed her inner state, but really she just wanted to piss off her mom and dad. And it worked, too. They were second-generation Indian Americans, and though they weren't as traditional as Ma and Pappa, they were both superconservative, stuffy lawyers. How they'd managed to spawn someone like Pinky, Ashish would never figure out.

"Um . . . thanks?" She tucked a lock of purple hair behind one ear and pushed back her rhinestone-studded glasses.

"She made it herself," Oliver said, grinning. "I'm constantly telling her to make me one. . . . Still waiting!" He put on a mock-salty expression and Samir laughed.

"Oh, hey." Hopping up, Samir said, "I'll go get everyone a drink. What do you guys want?"

"Don't worry about it; it'll take too long. You don't know our orders," Pinky said.

Samir smiled, but it was frozen and tight. "I know. That's why I asked what you all wanted. If you tell me, I'll remember for next time."

There was an awkward pause as they all digested that Samir thought there might be a next time. Then Oliver said, "I'll just come with you!" They walked off together.

"I need a potty break," Pinky muttered, standing up too, once the guys were gone. "Be back in a sec."

Ashish groaned. "Why the heck did Oliver invite him?" he asked Elijah. "Did he totally forget the catastrophe that was the holiday party at my place?"

Elijah shook his head. "You know Ol. He doesn't remember the bad stuff. And even if he did, he'd still have invited Samir because that's just how he rolls. He hates seeing people left out."

"I respect that," Ashish replied. "But man. I have a feeling we're going to have another screaming match on our hands before the night's through."

"Tell you what, let's work together to keep 'em apart," Elijah said, leaning forward. "Like, anytime you see Samir ask Pinky something, step in and answer. And I'll do the same if Pinky does her little snipy thing at Samir."

"Deal. Man, that's going to be exhausting."

"That's why God invented coffee."

Ashish laughed just as the door dinged. He looked toward it automatically—and then the world froze, except for her.

Sweetie walked in, talking on her phone and laughing that gorgeous, carefree, tinkling bell of a laugh. Her hair was pulled back into that high ponytail Ashish was beginning to grow very fond of, and she was wearing athletic pants and a bright-blue Piedmont T-shirt. She walked up and stood in line behind Samir and Oliver.

"Why do you look like you just swallowed a watermelon whole?" Elijah asked, craning his head to look at what Ashish was looking at. "Oh. Is that her?"

Ashish nodded. He pushed his shoulders back and was poised to go into his trademark swagger when he glanced down—and froze. "Oh, crap," he muttered.

"What?" Elijah asked.

"What the hell am I wearing?" Ashish pulled on his Ash/Pikachu T-shirt in horror. "I look like a freaking eighth grader." He sniffed experimentally at his armpit. "Damn it. Why didn't I put on deodorant before we came out?"

Elijah regarded him closely, one eyebrow raised. "Dude, you look and smell fine. Just go over there and say hi."

Ashish scoffed. "Uh, no. I can't."

"What do you mean you can't? Yes, you can. Just stand up, walk over there, open your mouth, and say, 'Hi, Sweetie.'"

Ashish almost dived for Elijah's mouth. "Shhhh! She might hear you!"

Elijah stared at him like he'd grown a shark fin. "Yeah, that was kind of the point."

Ashish shook himself off. *Jeez, Ash, get a grip.* "You're right. I'm gonna go over there. She's gonna love me. I'm Ash."

He grinned, and Elijah grinned.

He waited, and Elijah waited.

Ashish stared. Elijah stared back.

"You're not gonna go over, are you?"

Ashish's smile fell off his face. "Nuh-uh. It's fine. I'll just talk to her on Saturday, when we go out." His palms were actually damp. Not only had he lost his mojo again, his mojo was a distant memory, like it had belonged to someone else. How the heck had he *ever* approached girls? How had he ever done this so confidently, never even imagining that things might go horribly wrong? Then it hit him: It was because he'd never really cared about those other girls and they'd never really cared about him. But this already felt different. "You know, it's better that way anyway. I mean, it's not like we're serious or anything. It's not like I *owe* it to her to go—"

"Ash."

"—over there and say anything. I mean, this is preserving the mystery. I don't want to look all desperate anyway. Right? Right."

"Okay, you have *got* to breathe." Elijah took a deep breath. "Come on. Oliver taught me how to do this. You breathe in for the count of seven, and you breathe out for a count of three. Wait, or is it the other way around? Anyway, here we go. One . . ."

"Crap, crap, she's turning around. *Crap*." He grinned suddenly, still talking. "*CRAP*. She saw me." He waved overenthusiastically, still grinning, and stood.

He heard Elijah snort as he began to walk toward Sweetie. "Good luck, man," his friend said in a tone that suggested he meant, *You're totally going to screw this up, so, you know, all the best to you in your time of need*.

Sweetie stepped out of line and turned to Ashish. Thankfully, Oliver and Samir hadn't noticed yet, or he'd have them to contend with too. He and Sweetie walked a little distance away, close to a spinning card display.

"Hi," Ashish said, looking down at Sweetie. His heart fluttered a bit in spite of his extreme discomfort.

She looked up at him through the thick fringe of her coal-black eyelashes. "Hi." Holy crap. She had a faint dimple in her right cheek that he'd never noticed before. How was it that she just kept getting cuter every time they met? "How was your day?"

"Good." He smiled a half smile. "Distracting, though. There's something on my mind I just can't stop thinking about."

She dropped her gaze shyly for a moment before looking back up at him, and his head spun. SO. FREAKING. UNBEARABLY. CUTE. "Oh, yeah? What's that?"

He stepped a little bit closer. Her body heat washed gently over him. He could smell her shampoo—something minty and sweet— even with the strong coffee smell enveloping them. His entire body, all five senses, were tuned completely in to her, like a satellite rotating to keep in the earth's orbit. "Well, ever since I met this girl who challenged me to a race—"

"She challenged you to a race?" Sweetie said, quirking her mouth to one side. "That's pretty strange."

"Nah, I actually kinda dug it. She totally kicked my butt, too."

A hint of a smile played at Sweetie's mouth. Her full lips were lined in clear gloss, and Ashish tried not to stare. "Wow. She must be a pretty amazing athlete."

"She is," Ashish said seriously. "And see, now I kind of have a date with her Saturday. So I'm pretty nervous about making a good impression."

"Hmm." Sweetie pretended to consider this. "Well, I don't think you should be."

"No?"

"No. Because I think that girl probably feels the same way about you. So you can both just be nervous together on Saturday and it'll be okay."

"Yeah?" Ashish smiled.

"Yeah."

They stood there, grinning at each other like fools.

"Is this who I think it is?" Oliver's voice cut through the love haze like a knife. Ashish turned to see him and Samir approaching them with a tray of drinks. Oh, great.

Oliver grinned and continued. "Yeah, it sure is. You're Sweetie, right?"

Sweetie blinked. "Um . . . yeah."

"These are my friends, Oliver and Samir," Ashish said, trying to make a surreptitious *Go away* expression at Oliver, who seemed completely oblivious as usual. He just kept beaming at Sweetie. Samir, meanwhile, just looked confused. He still didn't know about everything that had happened over the weekend. That was going to be a fun conversation. Samir would totally gloat about Ashish taking his advice, even though this whole thing had squat to do with him.

"Oh, it's nice to meet you." Sweetie stuck out a hand, and both Oliver and Samir shook it.

"We're all pretty much dying to hear how Saturday goes," Oliver gushed. "Like, seriously. Elijah, my boyfriend, and I can't stop talking about it, especially since Ash has been so down since Cel—"

"Okay, time to go," Ashish said loudly. "Come on, Sweetie, I'll buy you some coffee."

"Well, if you're drinking coffee, and we're drinking coffee . . . ," Oliver, that unstoppable idiot, said. He shrugged. "Join us."

Ashish scoffed. "I'm sure Sweetie has way better things to do than—"

"No, I don't, actually," Sweetie said, looking at him with her eyebrows raised. Then, turning to Oliver, she beamed. "I'd love to join you guys. Thanks."

"Great! Just come on over to that table." Oliver gestured with his chin before walking away.

Samir, who hadn't said a word and had just looked increasingly confused, followed him, still frowning.

As Ashish and Sweetie walked up to the counter, she turned to him, one eyebrow cocked. "So. Is there a reason you don't want me to meet your friends?"

"Believe me, it's to protect you," Ashish said. Then he realized what she might be getting at, that he might be embarrassed because she was fat. "And, uh, I already showed them your picture today at lunch. That's how Oliver recognized you."

She looked away, but she was smiling. "Oh. Good."

Ashish's heart sang at the appearance of that somewhat-dimple.

Sweetie

Ashish insisted on paying for her drink. Sweetie found that charming, even though she supposed it had its roots in some kind of sexist thinking. But still. It was adorable, the way he seemed both nervous and intent on being chivalrous.

They walked to his friends' table in the back. Sweetie kept darting looks at him; he'd smile at her and then go back to glaring at them. She got the feeling that he'd been honest with her—he was apprehensive about this not because of her or how she looked, but because of them. Sweetie felt herself relax a bit. Whatever his friends were like, she could deal with it.

All four of the people at the table stopped talking (actually, it sounded kind of like they were arguing, but Sweetie couldn't be sure) when she and Ashish walked up. They sat on the couch beside each other, their arms brushing lightly as they got situated. Sweetie's stomach did a silly, flippy-excited thing and she tried not to let it show on her face.

"I'm so glad you could join us!" Oliver said. "This is my boyfriend, Elijah." He gestured to the muscular black boy next to him, who nodded but didn't give her the exuberant smile Oliver had. "Samir you've already met, and that over there's Pinky." He pointed to a dark-skinned Indian girl with rainbow-hued hair, about ten earrings in each ear, and a very opinionated shirt.

"'Sup." She nodded coolly at Sweetie.

The girl was extremely pretty in a kind of Goth, glamorous way. For an insecure minute Sweetie wondered whether she was one of Ashish's exes, but then she put the thought firmly out of her head. *That way lies madness and jealousy, Sweetie.*

"It's nice to meet you all," she said, smiling at each of them. "And thanks for letting me grab coffee with you."

"Sure!" Oliver said. "It's our pleasure." He elbowed Elijah subtly, and Elijah grunted assent.

"So what Oliver said about Saturday . . . You and Ashish are dating?" the other Indian-American boy, Samir, asked, his expression clearing like he'd arrived at a conclusion to a particularly bothersome mathematical problem. He was a tall, slightly lanky dude with neatly combed hair. He was the best dressed out of all of them, in a button-down shirt and neatly pressed khaki pants. He looked like a banker in the making. (Whereas Ash was wearing a Pokemon

T-shirt he'd probably had since eighth grade, which was kind of incorrigibly cute.)

"Well, yeah." Ashish shifted uncomfortably beside Sweetie, and she tossed him a look. What was that about? But he didn't make a move to do or say anything, so she continued. "But our first official date isn't till Saturday." Laughing, she said, "Ashish's parents have it all figured out."

Ashish cleared his throat. "Yep. So anyway, Pinky, do you have any more protests coming up?"

"Ashish's parents?" Samir asked, his eyes narrowing. "How did you guys meet, exactly?"

"Ashish's mom set us up," Sweetie replied. Was it just her, or was there something weird about Samir's expression and the way he was asking these questions? Why did he look almost . . . cocky?

"HA!" Samir said way too loudly, and Sweetie jumped. "So you decided to take my advice, didja? You could tell the S-Man knew what he was talking about."

Ashish rolled his eyes and sipped his coffee. "Yeah, sure. Whatever, bro."

"Oh, come on. Just admit it! You wanted a way out of your girl-less fog, and I gave it to you. I'm like the genius problem solver, just fixing up your life without a second thought."

Sweetie frowned and glanced at Ashish. He was still trying to appear nonchalant, but a muscle in his jaw twitched. And his shoulders were sort of hunched in, like he was trying to protect himself. But from what? And why was Samir being kind of an ass? No one was laughing.

"You just went around for *months* not being able to play, having trouble with the ladies, and now look at you! You should really have come to me a long time ago, dude. Like, when Celia cheated—"

"Shut *up*, Samir!" Pinky's voice was louder even than Samir's. Her eyes flashed behind her glasses. "Look around. Do any of us look amused? Doesn't that give you a hint that you should shut your damn mouth? News flash: Nobody likes you, and this kind of crap is exactly why!"

There was a frozen kind of silence. Sweetie didn't want to move her head in case it drew Pinky's attention, so she just swiveled her eyeballs around to look at everyone. Samir's face didn't hint at anything at all; it was completely devoid of expression. Elijah and Oliver both looked almost comical in their shock: Their eyes were wide, and their mouths hung open. Ashish was fair enough that his cheeks were tinted a faint magenta, but he refused to meet anyone's eye.

And then Samir's words floated back to Sweetie: *Like, when Celia cheated . . .* And hadn't Oliver been saying something about a Celia when Ashish interrupted him? Sweetie looked at Ashish more openly, remembering the picture she and the girls had looked at in the locker room that day after practice. She distinctly remembered Ashish's sad eyes.

And even though his mouth was turned up in a haughty smirk right then, there was a kind of woundedness in his eyes, a hardness to his jaw that came from feeling defensive, from being hurt. And it was because of this girl who'd apparently broken his heart. Sweetie felt a sickening kind of lurching inside her. She hadn't known, when she texted him, that he came with baggage from a previous girlfriend. And if she still had the power to make him look like he did, if she'd hurt him enough that his friends leaped to his defense at the mere mention of her name . . . did Sweetie even really stand a chance?

CHAPTER 15

Ashish

Well, this was just freaking awesome.

Not only had Samir decided to be an ass in front of Sweetie, he'd actually mentioned Celia and her cheating. Could a guy get no privacy around here? And as if that weren't enough, the way Pinky had erupted on him would definitely freak Sweetie out. First Pappa and his "contract," and now his friends behaving like wild jackasses.

The silence dragged on and on. It wasn't just that Samir had talked about his private stuff, either. The thing was, it still hurt to talk about Celia, to think about her, to think how it had gone from so good to so bad, how he'd been left behind—not that he'd say any of that to anyone. He barely thought about it himself.

"Well. If that's how you all feel." Samir hopped up from the chair and walked off, pushing the door open with the heel of his hand. They watched him go.

Nobody said anything. Then Ashish stood. "Yeah. I'm gonna go too." He looked at his friends and tossed the keys to Pinky. "Take the Jeep. Just bring it to school tomorrow."

"How are you going to get back home?" Oliver asked.

"I'll just call Rajat, my parents' driver. He can be here in ten minutes; I'll wait outside."

Pinky and Elijah protested, but Ashish shook his head at them and they fell silent. He looked down at Sweetie and smiled a little. "Um, sorry to just leave like this. But I'll talk to you later, yeah?"

She nodded slowly and he walked away. She'd probably call and cancel their date before Saturday. Whatever. To be honest, he was starting to think that maybe he wasn't ready to date again at all.

Outside in the parking lot, the air was cool and dry. Ashish walked over to the Jeep, grabbed a hoodie from the back, and put it on, zipping it up to his throat. Even though the parking lot was empty, he felt strangely exposed.

He leaned against the Jeep and texted Rajat, asking him to pick him up. This was nothing new; Rajat was pretty much on call 24/7 and had picked up Ashish at parties before when he didn't want to drive. Rajat was discreet, if nothing else. Ma and Pappa wouldn't ask any questions about why Ashish had come home from his study group in the family car, without his friends.

Someone cleared her throat behind him and he turned, expecting Sweetie. But it was Pinky. Her hands were deep in her jacket pockets, and she shifted from foot to foot, like she was uncomfortable. Neither of them were "feelings" people like Oliver was. "Hey."

"Hey."

They stared at each other. Then Pinky said, "You're leaving because of me, right?"

"Why would it be because of you?"

She sighed and leaned against the Jeep beside him. "I should've just let his bullshit roll off my back. But I can't. That guy annoys me so much. He's just so selfish and . . ." She sucked in a breath. "Anyway. I'm sorry I made a scene like that. Especially in front of Sweetie."

Ashish bumped her gently with his arm. "Nah, it's okay. I know you were just trying to look out for me. It's cool; you can't help but love me."

Pinky snorted. "Right. So . . . you excited about your date with her? She seems nice."

A car drove by and they both looked up, but it was a green Mustang. Relaxing back against the Jeep, Ashish said, "She is nice. But I think she's probably going to call the whole thing off. And honestly, maybe that's the right thing to do."

"What? Why would you say that?"

"I mean, just hearing about Celia makes me all . . . I don't know. Like I'm Mount Vesuvius and I'm just waiting to blow. I'm no shrink, but I'm pretty sure that means I've got some unresolved crap. Oh, and hearing what Samir said probably made Sweetie want to run away as fast as she can, which, let's face it, is pretty dang fast."

"Okay, one: So you're not over Celia. Isn't that what this is about? Going out there, getting back on the horse again? Giving another girl a chance? And two: If she runs, it's totally her loss."

"Aww, thanks, Pinky Dinky Doo." He put his arm around her and pulled her close. "You're such a good friend."

"Ugh!" She made a half-hearted motion to struggle and get away. "You know I hate when you call me that."

The bell above the front door of Roast Me tinkled and they both looked up. Sweetie stood a few feet away, looking at them. She waved a little awkwardly as she made her way over.

"I think that's my cue." Pinky extracted herself from under Ashish's arm. Turning to him, she said quietly, "Give her a chance, Ash." Her eyes were big and devoid of her usual Pinky sarcasm. "I have a good feeling about this one." Then, nodding at Sweetie, she walked back inside.

He looked at Sweetie, approaching in the purple-white lights of the streetlights. Even now she was beautiful. It wasn't just her physical appearance, though. Something about the way she held herself—that tentativeness, that open-eyed curiosity, that beguiling shallow dimple that popped out whenever she smiled or quirked her mouth—all of those things were attractive to Ashish, and he just couldn't figure out why. Maybe it was her pheromones. He'd read somewhere that if two people were suitable for each other, they'd find each other's smells really compelling. He flared his nostrils and tried to sniff surreptitiously.

Sweetie narrowed her eyes. "What are you doing?" She was standing about two feet away now, her head tipped back to look at him.

Crap. "Uh . . . nothing. Nothing at all." He stuck his hands into the pockets of his hoodie and looked out at the street. "You don't have to wait with me. It's kind of cold."

"I run warm," Sweetie said. "So it feels nice out here."

There was a pause. He could sense her question in the space between them but didn't press her. Honestly, the longer he could pretend that Samir hadn't wrecked everything between them before it had even had a chance to get started, the better. He could live in fantasyland for a little while longer. Just like he had with Celia. Apparently, he didn't learn lessons too easily. Wasn't that an indicator of intelligence, how fast you learned things? Well, he was lucky he had basketball as a way to get into college, then.

"Ashish . . ."

He forced himself to look at her but kept his face neutral. She, on the other hand, looked anxious, her big eyes full of questions. The urge to wrap his arms around her to comfort her was almost over-powering, but he managed to resist.

She swallowed. "What Samir said. About that girl Celia. Is it true?"

He tried a smile, but it didn't quite make it to his face. "What? My friends didn't fill you in the moment I left?" Oliver was the one who'd caused this whole mess by inviting Sweetie to sit with them in the first place. And by inviting Samir. It stood to reason the moment he was asked that he'd flap his lips to Sweetie.

She frowned a little. "No. All they said was that you'd had a hard time recently and I should talk to you about it."

Ashish rubbed a hand across his jaw. Oliver and Elijah were such good people. He really didn't deserve them. "Oh." Taking a deep breath, he continued. "Then . . . yes. It's true. I went out with Celia for almost six months. It was mostly long distance because she goes to SFSU, but still. It meant something." He laughed a little scorn-fully. "To me, the high school dumb-ass, anyway. We started to drift apart, but I felt sure that we could work it out. I mean, we were barely talking, but . . . yeah. I just thought what we had was real."

"So . . . what happened?" She asked it without judgment or greedy curiosity.

Ashish shrugged. "I went up to visit her at her dorm one day and her roommate told me she was out with some guy. She didn't even have the decency to tell me herself."

He heard Sweetie sigh, soft and low in the night. "I'm sorry."

"Yeah. Me too." He heard the bitterness in his voice but couldn't stop it.

She leaned against the Jeep too, and they both stared at the cars passing in the street for a while. "And you're not over her." It wasn't a question.

He turned on his side to look at her then. He needed to look into her eyes when he said this, so she really understood. "No, I'm not. And I don't know when—if—I'll ever be. So if we date, you have to realize . . . you're not getting all of me, Sweetie. And if that means that you need to walk away, I'll totally get it." He rubbed the back of his neck, agitated. "I'm sorry. I thought I could handle this, you know. Dating again, being with you. Because I like you. I really do."

"But you still see her when you're looking at me?"

Ashish shook his head; that wasn't quite right. "No, it's more like . . . she keeps darting into my line of vision when I'm looking at you. Like I haven't put all of that behind me yet. I'm not sure if I can connect with you on any kind of deep level because of her, Sweetie." It was kind of strange all of that came tumbling out. . . . Maybe he should be embarrassed. But he wasn't.

Sweetie leaned her head back against the Jeep as she looked up at the sky. Ashish felt his palms grow damp as he waited for her to say what was on her mind. He really cared what she thought, he realized. He wanted to be honest with Sweetie. He wanted her to know him, to fully know what he could offer and what he just couldn't. That was why he wasn't embarrassed about everything he'd just word-vomited out.

Finally she turned on her side too, to face him. "I still want to go out with you. It's not ideal for me to date a boy who's still hung up on someone else, I'll admit." She laughed a little. "But this whole dating thing for me is about something else too. You know how you wanted to date again, sort of like a palate cleanser to get rid of the Celia aftertaste?"

He nodded, smiling a little at the way she'd put that.

"Well, I wanted to date someone like you"—here she made a gesture toward his entire body—"to prove to myself that I could. My mom's always talking about how I need to get thin before someone handsome will give me a chance. And I knew in my heart that she was wrong."

"She is wrong," Ashish said forcefully, and she looked up at him in surprise. "I'm sorry, but that's total crap. You're beautiful. And you're incredibly talented, too. Any guy would be lucky to go out with you."

"Thanks." Sweetie smiled and looked down at her feet, her dimple almost slaying him. "Anyway, we both have things we want to achieve through dating each other, and it's not that one big, grand true love, right?"

Ashish nodded.

"So." Sweetie shrugged. "Let's just keep on with the plan. Maybe I'll help you forget Celia a bit, and maybe you'll help me see that I should listen to Amma less about what I can and can't do while fat."

Ashish smiled. "Really? You're sure?"

"Totally." She held out a fist for him to bump, and after a surprised pause he bumped it, laughing.

"You're cool, you know that?"

"Obviously." She stuck out her tongue at him, and then they were both laughing.

Car headlights swept over them, and Ashish looked over his shoulder to see the off-white Escalade with Rajat behind the wheel. "Oh, I should . . ." He gestured with a thumb over his shoulder. "Hey, do you want a ride back home?"

"No, that's okay. I drove." Sweetie smiled and stepped back. "But I'll see you Saturday at your house, right? So we can go to Pavan Mandir together?"

Ashish nodded. "Pavan Mandir. Get ready to get your worship on." He rolled his eyes.

Laughing, Sweetie waved a little shyly and turned to walk to her car. Ashish watched her all the way.

CHAPTER 16

Sweetie

The rest of the week raced by like, well, Sweetie on the track. Kayla, Suki, and Izzy kept her mind busy with talk of the upcoming Band Night at Roast Me. Saturday morning, just as Sweetie was finished with her shower and getting dressed, Kayla sent out a group text with the good news.

Kayla: we now have 12 bands ladies! Band Night is totally on!

Izzy: WHAT

Suki: F$%^#$@#@@$%F

OMG, Sweetie typed, sitting back against her headboard in her room. How did you make that happen?? Yesterday we were at 5!

Kayla: I told you before BGM

Sweetie: ??

Kayla: black girl magic ☺☺

Kayla: also I promised Antwan I'd seriously think about his promposal if he agreed to publicize at Eastman and got us to at least 10 bands

Izzy: haha well then I guess you owe him a date

Kayla: I was already going to say yes but this is way better than a corsage

Sweetie: hahahaha you are hilarious and ily

Kayla: ily2

Suki: okay so that's Kayla's prom plans and band night taken care of . . . what about you, Sweetie?

Sweetie: what about me

Kayla: don't play coy bb your date's in what an hour?

Sweetie: yeah just about . . . I'm NERVOUS you guys

Izzy: but this is just about proving to yourself you can do it right? So there's no need to be nervous!!

Suki: she's right you know . . . just remember that you're one kick-ass lady. He's the lucky one

Kayla: you've got that brown girl magic, too, S. You got this

Sweetie: OMG I'm crying. TY guys llysm

Kayla: love you too we're here for you

Suki: love your face

Izzy: Love you!! Have fun!!

Sweetie: k I'll text you guys when it's over

Suki: Yeah let's grab some fro yo or something and debrief

Izzy: Yessss

Kayla: I'm in

Sweetie: k!

Sweetie set her phone down and blinked away the tears. She had, hands down, the best friends in the world. She felt readier now than she had all week, just with a small pep talk from her crew. If Kayla, Suki, and Izzy believed she had this, then she had this. She trusted their judgment implicitly, even when she didn't trust her own. Speaking of trusting judgment . . . She grabbed her phone again and texted.

going on my first date today with Ashish Patel

Anjali Chechi: Okay you have NOT filled me in enough to drop that bomb on me

lol sorry will do that soon

Okay okay. Remember: SAFE SEX

Omg Chechi seriously we're going to Pavan Mandir

Okay you have NOT filled me in enough to drop that bomb on me

lolol I will I promise

Okay then talk soon!

Okay ☺

Just seeing Anjali Chechi's words on her screen made her feel even more secure. Ashish Patel, let's face it, was a small part of her life. There were others who knew her, who loved her, who felt like she was on totally equal footing with this basketball star who could be a model if he chose. Amma wasn't one of them, but so what? Sweetie walked up to her vanity, drew on some winged eyeliner, and smiled at herself. She was wearing a yellow *kameez* top with little red flowers on it and plain white *salwar* pants. Her *dupatta*, the shawl, was red with gold thread shot through. (It was a little warm for a long-sleeved outfit, but Amma had once told her her arms were her worst feature, and Sweetie had never quite been able to get over that.) She'd paired the whole thing with red sandals and a gold bindi, something she wore only to the mandir. Her hair hung in loose waves down her back and she felt almost beautiful today, and that was a good day in any book.

She still had more than an hour, so she walked over to her closet and pulled out her art supplies. She could finish working on the boxes for next week's farmers' market (she'd decided not to go with

Amma this weekend, as she had to get ready and be in the right head space for the date). She'd just set everything up on the dining room table and gotten comfortable when Amma walked in.

Sweetie glanced at her and then back down at the box she'd been tying the burlap ribbon on to. "Where's Achchan?"

"Taking a bath. He'll be out soon." Amma bustled around in the kitchen, putting things away. "Hopefully I'll sell almost everything today."

Sweetie made a vague, noncommittal noise in the back of her throat. She was still pretty mad about the whole thing with Ashish, to be honest. She still felt completely betrayed that Amma had told Sunita auntie that Sweetie wasn't good enough for her son. And so she didn't feel like looking at Amma right now, let alone talking to her.

"Want some chai?" Amma asked from the kitchen.

"No, thanks." Sweetie kept her eyes on the heart she was attaching to the corner of the box. She hoped Amma would go sit outside to drink her chai like she did when the weather was nice.

But no such luck. A moment later she was sitting two chairs down from Sweetie, watching her work while noisily slurping her drink.

Sweetie wanted to glare at her but managed to resist.

"That's nice," Amma said. "I like that color palette. Red looks pretty against the brown of the burlap."

"Mm-hmm," Sweetie said, reaching to snip off some more burlap.

"I'm making coconut chicken curry tonight. And *pal payasam* for dessert."

Sweetie glanced at Amma. Those were her absolute favorite foods. "But it isn't Onam." Onam was a festival from southern India, and

Amma was fairly rigid about making *pal payasam* only during Onam or for other special festivals.

Amma shrugged and sipped her chai. "So?"

Sweetie knew what this was: a peace offering. Amma and Achchan—and Sweetie by extension—didn't ever say "I love you" like her friends and their parents did. They made up not by talking about their feelings or sharing deep, intimate moments. Instead there were myriad ways of saying *I love you* or *I'm sorry* in their house: making someone's favorite dish; helping someone design the boxes for their sweets; being present at the farmers' market every Saturday so Amma never had to sit alone, or every track meet so Sweetie would always see a friendly face in the audience, no matter how far away the other school was; drawing a black dot in kohl on the cheek to ward off the evil eye; buying the right kind of soap before someone ran out.

But sometimes, like today, Sweetie wished Amma would say the words. That she'd say she was wrong or that Sweetie absolutely was good enough for whomever she chose to date, that her worth wasn't measured in dress size or pounds or kilograms. But that would never happen. So they sat there, in silence, until the bell on the big clock in the living room tolled nine o'clock. Sweetie got up, put away her art supplies, and smoothed down her hair.

Then, going back out into the living room, where Amma and Achchan were now, she said, "Okay, bye. I'm leaving."

Amma looked up from her *Bolly Gossip* magazine for a moment. "You're going to Kayla's house?"

"Yes. We're going to study for that calculus test." Sweetie's palms were drenched. She hated lying; it was hardly ever a good idea. She'd read once that if you were lying about something, it generally meant that your values were clashing with your actions. But the article hadn't talked about what to do when you knew, 100 percent, that you were right and your parents were wrong, but it had been ingrained into you from childhood that lying to them was the worst possible thing you could do.

The guilt only intensified when Achchan beamed at her. "My Sweetie, straight-A student and star athlete! So focused on her studies."

"I don't know about that," Sweetie mumbled, not quite able to meet his eye.

"No, it's true!" Achchan said, reaching out and taking her hand. He tugged on her and she sat in the oversize recliner, half squeezed in beside him, half on his lap. They'd sat like that since Sweetie was little, when he'd read to her from whatever book she was obsessed with that week. "I am very proud to call you my daughter. Your Achchan is very lucky, and he knows it."

Whenever Achchan began speaking about himself in the third person, you knew he was getting emotional. Sweetie tried not to let the guilt completely engulf her. She wanted to bury her face in his chest and wail, *I'm really going on a date with Ashish Patel!* And if it were just Achchan and her, she probably would.

But the thing was, she couldn't be honest right now. She knew how she felt, but she didn't know how to convince her parents—and Amma especially—that she was right about her body, that she didn't need to be thin to be happy, that there was absolutely nothing wrong with her. And until she could articulate those feelings and articulate them bravely and well, Sweetie knew, she'd have to keep the whole Sassy Sweetie Project under wraps.

Achchan patted her arm. "Are you okay, Sweetie?"

She glanced at him sideways. "Why wouldn't I be?"

"Everything fine with Kayla and Suzi and Icky?"

Sweetie laughed. "It's *Suki* and *Izzy*, Achcha."

He waved a hand, like, *I'm too old and too set in my ways to learn that.*

"Yeah, they're all fine. Everything's fine. I promise."

Amma glanced up from her magazine but didn't say anything.

"Okay then," Achchan said after a pause. "You got your cell phone? Call if you need anything."

She put her arms around Achchan's neck. "Thank you, Achcha. I will." She clambered off the recliner before the lump in her throat became actual tears in her eyes. "I really should go, though."

"*Sari*," Amma said. "Just text me when you arrive there and before you leave."

Usually Sweetie felt a little bite of annoyance at Amma's stringent rules. How many times had she been over to Kayla's? Was there really a need to text every single time? But this time she was too guilt drenched to feel annoyed. "*Sari*, Amma. *Pinne kaanaam.*"

"Bye."

Sweetie took off in her car before she could change her mind. *Come on. You said you wanted to be Sassy Sweetie. Don't be Stupid Soggy Sweetie now.* So she kept her foot on the gas pedal and kept going.

Ashish's house was imposing, even though she'd been here before, just last weekend. Back then she'd been in sort of a fog, worried about what his parents would say, wondering what the whole thing was about. But now . . . She tipped her head back and took in the gigantic mansion, which looked like it belonged on some Scottish moor somewhere. (Wait. Did Scottish moors have castles? Whatever. It was humongous.)

She took a deep breath, adjusted her *dupatta,* and walked up to the heavy-looking, ornately carved front door. She raised her hand to ring the doorbell, but the door swung open before she could.

Ashish stood there, smiling at her. His hair was perfectly mussed, his kurta and pants neatly pressed and, by the looks of it, starched. His brilliant smile held just a hint of anxiety around the edges, and he tugged repeatedly at his embroidered sleeves. "Ugh, why am I wearing this again? Oh, right, because my parents basically held me hostage until I agreed to." The idea of Ashish Patel not being totally comfortable either made Sweetie feel tons better. "Oh, wait. I meant, hey, nice to see you. Come on in."

Sweetie laughed. "Thanks." She walked in and looked around. The circular table in the center of the foyer held a huge vase full of fresh roses. The scent hung in the air, mouthwateringly sweet.

"So, fair warning," Ashish said, his eyebrows high. "My parents—"

"Sweetie *beta*!" Sunita auntie came clip-clopping through the open archway, her face bright in a full-on thousand-watt smile.

Ashish's face froze, his back to his mother. He mouthed, "Good luck," and then they both faced the onslaught together.

Sunita auntie came fully equipped with her *puja thali*—a silver tray on which were balanced various powders and other accoutrements. Sweetie had seen Amma with the same kind of *thali* during various special occasions (such as before final exams), and she knew what was coming. Ashish stood silently with Sweetie as Sunita auntie asked Lord Hanuman to look after them on this auspicious outing. Kartik uncle stood off to the side, watching everything with a face that gave nothing away. He'd be a tough one to win over, Sweetie knew. If, you know, she were looking to win Ashish's parents over, that is.

She felt a little bad for Sunita auntie, actually. She was obviously hoping for something miraculous and straight out of a romance novel, but she didn't know of Sweetie's and Ashish's hidden agendas.

A maid came and took the *thali* away, and then Sunita auntie slipped an arm through Sweetie's. "Come in, *beta*, come in. We didn't get a chance to properly welcome you last weekend, and for that I am truly sorry." The men trailed behind them as they walked in and took their seats in the mysterious second living room/den. Ashish sat beside her on the sofa, and his parents sat in armchairs across from them. "Your *salwar* is just so beautiful!" Sunita auntie continued. "Where did you buy it?"

"Oh, thank you! My mom got it for me on a trip to India last year. I couldn't go because of track, though."

"That's such a pity! It is so important to visit our ancestral home often. It helps us stay connected to our roots. Don't you agree?"

Sweetie glanced at Ashish, who was rolling his eyes so hard she was afraid they'd pop right out of his head. Turning back to Sunita auntie, she said, "I do, actually. And I do try to go every year. If I didn't, I think my Amooma—my grandmother—would have withdrawal."

Sunita auntie trilled a laugh. "Same with Ashish's grandparents! Photos are just not the same, are they?"

"No, they aren't."

For a slightly awkward moment, everyone just looked at one another in silence. Then Kartik uncle grunted to Ashish: "Jeep has gas?"

And that's how Sweetie knew—he wasn't nearly as scary or intimidating as he seemed. Underneath he really loved his son. "Jeep has gas?" was just another way of saying *I love you and I worry about you.*

"It does, Pappa," Ashish said.

"Okay then." Kartik uncle reached into his pocket and pulled out his wallet. He handed Ashish a bundle of cash—how much, Sweetie couldn't say, but the top bill was a hundred. She tried not to stare. "Take this."

"Pappa, it's okay, I have some money left over from my last allowa—"

"Just take." He thrust the money at his son.

Ashish took it quietly. "Thanks, Pappa."

Kartik uncle grunted in response. Sunita auntie clasped her hands, her eyes shining. "Well, I don't want to take up too much time. . . ."

Ashish and Sweetie stood in unison.

"*Thik hai*, Ma," Ashish said. "We'll see you both later?"

His parents nodded. Sweetie could tell from the barely suppressed energy in the room that it was all Sunita auntie could do not to hover and shepherd them to the door, maybe even smooth out Ashish's cowlick and kiss him on the cheek. Somehow she resisted. Sweetie was impressed; Amma could never show such restraint.

Outside, birds chirped in the trees beatifically. The trees whispered in the wind, and the fountain in the distance gurgled its silver song. Everything looked and sounded perfect: sunny and bright, cheerful and melodic. Maybe you couldn't buy happiness, but you could definitely buy something adjacent to it. Dealing with hardships had to be easier when you lived on what was basically a movie set.

Sweetie walked to Ashish's Jeep, but he shook his head and led her around the house to a series of garages instead. In one of those sat a shiny red Porsche, perched prettily on its shiny wheels. "I thought we'd take this instead," Ashish said. "Seems a little more datelike to me. I mean, if you're okay with it." He dropped his gaze and ran a hand through his hair as he said it, like he was afraid she'd think he was being silly.

Sweetie's heart squeezed in her chest. It was really sweet of him to make an effort, even though this wasn't a traditional first date in the strict sense of the term for so many reasons. "It's perfect," she said, and Ashish grinned, bright and happy.

Pavan Mandir was a forty-minute drive away. Sweetie tried not to focus on Ashish's perfectly muscled forearm, the way his big hand gripped the gear shift loosely, the confident way he shifted gears and sped up or slowed down through traffic. She tried not to notice the way his seat belt stretched tight against his muscled chest, or the way his pants hugged his thighs. Never having been in such close proximity to a boy, Sweetie realized something: Hormones were almost impossible to ignore. After clearing her throat to distract herself, she said, "Do you and your parents go to Pavan Mandir a lot?"

At the same time Ashish said, "You look really pretty today."

They both looked at each other for a second in awkward silence, waiting for the other to continue. Then they both burst out laughing. Sweetie pointed at him. "You first."

"Okay." He grinned that half-grin thing he did when he was feeling especially cocky. The one that did strange things to her heartbeat. "I think you look really beautiful today."

She gave him a suspicious look. "You said 'pretty' the first time. Why the change?"

Ashish laughed. "Does it really matter?"

"Oh, yes, it does. 'Pretty' is a step down from 'beautiful.' So you were lying either the first time or the second time." She put on a mock-serious expression. "Which was it?"

Ashish darted his eyes around like he was terrified. "Uh . . . I meant you're both pretty and beautiful? So, like, pretty to the beautiful power?"

Sweetie snorted. "That was a *really* bad save, but I'll let it go this time."

"Thank you. So to answer *your* question, I've been to Pavan Mandir mayyyybe twice in the last year."

"Seriously?" Sweetie couldn't imagine that. Her parents made the trek every other week, and she usually went along, unless she had something track related. "Why not? Are your parents not religious?"

"Oh, they are. Ma especially. But they gave up that battle in favor of other, bigger ones. I'm actually pretty sure that's what this whole first-date-at-the-mandir thing is about. They're forcing me to go. Parental units one, Ashish zero."

Sweetie frowned. "No . . . I don't think they're trying to one-up you, if that's what you're thinking." She paused, afraid she'd overstepped. "At least, that's just my opinion."

Ashish darted a glance her way. "Oh? Do tell. I'm curious to hear what you think of all of this."

"Well, I'm no parent, but . . . I think it's probably hard for Sunita auntie and Kartik uncle. You seem . . . pretty disinterested in Indian culture. I mean, you made it a point not to date Indian girls at all before me. So maybe they're not trying to get one over on you by making you go to the mandir for your first date. Maybe they're just trying to create, I don't know, like, a positive association for you or something. Maybe they're hoping you'll have fun and then you'll see it isn't so bad. Maybe to your parents, you not liking Indian culture feels like a rejection of them?" Sweetie stopped, sucking on her lower lip, afraid she'd make him mad with some of the stuff she'd said. "But obviously that's just what I think. And I don't know you or them very well at all."

Ashish was quiet for a while. Sweetie began to get more and more nervous that she'd totally wrecked any chance of a salvageable first date, when he turned to her, smiling, before turning back to the road. "I think you may be right. My mom actually said something to that effect—that maybe I think my culture's uncool because they've pushed it on me and I think *they're* uncool. Wow." He paused, thinking. "It's kind of sad. I never want them to feel like I'm rejecting them." Turning to Sweetie again briefly, he said, "I've lived with my parents for seventeen years and I would never have come to that conclusion. But it feels right now that you've said it. I wonder if you actually understand them better than I do."

Sweetie laughed. "Oh, I don't know about that. It's easy sometimes to have a clear perspective as an outsider. Know what I mean?"

Ashish looked at her again, and this time she saw respect and something that looked a lot like admiration in his gaze. She tried not to flush. "Yeah, I do. You might be one of the wisest people I've ever met."

"I don't know. . . . What about Oliver? He seemed pretty wise. So does your mom."

"Yeah, okay. But definitely in the top three."

"I'll take it." Sweetie grinned, more pleased than she let on.

CHAPTER 17

Sweetie

Pavan Mandir was a big, white, open-sided temple set on a hill that overlooked Frye Lake. *Pavan* meant "wind" in Hindi, and the temple got its name because it had no real walls or doors, just a series of beams and pillars that connected its ceiling to its floor. The wind off the lake swept in with abandon, leaving the temple slightly chillier than the day outside.

Sweetie loved it with all her heart. She had good memories of coming here throughout her childhood, letting the wind try to make off with her *dupatta* while her parents paid their respects to the Shiva lingam, the sacred stone, inside. The air always felt more cleansing in here, and no matter what worries she came with, Sweetie always left with a peace of mind that lasted all day.

They got out of the car and walked up the steps, before taking off their shoes to go inside. As soon as they set foot in the temple, the wind began to blow. Sweetie's hair floated around her, and giggling and holding on to her *dupatta*, she smiled up at Ashish. "I love it here."

He was watching her with an unreadable expression, his eyes intense and serious. She was just beginning to wonder what was going on when he smiled too. It was like the sun had suddenly burst out through thunderclouds; even Sweetie's bones felt warm.

They moved forward together to pray, and after taking the *prasad* offering from the *pujari*, they walked off to the side to look out over Frye Lake. The view was incredible: Wispy white clouds were smeared across the brilliant-blue spring sky, and the lake looked like a giant glittering diamond under the sun. They stood by a pillar, just watching and breathing in the air, for a long moment. A bird called in the distance, and another answered it in sweet song.

"This is actually really beautiful," Ashish said.

Sweetie looked to see him gazing down at the water, his expression thoughtful. "It's restorative," she said carefully. "I like to imagine my stress in a box that I leave at the steps here." Sweetie tied her *dupatta* like a sash at her hip so it would stay put. She smoothed her hair back into a bun, aware that Ashish was watching her every move. "I'm kind of glad my parents made it a bimonthly-ish habit for me."

"That's good." Ashish had a slight smirk on his face, but he spoke quietly. "I'm rethinking my position on this."

Sweetie smiled. She sat on the edge of the floor, her gaze still on the lake. "Let's sit here for a while, then," she said, sensing that Ashish needed this more than he was letting on.

After a pause he joined her. "Okay. Maybe just for a little while."

Ashish

They walked back to the Porsche in silence. It was weird, but Ashish felt . . . lighter. His chest felt less tight, like the bands around it had loosened just a bit. There was a surprising comfort in being around his family's religious culture too, in hearing the familiar words of the priest's incantations and smelling the sandalwood incense. Like being in a place that inherently understood him and one in which he could be still and be himself.

Ashish wasn't sure if he believed in God or not, but he couldn't deny that that particular temple felt really cleansing. It was the way the gardens at home looked after a lashing rainstorm . . . bright and colorful, dewy and fresh. All the dust and dirt they'd been collecting got washed away, and now Ashish knew how the gardens must feel. His dust and dirt had been washed away too—at least temporarily. Another plus? The stuffy embroidered kurta he'd been forced to wear wasn't even chafing his skin as much as it usually did.

He glanced at the clock on the dashboard as they slid into their seats. "I know we've already been to the mandir and we aren't contractually obligated to do anything together past that," he said in a slightly scoffing tone so Sweetie would see that he didn't care very much about what he was saying at all. "But do you want to go to lunch? I know the people who own this great restaurant. Besides, we'll be in public, so I think we'll be okay." His heart thumped a little unevenly as he waited for her response. Weird.

She smiled at him, completely guileless, and his heart pattered out a few more uneven thumps for good measure. "Why, I'd love to, Mr. Patel."

He took her to Poseidon, a restaurant not too far from Pavan Mandir. Pappa's business partner and good friend owned it, which meant the Patels were on a VIP list, which in turn meant they could get a great table pretty much whenever they wanted. The food was delicious, too. (Okay, and it didn't hurt that Zagat had called it "the most romantic seafood restaurant on the West Coast." This might not be a completely traditional first date, but dang it, he still had standards.)

"Wow." Sweetie looked up at the Grecian-inspired pillars and the enormous fountain in the courtyard, which was a statue of Poseidon holding his famed trident. "This is amazing. You know the owners?"

"Ah, peripherally. He's really my dad's friend. I've only seen him a handful of times at events."

They climbed up the wide steps and walked in. Gentle music greeted them in a foyer that boasted yet another Poseidon fountain (this one smaller) and an array of frondy plants in ornate pots. The skylight let in a dazzling amount of sunlight. The maître d', a dapper, short black woman in a suit, greeted them warmly. "Hello and welcome to Poseidon! Do we have reservations today?"

"We don't," Ashish said, stepping forward. "But I believe I'm on the P and T list. Ashish Patel."

The maître d' pulled up something on her computer, tapped a little bit, and then turned her A+ customer service–smile on Ashish. "Excellent. I do see you here, Mr. Patel. Would you prefer our conservatory or balcony?"

"Balcony, I think." Ashish looked at Sweetie, his eyebrows raised. "If that sounds good to you?"

She managed to nod, though she looked completely overwhelmed. Ashish always forgot what it was like to introduce new people to his world. Pinky, Oliver, and Elijah were so used to the flash that they barely blinked anymore. He smiled and winked at her, hoping to set her at ease.

"What's 'P and T'?" she asked as they wound up the spiral stairs, with the maître d' leading them.

"'Peeps and tweeps.' It's code for 'friends and important media.' I guess the PR consultant decided it was trendier—and is obviously a Twitter fan." Ashish chuckled. "Maybe 'VIP' is too blasé."

Sweetie laughed a little, but the sound was high pitched and nervous.

They were seated at a small, quiet table in the corner of the balcony, which had only three tables scattered along its huge stone floor; the other two were empty. Their view of the mountains in the distance was stunning enough, but right below them was a shimmering reflecting pool filled with koi and aquatic plants that were completely transfixing. Classical music played from hidden speakers.

"Koi in a Greek-themed restaurant?" Sweetie asked.

"This is America, the great melting pot, after all," Ashish replied.

After the waitress had taken their drink orders and promised to be back soon, Sweetie turned to Ashish. "This is really nice. Thank you for bringing me."

"Sure." He took a breath. "And, um, thanks for that moment at the temple. It felt good to just sit and be still for a while."

The waitress brought their Cokes then and took their orders. After she left, Sweetie said, "You're welcome. You know . . . it's okay to need some time to deal with this."

"With what?"

"Celia," she said, and he struggled to keep his face wince-free. "The breakup."

"Yeah, well, it's been three months," Ashish said, forcing a smile.

"What kind of loser wouldn't be over someone after three whole months?" He was aware he was sidestepping her question and not being completely honest about his feelings, but what was he supposed to do? Cry into his hands on their first date?

"You went out with her for twice that long. And it's not like there's a time limit on this kind of thing. I mean, not that I speak from experience, but if you really care about someone, it only stands to reason that it'll take a long time to feel okay again." She took a sip of her Coke and looked at him above her frosted glass.

Ashish sighed. "I guess. I can't wait to just get over her, though. Like, I kind of don't know who I even am right now. Samir was right that night at Roast Me—I'm not doing so well with basketball or girls or any of the other stuff that makes me Smoldering Ash." He stopped short, mildly horrified that he'd said all that.

"Smoldering Ash, huh?"

"Just a stupid nickname," Ashish said, looking at his drink like it was the most fascinating thing he'd ever seen.

Sweetie smiled, a gentle thing. "I like it." After a beat she added, "And that sucks." There wasn't a shred of discomfort or judgment in her voice. "I'm sorry it's been so hard for you." She reached out and placed her hand lightly on his for just a moment, rubbing her thumb slowly over the side of his palm.

His heart thundered. Well, *some* parts of him were definitely ready to move on. Interesting. "Yeah, well. Let's talk about less pathetic things, shall we?"

Sweetie took her hand back and smiled. "Like?"

"Lightning round," Ashish said. "Ready?"

She sat up straighter and nodded, mock-seriously.

"Sweet or salty?"

She raised an eyebrow. "Isn't it obvious from my name? Sweet."

He laughed. "Oh, right. Okay, then how about this: Movies or books?"

"Books."

"Slytherin or Hufflepuff?"

"Hufflepuff."

"Beaches or mountains?"

"Mountains."

"Cold or hot?"

"Cold."

Ashish leaned back, smirking.

"What?"

"You should know that every one of your responses to those questions was the exact opposite of what I'd have picked."

Sweetie laughed. "So. We're opposites. I don't think that's such a surprise, do you?"

"I guess not."

The waitress came then and deposited Sweetie's Greek-style marinated salmon and tzatziki sauce and Ashish's moussaka on the table.

"Okay, then," Sweetie said, leaning back and crossing her arms. "My turn."

"Bring it."

"*Downton Abbey*: Matthew Crawley or Henry Talbot?"

"I don't know what any of those words mean in that order."

Sweetie stared at him. "I don't think we can be friends unless you have at least a passing understanding of *Downton Abbey*."

"Sure. I'll get right on that." He grinned lazily.

"Okay, let's move on. Sunsets or sunrises?"

"Sunrises."

"Rain or snow?"

"Rain."

"Dogs or cats?"

"Dogs."

"Endings or beginnings?"

He held her gaze for a moment. "Beginnings. Definitely."

She dropped her eyes and reached for her Coke. After she'd had a deep gulp, she said softly, "Well, see? You answered exactly the way I would have for all of those questions."

"Except the *Downton Abbey* one."

"Right. Except that." She smiled, but it was a small, shy thing that he wanted to look at all day. "We'll have to rectify that someday."

Neither of them had even begun eating yet. Ashish unrolled his silverware. "Maybe if I break both legs and have nothing else to keep me occupied."

Laughing, Sweetie put a forkful of salmon in her mouth. Closing her eyes, she said, "Ohhhh. My. God. So good."

Ashish realized he could watch her make that expression all day. Clearing his throat to get his mind out of the very fun gutter it was swimming in, he said, "Gl-glood. I mean, glad. I'm glad you like it."

Sweetie opened her eyes and gave him a look that told him she knew exactly what he'd been thinking. Smiling, she looked down at her plate.

Great, Ash. That's what you want: Sweetie thinking you're a total perv. He shoveled his food into his mouth before he could say yet another stupid thing in the course of this meal.

• • •

They lingered over their food and then over dessert—Ashish made sure to tip the waitress generously for the privilege. And then, since neither of them wanted to leave yet, they decided to walk to the reflecting pool for a while.

It was easy with Sweetie in a way it never had been with Celia. Sure, it had been fire and sparks and heat and passion with Celia. (And then it had been ice cubes and thunderclouds and hailstorms and tears. Hers, not his, naturally. Ashish didn't cry.) (Okay, the tears had been his. But only a few.)

But with Sweetie time passed in gentle waves. A conversation with her was like a warm hug and a cup of hot cocoa on a cold day—comforting, familiar, a place you never wanted to leave. And the thing was . . . he found her really physically attractive, too. His brain still held on to the vestiges of Celia, sure he'd never be over her. But his body seemed not to be conflicted at all. It was a huge improvement, especially considering he'd barely been aware of Dana Patterson, cheerleader hottie extraordinaire. He thought he knew what it was: He was genuinely attracted to Sweetie's personality, and that just made her body even more attractive to him.

By the time he drove her to his house, the late-afternoon sun had stained the day gold. They sat in the garage, the Porsche turned off, everything quiet and dark and still. Sweetie looked at him and then darted her glance away, smiling a bit.

He turned in his seat to face her. "I had fun today."

She said softly, "Me too. You're good company. Except when you admit to not knowing anything about *Downton Abbey*."

Ashish rolled his eyes. She'd told him the premise. "*Downton*

Crappy, more like. I can't believe people like to sit around and watch ancient British people get dressed by their butlers."

Sweetie sighed. "No, they're dressed by their *valets* and *lady's maids*. Jeez. Weren't you listening?"

They laughed together. Then Ashish got serious. "You know, I wasn't kidding earlier."

Sweetie frowned. "About what?"

"That you look beautiful today." He reached over and wound a strand of her hair around the bun she'd tied at the base of her neck. Her eyes widened for a moment, but then she leaned into his touch. His heart sang.

"Thank you," she murmured.

Ashish shifted slowly in his seat, leaning forward an inch at a time to make sure she was okay with this. She held his gaze, her eyes dark and shining, until they fluttered shut. From just a breath away, she smelled heavenly, like sunshine and mint and something so soft it caressed his skin like silk.

Ashish meant for it to be a quick kiss. But once his lips found hers, her skin like velvet, he felt his hands cupping her face and gently pulling her closer; he couldn't get close enough. She tasted like dew and sweets, exactly how he'd expected her to taste. She made a quiet moaning sound in the back of her throat that drove him crazy, her own small hands sliding up against his chest and resting there between them. She was all soft, decadent curves—so different from any girl he'd ever kissed and still so incredibly, mind-blowingly sexy.

They pulled apart finally to catch their breath. Ashish smiled and rested his forehead against hers. Her eyes shone even more brightly, that faint dimple making an appearance and burrowing itself into his heart.

She giggled. "I don't know what to say except . . . wow."

He chuckled. "'Wow' is good. I totally agree with 'wow.'"

She swallowed and pulled away a little, looking down at her lap. "That was, um, my first real kiss."

He stared at her. It was ridiculous that this gorgeous, funny, sweet, intelligent girl had never been kissed. "I'm honored that I got to be your first, then. But also? I'm glad you didn't tell me that before. The pressure would've been too much."

She laughed a little, but it wasn't full of joy like her laughter usually was. "Right. Sure."

Ashish frowned. "What do you mean?"

She took a breath and met his eye. "You have a lot of . . . experience. With girls. And I don't. I mean, I have literally zero experience with boys. I'm not exaggerating."

"Hey." He touched her hand gently. "That doesn't matter to me. At all."

She looked at him like she was deciding whether or not to share something. Thrusting her chin out, she said, "And I'm not going to be easy just because I'm fat and no boy has ever dated me before."

Ashish froze. "I would never think that. Have I . . . have I somehow given you that impression?"

Sighing, she looked down at her tightly clasped hands. "No. It's just something I know guys think about fat girls. And it's not true at all."

Ashish put his hand under her chin and she looked back at him. "I don't think that. And any guy who thinks that is a total piece of crap. I don't care about your lack of experience. I want you to know we'll go at your pace, okay? I have no expectations at all, and I'm totally fine with taking it slow. I mean, my last relationship was extremely fast and look how that ended up."

She studied his face, as if checking for dishonesty. Finally, though, she smiled, full and bright. "Okay. I'm fine with taking it slow." Then, frowning a little, she said, "But kissing is good."

Ashish laughed. "Kissing is good; got it." Just to prove he really did get it, he leaned forward and kissed her again.

CHAPTER 18

Ashish

Basketball practice Monday after school was as lackluster as usual. Ashish bungled easy shots, he got hit in the side of the head because he was looking in the wrong direction, Elijah pretty much carried the game, and Coach ripped him a new one.

Ashish took all the ribbing from his teammates—both gentle and vicious—with humility. Yeah, he was sucking. Yeah, he knew. No, he didn't know how to fix it.

Something was off *inside* Ashish, something vital and passionate and competitive that had gone dormant after Celia dumped him. He'd secretly—and apparently stupidly—hoped that missing ingredient would come back after his date with Sweetie. But nope. It was obviously on an interstellar journey off in space somewhere.

He, Oliver, and Elijah were getting changed in the locker room when his phone beeped with an incoming text message.

Samir: Can I come by?

Sighing, Ashish typed a response. Just finished bball practice. Can it wait? Tomorrow?

He had basketball practice tomorrow, too. Tonight's fine. Maybe 7ish?

K see you then

Whatever Samir had to say, he could get it out of the way. To be honest, Ashish wasn't really happy with him at the moment. He'd called a few times over the weekend, and Ashish had just let it go to voice mail. What did Samir expect, when he'd blurted out all that crap to Sweetie and acted like a total douche? But it was obvious he wouldn't shut up until Ashish had heard him out. It was obvious he just wanted to give him some half-assed apology. Whatever. Ashish slammed his locker shut and turned to Oliver and Elijah. "Ready?"

But they didn't hear him. They seemed to be having a heated discussion about something on the bench. Oliver, the taller of the two, had his head bent down toward Elijah's. He was making extravagant hand gestures, the way he did when he was mad, and Elijah had on his closed-off, shut-down look. Totally weird. They never, ever argued. If something happened that they disagreed with, one of them would always laugh and kiss the other and say "Ah, my baby's so passionate" or something equally vomitous that made Ashish want to smile and poke his eyeballs out with a fork at the same time.

He stood there, wondering if he should leave, then discarding the idea. He didn't want to just abandon them. Maybe he should interrupt. . . . But they looked really into it. He needed to get home, though, or he wouldn't have time to grab dinner before Samir came over and gave him a headache. Ashish stepped closer and cleared his throat. "Uh . . . guys? You ready to go?"

Elijah looked away, but Oliver looked up at him. There were tears in his gray eyes. Ashish froze, completely shocked. Oliver was *crying*? What was going on?

"Hey, are you . . . ?"

But Oliver just rubbed his fists along his cheeks and dashed out of the locker room. Elijah bent to tie his shoes, totally avoiding Ashish's eyes. Okay, what was the protocol for this? He'd never been in the middle of a lovers' spat before. "Elijah, what—"

Elijah got up and grabbed his duffel bag with way more force than necessary. "Let's go."

Oh-kayyy. Ashish could take a hint. He followed Elijah silently, looking out for Oliver. But he was gone. Which was weird, because Ashish was supposed to be his ride. Surreptitiously he took his phone out of his pocket and sent a quick text.

Hey man you ok? Need a ride?

Oliver: Is HE getting a ride?

It didn't take Stephen King's imagination to get who "HE" was. Yeah

Then NO thank you. I can make my own way

Dude what is going on??

Why don't you ask him? He's the one with all the answers

"Who're you texting?" Elijah was looking over his shoulder.

Ashish put the phone away. "Oliver." Elijah made a motion to get into the Jeep, but Ashish put a hand on his arm. "What's going on, E.?"

Elijah tossed his bags into the back and turned to face Ashish, his arms crossed, his jaw hard. "What did he tell you?"

"Just that I should ask you."

"Okay, fine. Apparently, Oliver heard a rumor that I hooked up with some guy on the Eastman team two weeks ago."

Ashish was afraid to ask the next question but forced himself to anyway. "And is it true?"

Elijah scoffed. *"No."*

"Okay. So then what's the problem?"

"The problem is that Oliver wouldn't believe me. He said several people had seen me, and he knew the truth, so I should just come clean. Never mind that the Eastman team is totally homophobic. Never mind that they've given Oliver and me crap ever since we started going out. So I told him we should break up." Elijah rubbed a big hand along his jaw, agitated.

Ashish stared at him for a good ten seconds. "You said *what*?"

"We've been going out for two *years*, Ash. I'm his first serious boyfriend. And now he's acting like some jealous spouse. I just think, you know, if he can't trust me, then it's time we take a break. Maybe things are becoming too serious."

Ashish blew out a breath and tried to compose his face to look like something besides *You moron. You're making a huge mistake. How can you not see that?!* "Look, man. I'm no expert on serious relationships. But what you and Oliver have . . ." He shook his head and looked away. "People would kill for that, you know? People spend their entire lives looking for it. And you're kicking it to the curb because . . . he cares about you too much? You care about him too much? I don't even—"

"You're not in our relationship. You don't know."

Ashish didn't know what to say to that. "Are you saying you're not happy?"

"No. I'm saying I feel like I'm married. And I'm seventeen. I don't know what I want yet; I don't even know where I want to go to college or what I want to major in. How can I make arguably the biggest decision of my life right now?"

"You're scared. I get it—"

"No, you don't." Elijah shook his head. "You can't."

There wasn't much to be said to that. Ashish nodded. "You're right. I don't."

Elijah hopped into his seat through the Jeep's open side. "Can we just go?" he said, staring straight ahead.

"Yep." Ashish got in and started the engine. He glanced at Elijah again, but his friend refused to look at him. Ashish might not be an expert at relationships, but he knew a broken heart when he saw one.

"Samir is in the garden," Ma said as soon as Ashish walked through the door. "Everything is okay, *na*?"

Guess he wouldn't be eating dinner first after all. "Yeah. Everything's just fabulous." Sighing, Ashish set his backpack down on the floor in the den and crossed to the back door. He saw Samir through the panes of glass, sitting on a bench under a sycamore tree, his head bent, hands clasped loosely between his knees. He looked . . . beaten. There was no hint of defensiveness or annoying arrogance about him now at all.

It caught Ashish off guard. He walked down the path to the bench and sat next to Samir. The evening breeze was cool and stiff, riffling his hair and shaking the bushes around them. "Hey."

Samir glanced at him for only a second. "Hey. Thanks for letting me come over tonight, man."

"Sure. What's going on?"

"You haven't been answering my calls."

Ashish ran a hand through his damp hair and tried not to let his annoyance show. Samir sounded just as beaten as he looked. "After the stunt you pulled at Roast Me, you can't really blame me."

There was a pause as they listened to the wind sing in the trees.

"No, I guess not." Samir turned to Ashish and held his eye. "I'm sorry. That was really insensitive of me."

If he thought it would be that easy, he had to be kidding himself. "Yeah. It was."

Samir's gaze dropped down to his hands. "Is it true, what Pinky said? None of you like me?"

The landscape lights were on a timer, and they came on, casting a soft glow on all the trees and bushes around them. Ashish drew a breath, smelling roses and green stuff he didn't even have a name for. "Bro, can you blame us? You're constantly ragging us about stuff we're sensitive about. Me with Celia, Pinky with that whole green-hair phase she went through, Oliver and Elijah about their PDA. You don't make it easy for us to like you, you know?"

Samir actually looked surprised. "But . . . but that's what friends do. We tease each other. It's all in fun. I think Oliver and Elijah are the most solid couple I've ever known."

"Yeah, well, they're not so solid anymore," Ashish blurted out before he could stop himself.

"What?"

"They broke up. Damn it, I shouldn't have said anything. Just forget you heard it, okay?"

Samir shrugged. "And Pinky . . . I mean, I actually like her. I think she's really cool. No one else I know has the guts to try and pull off that shade of green."

Ashish threw his hands up in the air. "Well, you don't say any of those things! You just berate us and laugh at us and poke and prod at the thing we don't want to think about. It doesn't feel good natured, Samir. You just come across as a jackass."

Samir was quiet for a long moment. Then he laughed. "You know what's funny? Until the thing at Roast Me, I would've said you were my best friend. I mean, I knew Oliver, Elijah, and Pinky were probably top three for you, but I definitely thought I came in fourth. We've known each other a long time."

"Yeah. And you've tormented me that whole time." Ashish scoffed. He couldn't believe Samir had actually deluded himself into thinking they were best friends.

Samir glanced at him, his near-black eyes glowing softly in the light from the garden. "Right." He sighed. "I hope you know I am sorry about that. Really sorry." He got up and smiled a little, but it was a muted thing, not at all his usual annoying grin. "I'm gonna go."

Ashish held up a hand and listened to Samir's footfalls grow fainter as he wound back through the garden and went around the side of the house to the driveway out front. That was definitely weird. Samir was never humble or open or vulnerable or any of that stuff. Ashish felt momentarily bad, like maybe he should've gone easier on him. But man, the dude had definitely had it coming. And after the day Ashish had had, with basketball being awful and Elijah going off on him? Samir was lucky he hadn't just tossed him into the pond.

Ashish's phone beeped, and he fished it out of his pocket.

Sweetie: Unicorns or narwhals?

What? Grinning, he typed back, Definitely narwhals. You?

UNICORNS 5EVER

He laughed and then stopped, amazed at the sound of it tangling with the breeze in the quiet garden. Wow, he typed.

??

You just totally made me forget about the shot day I just had

Lol the shot day huh

Stupid autocorrect

☺ I'm sorry you had a shot day. But I'm glad I made you forget

Five more days

Ready to get your Holi on?

Yeah sweaty and covered in multicolored powders is just a regular Saturday to me

Give it a chance, Ashish!

I will, Sweetie. But only because you'll be there with me

Incorrigible flirt

Incorrigible beauty

I'm going now

K but smile

Why? You can't see me

But I'll feel you. It's like that Titanic song

GOING NOW

☺

☺

Ashish put his phone away, still smiling, and shook his head. Ridiculous. There was no way that text exchange could've traded his foul mood for this sparkling, happy one. Just no way. He must be light-headed from lack of food or something. Yeah, that was it. He needed food. He got up and made his way inside, purposely not taking notice of how he was skipping a little.

CHAPTER 19

Sweetie

Sweetie sat cross-legged on her bed, looking up in the lamplight at Jason Momoa. Okay, it was his poster, but still. "Jason," she said. "You've never steered me wrong. Should I do this?"

"Mm-hmm." Then she turned to Hrithik Roshan, her Bollywood heartthrob. "What about you? What do you think?"

She waited a moment and then sighed. "It's two a.m. and I'm talking to paper." Lying on her side, she tucked a pillow between her knees and looked out the window at the moon. She'd made a million pro/con lists, and she was no closer to making a decision.

"The problem is," she said, her voice too loud in her silent room. "The problem is, I know how badly this might go. But I also know how much this would help me prove a point about what fat girls can and can't do. So is the payoff worth the cost? How can I make that decision without being able to see the future?"

Suddenly Sweetie sat up and scrabbled in her nightstand drawer. She pulled out what she was looking for, and there in the darkness she shook that Magic 8 Ball like her life depended on it. "Should I sing at Band Night?" she asked, and then, hands trembling, looked at the answer bobbing slowly in front of her.

So that was that, then.

Sweetie took a deep breath and turned to her friends at the lunch table. "Signs point to yes."

Izzy didn't look up from her cell phone, Suki grunted as she read her book, and Kayla raised one eyebrow. "Eh?"

Really? Talk about anticlimactic. She pushed her hair out of her eyes and huffed. "Okay, I'll do it. The stupid Band Night thingy."

That got their attention. All of them sat up straighter and stared at her. "Really?" Kayla asked, her voice gleeful.

Sweetie nodded. "Yeah, I thought about it a lot, got some, um, psychic intervention, and decided that . . . I can't leave you guys hanging."

"No, you can't!" Suki reached over the table and grabbed Sweetie in a hug, her bony arms pushing into Sweetie's back. "I knew you wouldn't!"

"I could seriously kiss you right now," Kayla said, getting out her cell and furiously texting. "This changes everything. We're going to win the grand prize, no question."

"Yes!" Izzy said, clapping her hands. "Those duffel bags are ours!"

The grand prize that the owner of Roast Me had agreed to throw in after hearing about the huge amount of attention and interest Band Night had gotten from the high schools in the area—they were up to seventeen bands now—was $2,000 cash to the winning band. Izzy, Kayla, and Suki had decided that embroidered duffel bags would be a sweet gift for the track team, to go with their new jerseys.

"I don't know," Sweetie said, nibbling on her apple. "I still think we should give it to charity. Or, like, half of it to charity and half of it to funding uniforms for kids who can't afford them."

"Which is also charity," Suki said. Her parents were both doctors, so she didn't have too much face time with poverty.

"It's helping someone out. That's not necessarily charity," Izzy said loyally. "But I still feel like those duffel bags would be awesome. Have you seen the gold thread?"

"Yes, I have," Sweetie said. "You've showed me three times this week already."

Izzy giggled. "Oh, right."

"Antwan is pumped," Kayla said, putting her phone away. "Okay, and you've got the songs down?"

"Yeah. Since you've forced me to come to practice every single time you guys have gotten together, I don't think I'll have any problems," Sweetie said, rolling her eyes. "I'm just so nervous, guys. Like, bathed-in-sweat nervous."

"So what made you decide to do it?" Kayla asked, not unkindly.

Saying that the Magic 8 Ball or Jason or Hrithik had decided things for her would be easy. But there was a deeper reason, the reason she'd begun to seriously consider singing in the first place: the Sassy Sweetie Project. As Sweetie had lain in bed last night, thinking about how she'd single-handedly connived to get Ashish Patel's attention and then begun to date him, she'd gotten a surge of confidence.

When they'd kissed, she'd realized just how wrong it was that she'd never even tried to date a boy before because of those dirtbags who'd said fat girls were easy. And that made her wonder how many other things she'd subconsciously told herself she couldn't or shouldn't do because she was fat. Resisting fatphobic messages was one thing—but what about the insidious, internalized fatphobia she carried around?

She was a kick-ass athlete, a really good student, and extremely creative. But she had talents she never let shine because she had somehow internalized the message that no one really wanted to hear from a fat girl. Singing was one of those talents. So there might be jerks who laughed at her. But she knew that once she started to sing, they'd shut up. And if they didn't, so what? She wanted to sing for *her*, not for them. She would do this because her talent and her need to shine were bigger than her dress size, bigger even than Amma's prejudice.

"It was like what you said, Kayla. I just realized I need to stop being so afraid of what people are going to think. I mean, I'm still afraid, but . . ." She paused, feeling out her words. "But my need to prove something to myself is bigger than my desire to make people happy. If that makes sense."

Kayla grinned. "It makes total sense. I'm proud of you, sis."

"Me too," Suki said.

"And me." Izzy laid her head against Sweetie's.

She basked in their friendship, like warm ocean water. She could do this. She could *kill* this.

Thursday and Friday dragged by. Even with practice—which she totally dominated—it felt like time had begun to ooze, each second like thick oil working its way through a clock's every gear and knob. She kept seeing and hearing Ashish everywhere she looked—a tall boy with black hair, the way some senior laughed at some dumb joke, the boyish grin of some dude on a TV commercial. *Careful, Sweetie. You're not trying to fall in love with the boy.* He was an unstoppable flirt, but Sweetie knew not to read too much into it. He'd basically told her he couldn't fully give himself to her because of Celia. Besides, Ashish was one of those naturally flirty people. It was, like, his resting state. He had resting flirty face. Besides which, he was hurting, and she needed to respect that. She *did* respect that. This must just be temporary madness.

On Saturday morning Sweetie showed up at Ashish's house wearing an old white cotton T-shirt (the better to show off the Holi powders with) and a pair of old sweats. She felt a tug of self-consciousness as she stood at his front door, wondering if she had dressed down *too* much. Sure, they were just going to get their clothes ruined at Holi, the festival of colors where people actually had permission to throw colored powders at you and rub them into your face, but still. This *was* a date.

Then Ashish opened the door, a big, cocky smile on his face, and she relaxed. He was wearing a ratty tan T-shirt and old sweats just like hers. He hadn't even bothered to comb his hair. "Let's do this!" he said, shutting the door behind him and following her back down the stairs.

"Wait, aren't your parents coming?"

"Nah. They do the *puja* at the temple, but they haven't done the whole color thing in years. They say they're too old, but really I think it's that their clothes aren't old *enough*."

Sweetie laughed. "I can see that."

They walked to Ashish's Jeep. "I thought I'd drive this today, if you don't mind. Don't want to get the Porsche all messed up."

"Well, actually, I thought I would drive today," Sweetie said, raising her eyebrows.

Ashish hesitated for a moment. "Oh, okay, yeah, yeah." He walked over to her car and she laughed. Frowning, he said, "What?"

"You're not used to this, are you? Being driven on a date?"

He opened his mouth to argue, then shut it again. "No, I'm not," he said, and then he laughed as he got in the passenger side. "But I'm totally open to it."

"Good." Sweetie smiled, got in, and started the engine. "Because I am an excellent driver."

Ten minutes into the drive, Ashish turned to Sweetie. "So when you said 'excellent,' did you actually mean 'slowest ever in the history of humankind'?"

Sweetie frowned and glanced over at him. "I meant the safest. Ever."

Groaning, Ashish leaned over to look at the speedometer. "Thirty-two miles per hour! The speed limit's forty-five."

Sweetie slapped him away. "Get back on your side! And yes, I know. That's why I'm in the right lane. That's the speed *limit*, you know, not the speed minimum."

Chuckling, Ashish said, "Just another way we're opposites, then."

Sweetie cleared her throat and surreptitiously wiped her damp palms, one at a time, on her shirt and returned her hands to the appropriate ten o'clock and two o'clock positions. Time to get to the big issue: Band Night. "So, I had a question for you."

"Yeah?"

But before she could say anything, Ashish's phone beeped. And beeped again. And again.

"Whoa, do you need to take that?"

"Yeah, let me just . . ." He reached into his pocket and pulled it out. She heard him mutter under his breath, something that sounded like, "Oh, for . . ."

"Everything okay?"

He sighed. "Fine." She glanced at him, and his jaw was set. He was staring rigidly out the windshield.

"So obviously that's not true," Sweetie said softly. "You don't have to talk about it, but I'm a good listener. Just saying."

She saw his shoulders relax in her peripheral vision. "Sorry." Rubbing a hand over his jaw, he continued. "I'm just, uh, having issues with a friend. Pseudo friend. And my other friends. It's a messy time right now."

"I'm sorry." After a pause Sweetie asked, "Your pseudo friend . . . Do you mean Samir?"

"That obvious, huh?" Ashish's voice was low, tired. "He's not much of a friend, really. He's always saying the wrong thing, annoying us. I feel bad for him—I've known him forever—but man, that guy drives me up the wall. He's homeschooled and totally sheltered, but he thinks he's, like, the authority on everything and everyone."

"Maybe that's a defensive wall he's set up for himself," Sweetie said, nibbling on her lower lip. "Sometimes when people feel vulnerable, they lash out. Maybe he just doesn't know how to relate to you." She'd gone through a phase like that in middle school. Since kids were always making fun of her, she'd decided she'd turn the tables and become a little jerk. But being snarky and aggressive all day long was exhausting. Sweetie had decided it just wasn't her, much like being Amma's doormat wasn't her either. The answer lay somewhere in the middle, maybe.

"Complaining to his mom is definitely not the way to do it," Ashish replied. Then, seeing her confused face, he held up his cell phone. "That was my mom texting me. Apparently, his mom's been on the phone with her, telling her that I upset Samir Monday night. We had a talk that didn't go the way he wanted it to go."

Sweetie shook her head. "Friendships can be so tricky. I'm lucky enough to have three best friends and minimal drama, but even we go through our rough patches."

"Yeah . . ." He paused, and she felt the weight of unspoken words in the air. She waited. "And on top of that, Oliver and Elijah broke up. I was on the phone with Oliver until three in the morning, mostly just listening to him cry. And Oliver *never* gets on the phone, so that should show you how bad things are."

"Oh no." Sweetie felt genuinely bad; she'd really liked them. Especially Oliver, who'd been so soft and open and welcoming. "What happened?"

"I'm not even sure *they* know. They've been together since freshman year. Everything seemed to be going well and then it all just exploded." Ashish laughed. "Wow, listen to me just unloading on you. Sorry."

"It's okay." Sweetie looked at him for a moment to show him she was serious. "I like hearing about your friends."

He smiled. "Thanks. But weren't you going to ask me something when my phone went off?"

"Oh. Right." Sweetie swallowed. It was ridiculous to feel this nervous, really. "Um, so my friends and I are doing this Band Night thing at Roast Me. It's a week from Thursday at eight thirty. I was wondering, if you were free, if you wanted to come." When he didn't answer right away, she hurried on. "Um, not as a date, obviously. Since we're only allowed to do the four dates on your parents' list. But as . . . friends. Just to support us. The money we make's going to new team jerseys." *Stop talking and give him a second to answer, Sweetie, jeez.* She closed her mouth with a dry little click and waited.

He was doing his trademark smolder-smirk; she could see it in her peripheral vision. It was 30 percent smirk and 70 percent smolder, and she didn't even have fire protection in the car. She tried not to let her breath catch. "Of course I'll come," he said.

"Really?"

"Definitely. I want you guys to get new jerseys, come on. Plus, I heard about it already at Richmond and was planning to ask you if you wanted to go."

"Oh." She couldn't help the grin that spread over her face. A bonus date-but-not-really with Ashish Patel. She liked that idea. A lot.

"So do you want to come to my house to go together?"

Sweetie licked her lips. "Uh, about that. Actually, I'm going to have to go a bit early. I'm sort of . . . in one of the bands."

"Get out!" Ashish looked especially delighted. "What do you play?"

"I'm the lead singer." Sweetie tried not to grimace at how pretentious that sounded. "Only because Kayla and the others twisted my arm."

"You're joking. Would you believe it if I told you I was the lead singer in my middle school band? We were the Burning Bow Ties."

Sweetie gave him the side eye. "Oh yeah? How do I know you're not just trying to steal my thunder?"

Ashish raised an eyebrow. "If I was trying to steal your thunder, would I do it with the Burning Bow Ties?"

She laughed. "Okay, but you're going to have to convince me. Sing me something."

"Right now?"

"Uh-huh. Why? Are you scared?"

"Okay, okay, I will. But only if you accompany me."

Crap. Sweetie wished she'd kept her mouth shut. "No. I don't want to."

"Sweetie. You're going to be singing in front of a bunch of people on Band Night."

"Yeah, but I'll have the girls to back me up, other bands will be there . . . it won't be a one-on-one thing."

"Come on. I'm backing you up now."

She sighed. "Okay, fine. What should we sing?"

"You pick the song."

"How's your Hindi?"

"Passable. But Hindi songs? I slay them, not gonna lie."

Sweetie took a deep breath. Then she began to sing.

CHAPTER 20

Ashish

Ashish watched Sweetie openmouthed. She was singing that song "Meherbaan" from that movie, oh, what was it? Oh, yeah. *Bang Bang!*, with Hrithik Roshan. When he'd first heard the song in the movie, he'd liked it. It was a little sappy, but whatever. It was nice.

But now? It was like listening to music for the very first time. It was like warm gold being poured into the vessel of his soul.

He listened with every fiber of every muscle. He listened so intently, he forgot who he was.

Sweetie

Sweetie stopped abruptly and looked at Ashish, her heart racing. Why wasn't he singing along? Oh God. What if he hated her voice? Most people liked it, but music was such a subjective thing.

Um. Why was he staring at her like that?

"Ashish?"

"Yeah?" His voice was slightly foggy or something, like he'd been daydreaming. He blinked. When he spoke, his voice was normal. "Uh, yeah?"

"You're not singing with me."

He shook his head, like he was trying to clear it. "Oh, y-yeah, right. I'll . . . I'll sing. Ready?"

She nodded and began her stanza again, and this time he joined in.

Maybe choosing a song about someone falling in love and trying to decipher what it all means wasn't the slickest thing she could've done. But the song had just popped out and she'd gone with it without thinking about it too much. But even that was just at the back of her mind. What Sweetie fully noticed was how gorgeous Ashish's baritone really was. His voice was smooth silk scraping against sandpaper. It was inarguably beautiful.

Sweetie smiled to herself as they sang together, their voices dipping and tangling, soaring and falling. This was pretty near perfect, and their date had only just begun. Listening to Ashish sing in Hindi, Sweetie realized something: This was no longer just about the Sassy Sweetie Project anymore. She was falling for this boy.

They pulled up to Oakley Field just as they finished the encore version of the song (which they pretended adoring fans had asked them to do).

"So, people," Ashish said, holding an imaginary mic to his mouth as Sweetie put the car in park in the busy parking lot. "Who sang it better? Ashish Patel"—here he made a noise in the back of his throat like thousands of adoring fans cheering—"or Sweetie Nair?" The crowd in the back of Ashish's throat went waaayyyy wild. He bowed his head, conceding defeat. "The crowd does not lie." He looked up at her, doing his smolder-smirk. "Your voice is seriously *koyal* quality."

Koyal was the Hindi word for a bird that sang the most melodious songs. Sweetie smiled down at her hands. "Thanks. You're not so bad yourself." She looked up at him. "You should sing at Band Night too."

Ashish laughed and held up his hands. "I'd rather just come and drink all the half-price coffee, honestly. My singing days died with the Burning Bow Ties."

They got out and walked past a booth where people were selling colored powders. Ashish insisted on paying, as usual, and they bought a packet of each color, ranging from a sizzling violet that almost made Sweetie's eyes water to a rich bottle green to a brilliant mustard yellow.

"Do you think we have enough?" Sweetie laughed as they walked into the field proper, dodging streams of laughing, yelling people. Ashish was having trouble with the packets; as soon as he got his grip on one, another would begin to slip down. Sweetie reached out and snagged the peacock blue before it hit the ground.

"Always be overprepared, Nair," Ashish said. "It's the only way to survive one of these things. Look at them, milling around all innocently. But once the countdown is done, they'll morph into brightly colored, merciless hit people."

Sweetie raised an eyebrow and looked around at everyone, a mix of Indian people and people of other cultures. "I don't know. . . . They look fairly innocuous to me."

"Oh, you'll see," Ashish said darkly. "You may have been told Holi's the festival of colors, the festival of love, the symbol of spring and new beginnings. But there's a much more sinister side to Holi. At its heart, it's a cutthroat, bloody competition that's rarely talked about."

Sweetie laughed. "Well, I like how blended it is. Look at all these people—there must be, like, at least ten different ethnicities here."

"Yeah, it's pretty cool." They walked forward, close to the stage where the emcee would count down to when people could start throwing powders at one another. "Five more minutes."

Ashish's phone rang. "Dang it." He tried to get it, but his hands were full. Sighing, he dumped the powders on the ground. Then he reached into his pocket, pulled it out, and frowned at the screen. "Hello?"

Sweetie watched him go from confused to serious.

"Hi, Deepika auntie. . . . No, no, just at the Holi Festival . . . Right. I know. Yes, that's right. . . . Well, you know, Samir doesn't really make it easy to—" He listened for a few seconds, then sighed quietly. "Okay. I can come over and speak to him in a little bit. Maybe later this evening . . . No, I won't tell him I'm coming. Okay, bye . . . You're welcome. Bye."

Sweetie watched as he picked up the Holi color packets in silence. "Samir's mom?"

"Yeah. She wants me to go over there and talk to him. Apparently, he's been moping around the past few days and she's getting worried." He rolled his eyes. "She seriously treats him like he's a baby."

Sweetie pursed her mouth but didn't say anything.

"What?" Ashish sounded genuinely curious about what she had to say.

"I think when people act out of the ordinary like that, they usually have an important reason. Like, we might not see it, but to her . . . maybe there's something she's afraid of, you know?"

Ashish studied her for a long moment. "She had cancer quite a few years ago," he said quietly. "She beat it, obviously, but her diagnosis was when things really changed. Samir dropped out of fifth grade to be homeschooled by her." He shook his head and stepped closer to her. Her heart raced. "You're a really kind person, aren't you? Like, deep down."

Sweetie's heart thudded even harder as she looked at him, their eyes meeting over packets of color.

"Damn," he said, and chuckled.

"What?"

"I really wanted to smooth your hair away, but my hands are full. And dropping these things on the ground before doing it just didn't seem that romantic."

Sweetie laughed. "That's okay. You still get romantic points."

"Yeah?" He held her gaze and her smile faded.

"Yeah."

"Okay, people! The time has come! The moment you've all been waiting for! It's tiiiiime for the countdoooowwwwwn!!!!"

Ashish blinked and stepped away from her when the emcee's voice filled the air. It was almost like he'd been in a trance or something and had shaken himself out of it. "I really don't deserve any romantic points. Anyway, it's time to start."

His voice sounded a little duller now, and Sweetie frowned. What had just happened? They'd totally been having a moment, and now it was just . . . gone. And it wasn't about being interrupted, either. There was something else.

"Five . . . ," the announcer said.

All around them there was the excited rustling of packets as people ripped theirs open. Ashish was working on his without looking at her. Sweetie opened her mouth to say something, to ask him what had happened, but closed it again. Had she totally misunderstood the vibe between them? But how was that possible? He'd *said* he was trying to be romantic, right? So he wanted this to go in the same direction she did.

"Four!"

Sweetie ripped open her packet of yellow powder. "Hey," she said. "Everything okay?"

He looked at her and smiled, but it didn't reach his eyes. It wasn't the smirky smolder, just a garden-variety fake smile. "Yep."

"Three!"

"Ashish." She stepped closer. "You can tell me if something's bothering you."

"Two!"

But he just kept giving her that fake smile. "Nope, nothing's bothering me."

"One!"

She quirked her mouth to the side. "Okay, then. You asked for this."

He frowned and cocked his head just as the emcee said, "Holi *ayyyiiiiii*! Powders ahoy!"

She took the entire packet of yellow and dumped it onto Ashish's head. He stared at her for a moment, totally covered. His hair was yellow, his face was yellow, his clothes were hopelessly stained.

Oh, crap. Crap, crap, crap. He looked really mad. Had Sweetie totally miscalculated?

But then he began to guffaw. And before she knew what was happening, he'd dumped an entire packet of purple on her. "Hey!" She shrieked with laughter and began to tear open another packet. But he got there before her.

He rubbed red powder into her cheeks, yelling, "Have some blush, Sweetie!"

They were both laughing helplessly, both trying to tear open their mound of packets before the other one. Sweetie lunged at him with a handful of blue just as he lunged at her with a handful of green. They met in the middle and were wrestling so hard to get the colors on the other that they fell in a graceless heap to the ground. The people around them scattered, everyone laughing. The air was smoky with color.

Sweetie was under Ashish, and he pinned her with his arms, rubbing green powder into her hair, dabbing it onto her nose. She fought him off, laughing, and colored his neck with a vivid fuchsia. They were both squirming, trying to get away from the other, when slowly they stopped. Ashish had Sweetie's hands in his, splayed out to the sides. His knees were on either side of her. It suddenly occurred to her that this was all very . . . sexy.

He leaned down, looking at her lips. He was a riot of color, a total mess, but even so, she didn't mind when he pressed his lips to hers. She could taste the chalky cornstarch of the powder, but it didn't dampen the heat of this moment. She moved her hands to lock around his neck, and in that screaming chaos of the Holi Festival, he gathered her to him and kissed her until they were both light-headed, breathless, smiling.

When they pulled apart, he put a hand to his lips. The smile was suddenly gone, winked out like an imploded star in the night. Ashish scrambled off her and walked a few paces away.

Dizzy and struggling to catch up, Sweetie stood and went over to him. "What . . . what just happened?"

He turned to look at her, and his eyes were pained. "Sweetie, I . . ."

She could barely hear him. Shaking her head, she motioned to the parking lot, which was empty. He nodded and followed her off the field, both of them dodging the yelling, hollering, boisterous crowd of grinning, multicolored people.

She turned to him once they were alone and waited.

He rubbed his hair, unleashing a flurry of purple and yellow. It drifted down between them as he met her eye. "I'm sorry. I'm not trying to be unpredictable and bizarre."

"Okay. So what's going on?"

"I have this theory," he said in a rush. "You know how I said I'm basically incapable of connecting with anyone now because of . . . of Celia?"

Sweetie could see how it hurt him just to say Celia's name, and her heart clenched, both in sympathy and in envy. "Yeah."

"So it turns out I'm completely, irrefutably attracted to you." He swallowed, his big Adam's apple bobbing. He looked away and rubbed his jaw. "Um . . . *physically* attracted is what I mean."

Sweetie felt the warmth spread through her cheeks. "That's . . . I'm attracted to you, too, Ashish." She wanted to sing, just belt out something happy and upbeat and celebratory. But obviously she didn't. Ashish Patel, could-be *GQ* model, found her attractive. If she were Christian, she'd say "hallelujah." This was good news. This was really, really good news.

Ashish

This was bad news. This was really, really bad news. Just look at her face, all glowing and happy, her innocent eyes so guileless and shiny. She was going to hate him when he finished.

"But . . . don't you see? That's why it's no good. Kissing you and holding you is great. . . ." He sighed, a trembling thing. "God, is it great. But . . . that's not fair to you." He seriously could not believe he was saying all this. Out loud. To a hot girl. But Sweetie wasn't *just* a hot girl. She was . . . Sweetie. Ashish took a breath and put his ego aside. "The truth is, I can't give you the other side of the relationship. The, ah, emotional stuff, the commitment you deserve." He stepped forward and took her hands. "You should have that, Sweetie. Not just some guy who's going to swap spit with you."

She raised an eyebrow. "Okay, first: ew. I'm taking back those romantic points. And secondly, we've already talked about this at Roast Me, remember? Seriously, I think you're overthinking this a little bit."

"I am?"

"We've literally been out on one and a half dates. Three weeks ago neither of us knew the other at all. I'm no relationship guru, but I imagine physical attraction comes easy, but emotional stuff takes time." She shrugged. "And I'm willing to give it time. Are you?"

He stared at her. It couldn't be that easy. Could it? "I . . . I don't think it works that way."

Sweetie shrugged again. "Why not?"

"Sweetie, I really like you. You're cool. But—"

"Unless you're planning on running back to Celia in the next couple of weeks, what have you got to lose?"

Ashish looked at her steadily. "I don't want to hurt you."

"You won't." She smiled her serene smile. "I trust you. Anyway, let me worry about that, okay?"

"I . . . But . . . Are you sure?"

She squeezed his hands and her smile flourished into a grin. His heart sputtered and flapped around in his chest like a poor, frightened bird. "Yes. I'm sure. Ashish, you already think that I'm wise and kind. That's what you said. Were you lying?"

"Well, no." He didn't say that thinking someone was wise or kind didn't necessarily mean you were going to fall in love with them at some point. He thought Ma was those things too.

But then Sweetie went up on her tiptoes and kissed him, their hands pressed together between their bodies, and all logical, rational thought went flying out of his head.

There was seriously nothing like kissing Sweetie Nair. If everyone could kiss her, there would be no nuclear weapons. No arms races. People wouldn't want to drop bombs or steal money because they'd be too busy trying to sneak in another kiss. Kissing her was the solution to world peace. Ashish was sure of it. Actually, maybe it was better that no one knew that. Less competition. He wrapped his hands in her rainbow hair and pulled her closer.

They sat sipping smoothies at one of the food trucks.

"How's the vanilla avocado?" Sweetie asked.

He held out the cup so she could taste it. She made a face. "Not too bad for being *vanilla avocado*. Try my peanut butter chocolate banana."

He did and screwed up his nose. "Oh God. Too. Sweet."

She laughed. "Good thing you're not dating someone named Sweetie or anything."

He winked at her. "That's different."

She dropped her eyes in that shy way, and his heart trip-hammered. For someone who considered himself a bit of a player, Ashish realized he spent a lot of time being completely charmed by Sweetie. He told his heart to STFU immediately.

"So tell me something," he said, crossing his legs and throwing one arm over the back of his chair to distract from the feeling. "Your parents have no idea? What do they think you're doing?"

"Hanging out with the girls," Sweetie said. "Kayla, Izzy, and Suki have been really good about covering for me." She sipped her smoothie for a quiet moment. "But I still really don't like lying to them. I wish I didn't have to."

"You won't for long. We'll tell them in a bit, right?" He didn't say that at the end of the four dates, they would probably mutually decide to break up. Ma and Pappa thought he'd be madly in love with Sweetie. She was okay with him being physically attracted to her because she thought the emotional stuff would come later. He was sure that at the end of this he'd consider her a really good friend. But *love*? That just wasn't going to happen. He was tapped out. It was like he was a basketball full of love instead of air, and Celia had come by with a screwdriver, poked a giant hole in it, and drained it empty. The ball would never hold love again. It was damaged.

"Yeah," Sweetie said, answering his question. "I just hope Amma forgives me. Our relationship's a little complicated right now."

"Did you say you relate to your dad more?"

Sweetie leaned back and smiled that sparkly smile of hers. "Yeah. Achchan and I are really similar, and I don't mean just physically. We're almost like mind twins or something. I can tell he knows something's up. Just earlier he was asking me about Izzy, Suki, and Kayla, and . . ." She shook her head, her smile fading. "I really wanted to tell him. But if I do, I know he'll want to tell Amma out of some sense of loyalty. And that totally defeats the purpose of the Sassy Sweetie Project." She stopped short, her eyes wide.

CHAPTER 21

Sweetie

Sweetie's blood froze. She was literally a block of ice. Okay, not literally, but almost.

She did *not* just say that out loud. Please, God. Please let it have been an aural hallucination or something. PLEASE, FOR THE LOVE OF ALL THAT IS—

Ashish

"The *what*?" Ashish felt a grin spreading across his face. "The Sassy Swee—"

Sweetie leaned forward and put a small hand over his lips. He tried not to enjoy the feeling too much. "Never, ever repeat that. Ever."

"But—"

"Ashish, I am *begging* you."

He studied her expression, her wide, panicked eyes, and bit on the insides of his cheeks to keep from laughing. He held up his hands and spoke, muffled, from behind her hand. "Okay, okay. I won't say it."

She retrieved her hand and sat back down. She was sipping very primly at her smoothie when Ashish said, laughing, "But you gotta tell me what that entails."

She glared at him. "It entails standing up for myself, for what I believe to be true. It entails me overcoming sixteen years of crap messages from my mom and the media and other people in my life—both kids and adults alike—who think I'm less than them because of how I look."

Ashish softened. "Oh." He took her hand. "I really like it. I think you should get a T-shirt that says that, honestly."

Sweetie rolled her eyes. *"No."*

"Well, if you got me a T-shirt, I'd wear it. Proudly."

She studied his face, apparently assessing whether he was joking or not. "You really mean that, don't you?"

He nodded. "I think people who stand up for themselves, especially in the face of being told not to, are the kind of people this world needs more of."

She grinned suddenly. *Ouch.* She needed to have a warning beep or something before she unleashed that gorgeous thing on people. "Thanks, Ashish."

He bowed his head. "You're welcome, Sweetie." He looked up at her from under his eyelashes. "You know what? I had fun today."

"Yeah, me too."

"No, I mean, I *really* had fun. Here and at the temple. Doing Indian things. With a girl my parents picked out."

Sweetie laughed. "You sound a little shell-shocked."

Ashish shook his head slowly and took a sip of his drink. "I need to watch out before I turn into Rishi," he muttered. "Not that my parents would mind that."

Sweetie put a hand on his. "I don't know your brother. But I'm getting to know *you*, and I'll say this: I wouldn't want you to be anyone except exactly who you are."

It was pretty wild, but Ashish thought she actually meant it.

Watching her drive away was harder than he'd thought it would be. Being around her, her softness, her kindness, was changing him. He felt like a sharp rock that had been softened by a gently flowing river, succumbing to its beauty without even realizing he'd succumbed at all. When he was around Sweetie, his previous "playerness" felt ridiculous and childish. Being around her, he wanted to be good too. He wanted, he realized, to be worthy of her.

His phone beeped, and sighing, he pulled it out. It'd just be Samir or his mom again, freaking out. But the words on the screen froze him.

I miss you. –C

Ashish read the words over and over again. Celia missed him. She was the one who'd called it off. So . . . what did this mean?

What about Thumbs? he typed numbly, not even caring that it sounded totally bitter.

Oh Ash there's no one like you. I'm so lonely. Even in a crowd of people I feel completely untethered.

Whoa. This was serious. Celia never used words like "untethered" unless she was in a Mood. He waited.

Can I call you? Please? I know I don't have a right to ask

He should say, *Yeah, you're right. You have zero right.* Or, *Screw you and your untethered face, Celia.* He groaned and tipped his head backward. When would he learn? When?

Sure, his fingers typed.

His phone rang immediately. He answered but didn't say anything.

"Ash." Her voice, low and sultry, did things to his heart and body that he'd forgotten about. "Thank you for talking to me." She sounded appropriately apologetic, so he didn't say any number of biting things he wanted to.

Sighing, he walked around the house to the garden and along the pond path. "I'm actually not sure what you want to talk about. Are you okay?"

He could hear the smile in her voice. "You were always so caring. I miss that. There's no one here who cares about me. I'm just another body, floating around these halls."

"What happened to Thad?" Ashish asked, pulling a brown leaf off a rosebush and crushing it between his fingers. "I thought you were all 'swept off your feet' or whatever." He did the air quotes even though she couldn't see them. That was okay; sarcasm could travel phone lines just like smiles could.

"It was a mistake, Ash." Celia's voice was all choked up, like she was going to cry. He felt himself immediately softening, even wishing he could put his arms around her. There was no one more vulnerable than glamorous, beautiful, confident Celia when she cried. "I just . . . There's no one I can talk to here. I hate college. I hate it so much. I'm so alone!" And then she was full-on crying, sobbing and everything.

Ashish stood there, staring at the pond, stricken. "Oh, hey. Hey, don't cry, C. It's going to be okay."

"No, it isn't," she said, her voice muffled like her face was buried in her pillow. He could picture her then, her small body wrapped up in her bedsheets, her thin shoulders shaking, her mass of curls like a caramel-colored cloud around her.

It struck him that she was about as different from Sweetie as she could possibly be. What his friends had said about his usual pattern of dating skinny, conventionally pretty girls floated into his brain, jolting him with an electric shock of guilt.

Sweetie.

What was he *doing*? He shouldn't even be talking to Celia. But then he pushed the guilt away. He hadn't lied to Sweetie; in fact, he'd been up front about this. Celia still had a piece of him. That's just how things were. And he wasn't *doing* anything anyway; they were just talking.

He sank onto the bench and began to talk in that soft, soothing voice he knew she loved. She used to call it his "rumble." "It *will* be okay," he said calmly. "Like it always is. We'll get through this together."

By the time he was done talking with Celia, the sun was sinking, turning the sky the colors of the powders he'd rubbed into Sweetie's hair and cheeks earlier that day. It had been that same day that they'd kissed, when he'd pulled away, and it felt like ages now. After talking to Celia.

Not a good idea, a voice inside him said. *You're broken up for a reason.*

Yeah. So Celia was his first love. She was bright and colorful, the kind of person who, by smiling, made you feel like your entire world was on fire. She got him, and his cocky, arrogant side fit seamlessly with her. He never had to tone down his jockness or his flirtiness; all of that was what Celia liked about him. But Celia was also prone to drama. She was extremely touchy. She could be flighty and unreliable. And worst of all? He'd given her his heart and she'd nothing-but-netted it into the trash. She'd cheated on him.

Sweetie, on the other hand, was . . . To be honest, Sweetie was worlds away from him. She was sweet and soft and mild, a daisy growing among thorny weeds. Somehow, in spite of everything, she managed to round out his rough edges to fit with her soft ones. Somehow, it felt *right*. But still, Ash was terrified he'd inevitably break her heart because he couldn't be what she wanted, just like his friends had warned him. How could someone like him—selfish, never-made-a-relationship-last Ash—give Sweetie everything she wanted? Everything she deserved?

Sweetie was a different species entirely from Celia—and from everyone else he knew, to be honest. Heck, he'd never before dated anyone who'd come up with something as heart-meltingly cute, as ridiculously brave, as the Sassy Sweetie Project. As he walked to his Jeep to drive to Samir's house, Ash smiled suddenly at the memory of how she'd completely frozen after she'd blurted that out to him, looking like freaking Bambi in headlights. She was so unbearably adorable sometimes. His smile fading, he thought, *And that's why you need to be the man she deserves, Ash. You seriously cannot—canNOT—mess this one up.*

No pressure.

Sweetie

"Said, the universe couldn't keep us apart
Why would it even try?"

Sweetie stopped singing at the sound of applause and opened her eyes to see her friends clapping and cheering like she'd just won the gold at the Olympics. They were all gathered in Kayla's parents' four-car garage, half of which was empty and perfect for their rehearsal space. She rolled her eyes and laughed. "You guys. I'm not even done singing that part."

"Yeah, well, this is your second go-around, so I think we got it," Kayla said, her bracelets jangling at her wrist. "And you are in*spired* today."

"You could go to LA and be discovered," Izzy said, her hands clasped in front of her chest. "Seriously, Sweetie."

Suki narrowed her eyes. "Something's different, though," she said slowly, tapping a drumstick against her chin. Her long, silky black hair hung in waves down her shoulders.

Sweetie tugged self-consciously at her own bun. "Yeah. I've been practicing."

"Nuh-uh," Suki said, shaking her head. Then, widening her eyes, she grinned. "*Oh. I* get it."

"What?" Kayla looked from her to Sweetie, who was now studying her shoes with intense fascination. "What do you get?"

"Share with the class, Suki," Izzy said, and slurped at her Sprite.

"She's singing like this because she *believes* what she's singing now. It's a love song, guys." Suki snickered. "I'd say things with Ashish are heating up."

"Ohmigod, is that true?" Izzy said, and then choked on her drink in her excitement and had to be pounded on the back by Suki.

"Calm down," Sweetie mumbled.

"It's true, isn't it?" Kayla crossed her arms. "Yeah, I can tell by the way your face is."

"My face is how it always is!" Sweetie threw her hands up. "Sheesh."

"You mean '*Ashish*,'" Suki said, and then they all burst out laughing.

Sweetie glared at them, but she felt the smile tugging at the corners of her lips. Oh, come on. There was no way to be mad at them. Not when they were 1,000 percent right. "Okay, yes," she said, taking a seat on the worn, old corduroy couch that had been Kayla's mom's in college. "Things are going well. I mean, for me they are."

Kayla sat next to her and crossed her legs. "What do you mean, for *you* they are? What about Ashish?"

"He's still having a hard time with this girl he broke up with. We totally had a moment this morning at the Holi Festival. He kissed me. And I told you about our first kiss in his car, right?" She grinned around at her friends and they all nodded. "But then at the Holi Festival he pulled away right in the middle of it. We talked about it, but basically he had his heart shattered and now he's afraid, you know? So I told him I'd wait for him. He told me he's physically attracted to me"— Sweetie's cheeks burned in both happiness and embarrassment—"but he still feels this emotional distance. So I told him that'll probably come later, right? With time." She looked around at the girls again, but this time their grins had faded. "What?"

There was a beat of silence. Then Suki spoke. "You're okay with him only wanting you for your body? Because I'm pretty sure that's what you just said."

Sweetie felt her temper flare. Suki could be so blunt sometimes, even when she was wrong. "That's actually not what I said. Like, at all. I said the emotional connection will come later."

"Yeah. Meaning right now he just wants you for your body." Suki raised her eyebrows, like, *Duh.*

"It sounds like you guys are having a good time," Kayla rushed to add, seeing Sweetie's expression. "But, um, Sweetie . . . it sounds like you're really falling for him and he . . . might not be?"

"Right." She looked around at them all and shrugged. "He's not *yet*. But that doesn't mean things can't change. We've only been on two official dates, guys. And for me, this is about more than just Ashish. This is about me proving something to myself."

"We know," Izzy said, giving her a tentative smile. "We just don't want you to get hurt, that's all. Ashish didn't tell you that he would come around, did he?"

Sweetie was about to say that of course he had, but when she thought about it, she realized he hadn't. He'd just asked her if she was sure she still wanted to date him. "No," she said finally, her voice quiet. Then, straightening her shoulders, she added, "But that's okay. I know what I'm getting myself into. It's all going to be fine. Celia's out of the picture now, and it's the Sweetie Show." She paused and framed her face with her hands. "I mean, come on, guys. How can he resist this?"

They burst out laughing, and Izzy put her arms around Sweetie. "He can't."

"He won't," Kayla said, a little more darkly.

"Or we'll kick his arse," Suki added, and before Sweetie could open her mouth to protest, she launched into a kick-ass, thunderous drum solo that shook the walls and made the floor tremble.

Sweetie grimaced as she slid into her car and glanced at the clock on the dashboard. It was already past eight o'clock, and she hadn't even begun her giant economics project that was due Monday morning. Sweetie generally didn't spend her Saturday nights doing homework, but she probably should've started this behemoth of a project two weeks ago. She had a *lot* of work to cram into forty-eight hours. Sighing, she pulled into the parking lot of Roast Me on the way home to pick up an espresso and maybe some of those chocolate-covered coffee beans. She probably wouldn't need to sleep till *tomorrow* night.

Sweetie was waiting for her order when she felt a tap on her shoulder. She turned to see Oliver, Ashish's friend. Her face instantly creased into a smile. "Hey!" Then, remembering what Ashish had said about Oliver and Elijah's breakup, her smile faded.

He half smiled at her, and she noticed the dark circles under his eyes, the way he was all scruffy and unshaven, and his button-down shirt was totally rumpled. Not at all how he looked the last time she'd seen him.

"Hey," he said quietly. "How are you?"

"Double espresso for Sweetie!" the barista called out, and Sweetie went up to grab her cup. Oliver followed.

"Big night ahead of you?"

Sweetie made a face. "Econ paper. Bleh. I should've started eons ago, but . . ." She took a breath. This was uncomfortable. Not because Sweetie was uncomfortable with people's feelings. She wasn't. But because she didn't know whether she'd be totally overstepping a boundary by reaching out to Oliver now. They'd only ever talked once. "Um, Oliver . . ." He looked at her, his gray eyes dark and lifeless. "Ashish told me about you and Elijah. I'm so sorry."

He nodded, swallowing compulsively a few times. His eyes looked misty, and Sweetie realized with a jolt of alarm that he might be about to cry. Without even thinking about it, she put an arm around his waist (his shoulder was out of reach, dang basketball players) and led him over to the couches toward the back of the café, where they'd hung out that one time.

They sat on a couch together, and Sweetie handed him her espresso. "Here. You need it more than me. I'll get another one on my way out."

He accepted it with a grateful, watery smile and took two big swallows. "Thanks. That helps." He sighed a long, deep thing, holding the coffee cup between his knees, his head hanging low. "Man. I just . . . This doesn't feel real."

Sweetie put a tentative hand on his back. "I'm sorry. You guys seemed happy."

"We were." He laughed abruptly, the sound hard and dark. "I guess I should say I *thought* we were. But Elijah was obviously coming to other conclusions." In a wobbly voice he added, "I'm pretty sure he cheated on me."

"What?" Sweetie didn't know them very well, but the one thing she couldn't do was picture Elijah cheating on Oliver. Even to her inexperienced eye, Elijah had looked at Oliver like he was . . . he was the answer to some unspoken question. "He said that?"

"No. He wouldn't say anything. But so many people on the

Eastman team told me they'd seen him with some guy." He shrugged. "And he didn't even try to convince me when I confronted him. He just said that if I couldn't trust him, we should break up. After two whole years! Apparently, we're too close or something."

"But that's stupid," Sweetie blurted out without thinking. "Oops. Sorry."

Oliver smiled at her. "No, you're right. It is stupid. This whole thing makes no sense."

"I wonder . . ." Sweetie nibbled her lip, afraid again that she was overstepping. But then she decided if she were in Oliver's situation, losing the love of her life, she'd want someone to be straight with her. "I wonder if you know why you're having so much trouble trusting him. I mean, it's obvious to me you guys were happy. And you've been together for two years. So why did you believe those Eastman guys?"

Oliver studied his shoelaces so long, Sweetie was afraid he was trying to hold in a really angry outburst. But when he finally met her eyes again, he just looked confused. And hurt. "I don't know," he said, almost wonderingly. "That's a really good question. Why *didn't* I trust him?"

"And why didn't he try to convince you?" Sweetie asked, nodding. "Any ideas?"

Oliver thought about it for a second and then shrugged. "Not a one."

"Maybe it has something to do with fear," Sweetie suggested. "Maybe you're both afraid."

"Afraid?" Oliver asked. "Afraid of what, though?"

"I'm not sure. But maybe figuring that out is the starting point. The way you find your way back to each other."

"I don't know if that's ever going to happen. But thank you. I'm going to think about that."

Sweetie smiled. "Sure."

Oliver swallowed the rest of the espresso and got to his feet. "Well, I should go. I'm gonna hit the gym, try to work off some of this caffeine rush."

Sweetie nodded and followed suit. "Yeah, I should get going, too. Hey, Oliver. For what it's worth, I think Elijah's making a huge mistake. Whether he cheated or not . . . you deserved more than an insta-breakup."

Oliver reached down and hugged her. "Thanks, Sweetie. Ashish is right. You're a good person."

She smiled shyly up at him. "Ditto."

Oliver looked at her, his head tilted. "You've been good for him, you know. I mean, he's still totally flat when it comes to basketball and he doesn't sleep, but I can see a bit of a difference. He's a little less wilted."

Sweetie frowned. "I can't imagine anything worse than not being able to enjoy running. How long has basketball been like that for him?"

"Since the breakup with Celia. Almost four months ago, I'd say. It's tough." Oliver's phone beeped in his pocket, and he slid it out and glanced at the screen. "Well, I gotta go. See you soon, I hope?"

"Yeah, definitely. You should come to Band Night here a week from Thursday. I'm singing and I could really use the support."

Oliver paused. "Okay," he said finally. "For you." Grinning, he held up a hand and loped off.

Still thinking of what he'd said about Ashish losing his fire for basketball, Sweetie went up to the counter to order another double espresso. A plan had begun to form in her mind.

CHAPTER 22

Ashish

Ashish was almost to Samir's house when a text popped up on his Jeep's LCD screen.

Pinky: Yo meeting you at S's house

Huh. Weird. The system didn't let Ashish text while he was driving, so he continued on until he got there. And there, in Samir's sloping drive, was parked Pinky's lime-green electric car. She was leaned up against the side, texting furiously, her face lit up in the dark by the silver glow of the screen.

"Hey," Ashish called, hopping out the open side of the Jeep. "What are you doing here?"

She stashed her cell and looked up at him. "I ran into your mom at the aquarium; Saturdays are my day to volunteer at the flamboyant cuttlefish exhibit, and she was there for some board meeting thingy. Anyway, she said Samir's mom had called and she sounded all worried, so . . ."

They walked together to the front door. Ashish glanced at her. "Wait. Flamboyant cuttlefish?"

"Yes, it's a thing." Pinky sighed. "Just like the assassin bug was really a thing."

"I mean, come on. Can you blame us? 'Assassin bug' sounds totally made up."

Pinky rolled her eyes as she rang the doorbell. "Samir was the only one who believed me," she said after a moment. "Remember?"

"Yeah, I do," Ashish replied, looking at her. "He pulled it up on his phone and told us all to shut up."

Samir's mom answered the door then, looking slightly disheveled in a wrinkled sari and with frizzy hair.

"Hello, auntie," Ashish said. "We're here to see Samir."

"Oh, good, good," she said, standing to the side. Her smile didn't reach her eyes. "He'll be so happy to see you. I've been so worried, you know. Samir doesn't seem to be . . . himself. You can go up to his room."

They walked up the staircase together and knocked on Samir's bedroom door.

"Come in." His voice was muffled, almost flat.

Ashish turned the doorknob and walked in, with Pinky following close behind.

The first thing that struck him was that the room looked like a pit of despair. If you thought about the words "gloomy dungeon" in your head, you probably would conceive something very similar to what Ashish was looking at. Ashish had been in Samir's room many, many times over the years. It was always neatly organized and vacuumed (his mom cleaned it for him every day), with a potpourri bowl on the desk. Seeing it like this was almost . . . shocking.

There was only one lamp on in the corner of the room. Bedclothes were scattered everywhere, and Samir's desk was buried under piles of papers and food wrappers. It smelled musty and stale, like the windows and door hadn't been opened in who knew how long. Ashish glanced at Pinky, who was taking in all the same details with a totally neutral face. But because he knew her so well, he could see the look in her eyes: surprise. And worry. Samir was the nerdiest dresser of them all: His hair was always slightly oiled with coconut oil and brushed to the side, like some dude from the forties. He wore pressed button-down shirts and khaki pants all the time. Dude probably didn't even own a pair of jeans. He always smelled faintly of lavender lotion. The few times they'd been in his room, everything had been at right angles. Even his bedsheets had had creases.

"Hey, Samir," Ashish said. Samir was sitting in a beanbag, tossing a ball at the wall and then catching it on the rebound. He turned to look at them and nodded before going back to his ball. "Dude, what's going on?"

Samir didn't bother looking at him this time. "What do you mean?"

"Your mom called me, man. She's really worried about you."

"I'm fine," Samir said in a tone that suggested he'd said it many, many times these past few days. "So you didn't need to come over here with a pity party cake, okay?"

Pinky pushed a bundle of old clothes off his bed and sat. "We don't pity you, dude," she said. "But you're not acting like yourself and we're worried. That's all."

Samir smiled mirthlessly and looked over at her. "Really? But I thought no one liked me. So shouldn't you guys be doing a little victory dance?"

Ashish stepped in. "Look, man. I think we need to talk about that. I'm sorry if I hurt your feelings. The thing is, you have been a good friend at times. You've just . . . It's hard to realize that when there are so many times you've made fun of us or been—"

"A craphead," Pinky put in. Samir glared at her, but she went on. "Come on. You can't deny it. You've been really annoying and smug and holier-than-thou, and you just don't know when to let things go. Like, you drive them into the ground until no one but you is laughing and you still—"

"Uh, Pinky?" Ashish said, forcing a smile. "What are you doing?" He tried to keep his tone light, but he seriously wanted to throw a pillow at her face. She'd completely lost sight of the mission.

"Yeah," Samir said, narrowing his eyes. "What exactly *are* you doing?"

Pinky held up her hands. "I wasn't done. In spite of all those things, you *have* been a good friend. Like when you stood up for me with that assassin bug thing. Or when you stood in line for Bruins tickets for, like, two hours because they were all sold out online and Ashish was playing at an away game and couldn't get them himself. And I know Oliver really loves how you remember their freaking anniversary and none of the rest of us do." She paused. "Although I guess you won't need to do that anymore. Anyway, my point is, we do appreciate the things you do. And we're sorry for forgetting them because we got mad at you."

"She's right, man," Ashish added. "And the thing is, your advice about getting my parents to set me up with someone? It worked. Sweetie's really cool. I don't think I thanked you for that, but I appreciate it."

Samir was silent for a moment as he looked from Pinky to Ashish. Ashish held still, letting him process or whatever he was doing.

Finally he sighed and tossed the ball onto the floor. He turned so his body was facing them completely. "It's not just you guys. I *have* been a jerk. I mean, that thing with your hair, Pinky. I should've let it go when I saw that it was bothering you. And I didn't need to go on and on about you and Celia to the girl you were dating, Ashish." Another sigh. "The thing is, I act like a complete arsehole because . . . because I'm jealous. And that makes me defensive."

"Jealous of what?" Ashish asked, taking a seat on the blue mesh chair at Samir's desk.

"You guys are all so close. You go to school together. I left in fifth grade, and ever since then, things have been different. I'm just not a part of things anymore—how could I be? So I tried harder to fit in. I tried to be . . . more like you, actually, Ash. Cockier, more confident. I wanted to project this aura of, like, untouchability to cover the fact that I am, in fact, a totally overprotected homeschooled loser." He looked away and swiped at his jaw. "Whatever. It didn't work, and when I saw how *much* it wasn't working, I just . . ." He shook his head and was silent for a long moment. Ashish waited. He saw Pinky, sitting completely still in his peripheral vision. "I don't know what to do anymore. It's like I have these endless days and nights stretching out in front of me and it all feels so pointless and stupid. You guys were a great distraction." He smiled. "But I get that you don't want me to hang out with you anymore. It's fine; I'm not trying to weasel back in there or anything. I guess I'm just trying to figure out what's next, and right now that just looks like a big black hole."

"It doesn't have to be," Ashish said. "Firstly, I want you to come back and hang with us again. I mean, none of that defensive douchebag stuff, but just . . . yourself. The real Samir who peeks out sometimes. I think it's safe to say we all like him way better than the Ashish-clonebot." He raised his eyebrows at Pinky, who nodded enthusiastically. Samir managed a weak laugh. "And secondly, dude, you should talk to your mom about how you feel. Seriously."

"I don't—I can't." Samir rubbed his face and then shook his head. "She's . . . The cancer could return anytime. And it was so sudden before. She's scared. She says she isn't, she puts on this brave face, but I know her. Her mom, my *nani*, died of breast cancer. If I go back to school and she gets sick again . . ."

"You could go back to school and she could get sick again," Pinky said quietly. "But you could go back to school and she could be fine. She could get sick if you're homeschooled, or she could be fine. The thing is, we can't control what happens. No matter how much we want to, or how much we try to bargain with the fates or the universe or whatever . . . sometimes crap happens." She paused. "One thing I do know? I saw how upset your mom looked downstairs. What she wants more than anything is for you to be happy. And she knows you're not. So who are you doing this for?"

Ashish stared at Pinky, his longtime best friend/pain in the butt. He'd never heard her speak like that before. There was no hint of sarcasm, no rolling of eyes or sighing in great displeasure. He hazarded a glance at Samir, who looked totally bowled over too.

"I . . . I didn't look at it like that," Samir said. He blew out a breath. "You're right. There's nothing I can do to control what happens." He paused. "Who *am* I doing this for?"

"Think about it," Ashish said gently. "Only you can decide what you want to do, but just don't discount your own happiness, man."

"Yeah, because it makes you a total douche nozzle, apparently," Pinky said, rolling her eyes. Okay, she was back.

Samir chuckled, though he still looked somewhat dazed. "I'm definitely going to give it more thought. But right now I'd really like a distraction. So Oliver and Elijah are still broken up?"

"Yep." Ashish swiveled in Samir's chair. "Elijah's being a total dumb-ass."

"So is Oliver," Pinky said. "I mean, accusing Elijah of cheating? Does that sound like something he'd even consider doing?"

Ashish felt a flash of pain as he thought of Celia. How he'd trusted her and how he'd been totally wrong. "You never know. People do weird things sometimes." Saying it out loud just made him feel like a train wreck. Why was he talking to her again? Ugh. He'd spent hours on the phone with her just because she'd cried. "It's going to be interesting seeing them both together on Band Night at Roast Me," he added, just to take his mind off Celia.

"But they've been at basketball practice together, right? And that was okay." Pinky shrugged. "So maybe it won't be so bad."

"There's so much going on during practice, though," Ashish said thoughtfully. "And as soon as we hit the showers, Oliver jets out of there before he can so much as lay eyes on Elijah. They haven't really hung out together since the breakup."

"You know, it's odd," Samir said. "I always thought they'd end up going to the same college and then getting married after."

"We all kinda thought that," Pinky replied.

They were quiet for a long moment.

"This can't be it for them," Samir said suddenly into the silence.

"What are you thinking?" Pinky asked, one skeptical eyebrow raised.

"Something to remind them how good it used to be." Samir picked up the ball, threw it at his wall, and then caught it again. "Something that reminds them of what they're missing."

"Good luck," Ashish mumbled. Every time he'd so much as tried to bring up Oliver's name to Elijah, he'd been met with the Death Glare. "You're gonna need it."

Close to midnight, Ashish sat on his balcony with a Yoo-hoo, debating the merits of taking a shower then or later. He was pretty tired, but he knew he wouldn't be able to fall asleep anytime soon anyway. He scrolled through his Instagram feed—which was now pretty empty, after he'd deleted all the pictures of him and Celia and hadn't posted any new ones—and stopped at one that made him smile.

It was his brother, Rishi, with Dimple, the girl he was dating. They were both standing on a hill, with the San Fran skyline behind them. Their arms were wrapped around each other, both of them grinning so hard, their eyes were just little slits. They were practically bursting with sunshine and love. The caption read, *Seven-month anniversary of the first date. Think I'll keep her. Wait, she wants me to tell you guys that* SHE'S *the one keeping* ME. And then there was an eye roll emoji. If they weren't so ridiculously cute, Ashish would vomit. He liked the post and then wrote a comment: *Maybe come home sometime this century so we can all see the happy couple?*

His phone beeped almost immediately with a text.

Rishi-o: Done. When's the big game that all the scouts are coming to?

May 10th.

We'll be there. Ignore the screaming and cheering.

How are you?

Ashish sighed. Great. Rishi never asked him how he was like that. Ma had obviously blurted out something about his humiliating breakup. But before he could respond, another text came through:

Celia told Dimple you guys broke up

Oh. Ashish felt immediately guilty for the vote of no confidence he'd given his poor mother. Fine.

Dude. You don't have to do that with me. This is your bhaiyya

Ashish wanted to roll his eyes, but instead he felt this alarming lump in his throat. The truth was, no matter how much he'd hated Rishi for being the golden child, he was a good big brother. They'd had their ups and downs (okay, so before Rishi left for college, it had been a lot more downs), but in the end Ashish always knew that he could count on Rishi to be there for him. And what else mattered, really?

Not so hot in that case, he typed before he lost his nerve. But I'm dating someone new

His phone rang immediately, and Rishi's goofy face popped up on the screen. Sighing slightly, Ashish answered. "Yo, *bhaiyya*."

"Yo yourself, you gigolo."

Ashish did roll his eyes then. "No one uses that word."

"Except me. So tell me more about this new girl!"

"What's all that noise?"

"Oh, sorry. I'm at IHOP. It's sort of where everyone goes to pull all-nighters. All-you-can-eat pancakes for twelve dollars. We have a giant project coming up in art history about the cuneiform script that the Sumerians developed."

Ashish smiled. "Dude, don't rub your wild college life in my face." He was happy for *bhaiyya*. It seemed like college—and SFSU's art program in particular—really suited him.

"Sorry, sorry. Tell me, though. Who's this girl?"

"Her name's Sweetie Nair." He rushed to add, "Yeah, yeah, she's desi."

Rishi let out a theatrical gasp. "You dating an *Indian girl*?"

"I know, I know. And get this: I even let Ma and Pappa set me up. I figured if it worked for you and Dimple . . ." Ashish frowned. "I'm surprised they haven't told you all this yet." Usually his parents and Rishi were like BFFs. As weird as that might sound to other people—Ashish included—it really worked for them.

"I haven't called them in a while," Rishi said, sounding guilty. "College has just taken over my life. Between that and sneaking visits in with Dimple when I can . . ."

"I hear you."

"So Sweetie, huh? Is she helping you move on from the breakup?"

"Yeah, she is, actually."

There was a pause. Ashish tried to decide how to say what he wanted to say, what he felt deep inside.

"But?"

"But I'm not sure if it's going to work. We're so different. She's . . . I'm . . . My relationship track record sucks. And Celia . . . she really messed me up, Rishi."

Rishi's voice was soft when he spoke, judgment-free. "That's understandable. Celia was your first love, Ashish." He paused. "As for your track record—look, everyone's gotta start somewhere. You have to turn it around somehow. Why not begin now?"

Ashish swallowed and looked at the lit swimming pool in the distance. "Yeah. Maybe you're right."

"So this Sweetie girl . . . is she good?"

Ashish felt a small smile tugging at his lips. "Yeah, she's the best."

"Then give this a chance. You might surprise yourself. But you have to let go of everything that happened with Celia, all the hurt and confusion. Just cut the strings and let that . . . that kite fly."

Ashish raised an eyebrow. "That kite, huh?"

"Yeah. It's late, gimme a break." Someone called Rishi's name frantically in the distance.

Ashish chuckled. "You should go. Sounds like an art history emergency."

"It's a dangerous world, but somebody's gotta live it," Rishi said valiantly. "You okay?"

"I'll be fine. Talk soon, *bhaiyya*."

"Okay. Bye."

Ashish hung up and sat back, letting the cool breeze wash over him. Rishi hadn't really said anything earth-shattering, but Ashish still somehow felt better. Like he really would figure things out somehow, like maybe he wasn't as emotionally stunted as he feared.

His phone beeped again.

Sweetie: you up?

Huh. This was new. Sweetie didn't usually text after ten p.m. He typed, yeah but why are you? Thought you said you were an early-to-bed-er

ugh econ project don't ask

uh oh

i need a break so . . . I have a question

shoot

will you meet me at the corner of McAdam and Harper near where I live? And bring your tennis shoes

He smiled a little as he responded. is this another race? I think you've proved that you can kick my butt any day of the week. You don't have to try when I'm tired and weak

haha no this is something else

very intriguing

so you'll come?

obviously

☺ k see you in 20

Ashish felt a little burst of energy as he walked inside to get his shoes on and refresh his deodorant (just in case). (He also brushed his teeth. Just in case.) If he was going to be sleepless, then sleepless on a midnight rendezvous with Sweetie was by far the most interesting option. He grabbed his keys and left a note for his parents, but he was sure they wouldn't be up until the morning. Sleep came easily to everyone in their family. That had included Ashish until very recently.

He drove down to Sweetie's neighborhood and parked along the curb on Harper Avenue. Looking around, he saw immediately why she'd asked to meet him there. A small basketball court surrounded by a chain-link fence stood on the corner, quiet and empty. Smiling, he walked over to it, sat on a bench, and waited.

CHAPTER 23

Ashish

He was just about to text Sweetie a picture of himself looking all woebegone and lost when his phone beeped.

Celia: hey, you up? what are you doing?

He stared at the text for a long moment. He remembered what Rishi had said: *Cut the strings.* He slipped the phone back into his pocket.

"Hey."

Ashish spun around on the bench to see Sweetie walking up, her high ponytail bouncing, her smile bright like a sliver of moonlight in the near darkness. "Hey yourself." Standing, he reached out and pulled her into a hug. Without even meaning to, he inhaled the scent of her in one long, deep breath, which he let out slowly. His shoulders instantly relaxed.

She looked up at him and smiled, slaying him with that dimple. "You okay?"

"I am now." It was true, he realized. Everything felt good, peaceful.

She looked down at her feet, still smiling. Oh God. The adorability—that was a word, right?—was too much. Suddenly

Ashish couldn't remember why he'd ever been wary of asking his parents to set him up.

He grabbed Sweetie's hand and they began walking. "So, are you a basketball star too? Is your plan to just completely annihilate me in every sport?"

She laughed, the sound lighting up the quiet night. "No. This is all about *you* feeling like a star."

"Oh yeah?" He let go of her hand and turned to her, running his fingers lightly up her arm, delighting in her shivering. "Because there are a few things besides basketball that could make me feel like that."

Sweetie looked away and swatted at him, smiling. "Behave."

He held up his hands, thinking, *Man, no one does shy more beautifully than Sweetie.*

"I think we should play a round of basketball. Maybe get you to enjoy it again." She paused, biting her lip, as if she wasn't sure how he'd receive what she was about to say next. "I ran into Oliver tonight, and he told me you're still not feeling it." He crossed his arms, trying not to get defensive, and she put a small hand on his arm. "I just want to help. I can't imagine anything worse than not being able to enjoy running anymore."

Ashish forced himself to smile. She was clearly trying to make him feel better; there was no hint of pity or *Get over it already* in her eyes. "That's sweetie of you."

"Ha ha." Sweetie raised an eyebrow. "You can't deflect me that easily, Mr. Patel."

Judging by her outthrust chin, she wasn't going to let this go. "Okay, fine." Ashish let out a breath. "It *has* been pretty sucky."

She looked at him, those dark eyes like the most expensive black velvet, soft and infinite. "I can only imagine." Then, standing on tiptoe, she placed the gentlest, lightest kiss on his cheek, close to the corner of his mouth.

Ashish literally could not think of a single word to say.

"So this is my plan," she continued, completely oblivious to the effect she was having on him.

"Mmm, yes, plan," Ashish mumbled, blinking the lusty gauze curtain away.

"I want to have a basketball game, maybe something like horse. But we're going to make it interesting."

"Oh yeah?" Ashish raised an eyebrow. He could feel all parts of himself tuning in.

"Yeah. We can pick each other's positions to try to make the basket—the harder the better, obviously. And we have to sing the national anthem while we try to make the basket. You know, to make things interesting."

Positions. Harder. Ashish was trying really hard not to be a perv, but this was getting a little out of hand. She had said nothing to justify the thoughts running through his head. *Get a grip, jeez. Pun wholly intended.* "The national anthem, huh?"

"Oh, and I almost forgot." Sweetie stepped closer, her head tipped up to look at him. "For every basket you make, I'll kiss you." Her eyes glittered, and her mouth turned up in a half smile that nearly brought him to his knees. "And you seem to like my kissing, so."

Okay, so maybe she wasn't *completely* oblivious to the effect she had on him.

Sweetie

Sweetie had no idea where all that sass had come from. She had never, *ever* even *dreamed* of talking to a boy like this, let alone allow the words to actually leave her mouth. It was like pretending to be Sassy Sweetie was actually changing how she thought about herself. It was making her confidence level rise, melting those icy barriers she'd built before to keep out people who said she had very little to offer.

Like global warming, but with fewer sad polar bears.

She was supremely enjoying the dopey look on Ashish's face, actually. It felt incredibly good to know that, as hot and funny and nice as Ashish was, he seemed to be really into her, too. She flashed briefly back to what Kayla, Izzy, and Suki had said. How maybe she should play it safe because Ashish might only ever be physically attracted to her and unable to give her anything else. But it couldn't be true. Looking at him now, she could plainly see that it wasn't just her body he wanted. It was *her*. All of her.

She wrapped her arms around his waist and pulled him in. He automatically dipped his head toward hers, his eyes dark and serious. She closed her eyes and let her lips find his; his stubble scraped her jaw and she tasted him—his very Ashishness—with a sigh. His arms tightened around her, and she felt his muscles against her own soft curves; she felt every part of him come alive and fuse closely to her.

"Sweetie," he whispered, pulling away from her for a moment.

She looked at him in silence. He didn't say anything else, but she heard what he wanted to say, what he meant to say. That he was falling for her, too.

Ashish

He wanted to tell her so many things. That he was falling for her, but for some reason, Celia still tugged faintly at his mind, like a siren song floating across the ocean. He wanted to tell her Celia had texted him and that they'd talked. He wanted to tell her he'd never felt as happy, as at peace, as he did when Sweetie was with him. He wanted to tell her he was changing, becoming a better person, a gentler, kinder person, all because of her.

But something inside of him protested. *It's not fair to Sweetie to have that conversation right now,* it said. Rishi had told him to let Celia go. But first he needed to figure out why Celia was still on his mind, what that was all about. And until he did, he couldn't burden Sweetie with this. Maybe falling for Sweetie reminded him of falling for Celia, of getting his heart stomped on under her glittering heels. Maybe it was because everything with Celia felt unfinished, like he'd never gotten the chance to say his piece.

So Ashish *wanted* to tell Sweetie a lot of things. But in the end all he managed was her name.

Sweetie

"So. That was just a little preview." Sweetie grinned, and after the slightest pause Ashish grinned back. It didn't seem fully lit up, but she didn't let that bother her. He was probably just not used to feeling like this—finally leaving Celia and whatever hang-ups came with a breakup behind. Who could say? "Ready to play?"

"Let's do this." He swatted the ball out from under the crook of her arm.

"Hey!"

"Oh, what?" he said, spinning it on one finger. "You thought I was going to take it easy on you because you're so ravishing?"

Sweetie put her hands on her hips and pretended to look mad even though her mind just kept repeating, *Ravishing. You just heard the word "ravishing." In relation to you. From his lips.* "I expect nothing of the kind. Prepare to get your butt whupped."

Sweetie wasn't a basketball player, but she wasn't *bad*. It took Ashish almost ten minutes to get a basket that she missed.

"Whew, that's *H* for you," he said, shaking his head. "That could've been embarrassing if I got the first *H*."

Sweetie narrowed her eyes. "Why? Because I'm a girl?"

He looked genuinely perplexed. "No, because I'm the star here?"

She laughed. "Oh my God, the ego! Save me!"

He grinned. "Okay. So now I believe I've earned a kiss?"

She grew still, feeling suddenly trembly again. Her earlier hubris had disappeared. "Right," she said softly.

"You know what? Can I put it in an account and collect on the interest instead?"

Sweetie waited. "Um. What?"

Ashish grinned that cocky smile she loved, and her heart flopped around helplessly. "You know. I think it might work in my favor to collect on it in the end. One big kiss instead of a series of little ones."

Sweetie felt the heat flood her cheeks. She felt her knees wobble. All she could think about was him, wrapped around her. God, when had she gotten so kiss obsessed? The answer to that, of course, was when she'd begun dating Ashish. "Um." She cleared her throat when her voice came out a squeak. "Yeah. O-okay."

Ashish's grin got brighter. "Excellent. So. Warm-up's over."

"Right." Sweetie laughed, a tad hysterically. "That was the warm-up. I knew that."

Ashish's knowing smirk told her he wasn't falling for it. "Mm-hmm. It's my turn to pick the position. I say you go over there"—he pointed to some bushes—"and try to make the basket while crouching behind them. Oh, and don't forget the national anthem. Actually, you know what? I want you to sing me a song you'll be singing at Band Night."

"Seriously? Crouching *and* making me sing a pop song? That doesn't seem so fair for a *star*."

Grinning, Ashish tugged on the end of her ponytail. When she tilted her head back, he placed a gentle kiss on her neck. Sweetie could manage only a strangled gasp in the back of her throat; every nerve ending was vibrating with pleasure, humming with desire. "Forgive me," he murmured against her skin.

"Th-that's quite all right," she managed. On legs that felt like melting rubber, she walked to the bushes, stealing a backward glance at him. The way he was smiling at her, he looked . . . delighted. But why?

Ashish

Ashish was having a hard time not grinning like a damn fool. It felt so good to know that someone as kind, as sweet, as funny, as beautiful as Sweetie seemed to want him just as much as he wanted her.

His phone beeped in his pocket. He fished it out.

Celia: Are you mad at me

He stared at the message for a moment, his grin fading. Then he typed, No just busy sorry

Celia: Call me later?

He hesitated. This wasn't going to be easy. Yeah

Sweetie

Sweetie heard the beep and saw Ashish texting. "You need to get back home?"

He startled a little (guiltily?) as he looked up at her, but then her favorite smolder-smirk was back. He slipped his phone into his pocket. "No, it's fine. So you gonna make that basket? And sing?"

"Jeez, give me a minute, bossy," she mumbled, trying to get comfortable as she fell into a crouch.

She didn't make that basket or the next one or the next one. And no matter how ridiculous the positions she chose for Ashish—at one point she even had him climb the pole of the opposite basketball net—he managed to make them all. She challenged him to sing Bollywood songs, and he managed, even though his Hindi wasn't the best. He made her sing every song from the lineup for Band Night. And every time she missed and he made it, he'd say, "Don't forget. That's another kiss for later."

She had just missed the basket, earning her an *S*, when he began to lope toward her in the darkness, his eyes strangely intent. She straightened up, leaving the ball on the ground. "I—I still have an *E* left," she said hoarsely, though *why* she didn't know. If he was going to collect now, that was A-OK with her.

"I know," Ashish said softly, coming to stand so close to her, she could feel his body heat through her clothes. "I have a question, though."

His honey-colored eyes were hypnotizing in the dim light, twin planets she couldn't help but be mesmerized by.

"Okay."

He took another step closer. Their clothes brushed against each other. It felt like Sweetie's heart was tap-dancing its way out of her chest. "All those songs . . . you picked them."

Sweetie nodded, suddenly feeling a mixture of embarrassment and panic. Oh, no. Oh, no, no, no. He'd noticed.

"They're all songs about first love," Ashish said quietly, not breaking his gaze.

Sweetie swallowed. She wanted to look away, but she was frozen, helpless. "That's . . . that's not a question," she said finally, her voice just a husky whisper. Her cheeks burned.

Ashish put two fingers under her chin. She forced herself to hold still. "Sweetie Nair," he said, bending his head so their lips were less than a finger's breadth apart. "I really don't deserve you."

Her breath was coming faster. Sweetie knew what she wanted to say; the words were building behind her teeth, like a veritable ocean wave. But could she say them? Could she put herself out there like that, be honest and vulnerable? She thought of the Sassy Sweetie Project. How the whole point was to be brave in every facet of her life. How much she wanted to be *that* girl, the one living her life proudly and bravely, the one who wasn't afraid to get a little dinged with rejection. The one who'd pick herself up again, no matter what, because she knew that what she had to offer the world was spectacular. So she forced the words out, shaking her head. "That's not true. You're . . . you're the real thing, Ashish. You like to show everyone this cocky, arrogant front, but I see the real you. I see you, and you're sweet and funny and stubborn and vulnerable. You love with everything you have, and when you get hurt, you curl around yourself to protect the softest parts of you." She put a hand on his cheek, felt the stubble and the strong jaw there. Goose bumps broke out on her arms and legs. "But you don't have to do that with me. I won't hurt you." She paused, almost panting with the effort of keeping pace with her drumming heart. "And I . . . I think you know that. I think you're falling for me, too."

He stared at her for another long moment, and she began to wonder if she'd made a big mistake. If she'd misjudged. He *had* told her he was still kind of hung up on Celia, after all. What if he thought she was being presumptuous? But then Ashish smiled. A soft, sad thing, a wisp of a smile, really. "Oh, Sweetie," he whispered, bringing his mouth to hers fully. "How could I not?"

And then they were kissing and melting and sighing, and Sweetie was completely lost to the world.

Ashish

There was no lie in anything Sweetie had just said. Even as he kissed her, Ashish played her words over in his head—he *was* falling for her. He *did* know that she'd never hurt him, at least not intentionally. But here's what Sweetie hadn't said, and what Ashish knew to be true: He was still desperately, deathly scared, as uncool as it was to even admit that to himself. He was afraid of what would happen if he fell harder and faster and deeper than he was already falling. He was afraid of what it said about him that before this he'd had *one* serious relationship, which had ended in fire and flames. He was afraid that what he wanted to say to Celia, what he planned to say to her very soon, would go badly, that somehow he'd say his piece and *still* not have any closure.

So when he said, "How could I not?" he meant, *How could I not love someone as miraculous, as perfect as you?* But he also meant, *How could I not expect things to go 100 percent wrong in the end in spite of falling for you?* Ashish had a track record, and it wasn't a good one. Ashish was, in fact, terrified that every relationship of his was doomed to utter and spectacular failure, and that this one with Sweetie was no different.

But how could he say that to Sweetie? He wanted to laugh at the thought of it. Talk about an anti-aphrodisiac. Talk about killing things before they'd even begun.

So Ashish held his doubts and his mojolessness close to his vest, and he stood there, all alone in his cold, dismal pessimism. And then he pushed it all aside because he was here with her in this moment, and he was determined to enjoy it, dammit. Whatever happened in the future, whether he got his closure or not, Ashish was here with Sweetie *now*, and that was an incredible gift. He pulled her closer and kissed her deeper.

Sweetie

They lay in the cool grass together. They'd kissed so long, Sweetie's cheeks were slightly raw from being scraped by Ashish's stubble. She didn't care, though. The only thing that mattered was the feeling of his hard chest under her head, the feeling of his strong arm around her. She played with his hand as she looked up at the hazy sky and smiled.

"Ashish," she said.

"Hmm?" He sounded sleepy and happy, exactly like she felt.

"What's it like having a brother?"

"Hmm." He turned his head and kissed her temple. "I'm not sure how I feel about you thinking about my brother while you lie in my arms. Why do you ask?"

She shrugged. "I don't know. I've always wondered what it'd be like to have a sibling. I mean, I have my cousin Anjali Chechi, but it's not the same. She lives so far away, and we only get to talk on the phone. But I always thought it'd be so awesome to have someone there to bounce ideas off of all the time. To just have to talk to. Being an only child is lonely sometimes. And annoying. All your parents' focus is always on you."

Ashish laughed. "Yeah, I actually know a little about that. Now that Rishi's gone, my parents' laser beams are always swiveled and locked on to me. Actually, I shouldn't complain. That's sort of how I ended up here, with you." He kissed her cheek and she thrilled at the casual touch. "But . . . for the most part, Rishi is a really great big brother. I went through this phase of thinking we were the most poorly matched siblings on the face of this earth. You know, he's totally a golden child and I'm . . . er, what's darker than a black sheep? A black hole? I was always the black hole of my family." He laughed. "But Rishi's a good guy. His heart's in the right place, and I know he'll always be there for me, no matter what."

"Hmm. Will I ever get to meet him?"

"It's funny you mention that. He wants to come to my big game in May. I can introduce you two then."

Sweetie grinned up at the sky. "I'd love that. And I can introduce you to Anjali Chechi at my birthday party."

"That would be awesome," Ashish said. "How do you think your parents'll react to the fact that we've been dating behind their backs?"

"I don't think they'll be too happy, but . . . it'll be my birthday party. They can't get *too* mad, right?"

"Ah, Sweetie Nair," Ashish said, pulling her closer to him. "No one could get mad at you." And then he kissed her again.

As he got in his Jeep, Sweetie sighed. "So. I'll see you next Saturday?"

"Yep." He smiled and chucked her gently under the chin. "Just one week to go. I'll miss you."

She glanced down at her feet and smiled. "Me too." Then, looking up at him: "So, we're going to Gita Kaki's house then, right? Who's she?"

Ashish sighed. "It'd take an entire month to fill you in on Gita Kaki. Let's just say she's extremely . . . eccentric. And, um, just be prepared for some bizarre conversation. If you still want to go out with me after that, I'll consider it a big win."

Laughing, Sweetie leaned up on her tiptoes and kissed him again. It would never get old, being able to kiss him at will. "It'll take more than a batty aunt to keep me away, Ashish Patel."

His eyes shone and he beamed at her. "Good."

She watched him drive away until she couldn't see the Jeep at all. She missed him already. So far Sweetie had thought she was falling for Ashish Patel. When, though, should she begin to admit that "falling" had changed to "fallen"?

CHAPTER 24

Sweetie

Sweetie sat back against her headboard, freshly showered and in her Hello Kitty pajamas. Once a month on a Friday night, she and Anjali Chechi FaceTimed with each other. They couldn't get together to talk regularly, so this was the next-best solution they'd both devised. To Sweetie, these conversations were more than just chatting. They were a lifeline. When she'd had enough with Amma's constant haranguing and her self-esteem was hanging in shreds around her, seeing Anjali Chechi's caring face and hearing her tell her about her successful life had kept Sweetie from screaming and jumping out the window to run away from it all.

"Hey," she said as Anjali Chechi's smiling face popped up on her screen.

"Heyyyy, Sweets," Anjali Chechi replied. Her full face would never be considered conventionally beautiful: She still had scars from the chicken pox she'd gotten when she was little, she had a double chin, her hair was frizzy and untidy, and her eyes were too wide set. But to Sweetie, her face was home. It symbolized love and acceptance, and the feeling that things would work out just fine.

She relaxed and grinned.

"You look happy," Anjali Chechi observed. She never missed a thing with Sweetie. "I'm guessing this has to do with that boy you told me about?"

Sweetie felt her cheeks heat and she bit her lip and nodded. "Ashish Patel. We're going on our third date tomorrow."

"Third date! So things are getting serious?"

Sweetie adjusted herself against her pillows. "They are for me . . . and for him, too, I think." She beamed at just saying the words out loud. "We get along really well. Like, I think he's really cute and everything, but I also feel like I want to get to know him as a person. It's just like being with a good friend who's known me for years when we're together."

Anjali Chechi smiled. "That's so important. I'm really happy you're finding that, Sweetie. So Vidya Ammayi still doesn't know?"

"No, Amma's clueless. But we've decided to tell her at my birthday party. You'll be there for moral support, right?"

"Do you even have to ask?" Anjali Chechi made a *Come on* face.

"Thanks." Sweetie sat up. "And you're coming to my last meet as usual, right?"

"Again, I repeat: Do you even have to ask?" Anjali Chechi laughed. "You're going to kick everyone's butts this time around again, I assume?"

Sweetie raised an eyebrow. "Do you even have to ask?"

They laughed.

"The thing I'm currently nervous about, though, is my big performance next Thursday."

"Ah. Band Night?" Sweetie had texted Anjali Chechi all about it.

She nodded. "I picked the songs, and they turned out to be . . . love songs. I wasn't trying to do it, but it just happened. Do you think that's too cheesy?"

"Did your band members have a problem with it?"

"No. They said I have the right kind of voice for love songs, so they're cool with it. But now I'm all embarrassed. Going up onstage in front of all those people . . ." She surreptitiously wiped her hands on her pajama pants. "What if they laugh at me?"

A small crease popped up between Anjali Chechi's eyebrows. "So what if they do? You're getting up there and singing because you have a beautiful voice and you believe in yourself. What are they doing? Sitting in the audience passing judgment? That takes absolutely no courage."

After a pause Sweetie took a breath. "Yeah, you're right."

"Besides, you're going to have friends there too. And people who might judge you at first will totally see what you're capable of once you begin to sing. Don't you think they laughed at Adele before they realized she would command their respect?"

"Yeah. I'm still nervous, but you're right."

"It's normal to be nervous." Anjali Chechi's face relaxed into a smile. "Remember the story of my first surgery rotation?"

Sweetie snorted. "You bumped the instrument table with your hip and then tripped over your own feet and almost landed face-down on the floor."

"Exactly. And I was so nervous people would judge me because I was the only fat medical student in that room and that automatically meant I was lazy or a bumbling fool, right? But guess what? I'm an orthopedic surgeon now. And anyone who judged me or laughed at me that day?" She shrugged. "Don't even remember them. Do your own thing, Sweetie. The rest will fall into place."

Sweetie relaxed and smiled. "Thanks, Chechi. You're the best."

The doorbell sounded, and a few seconds later Amma called her name. Hmm, weird. She wasn't expecting anyone. Frowning, Sweetie turned back to the screen. "Uh-oh, I've been summoned."

"Go, go," Anjali Chechi said. "I'll be seeing you soon, right?"

"Right! And remember the thing for my party?"

"I remember." Anjali Chechi grinned. "I'm overnighting it tomorrow."

"Excellent. See you soon!"

Sweetie ended the call, plugged the phone into her charger, and walked out into the living room to see what Amma wanted.

As soon as she rounded the corner into the living room, Sweetie wanted to run back into her bedroom and change. Tina auntie and Sheena sat on the living room couch, dressed absolutely beautifully in what Sweetie was fairly sure were designer clothes. Their hair was perfectly styled, and they each had a faceful of makeup on. Whereas Sweetie's hair was still wet and hung in limp strands down her back. She adjusted the top of her Hello Kitty pajamas self-consciously, remembering how the buttons gaped.

Tina auntie gave her the once-over, before following it with an icy smile. "Hello, Sweetie. Ready for bed already?"

"No. I just like to change into pj's after practice." She went to sit by Amma. "Hi, Sheena."

Sheena did the chin-thrust/nod thing. "What's up?"

Amma said, "Tina auntie was wondering if you wanted to share a limo with Sheena to prom, *mol*. It's in two weeks, isn't it?"

"A week from tomorrow," Sweetie mumbled. She'd been trying hard to forget about it, honestly, and Kayla and Izzy were really good at not bringing it up around her. Suki thought the whole idea was idiotic and was boycotting it on principal. But Sweetie wanted to forget about it for different reasons. Firstly, Amma would never let her wear the dress she wanted. Sweetie would probably have to go in a long-sleeved, high-necked top and a skirt that brushed the floor. And secondly, no one had asked her.

She frowned. Wait. Why hadn't Ashish asked her? Sure, they went to different schools and had their proms on different days, but why hadn't he even brought it up? He seemed like the kind of guy who went every year, whether it was his prom or not. This was the first year that Sweetie was really eligible.

"Do you have someone to go with?" Tina auntie asked, and the look on her face very clearly said, *Of course you don't, you poor, sad, fat child.*

Sweetie squirmed a little. "Um, not really. I don't actually want to go at all."

Like she'd predicted, Tina auntie and Sheena both looked horror-struck.

"Why not?" Sheena asked slowly, like Sweetie was an unpredictable hedgehog who might fling all her quills at her or something.

Sweetie shrugged. "It's just . . . it's not my thing."

Sheena looked at her with open pity now. "I can tell my friends to dance with you, if that's what you're worried about."

Sweetie felt a hot wave of humiliation. But then it died down. And then she wanted to laugh. Because seriously, Sheena thought she was being *nice*. Like, she was so totally clueless that she thought implying no one would want to dance with Sweetie because she was fat and then offering to bribe her friends to do it was a *good thing*. Sweetie coughed to cover the laugh that wanted to burst out. She thought of Anjali Chechi bumping into the instrument table with her wide hips. She thought of who Anjali Chechi was now. And she smiled her most pleasant smile at Sheena. "That's very . . . kind of you, Sheena. But it won't be necessary. As I said, I don't want to go. So."

"But, *mol*, it might be really fun," Amma said. "You can ride in the limo."

Sweetie straightened her shoulders. Amma wanted her to go because it'd help the friendship or whatever she had going on with Tina auntie. She was desperate for Sweetie to try to bridge that gap for her, but that wasn't Sweetie's job. It wasn't her job to make other people feel comfortable. "Sorry, Amma. But I meant what I said." Then, turning to Tina auntie, she added, "Tina auntie, no, thank you. I don't want to share a limo with Sheena." She stood. "I have some homework to do, so I'm going to leave now. See ya." Waving, she turned and left as they watched in shocked silence.

Amma came into her room about twenty minutes later. "Why were you so rude, Sweetie? They were only trying to be nice."

"I don't think I was rude," Sweetie said, closing her book. She stuck her feet under the blanket at the foot of her bed. "In fact, I made sure to not be rude. But . . ." She took a breath. This time she wouldn't let the words gum up. "But I'm not a charity case, and I don't want to be treated like one."

Amma sat beside her on the bed. "You should go out with Sheena. She's a nice girl."

Sweetie held her gaze steadily. "I already have my friends."

Amma looked frozen, like she didn't know how to say what she wanted to say. "But, Sweetie . . . those girls are kind of . . . wild. They're tomboyish, no? Not Izzy, she's sweet. But Kayla and Suki are . . . are feminists, Tina auntie told me." She leaned forward when she whispered the word "feminists." "Sheena's a much better fit for you."

Sweetie bit on the insides of her lips to keep from laughing. "Amma . . . I'm sorry to have to tell you this, but I'm a feminist too."

Amma stared at her, her eyes wide in horror. She didn't notice when the red floral *dupatta* of her *salwar kameez* slipped off one shoulder. "Sweetie! Feminists don't get married. Stop that nonsense."

Sweetie did laugh then, openly. "Amma, what the heck are you talking about? Feminists can do whatever they want. They just want equal rights for women."

"*Ayyo, bhagavane*," Amma said, shaking her head. "Teenagers."

Leaning forward, Sweetie put a hand on Amma's. "Why do you think we see things so differently all the time?"

Amma frowned. "What?"

"We fall on opposite sides on almost everything, Amma." She swallowed the sudden lump in her throat. "We look different and we think differently and . . ." She shrugged. "It breaks my heart a little."

Amma looked at her steadily. "It breaks my heart too. But what can we do? You're the only daughter I have. And I'm the only mother you have. I suppose we must find a way to get along." Patting Sweetie's thigh, Amma got up to go.

"If I never lose weight but still end up happy in life, will you be happy for me?" Sweetie asked, ignoring the note of desperation in her voice.

Amma paused, one hand on the doorjamb. Over her shoulder she said, "If you don't lose weight and still end up happy, I will thank God for working miracles." Then she left, shutting the door quietly behind her.

A tear spilled over onto Sweetie's cheek, and she brushed it away with a fist. There were few things that made her feel lonelier than conversations with her own mother.

Ashish

Ashish and his parents sat in the gazebo, twilight twinkling around them. Pappa was "doing the barbecue," as he called it, or as Ashish thought of it, burning veggies on sticks and pretending it was kebab. Chef drew the line at grilling, though, so they were on their own.

"So beautiful," Ma said, taking in the scenery. The gazebo and entertaining patio were perched on the top of a small hillock on their property, so they had expansive views of their carefully sculpted five acres and the western hills in the distance. When Ma realized about two years ago that they only used the space for summer parties, she instituted monthly Friday-night grill-outs. Pappa was on board because he got to buy a giant spaceship of a grill, and Rishi had been on board because . . . well, because he was Rishi. But now that he was off putting out art history fires in college, Ashish was the only one who had to spend one Friday night every month eating charred bricks masquerading as veggie burgers and pretending to like them.

He glanced at Pappa, smugly turning over the veggie kebabs,

which already smelled like scorched plant flesh. Actually, this—hanging out with them here—wasn't that bad. He remembered trying to get out of these family nights every chance he had up until even a month ago, but right now Ashish couldn't remember why. His parents . . . his parents weren't so bad.

Ma looked over at him and smiled. "What are you thinking of, *beta*?"

Ashish shook his head and sipped his ginger beer. "Nothing. You know, I haven't said it yet, but, um . . . thank you. Thank you both." At Pappa's quizzical look (his face surrounded by a cloud of smoke), Ashish added, "I'm having fun with Sweetie. On the dates you picked."

Ma beamed, and Pappa said, "I knew it! I told you, Ashish, my ideas are—"

Ma cut him off with a look that Ashish couldn't see from his vantage. When she turned back around, she was beaming again. "Wonderful. I'm so happy to hear that." She put a hand on his arm and squeezed. "So the mandir wasn't too boring for you?"

Ashish took a breath. "No, weirdly enough. It was nice. Peaceful. And the Holi Festival was awesome." He grinned at the memories. "Sweetie's hair . . . I don't know if she'll want to go back to just plain black anymore."

"So! One might even say that your parents picked the best girl!" Pappa said, brandishing his spatula like a sword. "Compare Sweetie to Celia and—"

"*Kartik.*" Ma shook her head and sighed. "Ashish, ignore your Pappa. I'm sure Celia was very nice."

Ashish smiled, but it was a faded, left-out-in-the-sun-too-long version of his real smile. Celia. They'd finally talked after that night with

Sweetie on the basketball court. Ashish's heart legit cramped at the way he'd hidden this (temporarily) from Sweetie—the purest, most honest person he'd ever known in his life. He knew he had his reasons, but just thinking about it made him feel sick deep in the pit of his stomach, like he was coming down with the flu.

"What shall we bring?" Pappa asked, and Ashish realized they'd been talking to him while he was zoned out.

"Sorry?" he said.

"For Sweetie's birthday party," Pappa said, and clucked his tongue. "I think a nice DVD of that movie *Sixteen Candles*. All teenage girls love that movie!"

"Kartik, I already told you, that movie is well before Sweetie's time," Ma said, laughing. She turned to Ashish. "Do teenagers watch DVDs anymore?"

"Ashish, tell her *Sixteen Candles* is the diggity!" Pappa said, serving up the kebabs and burger-bricks onto plates.

"Pappa," Ashish said, massaging his temples. "It's 'the bomb diggity.' And no one says that anymore. And I don't even know what *Sixteen Candles* is. I have to side with Ma here, sorry."

Ma grinned triumphantly.

"Besides," Ashish continued. "This is all a moot point. You guys can't come."

Ma's grin fell off her face. "What?"

"Why not!" Pappa said, setting the plates down on the little table in the gazebo. "Sweetie will enjoy seeing us."

"Doesn't she like us, *beta*?" Ma said quietly, and Ashish wanted to smack himself for being so insensitive.

"No, of course she does," Ashish said. After a pause he added,

"Actually, I don't think there's anyone she actively dislikes. But, um, I think it'll be better this way. I'll get to meet her parents, charm them, get them on my side, you know? If you're there, I'll just be nervous."

"Of course," Ma said, patting his cheek. "You'll win them over so quickly, they won't even remember they had any objections in the first place! Isn't that right, Kartik?"

They both turned to look at Pappa. He pulled a bell pepper ("capsicum," as he called it) off the kebab stick, grunted, and said wryly, "Be sure to bring a very, *very* nice present."

"I'm no Rishi," Ashish said suddenly, and Ma looked at him in surprise. Pappa continued to chomp down on his veggies like a giant, oblivious rabbit. "I know that. I'm not going to charm her parents like . . ." He paused, wondering if he was really saying this. And then decided, *Yep, what the hell?* "Like Rishi charmed Dimple's before he even met them," he said in a rush, not meeting their eye. "But I have to try, you know? I really like Sweetie."

"*Beta*, you are every bit as charming as Rishi," Ma said, looking concerned. "You must never think otherwise."

Ashish looked at Pappa, but he was still focused intently on his food and didn't say anything. Because he didn't hear or because he had nothing to say? "Right," Ashish said, smiling at Ma for her benefit. "Sure."

"So you have everything ready like I asked?" Ashish asked Gita Kaki on the phone, pacing his bedroom the next morning. "Every single thing?"

Gita Kaki's voice squawked in his ear. "Yes, yes, *beta*. How many times I have to tell you?"

"Okay, thanks. Because we'll be there in just over an hour."

"*Haan, haan*, see you then. Oh, and Rishi, I have made *aloo palak* for you, your favorite!"

Ashish put a hand to his forehead. "No, Rishi is—I'm not—okay. I'll see you soon!" He hung up and slipped the cell phone into his pocket. Well, this was going to be interesting, anyway. If the worst thing Gita Kaki did was call him Rishi and force-feed him *aloo palak* (Seriously, yuck. Who the heck liked potatoes and spinach together?) during the visit, he'd consider himself lucky.

He was running downstairs to meet Sweetie outside—her car had just pulled up—when his cell phone pinged.

He pulled it from his pocket and checked the screen. It was Celia.

You told me to tell you when I was in Atherton next. I'll be there on Thursday. Seemed important. ☺ Wanna meet up?

Ashish stared at the words for a long minute. Yes, he typed quickly, an idea taking root. I have a thing that night though. Meet at 9:30?

The response came immediately. K, Bedwell?

Bedwell Bayfront Park was where Ashish and Celia had had their three-month anniversary date. It was where . . . well, where a significant turning point in their relationship was reached. He took a deep breath. Sounds good.

Then he put his phone away, squashed the guilt churning in his stomach at keeping this from Sweetie, and walked out the front door. *This is good, Ash*, he told himself firmly. *It's time.*

Seeing Sweetie smiling up at him through her windshield felt like standing in a hot shower right after getting soaked in cold rain. It was blissful; it solidified his resolve about what he needed to do

Thursday night. When she turned off her car, he opened her door and pulled her out gently by her arm. Then he enveloped her in a giant hug and sniffed the top of her head. "Ahhhh. Just what I needed. Peppermint shampoo."

She laughed and batted him away. "Okay, that's not weird at all."

"It's like crack. It's my Sweetie crack. It's Swack!" Ashish pulled her to him again and inhaled deeply.

She was laughing so hard now, she couldn't catch her breath. Watching her like that, Ashish began to laugh too. Finally they pulled apart, and he stood there, smiling at her. "Okay. You ready to get this show on the road?"

She nodded. "Let's do it."

They walked to the garage together, hand in hand, and he opened the passenger-side door to the Porsche. Then he paused. "Hey."

She looked up at him quizzically.

"You want to drive?"

Her eyes got wide and a smile began to seep slowly across her lovely face. Ashish could watch that forever. On time lapse. "Seriously? You'd let me drive your Porsche?"

He rolled his eyes to distract from how much he loved just staring at her like a creeper. "I don't think we're in any danger of the Porsche getting wrapped around a tree at the rate you go, let's be honest. I'm more worried we'll run out of gas before you get us there." He tossed her the keys. "It's a push button, but you can hold on to those. They'll make you feel more legit."

"Oh my God," she breathed, walking over to the driver's side. "I cannot believe I'm holding the keys to a freaking Porsche in my hand. Or that I'm going to be driving one."

Ashish laughed as Sweetie climbed into the driver's seat, gawking at the onboard navigation system and the sleek seats.

Sliding into the passenger side, Ashish reached over and kissed her cheek. "Ready to drive your first Porsche?"

"Absolutely."

He watched her as she backed out of the garage, feeling little pinpricks of guilt about the text he'd sent earlier. Ashish hated keeping this from Sweetie. But this was for the greater good. He had a course of action. Meet up with Celia, say his piece, hopefully *get* some peace.

Was he certain that would happen? That he wouldn't, once he saw Celia, suddenly become a blithering high school man-baby? No, he wasn't sure of those things at all. In fact, he was fairly terrified that he'd see Celia and realize, *Hey, forget getting closure, I could never even hope to orbit around closure's atmosphere.* But that didn't matter. He still had to try.

"So, does this Gita Kaki have any kids of her own?" Sweetie asked once they were on Highway 82.

"No, and that probably explains why she's constantly confusing Rishi and me," Ashish said. "Actually, I stand corrected: She thinks both Rishi and I are Rishi. Clearly, she has a favorite."

Sweetie laughed. "No way. How could anyone like Rishi over you?"

Ashish pretended to preen. "Hey, a guy could get used to flattery like that. Especially since pretty much everyone in my family prefers Rishi over me."

Sweetie darted a sideways glance at him. "You wanna know what I'm thinking?"

"You're thinking how this Porsche is the sweetest, smoothest ride you've ever had the pleasure of encountering," Ashish said.

Sweetie rolled her eyes. "Actually, I was thinking how you say Rishi's the golden child and people prefer him over you lightly and kind of sarcastically, but it seems like it bothers you more than you let on." She paused. "Do you . . . do *you* think it's true? That he's better than you somehow?"

Ashish looked out the window for a moment. Sweetie had a way of doing that, just getting to the core of things. It unbalanced him somewhat. Ashish liked to think he had the world by its throat. He was always one step ahead. Some people preferred Rishi—yeah, that was true, but it was okay because Ashish already knew it and expected it. But Sweetie . . . she said things in her soft, observant way. It made him feel like there was an empty part of him waiting to be filled, and he didn't even know with what or how he was supposed to feel about that.

He cleared his throat. "I guess. But it doesn't bother me."

Sweetie didn't say anything. She just reached over and put one hand on his knee.

"It doesn't," Ashish said more forcefully.

"Okay," she said amicably. "But just so you know, I don't think that. At all."

"But you've never met Rishi."

"I don't have to meet Rishi to know that I like you best of all." She grinned at him, completely disarming his defensiveness. "Okeydokey?"

He reached over and put one hand on the back of her neck, stroking the soft skin there. "Okeydokey," he agreed. Ashish didn't even laugh at how totally dorky it sounded. He was too busy feeling happy.

CHAPTER 25

Ashish

Gita Kaki lived in a luxury apartment complex overlooking the water. They parked underground in the visitor space and got out, stretching their limbs. Ashish walked around to grab Sweetie's hand, marveling at how natural it felt. It was only their third contracted date, but it felt like he'd known her a lot longer. Like if she started hanging out with his crew tomorrow, she'd fit right in with zero awkwardness.

Then he remembered his conversation with Gita Kaki and how he was counting on the least countable member of his family for something pretty important today, and felt his blood pressure rising. He didn't realize he was squeezing Sweetie's hand until she yelped. "Oh my God, I'm sorry," he said, rubbing her hand gently. "Are you okay?"

She quirked an eyebrow at him. "Yeah, but . . . are *you*?"

"Sure, sure. Totally fine." He forced himself to kiss her temple in a casual way. "Ready to meet some more of my 'interesting' family?" *And hopefully be wooed off your pretty feet?*

Sweetie bumped him lightly with her shoulder. "You don't have to say 'interesting' like that."

"Like what?"

"Like you really mean 'bizarre in the creepiest way.' I'm sure Gita Kaki's perfectly nice, her penchant for calling you Rishi aside."

He grinned as they got on the elevator and he pushed the button for the penthouse. "I'm so gonna enjoy saying 'I told you so.'"

As they traveled upward, Sweetie laughed suddenly.

"What?" he asked, smiling too. It was like her smile had a magnet that instantly attracted *his* smile magnet and . . . no, never mind. That analogy sucked. But seriously, the girl's smile was irresistible.

"I just realized everyone in your family is apparently ridiculously rich. Like, what's that about?"

He laughed. "I assure you, that's not true. Gita Kaki just happens to be another exception. Most of my other family is very middle class. Gita Kaki's husband, my Shankar Kaka, was an executive over at Google or someplace—I forget. Anyway, when he died, she inherited this apartment. They've owned it forever. My dad says none of her money's liquid, though."

"Yeah, because I totally know what that means." Sweetie laughed. "Oh my God, you're such a one-percenter and you don't even know it."

Ashish chuckled. "No, no, I'm not totally clueless. I know I'm rich. But I like to think I'm also down-to-earth."

"Oh yeah? Okay, quick, how much does a gallon of milk cost?"

Ashish stared at her, trying to keep his face neutral. Crap. Milk. Dang it, he should know that. But the problem was, their housekeeper, Myrna, did all the shopping. He didn't think he should share that little tidbit with Sweetie, though. *Oh, come on. Just throw out a number, Ash. Jeez.* "Like . . . twelve dollars?"

Sweetie stared at him. The elevator pinged right into Gita Kaki's foyer just as she burst out laughing. "You . . . think . . . milk . . . costs . . . twelve . . ." She lost it and began to guffaw again.

Ashish began to laugh too. "What? Is that too cheap?"

Sweetie lost it. She was turning a rather alarming shade of purple when Gita Kaki walked up to them. Frowning, she said, "Rishi, why is Dimple laughing so much?"

Ashish lost it too.

When they were both relatively calm, he did the introductions. "Gita Kaki, this is my friend Sweetie." It was an unspoken rule that you never introduced your girlfriends as girlfriends to the elders in your family; that was too unseemly. It had been drilled into Ashish since he was little, and from the totally unconcerned expression on Sweetie's face, he guessed her parents had a similar rule. It was kinda nice, actually. None of his other girlfriends—on the few occasions they'd run across someone in his family—had ever understood that. "Sweetie, this is Gita Kaki."

She folded her hands together. "*Namaskar*, auntie."

Gita Kaki responded in kind. "*Namaskar*."

They followed her into the living room. The entire far wall was made up of windows with a sweeping view of blue water.

"Wow," Sweetie breathed, walking up. "This is so beautiful."

"Thank you," Gita Kaki said, smiling approvingly. She loved nothing more than being complimented on her apartment, her most prized possession. And, according to Pappa, one of her only remaining possessions worth anything. "Shankar and I bought it when they first built this building. We were the first ones to sign on the dotted line. The architect was a very good friend. Can I get you anything? Juice?"

"I'd love a juice, auntie," Sweetie said, turning. "Can I help you get it?"

"No, don't worry," Gita Kaki said, already turning away. "Rishi, *pani*?"

Ashish rolled his eyes behind her back. "I'll have a Pepsi if you have one, Kaki."

She nodded and kept walking.

"The bad thing about her confusing me with Rishi is that she thinks I have all his gross eating and drinking habits too. Everything vegetarian, only water, the guy even likes spinach."

"So by 'gross' you mean 'healthy,'" Sweetie clarified, coming to sit by him on the couch.

He snorted. "If you want to call it that." He turned to her after checking that Gita Kaki was still gone. "Hey, fair warning—don't, um, stare when she shows you her . . . pet room."

Sweetie raised her eyebrows. "She has a pet room? What kinds of pets?"

But before Ashish could respond, Gita Kaki was back with their drinks on a silver tray.

They'd each drunk a few sips when Gita Kaki said, "So, Dimple. You've put some meat on your bones at college!"

Ashish froze, horror-struck. Oh God, no. "Gita Kaki," he said firmly. "This is *Sweetie*. And she's perfect as she is." Sweetie looked really uncomfortable. She wouldn't even meet his eye. Burning with anger, he took her hand.

"Sweetie?" Gita Kaki frowned. "What happened to Dimple?"

Ashish sighed. "I'm not Rishi. I'm Ashish. Sunita and Kartik's second son. Remember?"

Gita Kaki laughed. "Oh, yes, yes, of course! I'm sorry. You know, my spectacles aren't . . . uh . . ." She trailed off and took a sip of what looked like mango juice. "She's very pretty," Gita Kaki said suddenly. "I always like when women have curves. It's real! Not like those spaghetti noodles!"

"Um, yes," Ashish said, feeling his cheeks heat. "Me too." What a freaking weird-ass conversation. He sneaked a glance at Sweetie and saw her trying to hold back a smile as she sipped her juice. Well, now was as good a time as any, he guessed. "So, Gita Kaki. I was wondering if Sweetie and I could visit your, uh, pets?"

Sweetie looked at him in surprise, probably wondering what was going on. He tried to hold back his grin. Ha. Ha, ha, ha! She'd see soon enough.

"My pets . . . ," Gita Kaki said wonderingly. Then her gaze sharpened. "Ashish."

He waited, but there didn't seem to be any more forthcoming. "Uh . . . yes?"

"Do you know what the next big thing is going to be in courier services?"

Courier . . . services? What the heck? This was so not the steal-the-keys-to-Sweetie's-heart plan they'd discussed on the phone. He raised his eyebrows. "No?"

"Parrots." Gita Kaki nodded firmly. "Yes."

Ashish and Sweetie exchanged a glance.

"Parrots?" Sweetie asked, still polite as ever, as if this were all totally normal. Ashish wondered when she'd make a run for it.

"Yes, yes, parrots," Gita Kaki said testily, waving her hand, as if they were the difficult ones. Then she sat forward, her eyes gleaming. "See, unlike carrier pigeons, they wouldn't need to be trained to carry anything. Not to mention the money people would save on paper and ink! Do you know why?"

Ashish had a million questions. Why were they suddenly talking about this, for cripes' sake? Why did Gita Kaki think bird courier services were making a comeback? Was this some sort of hipster trend for the elderly? But he stuck with the simplest response. "No. Um, why?" He didn't dare look at Sweetie.

"Because you could just train the parrots to say whatever the message was! You know, 'happy birthday,' 'happy anniversary,' 'happy, er, Doughnut Day,' what have you!" She cackled happily. Then, snapping her attention to Ashish, she said, "Ashish. What's that song you kids all like?"

He stared at her. "Um . . ."

"The song, the song!" she said, getting irritated. Oh God. This was going to turn into an even bigger circus.

"Oh, um, 'Happy Birthday'?" Ashish said, grasping at straws.

"No, not 'Happy Birthday'!" Gita Kaki said, agitated. "Oh, I know! 'Macarena'! Sing that for me, Ashish. Sing it!"

"Gita Kaki, I have no idea what song that i—"

"Now, Ashish! Sing it!" she yelled, clapping her hands kind of savagely.

He stared at her. And then he started to sing. "Um . . . we all go to the Macarena . . . um, woo-hoo . . ."

A strange snorting sound emanated from Sweetie. Ashish darted a glance at her and noticed she was holding her glass of juice in front of her mouth and looking steadfastly down at the carpet.

Gita Kaki waved him off. "That's not 'Macarena'!" she said dismissively.

Of course it's not freaking "Macarena"; I don't know what that is! Ashish wanted to say. But Gita Kaki was already talking to Sweetie. "You see, Sweetie, even a complex song like that could be taught to the right parrot! They're so intelligent!"

Sweetie nodded politely, though Ashish could see the sparkle in her eye. Oh, man. He was going to catch so much crap for this later. "So are you going to start up a courier business, then? With the parrots?"

What? What? Why was she asking that? Why was she *encouraging* it?

"I'm so happy you asked, Sweetie!" Gita Kaki said, jumping up and going over to a rolltop desk in the corner.

Ashish turned to her and widened his eyes. "Don't," he mouthed.

She shrugged, like, *What?*

What did she mean, what? Wasn't it *obvious what*? But it was too late to say anything because Gita Kaki was coming back with two pocket folders. She handed one to Ashish and the other to Sweetie. "There," she said. "Now, that's everything you need to get started."

Ashish was too afraid to ask. He opened the folder instead and saw a flyer inside with a giant picture of a bright-green parrot in the center.

Your Guide to Getting Started as a
Parrot Trainer!

In just six short weeks, your parrots will be ready to deliver messages around the country! Make $$$$ from the comfort of your own home! A simple investment of $6,000—

Ashish shut the folder. Without looking at Sweetie, he reached over and took her folder too. "Um, thank you, Gita Kaki. We'll give these a closer look when we get home," he said. "And, um, now I was wondering if we could see the parrots. You know, to see their . . . training potential."

"Yes!" Smiling full throttle at him for the first time since she realized he wasn't Rishi, Gita Kaki stood and led the way to the back room.

"She actually has the parrots *here*?" Sweetie whispered as they followed at a safe distance.

"Don't ask questions," Ashish said, sighing. "They'll just open the doorway to Bizarro World, and you definitely don't want to take a trip there. Believe me."

Laughing, Sweetie held up her hands in surrender.

Sweetie

This was the most hilarious thing that had ever happened. Not just to her, but, like, in the history of time. Ashish the sweet, handsome, vulnerable, angsty jock had a great-aunt who wanted to enlist them in a pyramid scheme. With message-delivering *parrots*. Sweetie snorted again and then covered it up by coughing loudly. The look Ashish tossed her told her he didn't buy it one bit.

The only thing she didn't get was why Ashish wanted to see these parrots. He obviously wanted Gita Kaki to shut up about the whole thing. Shouldn't he be discouraging her completely and changing the subject?

But before she could ask, Gita Kaki had stopped in front of a closed door and was waiting for them to catch up. They hurried down the hallway just as a phone began to ring. One hand on the doorknob, she said, "Now, Ashish, I am trusting you with these precious babies. Okay?"

"Yes, Gita Kaki," he said solemnly, but Sweetie could hear the jubilation fizzing under his words at the thought of her leaving them. "I'll be very careful."

"And respectful," Gita Kaki added. Then she waited. After a pause, during which the three of them just stared at one another, she said sternly, "*Repeat* it, Ashish."

"And, um, respectful," Ashish said in a tone that implied, *I wish you and your stupid parrots would fly out the window in a cloud of green feathers and leave me alone forever.*

Gita Kaki nodded once, opened the door a tad, and then hurried off in the direction of the ringing phone.

Ashish breathed a sigh of relief. "Good God, I thought she'd never leave."

Sweetie smiled. "What? I kind of like her."

He threw her a look, and then they walked into the room. The first thing Sweetie noticed was the odor. It was sort of chalky and pungent, and she screwed up her nose.

"Oh, yeah, I forgot how bad they smell," Ashish said, going to open a window.

It was then that Sweetie realized what, exactly, she was looking at. It was a large room, with row upon row upon row of birdcages, each of them filled with two or three parrots. Most of them were bright green, but some of them had gorgeous, multicolored feathers—vivid reds and peacock blues and brilliant, happy yellows. They were all looking at her, cocking their heads and quietly squawking.

"Wow. These are so cool," Sweetie said, moving closer to take a look at them. "There must be, like, fifty here."

"Fifty-six, to be exact," Ashish said, turning back to her. "She's had some of these for more than twenty years. They're like her kids; each one has a name, and she insists they all have distinctive personalities, too."

"That's amazing," Sweetie breathed, reaching out to stroke one of the cage bars. "It's kind of sad that they have to live caged, though."

"It is," Ashish said. "But maybe they're happy like that. Maybe they don't even know what they're missing because this is all they've known."

Sweetie straightened and looked at him. They studied each other in silence.

And then one of the parrots in the cage behind them, a big, beefy one, screeched, "FEED ME, DAMMIT!"

Sweetie jumped and spun around. The parrot stared at her with its beady eyes. Clapping a hand over her mouth, she began to laugh. "Oh. My. God. Did that bird just curse at me?"

Ashish laughed. "Yeah, that's Crabby. He's been like that for as long as I can remember. No food for you yet, Crabby," he said to the bird. "You need to wait your turn."

"BALLS!" the bird yelled, and Sweetie began to snort helplessly again.

Ashish chuckled. "Yeah, he's hilarious until you keep getting woken up at night because you're spending summer break here and you share a wall with him."

Sweetie wiped her eyes. "Oh my God. A deranged parrot. This just keeps getting better."

Ashish walked up to her and her smile faded. When he was just a hair's breadth away from her, he took her chin in his hand. "Being with you can't really get any better."

Sweetie smiled up at him before standing on tiptoes and kissing him softly. "What about now?" she whispered against his mouth.

His arms tightened around her waist, and he pulled her snugly against him. She felt something very interesting against her hip, and her heart fluttered. He wanted her. He wanted her as much as she wanted him.

"GET A ROOM!" Crabby said behind them, and they flew apart.

"Okay, that's new," Ashish said. "Stupid third wheel."

Sweetie sputtered a laugh. "Technically, he's one of fifty-six wheels," she pointed out. "Speaking of, why are we in here? I thought the whole parrot pyramid scheme was giving you the heebies."

"Oh, it was," Ashish said, raising his eyebrows. "She's always been eccentric, but that was the first time she's tried to enlist me in one of her harebrained ideas." He shook his head. "Anyway, I have something to show you. Or, I guess, ask you."

"Oh yeah?" She smiled, pleased. There were few things as exciting as surprises. "What's that?"

But instead of answering her, Ashish raised his hands and clapped three times.

Sweetie could hardly keep up with what happened next. There was immediate and cacophonic squawking. It took her a moment to realize the parrots were speaking English words.

"With! With!" one in the corner squawked.

"To!" a multicolored one behind her said.

"You!" a third one screamed after a pause.

"Me!"

"Go!"

"Stop!" Ashish yelled, clutching his hair. "You stupid birds! Stop!"

"Will!" a parrot behind him said into the following short silence, almost defiantly.

"With!" the first one said again.

"You already said that!" Ashish yelled. "Stop it! What are you doing?"

"Damn! Hell! Stop!" Crabby chorused, invigorated by the panic in Ashish's voice.

Sweetie began to laugh. "What is going on?"

"You!" the one parrot screamed again.

"Me!"

"To!"

Sweetie's stomach hurt. Tears began to stream down her cheeks, she was laughing so hard. "What . . . what are they doing, Ashish?" she asked when she could breathe.

Ashish studied her for a moment, his expression livid. Then, seeing her bent over helplessly, he began to laugh too. "The idiotic birds were supposed to ask you to—"

"Prom!" one of the birds said. "Prom! Prom!"

Ashish shrugged. "Yeah, that." He turned to the last bird. "Thank you, Petey. Very helpful."

Prom. This was about prom. "You're asking me to prom?"

"*Your* prom," Ashish clarified. "I've, ah, been suspended from Richmond's proms for some shenanigans last year, so that's kind of our only option." Sighing, he added, "Anyway, these annoying hellbirds were supposed to help me ask you. In a very orderly fashion. I spent all last Sunday afternoon training them, and Gita Kaki assured me she was keeping up with it throughout the week. Which, I don't know. What else did I expect, right? Total train wreck."

"At least I know where Gita Kaki got her inspiration for that whole courier-services thing."

Ashish groaned and covered his face with his hands.

Smiling, Sweetie stepped closer to him and gently moved his hands off his face. Circling her arms around his narrow waist, she said, "By the way, this isn't a train wreck. It's the most romantic thing ever."

"Seriously?" Ashish cocked an eyebrow. "Oh, right. I forgot I'm your first boyfriend; the bar's pretty low."

She laughed and slapped him on the chest, reveling in the way her hand bounced off the muscle there. And the way he'd casually called himself her boyfriend. They were boyfriend and girlfriend. Ashish Patel was her boyfriend. She tried not to squeal in pure, giddy glee. "Seriously. This is the sweetest, most adorable thing I've ever heard of. Thank you." She'd never even dreamed she'd get a promposal from a boy at all (or, technically, from a parrot), let alone a boy as perfect as Ashish, or one into which the boy had put so much effort.

He kissed her on the nose. "So?" he said softly, those honey eyes melting her bones, turning her blood to lava. "Sweetie Nair, will you go with me to prom?"

She gazed up at him through the fringe of her eyelashes. "Yes, Ashish Patel," she whispered. "I'll go with you to prom."

Smiling broadly, he leaned down and kissed her. And that, among the smelly, squawking, unbalanced parrots, was the most romantic moment in Sweetie Nair's life.

Ashish

Ashish held her close, his heart leaping with joy. She really did love his madcap promposal; he could see in her eyes that he'd pulled it off somehow. And right on the heels of that joy came the nagging guilt, because he still hadn't told her everything about Celia. She'd see why he had to do it this way, though, right? Ashish desperately hoped she would. He might be a little thick when it came to love, but one thing was clear even to him: If Celia leaving him had broken his heart, Sweetie breaking up with him would pulverize it to nothing.

CHAPTER 26

Sweetie

They spent another couple of hours eating lunch and visiting with Gita Kaki and left shortly after that. Neither Ashish nor she was in any hurry to stick around and hear more about Gita Kaki's mad scheme to take over the world with tropical birds.

"But are you sure she doesn't have, like, dementia?" Sweetie said as they got into the elevator. "That's a serious thing, you know."

Ashish laughed and squeezed her hand. "I'm sure. She's been like that since I was a little kid. She's just . . . different. She has no problems taking care of herself, though, believe me."

"Or her parrots," Sweetie said. "Can we come back and visit her soon?"

"You have to be joking."

"I'm not," Sweetie protested as they got out of the elevator and walked to the Porsche. "She seems lonely, and I think she really liked us visiting her. Plus, I feel like we really hit it off with Crabby. Maybe next time we could even bring Dimple and Rishi."

Ashish threw an arm around her shoulder and pulled her to him. She snuggled in against his warm body. "You are the literal sweetest, you know that?" After kissing her on the top of her head, he continued. "Yes, I guess we can come visit her soon. But let's give it, I don't know, like, six months?"

She smiled happily. "Sure."

Ashish took her face in his big hands, and her heart sped up as she looked into those eyes. "Hi."

"Hi," she breathed back, her muscles going all liquidy.

He smoothed a curl off her forehead. "I really like you, Sweetie Nair."

Her heart did a couple of somersaults in her chest. "You really like me?" This moment was like winning the lottery on her birthday while eating Amma's *pal payasam*. She was afraid to blink, just in case she woke herself up and this whole thing turned out to be a dream. A very, very, very nice dream.

"Obviously," Ashish said, his cocky smirk back.

He paused. The cocky smile disappeared, replaced by vulnerability. He blinked and looked away before meeting her eyes again. "Do you . . . do you feel the same way?"

He was actually unsure, Sweetie realized with wonder. He seriously didn't know the effect he had on her. He had no idea how hard she'd fallen, how hard she continued to fall every single moment they were together. But she couldn't say all of that. She didn't want to freak him out too early in their relationship. "Obviously," she said instead, grinning.

He smiled then, jubilant and bright. Stroking her dimple with his thumb, he leaned down and planted the softest, sweetest kiss on her lips. "Then I'm the luckiest guy on the planet."

Sweetie didn't even remember the drive home (which was fine, since Ashish drove). She was fairly sure the Porsche carried them through the clouds, though, and that they never touched the ground at all.

Ashish

The whole Richmond gang (plus Samir) were hanging out on the balcony at Ashish's place Wednesday night. Myrna had brought them out some fresh-squeezed lemonade, and she'd opened the umbrellas placed at the various clusters of sofas and tables so they could all just lounge around and "study for finals." Really they were just shooting the breeze, drunk on that end-of-the-school-year exhilaration.

Well, *most* of them were drunk on the exhilaration. Oliver and Elijah looked like they were being led to a dinner date with Hannibal Lecter. Neither of them had so much as looked at the other, let alone said a civil word or two. Ashish could feel the tension crackling between them. He didn't get too close, in case he got zapped like those poor bugs in those . . . whatever they were called. Bug zapper thingies.

"Yo, Dreamland," Pinky called from across the balcony. She was sitting on a little settee with Elijah, and Samir was across from them, his nose buried in some comic. He didn't have the same final exam anxiety they had, being homeschooled. On the flip side, he didn't really have that end-of-year exhilaration, either. When your home was also your school, it sort of sucked the joy out of summer break. "I'm talking to you."

Ashish blinked. "Sorry, I couldn't understand you with that thing in your lip." Pinky had gotten her lower lip pierced last weekend at some hippie forest festival, to her parents' complete horror. The fact that it glowed in the dark—something she liked to boast about at random intervals—did not help the situation.

"Har, har," she said, though it was obvious that she had trouble speaking with it in. Not that Pinky would ever admit to making a mistake like that, especially one that vexed her parents so much. "We were talking about Band Night at Roast Me tomorrow. Are we all going together or what?"

Ashish darted an uncomfortable glance at Oliver. "Um, yeah, I could drive you guys in the Escalade."

"I'll just meet you guys there," Oliver said immediately, without looking up from his biology textbook.

"There's plenty of room," Elijah said stiffly from the settee.

"I know how much room there is, thanks," Oliver replied equally stiffly.

"What's the big deal?" Elijah said, standing up suddenly. "You're here at the same time I am. It's the same thing as being in a freaking car for twenty freaking minutes, Oliver."

Oliver set his textbook down with a slam. Ashish tried not to wince; if the glass of that tabletop cracked, Ma would have his head. Not that that was important when his two best friends were having a lovers' quarrel, obviously. It was just a random, errant thought that deserved no more airtime.

He surreptitiously slid the textbook over with his pinkie to check. Yessss. Crack-free.

"I didn't know you were going to be here!" Oliver said, his cheeks aflame. He always got really red when he was mad. Uh-oh. Ashish met Samir's eye across the balcony and tried to telepathically convey: *Crap. What do we do now?*

Pinky smiled and held up her hands. "Hey, guys, chill. Let's all just sit around—"

"*You* told me it was just going to be the four of us," Oliver said to her, his eyes going all dark and cloudy.

"And you told me Oliver couldn't make it," Elijah said, glaring at her.

She folded her hands and put them in her lap. "Oops," she said, forcing the fakest-sounding chuckle of all time. "I guess I got mixed up."

Elijah shook his head. "How do you get freaking 'mixed up' with somethi—"

"Oh my God!" Samir said suddenly, throwing himself off the chair and onto the floor.

Everyone stopped and stared at him.

"What the heck are you doing?" Oliver asked finally.

Samir looked around at all of them. "It felt like . . . like a charley horse or something on my leg. . . ." He massaged his thigh unconvincingly. "Er . . . it seems to have gone away now."

"Good. I'd hate it if you died from a charley horse," Ashish said loudly, glaring at Samir. Did he really think that was going to distract Elijah and Oliver from their fight? The dude was deluded. If his big plan to get them back together was of the same caliber as this move . . . RIP, Elijah and Oliver's relationship.

Oliver sighed and picked up his textbook. "I'm out. See you guys."

"Oliver, wait," Ashish said. Seeing his friends like this made him feel like he'd eaten some of Gita Kaki's (in)famous *aloo palak*. "You don't have to go."

Oliver tossed a glance at Elijah. "No, I really do," he said. "I'll text you later."

Elijah exhaled when the French doors had closed behind Oliver. He sat back down on the settee, his head in his hands. "He can't even stand to be in the same space as me. If you'd have told me that even a month ago, I would've called you an idiot."

Pinky put her hand on his shoulder as Samir dusted his pants off and took his seat again, looking completely upset for Elijah. Ashish knew how he felt.

"I still love him, you know," Elijah said, putting his elbows on his thighs and looking down at the floor. "These past couple of weeks have been hell. I can't sleep. I can't concentrate." He glanced at Ashish. "You saw how I was at last practice."

It was true. Elijah's head hadn't been in the game at all, and everyone could tell. If Oliver saw, though, he just ignored it. "If you feel so awful," Ashish asked softly, dragging a chair over, "why don't you just tell him? Just lay it all out?" Ashish scratched the back of his neck as his words filtered down to Elijah. Being up front wasn't always the best option. If anyone knew that, he did. Feeling like a hypocrite, he added, "Um, you know, if you want to."

Elijah laughed a little. "Man, I am really happy for you that you've found love or whatever. But being honest isn't always the way to go with the object of your affections."

"No, I actually totally get that," Ashish mumbled. Man, the day he could put this whole Celia thing behind him couldn't come fast enough.

Elijah continued as if Ashish hadn't spoken. "Especially when he seems to hate your guts."

"What if it's just a front, though?" Samir asked. "Sometimes people put up these fake walls because they're afraid. Maybe Oliver just wants you to make the first move."

Pinky looked at Samir and smiled a little. She was probably remembering the same conversation Ashish was—the one they'd had with Samir in his room. "Have you tried calling him?" she asked Elijah.

"No. Picked up the phone a million times, but I just can't bring myself to do it. I just keep going back to the day when he accused me—*me*—of cheating on him. How he just wouldn't believe me." Elijah shook his head and scratched his chest. "I've never given him a reason to not trust me. And for him to just dismiss the past two years like that . . ."

"Do you still feel like you're too young to be in the relationship with him?" Ashish asked gently. "Like what you said the day you guys broke up?"

Elijah smirked. "That's the funny thing. I did feel like that, but then what you said kept replaying in my head, Ash. Most people spend their lifetimes looking for something like this, you know? If it felt wrong, it'd be another thing, but Oliver and I belong together, like . . ." He trailed off, his eyes on the horizon, preoccupied with memories. "Anyway," he said, seeming to come to. "What does it matter if he won't even be in the same room as me, right?"

"But—" Pinky began.

Elijah held up a hand. "I want to forget about what just happened, please."

"Okay," Pinky said softly, putting her skinny arm around his broad shoulders. "Okay, Elijah."

They were subdued after that. Ashish caught Samir looking thoughtfully at Elijah a couple of times. He'd have to ask him what that was about. He'd been pretty secretive about it, but Ashish wondered if the look had anything to do with Samir's plan to reconcile them.

Ashish had been surprised how much Samir had changed since their talk in his room. He'd stopped being such a jerk and was actually pretty cool now. And he and Pinky had even hung out together a couple of times without killing each other, which should probably go in *Guinness World Records* or something.

His phone buzzed. Fishing it out, Ashish saw a text message from Oliver. This sucks

He typed quickly, Yeah sorry man

Is E upset? Or glad that I left?

He doesn't want to talk about it so I'd say upset

Good

You don't mean that

The response came back after a long pause. No I don't

Still coming to Band Night?

Yeah I'll be there.

Okay. I'll give you a ride. The others can ride with E

Thanks man. See you tomorrow

It was like watching Romeo and Juliet—er, Julius—fight. They were meant to be together; why the heck couldn't they see what the rest of the world saw?

Shaking his head, Ashish pulled up the Flowers2U app and placed an order. He was just slipping his phone back into his pocket when it buzzed again.

Celia: Tomorrow at 9:30?

Ashish took a deep breath. *This is it, Ash. This is your chance for closure.* Yep

Can't wait. I miss you

We need to talk

Yes we do, gotta go but I'll see you then

Ashish set the phone on the table and looked off into the distance. Tomorrow. There'd be a lot to say tomorrow.

"Who was that?" Pinky asked, coming to grab another glass of lemonade.

"The Ghost of Christmas Past," Ashish said, turning back to his books.

Sweetie

Demonic possession. That was the only explanation. That was the only reason she, Sweetie Nair, would conceivably have signed on for this.

She stood off to the side with Kayla, Suki, and Izzy. The other bands were already there, and Roast Me was buzzing with an excited, suppressed energy. Every chair in the place was full (the owner, Andre, had put in at least three dozen chairs, and people were even standing at the back, coffee cups in their hands, grinning like nothing was wrong—like Sweetie wasn't just realizing she'd made the *worst* mistake of her life). She turned to Izzy, her eyes wide, and grasped her friend's arm.

"I can't do it," she said, her heart thumping. Sweat was breaking out on her upper lip. Ew. "I'm sorry, Izzy." Kayla and Suki, hearing her tone, turned, frowning. "And I'm sorry to all of you. You're like sisters to me, but even that has a limit. Even *blood* has a limit. And someone's going to be bleeding if I have to go up there, okay?" She laughed hysterically and jabbed a thumb at the stage.

Kayla pushed past Izzy and put her strong hands on Sweetie's shoulders. "Breathe," she commanded, looking Sweetie straight in the eye. Kayla was wearing black sparkly eyeliner and bright-fuchsia lipstick, with studded leather pants and a glittery top. She looked amazing and totally at home here. Unlike Sweetie. "You're going to be fine. I promise. You've been singing since you were a snotty five-year-old who could barely hold her scissors straight, and you've been blowing people away with your voice since just about then."

Sweetie smoothed her red-and-white polka-dotted dress down. On Kayla's insistence, she'd worn a black lace tutu underskirt with it, which peeked out the bottom. Now she was afraid it looked like she was trying too hard. "But those people—"

"You look amazing," Suki said from beside Kayla, reading her thoughts. "I mean, like, totally retro glam chic." Suki had dyed her hair a pale lavender and wore a long-sleeved sheer black lace top with deep-purple sparkly jeans. She looked like a runway model and didn't give fashion compliments easily, which instantly made Sweetie feel better.

"Thanks," she said, smiling. "You guys look gorgeous, too. All of you." Sweetie gave Izzy a quick squeeze around the waist.

Izzy was dressed in a light-pink floral dress, which she'd paired with combat boots. Her curly blond hair was in two thick braids. "I don't think I know anyone else who could pull off what you're wearing," Sweetie told her friend, and was rewarded by that warm, braces-accented smile she knew almost as well as her own.

Izzy laughed. "I got the idea from Pinterest."

"Well, it's freaking fabulous. *We're* freaking fabulous." Sweetie was relaxed now, she realized. She gathered her friends in a group hug. "I love you guys. This is going to be all right, right?"

"Better than—oh," Suki said, raising an eyebrow. "Incoming hottie, on your six."

Her friends melted away just as Sweetie turned to see Ashish striding toward her dressed in a button-down green shirt and dark jeans, that cocky smile on his face, his eyes lit up like neon signs. She grinned, feeling her heart leap in her chest. God, he was handsome. The way the shirt strained against his shoulders, the way those jeans hung from slender hips . . . *Okay, eyes up, Sweetie.*

He took her hands and kissed them gently, one at a time. Sweetie concentrated on not swooning. "You . . . look . . . incredible," he said, letting go of one of her hands to stroke her cheek. "Wow. That eyeliner . . . that lipstick . . . that dress . . ." He shook his head. "Wow," he said again.

Sweetie trilled a laugh. "I'm gonna have to start wearing this outfit more often. But seriously, you don't look so bad yourself." She gestured at his body and then leaned in close, putting her nose right up against his neck, thrilling in the way his breath caught in his throat at the contact. "And you smell really good too," she said in a voice that was just slightly husky.

"You saying I usually stink?" Ashish asked, and then laughed. "I wore some cologne tonight. You know, this being a special event and everything."

"I'm honored," Sweetie said, putting one hand to her chest. Ashish's eyes lingered at the cleavage highlighted by the sweetheart neckline of the dress, but he made a valiant effort to bring them back to her eyes. She knew the feeling.

"So, you nervous?" he asked. "Because you don't need to be, you know. Your voice is . . . gilded."

"Gilded? Have you been reading the thesaurus again?" Sweetie asked, raising an eyebrow.

"Enthralling," Ashish said, stepping in closer. She could feel his body heat swirling around her like a luxurious blanket. Her head almost swam with desire. "Just like you." He touched his lips to her throat, lightly. "I really like you," he whispered against her skin.

She couldn't speak for a full three seconds. "Obviously." She'd tried for a debonair, nonchalant voice, but it came out as a squeak.

Ashish pulled back and grinned at her. "Obviously." Kissing her knuckles again, he asked, "So what time's your set?"

She blinked at the change in topic and then laughed. "Why, you got someplace important to be?"

He didn't laugh. Sweetie's smile faded. "Um, at nine."

He nodded, drumming his hands on his thigh. "Okay. I, uh, have somewhere to be at nine thirty, so you might not see me right after. I'm sorry." He seemed nervous suddenly, on edge.

Sweetie frowned, a little disappointed. "Oh, well, that's okay. At least you get to see me sing, right?"

His face relaxed into a small smile and his eyes warmed up, like he was really seeing her again. "Right. Hey, let's take a selfie together." He pulled his phone out of his pocket, and Sweetie scooted in close to him.

They both smiled huge, goofy smiles. Sweetie smothered a laugh; she hadn't realized she was smiling that big, and she didn't think

Ashish had either. They were both just really, really, almost drug-induced-level happy. The last time she'd felt this floaty was when she had a root canal and the dentist gave her some laughing gas.

I'm so incredibly lucky, she thought as the phone made its clicking shutter sound. We're *so lucky*.

"Yo, Ash!" Pinky's voice cut through the crowd. Standing on tiptoes, Sweetie saw her at the counter at the far end of the room. "It's buy-one-get-one with Frequently Caffed cards tonight! I need yours!"

Ashish rolled his eyes. "What happened to yours?" he shouted back.

"Left it at home! Pleeeease?"

"Seriously?" he muttered, setting his phone down on the table to get out his wallet. "Pinky's got a caffeine problem." He turned to Sweetie and smiled. "I'll be right back."

She grinned. "Okay."

It was only when his phone beeped that she realized he'd left it behind. Her eyes automatically went to the screen.

Sweetie froze, the floaty feeling gone; her heart dropped like a hunk of cold lead. It was a text from Celia.

Can't wait to see you at Bedwell. 3 more hours. <3

I'm wearing my red halter . . . same as that one time ;)

It beeped again, but Sweetie forced herself to look away. She didn't want to see any more. She didn't *need* to see any more.

CHAPTER 27

Sweetie

Sweetie was turning away, numb, when she felt a big hand on top of her head. Her heart racing, she turned, expecting to find Ashish, but saw Oliver smiling at her instead. "Heyyy, girl. Ready for your big night?"

"Yeah—but wait." She frowned. "Did you just palm my head?"

Oliver's grin turned sheepish. "Sorry about that. Hazards of being a ballplayer, you know. Any circular object, you just wanna . . ." He made a palming motion with his hand and then waved it off. "Anyway. You look amazing, by the way."

Sweetie managed a watery smile. "Thanks."

Oliver frowned. "You okay?"

"Oh, yeah, totally." She picked up Ashish's phone with as straight a face as she could manage. "Could you give this to Ashish? He left it on the table. And, um, just tell him you found it. Okay?"

Oliver paused and then nodded. "Yeah, all right. Hey, if there's anything you want to ta—"

"No, I'm good." She took a deep breath and put a hand on his arm. "So, how are you doing? With the whole breakup thing?"

Oliver shrugged, looking over her head at something for a moment. "Ah. You know. It sucks. It hurts. I keep expecting it to go away, to get better with time, but it's just gotten worse. I miss him like a . . . like a freaking limb or something." He cleared his throat and smiled at her, a broken thing. "Do I sound pathetic or what?"

Sweetie squeezed his arm. "Not pathetic. Just like someone in love."

He snorted. "Yeah, what's the difference?"

She raised her eyebrows and nodded. He had a point.

Kayla, Suki, and Izzy came up then. "Hey, we've got to go over to the band area," Suki said. "The first band's about to start their set."

"That's my cue," Oliver said. "Break a leg, girls!" He turned and melted away into the crowd.

"Where's Ashish?" Izzy said.

Sweetie's smile faded as her heart thumped brokenly in her chest. "Oh, getting Pinky two-for-one coffees with his Frequently Caffed card. Don't ask," she forced herself to say in a normal voice, seeing Izzy's eyebrows knit together. "Apparently, Pinky's got a caffeine addiction."

"Well, do you want to wait for him for a couple of minutes?" Kayla asked.

"No," Sweetie said. "I'd rather not, actually."

She began to walk toward the band area on the right side of the coffee house.

"Wait, wait, what happened?" Kayla asked behind her.

Sweetie kept walking. "Don't want to talk about it."

She could practically feel the looks the three of them were exchanging behind her back.

"Did he hurt you?" Suki asked when they'd all come to a stop in the band area, her eyes sparking. "Because I will kick his—"

"No, he didn't hurt me. I just . . . I just want to forget about it for tonight, though, okay?"

The three of them nodded reluctantly.

A guy grabbed Kayla around her waist and she spun around, smiling. "Antwan! What are you doing here? You're supposed to be over there, with the plebes."

The tall black boy in hipster glasses laughed. "Plebe? Ouch. Don't forget who you're taking to prom."

Prom. The word settled in Sweetie's heart like a splinter in soft flesh. Why had Ashish bothered to do all of that, to ask her to prom, if he was still messing around with Celia? Why bother to go on these four dates at all if he was still seeing her? He'd put so much effort into telling her how he really felt, that his heart still belonged to Celia. And then, more recently, that he really liked *her*, Sweetie. Had she misread all his signals? Had she been completely foolish and starry eyed, like the dating amateur she was? Or . . . was it all a ploy? She remembered those dirtbags talking about how fat girls were easy. Was that all this was? Had Ashish been playing her the entire time?

An abyss opened inside Sweetie's soul. She wanted to cry and throw things. She wanted to scream and hit something. The Sassy Sweetie Project had been going *so well*. And part of that had been her relationship with Ashish. Part of it was knowing that a boy like him could find her not just desirable—the opposite of what Amma thought—but that they might actually be *happy* together. She'd finally begun to accept that what she'd always believed in her core—that her weight did not signify anything bad about her, that she was just as worthy and talented as any thin person—was true, in spite of what anyone else might say. And now . . . now it turned out Ashish had been toying with her. He'd decided she was not actually a whole person, with feelings and a heart. And why would he think that? Her appearance, of course.

Molten fury pulsed in her, like a volcano about to erupt. She balled her fists and took a deep breath. She counted backward from a hundred so she wouldn't begin flipping chairs and Hulk-smashing the wall. *Nothing has changed, Sweetie*, she told herself. *He broke your heart, but that says more about him than it does about you. You're still the girl you were yesterday. You can still continue the Sassy Sweetie Project. You don't need him; you never did.* Her heart rate began to slow. She unclenched her fists.

Well, if this had all been an act, she had to hand it to him. He was an excellent actor. She'd fallen for it, every bit of it. Heck, she'd fallen for *him* in the process.

Tears threatened and Sweetie blinked them away. She wouldn't let him ruin her night or her makeup. She was going to go up there and put on the best show Atherton had ever seen. So what if they were love songs? She'd sing them with every fiber of her battered being. She'd bring everyone—including Ashish, *especially* Ashish—to their knees.

Ashish

"Hey, man. You, uh, left your phone." Oliver dropped the phone into Ashish's palm with a weird expression on his face. Like, half judgy, half curious.

"Huh. Thanks." Ashish frowned, pocketing it. "Um, everything ok—"

"Why are we doing this?"

Ashish turned to find Elijah on his other side, staring intently at Oliver, who scratched his jaw and looked away. "We're doing this because you wouldn't deny sleeping with someone else," Oliver said.

Elijah stepped in closer. Ashish realized he was in the middle of their couple sandwich and discreetly backed up a half step. Should he leave? Nah, that'd be too abrupt. Besides, he needed to moderate if things got too feisty . . . uh, in a bad way feisty, not the good kind of—anyway.

"You should've trusted me," Elijah said. "You know how I felt about you." His voice dropped a notch. "How I *feel* about you."

Oliver bit his lip, and his eyes got misty. "Maybe . . . maybe you were right. Maybe we got serious too quickly. Maybe . . . maybe we should see other people." His voice wobbled and he shrugged.

"I know I said that, but I reject that idea out of hand. I reject the idea that we don't belong together." Elijah stepped even closer to Oliver and took his hands in his. "The thing is, Ollie, I feel so incredibly fortunate to know you. Love is unpredictable and so . . . so freaking elusive. I just can't stop thinking about how damn lucky I am."

Oliver looked steadily into Elijah's eyes. "You're just saying that because you're lonely."

"I'm not," Elijah said without missing a beat. "I'm saying that because it's true. I love you. Don't you remember the good times? Don't you remember how it used to be?"

"I'm starting to forget," Oliver said, taking his hands from Elijah's.

"Dude." Samir grabbed Ashish by the arm and turned him around, and Oliver walked away.

"Sense the mood," Ashish hissed, turning back to Elijah. He put a hand on Elijah's shoulder, but Elijah shrugged it off and strode away, not meeting his eye. Sighing, Ashish turned back to Samir, who was basically dancing from foot to foot, impatient with news. "What's going on?"

"Yo. It's all set." Samir flashed a set of very white, very straight teeth.

Ashish waited. "Is that supposed to make sense to me?"

"Everyone, please take your seats," Andre said into the mic onstage. "The first band is just about ready to begin their set. Please find a seat."

"Damn," Ashish said, looking over his shoulder. "I wanted to wish Sweetie luck one last time." But he saw the bands were all sequestered over to the far right. He couldn't even see her, thanks to the line of tall dudes in the front.

"Forget about all that," Samir said as they made their way to their seats. The yellow overhead lights in Roast Me switched to multi-colored ones, and the crowd whooped and clapped. There were so many people, those who couldn't find a chair were crammed into the back. "I have the definitive answer to Oliver and Elijah's problems!"

Ashish looked at Samir as they sat. "Bro. What did you *do*? Is this what you've been plotting?"

Samir frowned. "Plotting?"

"Yeah, I saw you on the balcony last night, looking all Brutus-like."

"Okay, but Brutus was the bad guy. I'm not betraying anyone, I'm bringing the lovers together."

"If you can do that, I'll have to call you David Blaine." At Samir's confused expression, he shook his head. "Go on. I'm listening."

"So I went and spoke to the first band when we got here, and they're on board. They're going to play 'Crazy in Love.'" He looked all gleefully expectant.

"That old Beyoncé song?" Ashish asked, totally confused.

"Not *just* that old Beyoncé song, Oliver and Elijah's song," Samir said in a tone that suggested it was common knowledge.

"Um, what? How do you know that? I don't even know that and I hang out with them every single day."

Samir crossed his arms and looked a little abashed. "Let's just say when people don't like you, they don't talk to you. And if they don't talk to you, you learn a lot by just listening and learning."

"Ah." Ashish felt a pinprick of sympathy for Samir. Being disliked and ignored had to have sucked big-time, but he'd still stuck by them. "So okay, back to your nefarious plan."

"If by 'nefarious' you mean 'ingenious,' then okay." Samir smiled and leaned forward again. "So, the first band's going to play that song, and before they begin, they'll say, 'This message is from an anonymous audience member. When two people are meant to be together, things just fall into place. This song goes out to the man of my dreams.' And get this." Samir leaned even closer, all excited. "I've sent Oliver and Elijah each a note that says the other one dedicated the song to him!"

Ashish stared at him. "You what? When does that ever work out well in the movies? And let me tell you, it's usually the messenger who ends up shot. So don't come crying to me if that happens to you."

"O you of little faith," Samir said. "Just watch and see. Those two just need to get together and talk to each other without all that anger and guilt in the way. This is going to be amazing."

"Ye."

Samir glanced at him sideways. "Gesundheit."

"No, it's not 'O *you* of little faith,' it's 'O *ye* of'—you know what? Doesn't matter. I hope you're right, man. They were just talking to each other, and . . . I feel like their whole problem is that this love thing just hit them between the eyes when they weren't expecting it. They need to understand how lucky they are to have found it at all. I think Elijah has, but I'm not sure about Oliver." Ashish craned his neck to find Oliver. He saw him opening a little note, reading the message, and then putting it away in his pocket just as the first band began to introduce themselves up onstage. He couldn't figure out from his expression what he was thinking. He found Elijah a couple of seats down from him, opening a note too. Elijah's eyes immediately began searching the crowd for Oliver.

Ashish's heart hitched. He really, really wanted this to work out for them, he realized. And maybe Samir's plan seemed totally hokey, but he couldn't help hoping. He turned to Samir. "I'm glad you're trying this," he said. "Thanks."

Samir nodded.

Pinky settled in beside him with a giant blended coffee. Her eyes glittered, feverish and bright. "These are buy one, get one! I got this one for free! Free!"

Ashish rolled his eyes just as Samir laughed.

His phone buzzed in his pocket and he pulled it out. He had three text messages from Celia he hadn't read yet. A fourth one had just come in: a picture of her in a bath towel.

Getting ready for you, the caption said.

Swallowing, Ashish put the phone away.

Sweetie

The first band, Hot Cup of Tea, finished up right at their allotted five-minute mark, and the second band went on. They were all guys, dressed in black, with fake tattoos up and down their arms. They called themselves Torn.

Sweetie stood staring at them as they began to play. She felt like she was here but not really. The world felt like it was at a remove. She laughed a little and joked with Suki, Kayla, and Izzy, all of whom were hopped up on free espresso shots courtesy of Antwan, but Sweetie couldn't fully get into it. She'd given up trying to find Ashish in the crowd when the guys from Torn had been in front of her blocking her view (darn tall people), but she could now see unhindered.

He was sitting in a chair next to Samir and Pinky, and he was looking at his phone. He had the weirdest look on his face as he put it away. Sort of like anticipatory determination. Sweetie pulled in a deep, shuddering breath and looked away. She didn't even want to know what he was anticipating.

Torn wasn't half bad, and when they finished four and a half minutes later, it was Sweetie, Kayla, Suki, and Izzy's turn. They walked up onstage with their instruments (all except Sweetie, who wasn't playing one, and Suki, who was using the drum set that someone had loaned to Roast Me for the night). Like he did with Hot Cup of Tea and Torn, the emcee introduced all of them by name and what they'd be doing that night. There was immediate cheering from Antwan's crowd and Ashish's crowd. Sweetie was kind of glad the spotlights made it hard for her to see the audience. She didn't want to see Ashish being supportive and sweet right now. Not when she half wanted to murder him and half wanted to sob against his chest.

She had a moment of panic at the thought of all those pairs of eyes on her—the last count had been at sixty-eight audience members. She thought she looked adorable in her dress, and so did her friends (and apparently Ashish, but she didn't want to think about that), but people in general did not echo that sentiment. She began to self-consciously tug at her dress, wishing she'd worn a cardigan or something to cover up her arms, then forced herself to stop. This was about the music, *just* about the music. She could do this. So what if they laughed at her? She thought of Anjali Chechi's words. *You're getting up there and singing because you have a beautiful voice and you believe in yourself.*

And she began to sing.

She'd heard people muttering to themselves and laughing a bit—usual not-completely-engaged audience stuff—as Kayla introduced their band. But when she filled the coffee shop with her music, the silence fell like a hammer. It was immediate, absolute. Sweetie closed her eyes and felt the music flood her blood; it wrapped around her bones like sinuous vines and filled her heart to bursting with light.

Ashish

Ho-ly cra-ap.

It was like watching something heavenly, something unearthly, come into being right before his stupefied eyes.

She was a goddess. She was . . . she was unspeakably . . . stunning. There were no words that did her justice in that moment.

Ashish couldn't look at anything except Sweetie. The entire world melted away.

CHAPTER 28

Sweetie

Sweetie had a moment of clarity, of near panic, when she wondered what she looked like to the audience. Were they totally distracted and grossed out by her arms? By her stomach? Her thick calves? What about Ashish? He was probably just staring at his phone and thinking about stupid Celia in her stupid red halter.

She put even more of herself into her song, in a desperate attempt to forget everything else.

Sweetie didn't give the audience much of a chance to jeer—or cheer—between the two songs she was singing. This was for her own mental health. It was easier at track meets—she was on the track, running past them, so everyone just looked a blur. Plus, most people could barely see anything from the bleachers besides a girl in a blue-and-gold track uniform streaking past them. But this . . . this was almost as bad as if she'd invited everyone to come watch her sing in the shower. Almost. There was nothing else for them to focus on *but* her. And Sweetie knew what people were like. She didn't want to give them a chance to shout out humiliating comments about her weight or for them to laugh at her. She didn't want to let the girls down, and if she heard anything like that, it'd be really, really hard for her to keep going. Especially after what had happened with Ashish.

As the last note of the second, and final, song drifted through the air and spiraled into silence, Sweetie's palms broke out in a sweat. This was it. She had nothing more to give them; their judgment would come now and she wouldn't be able to stop it.

The room almost cracked in half with the force of their applause.

At first Sweetie wasn't sure what was happening—this applause sounded so different from the applause the other bands had gotten. She wondered if it was the acoustics of being onstage. But then she saw shadowy shapes getting to their feet and a rhythmic chant began to go up. It took Sweetie a moment to realize they were saying her name. And then she realized they were giving her a *standing ovation*. She turned to Kayla, Suki, and Izzy in complete surprise, grinning, and they were all grinning back at her, too. Suki raised one fist in the air and whooped—the audience went even wilder. Sweetie closed her eyes, letting the sound of their cheering and her name wash over her. Her heart was a helium balloon, lifting with pure, giddy joy. They loved her. They *loved* her. They didn't care what her stomach or her thighs looked like. It was like they could see the light she'd always nurtured inside of her and were acknowledging that, yes, it was just as special as she'd suspected and, yes, she had something extraordinary to offer the world.

There were chants of "Encore, encore," but Andre came on the stage and said that, in the interest of time, there'd be no encores. (He got booed bad. Sweetie didn't envy him.)

As she made her way off the stage, a man came up to her holding the giantest bouquet of pink peonies—her favorite. "Sweetie Nair?" he said (he pronounced it like it rhymed with "hair," but she didn't even correct him because FLOWERS).

"Yes?"

"These are for you." He smiled and thrust the bouquet at her, got her signature, and left.

"Oh my God!" Izzy said beside her, her eyes like giant brown beacons. "Who are those from?"

"I think I know," Suki mumbled. "Let's just be glad Antwan has Kayla, uh, *ocupado*, or she'd take those from you and get the entire crowd to stomp on them."

With slightly trembling hands Sweetie opened the card: *The only flower that seemed to even remotely match your beauty. Got these in advance because I knew you'd enrapture everyone . . . just like you did me. Obviously. —A*

Biting her lip to keep her emotions from engulfing her, Sweetie looked over to where Ashish had been sitting. His seat was empty.

She pushed the flowers at Izzy. "Here. Keep them. Or throw them away. I gotta go."

She pushed her way past everyone and stepped outside into the cool night.

There was a bench outside, around the side of the building. Sweetie went there, shivering lightly in the breeze. Her eyes were brimming with tears, but she didn't bother to wipe them away. Her mascara would smear and make her look like a raccoon. So what? She sat on the bench and stared off into the distance at the halo caused by the streetlights down the road.

"Mind some company?"

She turned to see Suki and Izzy loitering a few feet away. She waved them over. They sat on either side of her in silence. Izzy had the giant bouquet of flowers still, and she set them by her feet.

"You were amazing tonight," Izzy said. "No crappy-arse boy can take that away from you."

Sweetie managed a small smile. "Aww, thanks, Iz—"

"And you're an amazing athlete," Izzy continued fiercely. "He can't take that, either. You're totally going to kill it at the big meet next Friday."

"Hey, girls." They all looked up at the female voice to see Kayla walking toward them.

Sweetie wrapped her arms around herself as Kayla squeezed in beside Izzy and the giant bouquet. "What happened to Antwan?"

"I told him my girl needed me. Sisters before blisters, am I right?"

Suki snorted. "Did you just call boys 'blisters'?"

"She's right," Izzy said, rolling her eyes. "They're irritating and painful and unneeded."

Sweetie laughed weakly. "Thanks, guys. I'm glad you didn't let me come out here alone."

Izzy put her hand on Sweetie's just as Kayla said, "Of course we didn't let you come out here alone. Now the only question is, do we put itching powder in Ashish's shoes or in his jockstrap?"

"I ain't touching either of those things," Suki said.

Sweetie shook her head. "I just don't get it, you know? That card in those flowers . . . it's so incredibly sweet. And everything we've shared . . . I felt like it was all real."

The girls were silent. Then Suki said quietly, "Do you feel up to telling us what happened?"

Sweetie filled them in on the gist of everything. They were silent while they took it all in.

"He said he really likes you while at the same time he was obviously planning this ridiculous thing with Celia behind your back?" Izzy said. Her voice was quiet, dangerous. The thing about Izzy was that she was the sweetest, most innocent one of the four of them. But if you crossed anyone she loved, she turned into Princess freaking Xena. She grabbed the giant bouquet and stood. "Come on."

They all stood with her. "Um, where are we going?" Kayla asked as they followed her to the parking lot.

"I'm going to shove this bouquet up Ashish's—"

"That won't be necessary," Sweetie said. "Really."

"Okay, so I agree that the shoving is unnecessary," Suki said. She grinned suddenly. "Would be fun, though. Anyway, I think Izzy's onto something with the confrontation thing."

"I just want to go home, honestly," Sweetie said. Suddenly she felt very, very tired.

Kayla turned and took her by the shoulders. "Sweetie," she said, her dark-brown eyes glittering under the streetlights. "This jock totally took you for a ride. He thought you were gullible enough to fall for his lies, and then he decided he wanted to hook back up with his ex *while telling you* that she'd broken his heart so badly he couldn't emotionally connect with you. He's scum. Are you really going to let him off that easy? Do you really want him to have his little hot-and-heavy date in Bedwell with zero consequences because he bought you some expensive flowers? I mean, I know that's not why you want to go home, but that's exactly what he'll think."

"Guys like Ashish are used to getting their way. They think that because they're hot and they can slap a ball around, they can get away with everything short of murder." Suki's black eyes sparked with anger. "Come on."

Izzy held the bouquet in one hand and thumped it against the palm of her other hand, like a Mafia boss. "You know you want to."

Sweetie sighed. They were right. Ashish shouldn't get off so easily. Besides, wouldn't it feel good to let off some steam? To let him know that she wasn't some easy, pathetic girl he could just take for a ride because he was her first boyfriend or because she was fat? She straightened her shoulders. "Fine. Let's do it."

"That's my girl," Suki said, swiping under Sweetie's eyes with her fingers to get the smeared mascara. "Let's kick some jock butt."

As they sped out of the parking lot in Kayla's Suburban, Sweetie caught sight of two figures under the eave of the building. They were wrapped around each other, kissing. With a smile, she realized it was Oliver and Elijah. Well, at least the night had ended well for someone.

Ashish

It was exactly like the last time he was here with Celia. Ashish was having a major case of the déjà vus, combined with a heapin' helpin' of the heebie-jeebs.

She was wearing the same red halter with those tiny blue shorts and those killer cowboy boots. Her hair was up in a bun, with just a few curls escaping around her face. She'd spread out a picnic blanket—complete with LED candles—on one of the little green hills overlooking the bay. Ashish was pretty sure it was the exact green hill as the last time.

Leaving the parking lot (Oliver had told him, kind of mysteriously, that he had a ride home, so Ashish had been able to leave alone), he walked up the hill and sat cross-legged beside Celia. She smiled at him, her skin glowing from the light of the candles, her hazel eyes shimmering. She was beautiful—he couldn't deny that.

Celia reached over and put a hand on his arm. "Thanks for coming. It's so good to see you." She scooted in closer, so their thighs were touching. "God, I've missed you, Ashish." She trailed a finger up his forearm.

Ashish put a hand on hers, making her stop. "Celia," he said, holding her gaze. Her smile faded slowly at whatever she saw on his face. "I'm dating someone."

She shook her head. "But it doesn't feel as right as you and me did, does it?"

Ashish took a deep breath, filling his lungs with the distinct scent of the bay. "It feels . . . more right. I'm not saying that to hurt you, Celia. But Sweetie, she's . . . . she's like the other half of my jagged soul, you know? She's got the soft edges that fuse with my hard ones. She's so easy to be with." He shook his head. "There's something about Sweetie. Something I can't explain. I just l—" He stopped short and stared straight ahead at nothing. *Oh my God*, he thought to himself. *Oh my God.*

"What?"

"I love her." He grinned, thinking, *You freaking love her, Ash. I can't believe you didn't see this until now. You idiot! You. Love. Her.*

He laughed a little maniacally, exhilarated. He wanted to fly. It was quite possible he *could* fly, because he was so dang happy. This was like Balltopia. This might even be better than Balltopia. He loved Sweetie. Ashish and Sweetie, sitting in a tree, k-i-s-s-i—

Celia took her hand out from under his and wrapped her arms around her legs, pulling her knees up to her chest. "So you don't miss me at all?"

The tremulous pain in her voice crashed Ashish back to reality. The grin fell off his face. "No, no, hey, C." He squeezed her arm and sat with her for a moment in silence. "It's not that I don't miss you. Honest. In fact, for the longest time I couldn't even function. I'm still getting myself back all the way. But you could tell, couldn't you, when we were together, that something was off? The whole reason you went out with that d-bag behind my back—"

"I was wrong. I'm so, so sorry about that, Ash. I was wrong and horrible." She turned her head to look at Ashish, and her eyes were swimming in tears that were golden in the light. "You were the only one who ever understood me, Ash. This past year at SFSU has been horrible. I'm so lonely all the time. I don't have any friends. Maybe if you and I were dating, I could convince my parents to let me move back home. I could . . . I could go to Menlo College—"

Ashish put a hand on her shoulder. He'd never seen Celia like this; it broke his heart. "C . . . ," he said gently. "You don't need me as an excuse to move back home. Your parents will understand that it's too soon for you to move out."

She swiped at her eyes. "But they won't, though. They were both so happy for me to 'leave the nest,' as they kept calling it. They kept saying they were so proud that I was finally beginning my life independent of them. I know they'll just think I'm this giant failure if I move back home because I can't hack it away from them. But if it's because things are getting serious with you . . ." She sniffed and sobbed at the same time. "Oh God. I just heard it. Like, for the first time, you know?" She put her chin on her knees. "I'm such a pathetic loser."

"Hey." Ashish waited till she met his eye. "Celia Ramirez is many things, but *loser* ain't one of them. Okay?"

She smiled a little. "I also said 'pathetic.'"

Ashish laughed. "Okay, I'm not gonna lie, walking up here and seeing how you'd re-created our date at Bedwell was a little unsettling." He put an arm around her shoulder. It felt easy now, like something he'd do with Pinky, with no other connotations surrounding it. "But I get it now. You're just sad, C. There's nothing wrong with that. And sure, your parents might be momentarily disappointed that you don't want to launch yet. But they're going to be happy that you felt you could go to them with this, you know?" He snorted. "And seriously, if they're anything like my parents, they'll probably be secretly pleased that you came back. I think Ma and Pappa want Rishi and Dimple to stay home once they're married . . . and they probably wouldn't even mind it now."

Celia laughed. "I can see that." More seriously, she continued. "And you know what? You're right. I bet they'll just be relieved that I reached out. I mean, I've even gone to see the campus shrink a couple of times." She took a deep, shuddering breath.

Ashish patted her on the back. "I'm sorry it's been so rough. I guess that's the side of college you don't hear about too often, huh?"

"Yeah. There's a lot more to it than people think. It's not all fun and parties, even for someone like me. Mostly, it's just so big. . . . I kinda got lost, you know?"

"Yeah. But you'll find yourself again."

"Thanks, Ash."

They sat together for a few more minutes and then began packing up.

"You know, something about you is different." Her hands paused on the picnic basket as she studied him. "But in a really good way. I'm . . . I'm happy for you, Ash. This is what you deserve." She smiled softly, a little sadly. "So. This girl you're dating. Tell me more about her."

Ashish felt the maniacal, exhilarated grin reacquaint itself with his face as he said her name. "Sweetie Nair. My parents actually set us up."

"Shut. Up."

Ashish laughed. "Yeah, I know. That caught me off guard too. But she's kind of perfect for me, actually. She's athletic and kind and charming without even realizing she's being charming. . . ." Shaking his head, he picked up the picnic basket and the blanket and began walking down the hill, toward the parking lot. "She makes the planet brighter just by being on it."

"So if Sweetie's so perfect, what's she doing with a dope like you?"

Ashish laughed. "Actually, I ask myself that every single day, pretty much." His heart wanted to burst into light at the memory of Sweetie singing her heart out. In the distance a Suburban roared into the parking lot, gravel skidding and bouncing, but Ashish didn't pay much attention. He was too busy thinking about how he was ready to take the next step with Sweetie.

She'd stuck by him when he was in pain and dazed with heartbreak and demojofied. Gently, gently, she'd brought him back to his parents, showed him how wrong he'd been about not dating Indian-American girls, how idiotic and empty the whole "mojoless player" thing was. Gently, gently, in her Sweetie way, she'd changed the core of him. She'd shaken his world and reshaped it into something bright and light and colorful. It was obvious what he needed to do next.

He needed to say those three little words to her. Three little words that would change their lives forever. Ashish grinned; he felt free. He was no longer afraid of screwing things up with Sweetie. From now on, everything would be smooth sailing between them.

CHAPTER 29

Sweetie

"You f-fart goblin jerkwad!"

The words shot out of Sweetie's mouth before she could stop them; it was the only insult she could think of that came close to expressing her wrath. Ashish was walking toward the parking lot with a girl who had to be Celia, with her gorgeous red halter and short shorts, her perfect cowboy boots and artfully arranged bun. She was half Sweetie's size, too. It shouldn't bother her, but it did. It stung like hell.

Ashish's head snapped up as Sweetie slammed the passenger door shut and stalked up to him. "Sweetie?" He looked totally bewildered. "What . . . what are you doing here?"

Her girls flanked her as she crossed her arms. Celia looked completely terrified, her doe eyes swiveling this way and that as if she were looking for a quick exit. "Do you think I'm stupid, Ashish?" Sweetie said. "Did you seriously think you could continue to date Celia behind my back and I wouldn't find out about it?"

"Wh-what?" He jerked his head to look at Celia, as if remembering for the first time that she was with him. "No, it's not—"

"Save it, Ass-sheesh," Izzy said, taking a menacing step closer to him.

He rolled his eyes. "Never heard that one before."

On Izzy's right, Suki brandished Ashish's bouquet at him and, as he watched, broke them in half over one thigh.

"Hey!" he said. "Those were for Sweetie!"

"Well, she doesn't want your janky frakking guilt flowers," Kayla said from Sweetie's side.

"They're not guilt fl—" Turning to Sweetie, Ashish said, "Could you call off your goon squad? This isn't what you think it is. Let me explain. Come on, Sweetie, you know me."

She felt herself wavering. He looked so genuine, so completely confident in what he was saying.

"Goon squad? You're lucky we aren't throwing your bony butt in the bay," Suki said, pushing forward and narrowing her eyes, her hair swinging out to cover half her face. "Dirtbag."

"You mess with Sweetie, you mess with frakking all of us," Kayla said, stepping forward too, her arms crossed. "Now, you choose. Do you want to get kicked in the frakking nads by Sweetie or by me?"

"What?" Ashish squeaked.

"W-wait."

Sweetie turned at the female voice. Celia tucked an errant strand of hair behind her ear and stepped forward slightly, licking her lips. She looked extremely nervous. "Ash is right. There's nothing going on between us."

Kayla cleared her throat and pointedly looked down at the—ugh—blanket. Sweetie's insides shriveled at the thought of them doing it on that checkered red-and-white fabric.

"I know it looks bad," Celia said. "But it was all me. I wanted to get back together with Ash—at least, I thought I did—but it was all a mistake. We were just talking tonight, and he made me realize some things about myself." She shook her head. "But more importantly for you, I realized that this guy is head over heels for you, Sweetie. Seriously."

Ashish rubbed his jaw, his eyes studying Sweetie closely, half hopeful.

Sweetie looked at him, frozen. Those eyes she loved so much, like dark honey drizzled into a cup of tea. Even now they looked totally honest, completely guileless. Could it be? Was Celia speaking the truth?

"Nice try," Izzy said, flashing her braces-covered teeth in a snarl.

"They probably get off on cheating or something," Suki said in disgust.

"Sweetie." Ashish's voice was clear, and he looked right at her, no hint of deception on his face. "I would never hurt you like this. Tell me you know that."

Sweetie stood there quietly, looking at him, studying him, willing what he was saying to be true. But the blanket. The text messages. The fact that he was here at all, that he'd kept all of this from her in the first place . . .

"She doesn't have to tell you anything, jackass," Suki said, kicking off one boot. When she picked it up, the rest of the girls followed suit, kicking off one of their shoes, picking them up, and advancing on Ashish.

"What is this?" he said, looking at them warily.

"Oh, you'll find out," Izzy said, smiling.

"Stop!" Sweetie called out.

They turned to her. "Are you sure?" Kayla said. "Because there are four of us and only one of him."

"Take your shoe off," Izzy said, practically bouncing up and down. "Come on, Sweetie, it's gonna feel so good!"

"I just wanna go," she said quietly, and turned back to the Suburban. After a moment, the girls caught up with her and piled in.

Even as she refused to listen to Ashish calling her name, something inside Sweetie protested. Could this really be true? Was Ashish just a big cheater? Were he and Celia just feeding her an old, tired story she'd be a total fool to believe? But why? What would be the point?

Well, maybe they needed Sweetie to believe so they could continue their tryst in all the secretive excitement. The thought made her sick. But really. Would Ashish, *her* Ashish, do that?

"Jerkface douche-canary," Suki said, as Kayla started up the car.

"We should've tap-danced all over his face in our heels," Izzy said to her. "I can't believe he just stood there with Celia and refused to admit anything."

The more they spoke, the worse Sweetie felt.

"Guys, I . . . I just can't . . . Ashish is not . . ." She shook her head, holding back tears, as Kayla whipped out of the parking lot. "I didn't get a dirtbag vibe from him at all, you guys. Even right then. I just didn't feel like he was lying. Did you?" She turned to Kayla, who was usually a really good judge of character.

Kayla kept her eyes on the road for a long moment. Then, looking at Sweetie out of the corner of her eye, she said, "I didn't get a lying vibe either, honestly."

"But let's look at the facts," Suki said from the backseat. "One: He was dating you and simultaneously texting Celia without telling you. Two: He told you he really liked you while simultaneously planning this whole looks-like-a-date-with-benefits thing behind your back. Let me ask you, when you saw him earlier tonight, did he give any hints at all about what he was up to later?"

"No," Sweetie said quietly. "He just said he had somewhere to be at nine thirty."

Suki sat back. "I rest my case."

"You don't want to be that girl, Sweetie," Izzy said from beside Suki. "The girl who becomes a doormat and gives the dirtbag guy a thousand chances just because he's cute and can lie well."

"No, I don't," Sweetie agreed. "I definitely don't." The one thing she'd always had, the one thing she'd hung on to in spite of everything she'd been told about herself—that she was ugly, that she was lazy, that no one would love her until she was thin, that she wasn't a serious athlete because she was fat—was her self-respect. And she'd be damned if she was going to let Ashish Patel take that from her.

Kayla dropped Sweetie off in front of her house. They'd spent the rest of the ride back singing songs from Band Night—which, by the way, had been a total success. According to the text from Antwan that had just come in, they'd raised enough money for the new jerseys and then some. They'd even decided to donate the overage to a charity for underprivileged women athletes.

As soon as the Suburban disappeared around the corner, though, Sweetie's temporary high melted away. It hadn't been completely genuine anyway; it had been painted on over her sadness and disappointment. Now that she was alone, those emotions showed through, and Sweetie felt completely drained.

She let herself into the house and walked to her bedroom.

"Band Night *engane indaarnu?*"

Sweetie turned, her hand on the doorknob, to see Amma in the hallway in a nightdress, her hair in a neat braid. Her eyes were puffy, like she'd been asleep. Which she probably had—it was past ten thirty, and Amma and Achchan were usually in bed by ten p.m. tops.

"It was good," Sweetie said. "We made all the money we needed to make for our jerseys." There was no point in telling Amma about the standing ovation. The way people had gone mad cheering for her. Amma would just ask if Sweetie was sure they weren't actually screaming out insults about her weight or something.

Amma clapped her hands. "Very nice! Will you sing me some of your songs? Maybe this weekend?"

Sweetie laughed a little. "Okay." Then, after a pause, she added, "Thank you for letting me go. I know you and Achchan don't like me staying up late on school nights."

Smiling, Amma came forward and put her hand on Sweetie's cheek. "I think I am starting to understand that my daughter is blossoming into a woman," she said softly. "And perhaps it is time for me to begin backing away just a little."

Sweetie swallowed the sudden lump in her throat. She felt tears threatening and blinked hard. "But not too much," she said, leaning down to hug Amma. What was it about a mother's hug, anyway? It made her want to burst into tears at the same time that it made her feel infinitely comforted. Like the suckiest thing possible had happened, but somehow things would work out because Sweetie always worked things out.

"Not too much," Amma agreed, making circles on Sweetie's back with her open palm like she used to do when Sweetie was little. After a pause she said, "Sweetie, *mol* . . . all that what Tina auntie was saying? About prom?"

Sweetie straightened and looked into her mother's brown eyes, the exact same hazel shade as her own. "Yeah?"

"She's wrong."

Sweetie's eyes almost bugged out of her head. "Really?"

Amma thrust her chin out. "You know, when I was small, my family had no money. At school the girls and boys would tease me because my uniform was always too short and my socks were full of holes. So when I grew up, I decided my child would never feel like that. I made sure you always had nice things. I didn't want you to be teased. Then . . . with your weight . . ."

Sweetie felt something inside her harden against what she knew was coming.

"With your weight, I thought people would make fun of you anyway. I wanted you to be friends with a girl like Sheena, you know. Fashionable and cool. So I became friends with Tina auntie. But I started to realize you're not . . . you're not like Sheena. And you're not like me. You're Sweetie." She smiled and shook her head a little. "After we talked, I realized that you can make your own decisions. If you don't want to go to prom, who is that Tina or that Sheena to tell you it's wrong? You do what you want, *mol*. And just forget about everyone else. Even your old Amma."

Sweetie smiled through the tears in her eyes and shook her head. Maybe this wasn't everything—Amma wasn't apologizing for all the comments she'd ever made about Sweetie's weight. She wasn't reversing her position on what Sweetie could or couldn't wear. But this wasn't nothing. This wasn't insubstantial. This was her mother admitting that maybe, maybe Sweetie didn't have to be *exactly* like the other girls. This might just be the first crack in Amma's intractable armor. "I can't forget about my Amma any more than I can forget about myself," she said in a high, choked voice. "You know that."

Amma pulled Sweetie's face down and kissed her forehead. Sweetie closed her eyes and soaked it in.

Ashish

Okay, how was this possible? How had he gone from neatly tying things up, from finally arriving at the conclusion that he was irrevocably in love with Sweetie to having her call him a fart goblin jerkwad, whatever *that* was, threatening him with her Mafia girl gang and then storming off into the night? *How?*

The LCD screen in his Jeep lit up with an incoming text.

Pinky: ZOMG you'll never believe it but Samir's madcap plan worked!! O and E are back together!!!!!!

"Madcap," eh? He guessed by the exclamation point bonanza that Pinky was still sucking down the coffee. He smiled to himself in spite of everything. So Oliver had probably gotten a ride home with Elijah. That was awesome; those two deserved to be together.

And so did he and Sweetie, dammit. They deserved to be together because they were made for each other. How could she believe he was capable of leading this huge double life?

Then again, you didn't really give her a reason to think the best of you, now, did you? a tiny internal voice insisted. *You've been talking to Celia behind her back. How was she supposed to know that there was nothing more nefarious going on?*

How had she found out, anyway? At no point had his phone been unatten—

Oliver had given him the phone and he'd been sort of weird. What if Oliver had seen the messages and told Sweetie?

Ashish dismissed the idea out of hand. No, Oliver would talk to him first before he did anything like that. So then what? Oh God. He'd left the phone on the table after they'd taken a selfie, hadn't he? And Celia had probably texted him then, right in front of Sweetie.

Ashish groaned and gripped the steering wheel tighter. Okay. There was nothing else to do. He had to see her.

He pulled off the side of the road and texted her.

Will you come talk to me? At that playground on the corner of McAdam and Harper

It showed as read almost immediately. One minute. Two minutes. Three. Four. Ashish was starting to think that she was ignoring him when the response came back.

Sweetie: Nothing to say

Please

Why?

Because I love you an idiotic amount, he wanted to say. *Because I can't imagine waking up tomorrow with you still thinking the worst of me. Because I can't lose you over something as stupid and small as this misunderstanding.*

Because it's you and me, he typed instead. Please

Three minutes later: Ok. When?

His heart leaped. 20 minutes

He started the car again and pulled back onto the road, his entire body clenched with an almost painful, crushing hope.

CHAPTER 30

Ashish

His headlights picked her up as soon as he pulled into the parking lot. She was sitting on the bottom rung of the jungle gym. He felt a pinprick of hope at the realization that the rung was wide enough that he could squeeze in beside her. She'd left room for him still. That had to count for something, right?

He turned off the car and walked over to her, his footsteps soft and silent on the rubbery stuff they used on kids' playgrounds. Maybe it *was* rubber. Whatever. No time for that now. "Hey." He stood beside her, not wanting to sit and invade her space until she'd told him it was okay.

She looked up at him. Her hair was wet, like she'd just taken a shower, and she wore sweatpants and a big sweatshirt. Her eyes were puffy, like she'd been crying, and Ashish's heart broke at just how beautiful she was. He couldn't wait to set things right. He *would* set things right. Sweetie would never cry because of him again.

"Hi," she said softly. She scooted over a bit.

Taking the invitation, Ashish sat next to her. He could feel her body heat; he could smell her sweet peppermint shampoo. He wanted nothing more than to gather her in his arms, to kiss that velvety mouth, that irresistible dimple, that soft throat. But he held back with everything in him. "Thank you for meeting me. I know it's late and you probably don't want to even look at me."

She shrugged.

"Sweetie . . . remember when I said I couldn't give myself to you all the way because—"

"Because of Celia." Her voice broke a little on Celia's name, and Ashish wanted so badly to blurt out the truth, how things really were. But he had to take it slow. "Yeah. I remember."

She got up and walked off to the tire swings. She sat on one and began to gently swing. Ashish followed her and sat on the one next to hers.

"You don't have to remind me," Sweetie said softly, her words twining with the creaking of the chains. "I know you didn't make any promises. But then you said you really liked me. And you went to all that trouble to ask me to prom. I thought . . ." She swallowed, and when she spoke, her voice was all choked up, shattering whatever was left of Ashish's heart. "I thought that changed things. That you were, um, falling for me."

He took a breath. "Things *were* changing. I *was* falling for you. Actually? I've already fallen."

She looked up at him sharply, her features shadowed in the dim light from the streetlight a few yards away. "But then . . . then why were you talking to Celia at all?"

Ashish kicked the dirt, the entire swing juddering at the impact. "I won't lie. When Celia first texted me, right after you and I went on our second date, I couldn't help but talk to her again. She'd broken my heart, and . . . and I guess in some way that meant she still had power over me. She sounded so down, so lonely, that she got to me. There was history there, you know? But then, as you and I got to know each other better, I realized something. Celia was someone I *used* to love. Past tense. And that would never change. She's made some mistakes, but I think she's a good person, and . . . and that's it.

"I couldn't stop talking to her because there was a part of me that felt like I owed her that. She sounded like she didn't have anyone else to talk to. She seemed really fragile. But also the bigger reason was that . . . I just really needed to see her one last time to put this whole chapter of my life behind me. I was desperate for closure, Sweetie, and the only way I felt I could get that was to see Celia face-to-face, to tell her it was over to her face. So when she asked to meet, I said yes. Once we did, I told her right away that I wasn't interested. That I only had eyes for you." He waited, watching her expression, seeing how she was taking it. "And seeing Oliver and Elijah and everything that happened with them . . . I began to realize that it was completely stupid to turn my face away from true love. So what if it was unexpected? So what if you and I make absolutely no sense on paper? So what if I'm doomed to be unhappy because I suck at relationships and I'll probably mess this up along the way? Like I'm already messing it up? For now it works. It's *right*. And I know now I'm damn lucky to have you. For as long as you'll have me. I'm done being afraid."

She shook her head and looked down at her feet. "But why didn't you just tell me all this before?"

Ashish swallowed. "I thought that it would be better if I could tell you once everything was wrapped up. I could just say, 'Hey, this thing with Celia is completely behind me now.' I'd have closure, and it'd be completely honest. I already knew I didn't have feelings for her, but she still had this . . . this hold on me, you know? Like the ghost of our relationship was always there when I was with you, and I thought once I just met up with her and got everything out in the open, that ghost would finally dissipate. Plus, I didn't want you to see me as this . . . this weak dude who couldn't deal with his ex. But I realize now that it was stupid of me. Of course you'd want to know if I was talking to her. My brother Rishi's this super-selfless dude, you know? He's always putting everyone else before himself. He's happy doing that, and people love him for that. But me? I'm the opposite. I've always just thought of myself. When I thought about others, it was about them in relation to me. It doesn't come easily to me to think of others. I never really cared about it before—I just thought that's the way I was. Ash, the selfish player who doesn't even want to acknowledge the Indian part of his identity.

"But you . . . Sweetie, you've changed me. And you make me want to continue to change in the best possible ways. I should've just told you everything I was feeling, but I got all idiotic and selfish." He got up and went around to where Sweetie was sitting and knelt before her in front of the swing. Taking her hands, he said softly, "I'm so, so incredibly sorry for hurting you. That was the absolute last thing I ever wanted to do."

Sweetie watched him quietly, with only the occasional chirping cricket breaking the silence between them.

"Really? The *last* thing?" Sweetie asked finally.

He nodded, a little confused by the way she'd said it.

"What about eating a live toad—with warts—or hurting me?" Her dimple made an appearance.

Ashish kept his expression serious, though his heart was leaping like a happy fish. "Did I mention I love *cuisses de grenouilles*?"

"Er . . ."

"French for 'frogs' legs.'"

Sweetie snorted. "Okay. Dancing naked in front of the Bruins or hurting me?"

"The Bruins better get ready to see somethin' really special."

Sweetie giggled. "You're crazy."

"Crazy about you." Ashish held her eye until her smile faded and she was serious too. "I love you."

Sweetie looked like she was choking on something. After a long moment, just when Ashish was thinking he couldn't take the suspense anymore, she said, "Y-you love me?"

He grinned. "Obviously."

She placed her tiny, soft, irresistible hands on his cheeks. He closed his eyes for a moment, reveling. "I love you too, Ashish." She leaned in to kiss his lips, first tentatively, then with more hunger. "Obviously," she whispered against his mouth.

Ashish's grin got even bigger. To be honest, he didn't think he'd ever stop grinning.

Sweetie

Everything was perfect. Sweetie didn't know if Suki, Kayla, and Izzy would think she was being soft by forgiving him. But this felt right to Sweetie. And that was all that mattered. He'd apologized. He'd given her an explanation that she felt was the honest, right one. He'd told her a little bit about the hard time Celia had been having at college, and she was glad Celia had had Ashish to turn to. (Andddd she was glad their whole text thing was over now. Come on. She was only human.)

But there was still one niggling thing left. Something she had to tell Ashish, so he knew how things were with her, too. So he could be prepared.

They were sitting on the ground now, Sweetie's head on Ashish's lap. He played with her hair, his big fingers warm and comforting.

"Ashish . . . ," she began, feeling suddenly nervous. She wiped her palms on her sweatshirt.

"Hmm?"

"Do you remember me telling you that I wanted to use our free pass on my birthday party?"

"Of course. This weekend. I even have a present all picked out."

"Really?" She grinned up at him but then became serious again. *Focus, Sweetie.* "So, there's something you should know. I wanted to tell my parents about us."

"Yeah, you said. Dude, I'm so prepared. I have my impress-the-parents outfit ready to go. Button-down shirt, khaki pants, the whole nine."

"Great, but listen." Sweetie sat up and met his eye. "Ashish, if my parents say no, if they still don't want us to date . . ." She took a breath. "I'll respect their wishes."

Ashish's expression froze. "You mean you'll break up with me?" he asked in a voice so quiet, so vulnerable, that Sweetie's eyes immediately filled with tears.

She put her hand on his. "I'm sorry," she said, biting her lower lip. "But I just can't go against my parents' wishes. As misguided as they are about some things . . . in the end they matter. A lot." She laughed. "I know it sounds hypocritical after I've dated you behind their backs for the past month. But that was for me to prove something to *myself*, and I have. I know what I've always believed to be true *is* true—my ability to find romantic love isn't tied to my weight. And I'm worth so much more than what bigoted, ignorant people might think."

"So the Sassy Sweetie Project is a success?" Ashish asked, smiling.

"Totally." She laughed and swiped under her eyes. "But now that I've done what I set out to do . . . I need to tell my parents. And if they still don't understand . . ."

"We'll have to break up." Ashish nodded. Took a deep breath. "I get it."

"You do?" Sweetie had expected more pushback, what with him being the original rebel and everything.

"I do. I mean, it totally sucks, but I get it. You're like Rishi in some ways. You're the golden, dutiful Indian child. I guess that's one of the reasons my parents wanted us to date."

Sweetie shook her head. "I don't know about that." She put a hand on his cheek, feeling the light stubble there. "Thank you for understanding. If they don't agree . . . my heart will be broken. Completely."

Ashish stroked her cheek, his eyes honeyed sadness. "Then I guess we'll just have to make this moment really count."

He leaned in to kiss her, and when she tasted salt on his lips, she realized she was crying again.

• • •

Sweetie sat at her desk, looking at the selfie of her and Ashish they'd taken Thursday night at the playground. It was dark, and there were shadows in all the wrong places on their faces, but she could still see the love, the light, shining out of them both. She'd never been this happy. Never.

It was the day of her seventeenth birthday party. She should be bubbling with excitement as she usually was, thinking of all the gifts her parents' friends would bring. Because, to be completely honest, this birthday party thing was really for her parents to socialize with their friends and show off their (or rather, Amma's) party-planning skills. Why else would they throw it on the morning of junior prom? Out of the seventy-five people invited, Sweetie had insisted on only five: Kayla, Suki, Izzy, Anjali Chechi, and Jason Chettan (who were technically both her and Amma's guests). Ashish was the stealth guest of the day; he'd promised not to eat or drink anything, so as not to upset the delicate balance of food/drink-to-guest ratio that Amma had spent months perfecting.

Sweetie's actual birthday wasn't for another two weeks, but her parents had been worried all their friends would be vacationing and wouldn't be able to come. Then who would see and be impressed by the peacock ice sculpture? The fully catered lunch and the open bar? Who? Which was usually fine, because more parental-unit friendlies meant more fabulous presents.

But Sweetie wasn't as excited as she usually was. The day outside was weirdly overcast, which matched her mood pretty well. It could all go horribly wrong today. Sweetie hoped it wouldn't . . . but she also knew Amma. She felt like she'd been training the last month for this one day. This was her big relationship meet.

Ashish had insisted on making a list last night when she'd confessed to him how afraid she really was that things would go completely awry. Ashish was weirdly optimistic for having such a smirky-jock persona. She studied his list with a half smile.

Why Sweetie's Parents Will Love Ashish
and Totally Agree to the D...

- Ashish's cute smile
- Ashish's impeccable sense of dress
- The flowers Ashish will bring for Sweetie's mom
- The toffees Ashish will bring for Sweetie's dad
- The fact that Ashish is a killer ballplayer
- Ashish makes Sweetie happy
- Cute butt

Sweetie laughed when she read that last one. She hadn't seen it last night; he'd obviously added it on when she wasn't looking. She flipped the page to read the list on the back, which she'd written. (Ashish's editorializing was in parentheses.)

Why Sweetie's Parents Will Hate Ashish
and Totally Kick Both Their Butts

- They've dated for more than a month in secret. (But what's a month in the grand scheme of things? Seriously. A month is like a blink to adults. Like half a sneeze.)
- Sweetie hasn't lost any weight since the last discussion with Amma re: dating Ashish. (Your Amma will see

that I think you're the most beautiful girl in the world, so this is a moot point.)

- Amma specifically said no to Ashish . . . not just to dating *any* boy, but specifically to *Ashish*. (Has Amma ever met Ashish? Mm-hmm, didn't think so. My superpower is charming any adult. Not even kidding. Just cross this off your list now.)

~~g, Sweetie~~ folded the page and tucked it into a notebook at the bottom of her drawer. To be honest, she was looking forward to the hiding and lying being over, one way or another. Her phone beeped.

Kayla: I can't believe your parents are throwing this party the day of prom

I know right?

So I have to get my hair and makeup done . . .

WHAT???! You have to come! I told you, A is going to be here. I need support

You think I'd miss that? I just need to leave by 2:30. So if you could spill the beans before then . . . I got the latest appt I could

Thanks. I'll definitely tell them before then. Otherwise I'll burst

So. I hate to be the pessimist but what if they say no? Will you still go to prom?

Idk . . . I thought about it too. If I go I'd have to go without Ashish but Idk if I could

Don't blame you. Love you

Love you too

Sweetie set the phone aside and walked to her closet. She opened the door and stroked the dress she'd be wearing to the party, which was also going to be her prom dress. Two big surprises in one day. Poor Amma.

CHAPTER 31

Ashish

Ashish looked in the floor-length mirror in the corner of his room.

Steel-blue button-down shirt tucked into pants: check (Ma had told him it made his eyes really pop, and dang if she wasn't right).

Khaki pants: check.

Black shoes buffed to a glossy shine: check (and thank you, Myrna, for saving him at the last minute from applying what had actually been car grease instead of shoe polish). (To be fair, Ashish never ventured into that part of the house, and the jars weren't labeled.)

Hair neatly combed instead of stylishly spiked as usual: check.

Face neatly shaved: check.

He smoothed down his shirt and took a deep breath. He'd done everything he could; this was it. In ten minutes he'd be leaving for the party. And then . . . either things would be amazing or they'd flop.

Ashish couldn't see this whole thing with Sweetie ending. He didn't know if he was deeply in denial or what, but how could her parents not see how happy they were together? How could they stick stubbornly to their guns when Ashish turned on the full-throttle charm? Impossible.

He slid his phone out of his pocket and, sitting on the bench at the end of his bed, sent a text.

Whatever happens today . . .

Mein tumse pyaar karta hoon . . .

Pyaar karta tha . . .

Aur pyaar karta rahoonga.

Smiling, he put the phone away. The Hindi lines were cheesy movie dialogue that meant, "I love you, I've loved you, and I'll always love you." But he meant it. God, did he mean it.

There was a brief knock, and then Ma and Pappa stepped in. Ma smiled a little and Pappa put his arm around her shoulder.

"How are you, *beta*?" Ma asked, one hand at her chest.

"Fine. Just a little . . ." He shrugged, trying to downplay the nerves.

"Terrified?" Pappa asked. "Want some Pepto Bismol?"

Ashish glared at him. "No, thank you. I'm not terrified. Merely . . . anticipating."

"Of course you're not terrified," Ma said at the same time that Pappa said, "You know, there's no shame in admitting the fear that can grip the intestines! When I was on the way to ask for Ma's hand in marriage, I almost had to jump off the bus to relieve—"

"Pappa, *please*." Ashish tried not to grimace. "I mean, I really appreciate your, uh, sharing. But I think I'll be okay. I mean, Sweetie's parents have to like me. Everyone likes me when I'm charming. Ma always says that."

Ma came to sit by him on the bench, her silk *salwar* swishing.

"You're right. When you're charming and people see your smile . . . oof. *Chanda-sooraj munh chhupa ke baith jaate hain.*"

Ashish rolled his eyes. "I seriously doubt the moon and the sun hide their faces because of my smile. . . . Oh, wait. Is this one of those over-the-top Hindi things?"

Ma laughed. "Yes." She kissed his cheek and then proceeded to rub off the lipstick. "*Beta*, I want you to know that Pappa and I think you're perfect."

Pappa grunted, which didn't exactly sound like assent, but Ashish rolled with it. "Thank you. Not as perfect as Rishi, but good enough, right?" He smiled and adjusted his cuffs casually to show it was all a joke to him, even if that wasn't strictly true.

Ma frowned. "Ashish . . ."

"It's okay, Ma. I know I haven't been the easiest kid."

"Easy?" This time it was Pappa who spoke up. "No. You're not easy."

Ashish shrugged, like, *Yeah, what'd I say?*

"But," Pappa continued. "You're passionate. You're brave. No one in this family has ever tried to do the things you've done, Ashish, because none of us have the fighting spirit you do."

Ashish stared at Pappa, not able to think of a single word to say.

"Have you ever tried to eat curry that hasn't been seasoned?" Pappa asked, almost aggressively. "It's bland. It's boring. No one likes it." He cleared his throat. "That's what our life would be like without you," he finished gruffly, crossing and then uncrossing his arms.

Ma smiled at him and then at Ashish, tears in her eyes. "I couldn't have put it better myself."

"Wow," Ashish said, looking down at his feet. "Um, thank you. Both of you." He literally could not believe that those words, in that order, had come out of Pappa's mouth. Could it be true? Did his parents really love him just as much as Rishi, even if he was such a pain in the ass? He'd have to think about it more later.

"*Beta*, but are you sure you don't want us to come with you?" Ma asked, pulling him out of his mini reverie.

"You said I was perfect." Ashish smiled. "So how could Sweetie's parents not be won over in about three seconds?"

"True . . . ," Ma continued, putting a hand on his. "But sometimes people can't see past their own—oh, *kaise kehte hain*—hang-ups. The things that make them feel a certain way, but they don't know why. For Sweetie's mother, that is Sweetie's weight. I would hazard that the reason the weight bothers her is because she has some things that weigh on *her* mind, hmm? So in a way, it has nothing to do with Sweetie. Or you."

Ashish hadn't quite looked at it like that. What if Sweetie's parents refused to be charmed by him because of what he represented? Something that bothered them and they couldn't come to terms with that had nothing to do with him or Sweetie? He couldn't control that.

"No, you can't," Pappa said, and Ashish realized he'd spoken that last part aloud. Pappa stepped closer and put a hand on Ashish's shoulder for just a moment. "There are things in life beyond your control, Ashish. You'll only make yourself mad trying to change them."

He looked up into Pappa's face, into those dark, almost-stormy eyes. "So what should I do?"

"Be honest. Own up to your feelings and your actions. Then step back. A man always knows when to step back."

"Uh-uh," Ma said, wagging her finger at Pappa. "A wise *person* always knows when to step back."

Ashish sighed. "I'm not so wise," he said. "But I *am* a person. So at least I have half of this in the bag?"

Ma and Pappa both chuckled. "Best of luck, *beta*," Ma said, getting up. "You have our blessings."

Even a year ago Ashish would've said a blessing was worth about as much as the air you used to say it. But now . . . now it felt different. They'd seen him at his lowest. They'd known what he needed even when he himself didn't. Ashish was grateful for his parents' wisdom. He hugged them and walked out, his heart pounding.

Sweetie had given him her address, but even without that, it wouldn't have been hard to find her house. It was a pale-blue stucco, with a heavy wooden front door that stood wide open. Hordes of mostly Indian people were entering at a steady pace, and Ashish could see that the big living room inside was packed too. Children were shrieking and playing in the side yard and disappearing around back. A waiter in a tux was maneuvering around them with a tray of drinks. Lively Hindi party music played.

Ashish had to park down the street—there was no room nearby, even though he was right on time—and as he got out of the Jeep, his palms got just slightly damp. Wow. Nervous. He'd never been this nervous outside of a basketball game, and even then it had been a long time since that had happened. He swallowed, then picked up the box of toffees, the bouquet of Gloriosa lilies, and the gold-and-purple-wrapped box that contained Sweetie's present. Well, part of it, anyway.

As he walked up to the house, he noticed that most of the people here were in suits and expensive-looking brocade kurtas. Even the teens and middle-school-aged boys were in ties. Dang it. Pappa always said to keep a tie in the dash, just in case. But of course Ashish never listened. He thought that sounded like the stuffiest idea in the world. *Great job, Ash. Your stupid rebellion might just cost you the love of the most amazing girl in the world.*

I'm here, he texted Sweetie as he walked up the driveway.

Then he took a deep breath and followed a family with four shrieking children inside.

Wow. This was . . . intense in a weird way. Ashish had been to a lot of parties with his parents, but this one was a blend of über-high-end, snooty waiters circling with drinks and hors d'oeuvres and extremely middle-class Indian families laughing and joking and letting the children climb all over the furniture and one another (Ashish knew about the latter kind from the rest of his family, who were scattered around the country and India). The waiters kept dodging the kids as they wove around their legs, and the party music kept thumping, making the entire scene look like something from the world's most suburban circus.

A small hand on his arm had him spinning around, a smile on his face. But it wasn't Sweetie. A tiny Indian woman, about Ma's age, looked up at him from behind cat-eye glasses. She was dressed in a cream-colored sari with a golden border. "Hello," she said. "I'm Vidya Nair, Sweetie's mother."

"Oh. *Namaste*, auntie," Ashish said, immediately trying to fold his hands together. Except he was holding a giant pile of things and couldn't quite manage. The bouquet of lilies almost slid out of his grasp and fell on the floor. Crap. Ma would kill him; she'd picked these out with the help of her friend who was an expert on all things botanical. They were apparently very rare and expensive. Doing a dance worthy of the suburban circus, Ashish managed to salvage the flowers and held them out to Sweetie's mom. "These are for you. Special from my mother, Sunita Patel." He smiled in his most charming, can-do way. "I'm Ashish Patel."

Sweetie's mom took the bouquet but didn't look nearly as impressed or pleased as Ma had predicted. Dang. "Yes?" she asked.

It took Ashish a minute, but then he figured it out. She meant "Yes?" as in *And what are you doing here, you chump?* He swallowed. His armpits were starting to prickle with nervous sweat.

"Ashish, you came!"

Ashish turned just in time to see a familiar-looking black girl bound up to him and wrap her hands around his arm. She looked at Sweetie's mom. "This is my good friend Ashish," she explained, tugging his arm with exceptional force for someone her size. He tried not to wince. "So glad you made it," she said to him, smiling savagely now.

That's when it hit him. This was one of the Mafia gang girls from Thursday night. Well, that explained the arm ripping. "Oh, um, yes," he hurried to say. "I, uh, um . . . traffic."

The girl gave him a raised-eyebrow *You're an idiot* look. Oh, well. He was used to that look from girls.

Vidya auntie's face relaxed just a touch. "Kayla, will you please show your friend where to put the present? And have you seen Sweetie?" Her face moved back into frown territory, and Ashish felt bad for Sweetie, wherever she was.

"Not yet," Kayla said. "But I can go up and see if she's in her room?"

"No. I'll do that." And Vidya auntie turned with the determined air of someone who was about to call for a beheading.

Kayla let his arm go and turned to face him, her head cocked. "I'm not sure about you. I mean, I know Sweetie wants you here, but . . . I don't know. I feel like you're the kind of guy who ends every party with a lampshade on your head, hitting on some innocent girl from Minnesota."

Ashish blinked. "Um . . . what?" Did that make sense anywhere except in Kayla's head?

"I don't know. You've just got that look." She paused. "And believe me, there is definitely a type of guy like that."

Ashish pursed his lips and bobbed a slow nod. "Okay. I have, like, zero idea what to do with what you just said. But I *can* tell you I have big plans for me and Sweetie, and none of those involve lampshades or Minnesotan girls."

Kayla laughed. "Fair enough. Let's find the present table."

Sweetie

Sweetie sat in front of her vanity, staring at herself in the mirror. It was time. She just needed to do it. Be brave. Remember the Sassy Sweetie Project.

Her locked doorknob jiggled, and she turned, her heart pounding.

"Sweetie?" Amma said from the other side of the door. "What

are you doing hiding in your room with the door locked? Come on! Guests are here."

"Yes, Amma," she called. "I'll be down in a minute."

"It doesn't look nice to keep them waiting, *mol*," Amma said, her voice all twitchy. She loved throwing parties, but she hated actually having to entertain. It made no sense to Sweetie. "They're asking about you."

"Just finishing up my . . . um, makeup," Sweetie said, looking at her T-shirt in the mirror. "I'm almost done."

"Okay, okay," Amma said, sounding resigned now. "Five more minutes!"

"*Shari*, Amma," Sweetie called, collapsing against the back of her chair in relief. Okay, five more minutes. She could do this.

Her phone beeped.

Anjali Chechi: Flight just landed. On our way soon! You got it, right? Are you wearing it?

Yeah, it came in the mail two days ago. Not wearing it yet. I'm not sure I can do it. Maybe I should just wear the one Amma picked out. I mean, the dress, Ashish, prom—maybe it's all too much on the same day?

Anjali Chechi: I won't force you, Sweetie. But just think about what you'll regret doing: Being a BAMF or not being one?

Sweetie laughed to herself. Not being one.

Anjali Chechi: Smart girl. See you soon. xx

Sweetie rose with a renewed vigor. Ashish had already texted her about five minutes ago. He was downstairs. Poor dude . . . She didn't even want to think how he was coping down there without her.

She took the outfit out of her closet and forced a brave smile. She was Sassy Sweetie. She was a BAMF.

CHAPTER 32

Ashish

Okay, Sweetie's family knew way too many people called Padma. He'd just been introduced to an ancient great-grandma, a middle-aged, slightly angry-looking woman who claimed to be the best entertainment attorney in the state, and a tiny girl with masses of curly hair, and they were all Padma. How was he supposed to remember any of this? *Was* he supposed to remember any of this?

Where was Sweetie?

The suspense was getting to be too much. Ashish felt like he was constantly on display, even though no one really seemed to be paying attention to him. Except for the Mafia girl gang, all of whom had come up and introduced themselves and talked to him a bit. He'd gotten the distinct feeling that they were sizing him up, looking for hints of douchebaggery, but they seemed pretty comfortable with him now. The girl with the braces, who looked to be about twelve, Izzy, had even apologized for calling him Ass-sheesh that night. (And for calling him Pa-hell, which he hadn't known she'd called him until she told him and then blushed bright red when she realized she'd only called him that behind his back; apparently the girl had a talent for mean puns.)

He just wanted to get this show on the road. He wanted to tell Sweetie's parents exactly who he was and why he was here and lay it all out for them.

Sighing, he wandered over to the bottom of the stairs and happened to glance up.

The world shrank. There was only her.

Sweetie stood at the top of the stairs, her eyes closed, her lips moving like she was praying or talking to herself or something. She wore this bright-yellow Indian outfit—Ashish thought it was called an Anarkali, but he wasn't sure—which was basically like a long, ankle-length dress with fitted pants underneath. The top of the dress was a halter, and the area around her throat and chest was covered in tiny diamonds that caught the light and shimmered with the tiniest movement. Her bare arms were smooth, fists clasped at her sides. That amazing mint-scented hair was in loose curls, hanging past her shoulders like a shiny black waterfall.

Ashish stared. He shouldn't; he knew that. She was obviously having a private moment before she came downstairs. But he couldn't help it.

She was a goddess. She was . . . pure beauty. Pure love. She was everything he'd never wanted but had to have.

She was everything, period.

Sweetie

She was terrified, period.

Out-of-her-skin terrified, actually, if you wanted to get technical.

It literally felt like her heart, her muscles, her bones, all of her internal organs, wanted to exit her body and make a run for it. Just to not be there.

Why had she decided to do all of this on the day of her party? Why?

She opened her eyes, resigned to going downstairs and torpedoing . . . oh, *everything*.

She opened her eyes and looked right into Ashish's. And the world shrank.

He was staring at her in absolute wonder. The way you stare at a double rainbow. The way the earth stares at the sun. The way that squirrel outside had stared at the peanut-butter-covered pinecone she'd set out for it last winter. Reverentially, like he couldn't believe his luck.

Sweetie smiled, and he actually grasped the banister, like she'd almost knocked him over.

Right. *This* was why she was doing all of it. Ashish Patel. He was not the *only* why, but he was a big part.

Sweetie descended the staircase toward his waiting arms.

"Hi," she whispered, walking up as close to him as she dared.

He stepped closer, smiling down at her. "Hi."

Her heart stuttered. He looked amazing. That shirt with those eyes—OMG. And he smelled . . . mmm. Lemons and something spicy. "You look—" she began just as he said, "Pulchritudinous."

She paused and then laughed. "What?"

"It's an SAT word I've always had trouble remembering. It means 'beautiful,'" Ashish murmured, his eyes roving her face in a hungry way that made her bones all jellified. "But I don't think I'll forget again. You . . ." He shook his head. "You have the power to reduce me to vapor." He trailed a finger lightly down Sweetie's arm and she shivered, unable to look away. "My heart is yours, Sweetie Nair. Completely."

There were a million people around them. Her parents were tucked away somewhere. Children shrieked; a glass shattered. The sound system was playing a remixed version of "Sheila ki jawani," one of the most horrendous Bollywood songs ever created. And still, somehow, Sweetie felt drunk with the magic of first love.

She took a breath. Touched Ashish lightly on the chest. She imagined she felt his heart thumping feverishly against her finger-tips. "Obviously," she said, her face completely serious, "I love you, Ashish Patel."

He smiled. "Obviously I love you too."

"So what's the plan?" he asked, once she'd led him to the unoccupied study. She left the door open because she didn't want any of the nosy uncles or aunties telling Amma that her daughter had ensconced herself in a closed room with a boy. Or worse, for Amma to find them like that.

"I'm just waiting for Anjali Chechi to get here," Sweetie said, twirling a lock of her hair around her index finger.

"Your favorite cousin, right? The orthopedic surgeon?"

Sweetie smiled, pleased that he remembered. She'd mentioned Anjali Chechi only once or twice before. "Yeah. And her husband's really cool too. You'll like him."

"So they're sort of like buffers between me and your parents?"

"Human shields, more like," Sweetie murmured.

"Hey." Ashish put a hand on her arm. "Whatever happens, it's all going to be okay. I promise."

She smiled and stepped back a little.

He frowned and took his hand away. "You all right?"

"Yeah." She laughed, feeling her cheeks heat up. "Um, I've just always had a thing about my arms, you know? I never leave them uncovered."

Ashish looked at her steadily. "You're beautiful. And your arms are beautiful."

She studied his expression and realized she believed him.

"Sweetie!" They both turned to see Achchan walk in, grinning widely. "How's my birthday girl?"

Sweetie laughed as he put an arm around her and kissed her cheek, his mustache prickling her skin. "It's not my birthday for another two weeks, Achcha."

"Right, right. Today is all about the presents, your favorite part!" Then he took in her outfit, his eyes widening. "Beautiful!"

Sweetie smiled and tugged at her Anarkali. "Thank you." Achchan was clueless. He had no idea of the entire mini war Sweetie and Amma had waged about this. "Oh, and, Achcha, I'd like you to meet Ashish Patel."

Achchan's eyebrows wrinkled, like he was sure he'd heard that name somewhere. But he shook Ashish's hand anyway. "Hello, hello! Do you go to Sweetie's school?"

"No, uncle. I go to Richmond Academy." Sweetie felt a swell of pride at Ashish's firm, confident handshake.

"Ashish is their star basketball player," Sweetie said, putting a hand on his arm and then taking it off quickly when she realized what she was doing. WITH. ACHCHAN. RIGHT. THERE. "But he's too modest to say that."

Ashish laughed, looking down at her with so much admiration and pure love, her bones filled with helium and she almost floated off into the stratosphere. "That's funny coming from the track star of Piedmont."

Achchan looked from Sweetie to Ashish and then back at her again, a slight crinkle between his eyebrows, like he was trying to figure something out. Sweetie looked steadily at him, her heart pounding. If he asked her, she'd tell him the truth.

"There you are!"

Sweetie turned at the familiar-as-her-favorite-Hello-Kitty-pajamas female voice to see Anjali Chechi come bouncing in, Jason Chettan close on her heels. Anjali Chechi was always full of a kinetic, effervescent energy. Even her curly hair was exuberant—it reached out in all directions from her head like it just couldn't bear to be contained, even though she'd tried to tame it into a bun at the nape of her neck.

Her grin was at a thousand percent as she gathered Sweetie in a hug and then held her at arm's length. "Oh my God," she said, her eyes shining. "You're a vision. Seriously."

Sweetie smiled shyly. "Thank you for getting this for me."

Anjali Chechi waved her off. "You were the brains of the operation. I was merely the muscle." She turned to Achchan with a smile. *"Namaskaram."*

"Anjali, Jason!" Achchan said, beaming. He thought of Anjali Chechi as his adopted daughter. "Have you tried the chili prawns appetizer? They're serving them in small glasses! Let me show you."

Anjali Chechi laughed as Achchan led her away.

Jason Chettan put his thumbs in his pockets. "So, uh, has your mom seen you in this yet?"

Sweetie sighed. "Not yet. I'm sort of hiding in here. This is Ashish, my . . . friend."

Jason Chettan reached out and grasped Ashish's hand. He was short, only five feet five, and Ashish towered over him. "I know that description's not *completely* true, but we can stick with that for now." He winked.

Ashish grinned. "At least we have you for support. Sweetie tells me this is going to get intense."

Jason Chettan whistled low and long. "Oh, yeah. Vidya Ammayi is . . . ah, let's say very particular about the way she sees things."

Sweetie groaned. "Speaking of . . . I should go say hi and get it over with. I want to give her space to freak out about my outfit before we tell her about us."

Ashish reached out and squeezed her hand. "Okay. We're telling her after lunch?"

Sweetie gulped and nodded. "Yep. Exactly ninety minutes to go." She looked at Jason Chettan. "Will you keep Ashish company while I go make the rounds?"

"Of course." Jason Chettan grinned. "He probably needs a lot of lessons on how to stay alive while dating someone in this family."

Sweetie swatted him on the back, gave Ashish a *Love you, see you in a few to prepare for battle* look, and left the study.

It took Sweetie twenty-two minutes to walk around the house before she found Amma because she kept getting stopped. She didn't even have a chance to go out into the backyard and see the giant peacock ice sculpture. People wished her a happy birthday and asked her about her grades (the ubiquitous Indian question), her plans for college (ditto), and her plans to lose weight (tritto). Each time her answers were the same: "Thank you," "They're great," "Not sure yet," and "None whatsoever." The aunties and uncles seemed dissatisfied with the fact that running hadn't helped her lose weight and that she didn't seem particularly interested in doing so, but Sweetie would smile, press her hands together, and move on after five minutes.

Finally she ran into Amma in the kitchen, telling a waiter to shelve the appetizers so guests didn't lose their appetite for lunch.

"Sweetie, *mol*, I've been looking everywhere for you," she said, bustling up to Sweetie. And then she stopped.

Sweetie's heart raced as she watched Amma's face slacken as she took in Sweetie's outfit, a slow drag from top to bottom and back again. "What is this?"

Sweetie straightened her shoulders. "My Anarkali. The one I told you I wanted."

"Go upstairs this minute and change." Amma's voice was a hiss, low and biting. "This is not how we behave in front of guests."

"Amma, I'm not changing," Sweetie said. Her heart was pounding so hard, her voice actually wobbled with the effort of trying not to hyperventilate. "I'm wearing this. You don't have a problem with Sheena wearing halters."

"Sheena doesn't need to cover her body," Amma said, looking around frantically. "Sweetie, people are going to laugh at you. They're going to make fun of you."

It was the same old conversation, the same path they'd walked thousands of times since Sweetie was little. She knew why Amma was so insistent. She was genuinely afraid for Sweetie. She wanted to protect her. She thought differently from other parents, the ones who showed off their imperfect kids flamboyantly and proudly, with no regard for what society might think of them. To Amma, *those* parents were in the wrong. She'd never understand how exposing your child to possible ridicule might be a strong thing to do or a way to give a middle finger to the world. To Amma, the world was cruel, and her only daughter had to be protected at all costs.

Sweetie took a step toward her mother. "I don't care if they laugh at me, Amma. Will it hurt my feelings? Probably. Will it make me cry? Maybe. But don't you see? Covering myself up, telling myself I can't show my skin because I'm not good enough to do that, is way worse for me. I can't live like that. I can't constantly feel like half a person because of my weight. I need you to see that. I need you to love me as I am. Please." As she finished, her throat was tight and painful and tears dripped down her cheeks. She didn't bother to wipe them away.

Amma stared at her. "You think I don't love you as you are?" She looked away and shook her head slightly. Then, turning to Sweetie, she asked, "Have you been in the backyard?"

Sweetie frowned, slightly confused. "Not yet. Why?"

Amma took her hand firmly and began to lead her to the back door. "*Varu.* Come."

Sweetie followed Amma in a complete daze. What was she doing? They stepped outside and Sweetie saw the giant peacock in the corner, sweating in the heat. And then she turned.

It sat proudly on a table, surrounded by ecstatic children. "The chocolate fountain," Sweetie said softly. An enormous one too, just like she wanted. "You got it."

Amma looked at her steadily. "Yes. Because you wanted one. And because I . . ." She swallowed. "Sweetie, you are my daughter, my *mol*."

Sweetie heard what Amma was saying: *I love you. You're everything I care about in this world.*

She smiled, her eyes filling with tears. "Then please understand, Amma, that I am happy like this. I'm happy being fat. To me, 'fat' isn't a bad word. It's other people who've made it like that. It's as much a part of me as being an athlete or Indian American or a girl. I don't want to change it, and I don't want to hide it. *I'm* not ashamed, even if you are."

"I am not ashamed of you," Amma said fiercely. "I could never be ashamed of you."

Sweetie looked at her feet and then back up at Amma. A small toddler girl pushed between them and went running off toward the ice sculpture. "But you didn't want me to date Ashish Patel. Because I wasn't thin enough for him."

Amma sighed. "The Patels are very different from us, Sweetie. When you deal with people like that, you have to be image conscious. Otherwise, the rumors are vicious."

"But that's what I'm trying to say. That's about other people. Sunita auntie wanted me to date Ashish. *You* were the one who said no. You have to let go of your fear of what other people will say, Amma. At least when it comes to me. Because when you try to hide me, it tells me you're ashamed of me. That you think I'm not as good as other people's kids."

Amma put her hand on Sweetie's arm. "I have the best daughter. The best. I am not asham—"

"Vidya!"

There was a beat, and Sweetie's heart swelled with hope. What? What had Amma been about to say?

"Vidya. Hello!"

Reluctantly, they turned to see Tina auntie walking up to them, wearing a turquoise sari.

"Oh, hello, Tina," Amma said, smiling. "I'm so happy you could come! Where's Vinod?"

Vinod was Tina auntie's husband, who appeared to always be in a meeting. "In a meeting," Tina auntie said, and Sweetie bit her cheek to keep from smiling. "And Sheena couldn't come. She had another party to go to." Turning to Sweetie, she said, "Happy birthday, Sweetie."

"Thank you, Tina aun—"

"Oh." Tina auntie pursed her lips as she caught sight of something behind Sweetie's back. "Chocolate fountain?"

Amma smiled. "Yes. Sweetie really wanted one."

Tina auntie's lips got even thinner, until they were barely visible at all. "Want or not want, we must give our children what they need," she said. Sweetie felt her cheeks heat up, half with embarrassment and half with anger. She knew what was coming. Looking Sweetie up and down, Tina auntie added, "Without proper coverage, it's obvious Sweetie's weight is—"

Sweetie opened her mouth to excuse herself, but Amma spoke before she could. "Tina, that is enough."

Sweetie snapped her mouth shut and stared at Amma in shock. Tina auntie mirrored her expression.

"You will not speak to my daughter or me that way," Amma said, straightening her shoulders. "You are a guest in our home. Please do not overstep your bounds." Putting an arm around Sweetie, Amma continued. "Come, *mol.*"

As they walked away, Sweetie shook her head. "Amma . . . wow. That was . . . that was . . ."

"Belated," Amma said. "I should have been standing up for you a long time ago, Sweetie." They came to a stop under a shady oak.

Sweetie smiled tearfully. "It's okay, Amma." She took a deep breath and plunged ahead. "And, um, I have something to tell you. I was going to save it for later, but . . ." She swallowed. Looked across the backyard. And saw Ashish watching. She waved him over.

Amma turned to see him and then turned back to Sweetie, her eyes narrowing, her earlier softness evaporating. *"Enta ithe?"*

"I'll explain everything," Sweetie said quietly as Ashish came to stand beside her. "You might want to call Achchan over too."

Amma looked from Ashish to her, her face hard. "Let us talk in the study." She turned and strode off without waiting for Sweetie or Ashish.

CHAPTER 33

Ashish

Seeing Sweetie's face fall as Vidya auntie strode away was the worst thing. She looked like one of those chocolate Easter bunny GIFs, where someone turns on a blow-dryer and melts its face off. Sweetie's face practically touched the ground.

"Hey." He put a hand on her arm. "It'll be okay."

She smiled at him, but he could see the effort that she was putting into it. "We were having such a good conversation, you know? We were really connecting. I *thought* we were, anyway. I thought she was finally seeing things my way."

"Maybe she still will," Ashish said. "You know? This ain't over yet."

Sweetie snorted. "You sound weird when you say 'ain't.'"

"Do I? I can't pull it off?" he asked as they began to walk inside. "Huh. I always thought I had sort of a Dean Winchester vibe."

Sweetie laughed. They passed by Anjali and Jason, both of whom were talking to an older Indian couple. Sweetie put her hand on Anjali Chechi's back. When she turned, Sweetie said, "Study. Now. Please."

Kayla, who'd been grabbing a new mango juice at the bar, walked up to them. "Hey, hey." Then, seeing Sweetie's expression, she added, "Uh-oh. Is it time?"

Sweetie nodded once. "She wants to see us in the study."

Kayla winced. "Ooh. Do you want me to come?"

Sweetie sighed. "No. I think she wants it to be a private, family-only thing. Even Anjali Chechi and Jason Chettan are going to be pushing it."

Kayla hugged her. "Okay. Well, you tell me if you change your mind. I'll hang around close by."

Sweetie closed her eyes and hugged her friend back. "Thanks."

Their grim party of four walked to the study and closed the door behind them. This being a regular house, there was barely enough room for all six of them to fit comfortably. Ashish stuck close to Sweetie, figuring she'd need the support. He wiped his palms surreptitiously on his pants. He had to admit, this didn't look good. The way her parents were staring at him and Sweetie . . . it was like they'd done something way worse than dated for a month without telling them. Like they'd stolen all the penguins from the Antarctic or something. That'd be weird, though.

Whatever happened, Ashish decided, however much her parents yelled, he would hold his tongue and his temper. He'd be respectful to his elders, something his parents had always drilled into him, but that had never really sunk in before now. He wouldn't give Sweetie's parents any more ammunition than they already had. Because he refused to believe that them saying no would be the end of it. Surely they'd come around, right? Or in a week or two Sweetie would realize she couldn't live without him any more than he could live without her? This couldn't be the end. Not when there was so much between them. Not when it seemed like his entire life had been a series of moments leading him to her.

Sweetie's parents looked extremely tense: Vidya auntie sat on a chair with her arms crossed, and Soman uncle leaned against the desk, his hands gripping the edge. Anjali and Jason sat on a futon across from them. Ashish and Sweetie remained standing, close together, by the door.

"What is going on, Sweetie?" Soman uncle asked, looking at her sadly. There was no anger in his gaze, unlike Vidya auntie's.

Sweetie took a deep breath. Ashish could feel the heat wafting off of her, could practically hear her thundering heart. He wanted to reach out and hold her but held still instead. "Achcha, Amma . . . Ashish and I have been dating. For a little over a month."

Vidya auntie got even stiller, if that were possible. Soman uncle looked like he might actually cry.

"After I told you no?" Vidya auntie said finally, shattering the silence that weighed about a thousand pounds. "You went behind my back?"

Sweetie flinched a little at her mother's tone, and Ashish had to clench his fists to keep from reaching for her. "I did," Sweetie said softly. "Because . . . because I felt you were wrong."

Oh God. The look on Vidya auntie's face. He could already tell this was not going remotely according to plan. Ashish surreptitiously slipped his phone out of his pocket.

HELP, he typed, and quickly pressed send. If he knew his parents, the fact that he'd told them not to come probably didn't mean much. They had no respect for his boundaries. But more than that, they were his family, which meant they were always doggedly there for him.

He really, really hoped they hadn't suddenly decided to change.

Sweetie

Sweetie knew what she'd said was really pushing things too far. She'd never told Amma outright before that she was wrong. It was a hugely disrespectful thing to do, but she figured she'd gone this far. She was already confessing to dating Ashish behind their backs for more than an entire month. Why not jump in with both feet? Why not fully be that girl who dared to stand up on that stage and sing her heart out in front of total strangers? Why not be the girl who dared to text Ashish Patel, the Richmond jock, and then dared to challenge him to a race? Why not be Sassy Sweetie completely? If track had taught her anything, it was that you didn't take home the gold unless you completely committed.

There was another beat of silence, and then Achchan spoke. "But . . . why didn't you tell *me, mol*?"

Sweetie's heart broke at the tone of Achchan's voice. He didn't sound thunderously mad like Amma; he just sounded beaten, so completely hurt. She knew what he was trying to ask: How had she allowed this giant secret to grow between them? Achchan and she, twin souls, had never been so far apart as they were at this moment. And it was all because of her. Because of the choices she'd made. "I . . ." She swallowed, trying to blink back tears. "I wasn't trying to hurt your feelings, Achcha," she said finally. "I just didn't know what else to do. I—"

"I, I, I!" Amma said. "Selfish. This is what you are, Sweetie. So selfish. The decisions you've made have been only to benefit you! You didn't think of your family once! You just wanted to go gallivanting around with this boy"—she thrust her chin at Ashish—"and you didn't care about anything else."

"Wait a second, Ammayi," Anjali Chechi said, shaking her head. "That's not fair. Sweetie has the option to be selfish. She's not quite seventeen years old. If she can't think about what she wants in this life now, when can she?"

Amma waved her hand. "That kind of American mind-set has no place in this home."

Sweetie felt her heart break even more. "So you're saying someone like me has no place in this home," she said quietly. "Whether you mean to or not, Amma, that's exactly what you're saying. I'm Indian, yes. I respect my culture, yes. I love my parents, yes. But I love myself, too. I respect myself, too." How was it possible that she and her mother fell on opposite sides of this one, more-important-than-anything issue?

Achchan stepped forward. "We would never say that you have no place in our home or even think it. You're our only child." He turned to Amma and raised his eyebrows.

"There's no need for all this drama," Amma said. "Sweetie, I have told you. You are my daughter. But you have lied to us for a month. There is nothing more to say. I don't know what ideas this boy filled your head with and what all he made you do—"

Ashish cleared his throat and Sweetie looked at him, wide

eyed. *Please don't say anything*, she tried to transmit psychically. *You'll only set this train wreck on fire.* But if he got the message, he didn't listen. "Auntie, if I may," he said in a voice that was both firm and respectful. Sweetie would have to take notes on how he did that. When she tried to be firm and respectful, it just came out all squeaky. "Sweetie and I have done nothing that we are ashamed of. To be honest, my parents knew about us dating. They were on board, and although they weren't enthused about the fact that you both didn't know, they made sure nothing untoward happened. In fact, they made us sign a contract. We went on three dates that were fully parent sanctioned. Of course, we did meet up on one or two other occasions, but again, nothing happened that would make me hesitate to look you both in the eye." He squeezed Sweetie's hand briefly before letting it drop again. "Sweetie is a remarkable person. She's taught me so much about myself. She's taught me what it means to be kind and gentle while also pursuing what you know is right in your heart. I have never met anyone like her."

By the time he stopped speaking, everyone was staring at him, openmouthed. Sweetie wondered if he knew the kind of effect he had on people. Not just on girls, but on people in general. Ashish was the kind of guy who made you pause and listen when he spoke. His words, confident and strong, were clad in iron.

Achchan grunted. "Well, I—"

There was a knock on the door.

Looking just as confused as the rest of them, Jason Chettan opened the door. Ashish's parents traipsed in, dressed like royalty. Sunita auntie's face immediately creased into a smile as she gathered

Sweetie into a hug and then stroked Ashish's hair, before turning to Achchan and Amma. She pressed her palms together.

"Hello again, Vidya," she said earnestly. "Please allow me to apologize for stopping by uninvited. Sweetie did tell us this was a family event, but I really wanted to speak with you in person about everything that's happened, and I knew Ashish was here. . . ." She paused. "Oh, my manners have deserted me today. This is my husband, Kartik."

Kartik uncle shook hands with Achchan, who looked like he might faint. "You're . . . Kartik Patel," he said, as if he'd just made the connection. "Of Global Comm."

Kartik uncle smiled. "Yes indeed. And Ashish tells me you yourself are in engineering? I had wanted one of my sons to go into the profession, but alas, neither of them shows any aptitude at all!"

Achchan beamed. Amma looked by turns discombobulated and furious, as if she had no idea whether to welcome the Patels like a good host or to kick them out.

Sunita auntie stepped closer to her and put a hand on her arm. "Vidya, I take it that Ashish and Sweetie have told you about them dating." Looking straight into Amma's eyes, she continued seriously. "I am so sorry that we encouraged the children to date behind your backs. Our intention was never to disrespect you or undermine your authority. You see, Kartik and I thought long and hard about it, and in the end we felt that when teenagers are determined, they'll find a way to do what they want to do." She studied Amma's expression, which was still stony, and continued valiantly on. "I didn't think, from talking to you, that you disapproved of Ashish or our family. Simply of . . . Sweetie's physical appearance as compared to our son's. That's why we agreed to this at all. But through everything, we wanted to make sure they didn't do anything we wouldn't be able to tell you about. They went to the mandir on their first date." She smiled. "And then to the Holi Festival, and then to visit Ashish's Gita Kaki in Palo Alto."

Amma looked from one face to the next. Sweetie's heart thudded as she waited for her mother to speak, to say something, anything. Finally Amma spoke, her voice trembling. "But Sweetie and Ashish are not compatible. How can they be when Sweetie is . . . ?" Turning to Ashish, she said more firmly, "Sweetie has a lot of self-respect. She won't just do whatever you want because she's . . . she is not . . ."

Ashish shook his head. "I think Sweetie is the most beautiful girl I've ever seen, auntie. I promise you, when I look at her, I can't believe that I got so lucky. I would never disrespect her. Never."

Amma looked around at them all. Sweetie held her breath; this felt like a turning point. Amma had to see Sweetie's side now. She *had* to.

Shaking her head, Amma said, "You are trying to manipulate me, Sweetie. You think by inviting Sunita and Kartik Patel here, I'll change my mind?" Her eyes flashed. "This is over! I forbid it!" Then she turned and stalked out of the study.

Everyone froze as the door slammed behind her. Ashish reached out to squeeze Sweetie's hand. Her lower lip trembled and she bit it, her eyes filling.

People began to speak all at once.

Ashish: "It's okay, my love—"

Sunita auntie: "Oh, Sweetie, she'll change—"

Kartik uncle: "Do you have any Pepto Bis—"

Anjali Chechi: "Ridiculous—"

Jason Chettan: "Give her some time—"

Achchan: "Let me just go and see what she's—"

"No," Sweetie said suddenly, loudly, her voice sluicing through the air. They all stopped to look at her. "I'll go," she said, meeting each of their gazes one by one. "Let me go speak to her."

"Are you sure?" Ashish said. "Do you want me to come with you?"

Sweetie smiled a little. "No. I need to do this by myself."

There was utter silence in that tiny room packed to the gills with Patels and Nairs as Sweetie swept out after her mother.

Amma was in Sweetie's room, as Sweetie knew she'd be. She was looking at all the track trophies Sweetie had won over the years. Sweetie watched her from the doorway for a silent moment before walking in and closing the door behind her.

"Amma," she said, twisting her hands together in front of her and then forcing herself to stop. She had nothing to be nervous about. She was right; she knew she was. This was her moment to be honest, to be brave, like she'd always wanted to be. To let her words match her thoughts, to finally stand up for herself. To be Sassy Sweetie. "What was that about? Why are you so upset?"

Amma stroked one of the trophies on Sweetie's shelf and smiled. "I remember when you first told me you wanted to join the track team. You were in fourth grade. I took you to try out for the Atherton Kids Athletic Team, do you remember?"

Sweetie shook her head. "I never ran for them."

Amma's smile faded. "No, you didn't. When we got there, the coach took me aside. He told me you were too . . . 'unhealthy' to run. He said it was a medical matter. If something happened to you, the organization would be liable."

Sweetie felt her cheeks flush. "He was an idiot, then."

"I took you back home," Amma continued, as if Sweetie hadn't spoken. "I told you the team was full. When you got to middle school and decided to try out without telling me, I couldn't stop you. I thought maybe you should do golf or shot put. But you had your heart set on running. And when you got on the team, you were so proud. Then two months later I got the call from your coach."

Sweetie remembered the call. She'd begged Coach not to call Amma, but she hadn't listened. There were two girls on the team who bullied Sweetie incessantly. Coach had gotten involved as much as she could, but the girls were mean only when she wasn't looking, and Sweetie refused to tell on them. Finally, when Coach had found her crying yet again in the locker room, she'd said she had no choice but to get Amma involved. "You tried to take me off the team," Sweetie said.

"To protect you." Amma turned to face her. "To keep you safe."

"I didn't need you to do that," Sweetie said. "I joined again anyway. I forged that letter from you, remember? Coach let me back on. I became the strongest, fastest runner, and then the girls didn't bother me so much anymore."

"You had a happy ending that time," Amma said. "A lucky happy ending. It won't always be like that, Sweetie. Life is not lucky or happy for girls and women who are different."

Sweetie studied Amma thoughtfully. "How do you think life would be different for me if I were thin right now, Amma?"

"You'd have more opportunities," Amma said.

"You would want me to be appreciated for my talents, right? For people to see past my outer appearance to who I am inside?"

Amma nodded.

"You'd want me to be asked to prom, to go to a good college, to find love and friendships?"

Amma nodded again.

Sweetie shook her head. "Don't you see, Amma? I already have all that. I was up on a stage, singing my heart out, and people *got to their feet to applaud* because they wanted more. I have friends who'd stand by me through anything. I'm going to get into a great school because I have some of the highest grades in my class *and* I kick butt as an athlete. I have a boy who loves me with all his heart, who came here with his parents to win yours. And guess what? I don't need Sheena's charity because Ashish asked me to the prom. See, Amma? I already have everything you want for me. I have it all, and I have it as a fat girl. I'm not afraid to live my life as I am *right now*. I don't need to change. I'm not afraid, so why are you?"

Amma and she stared at each other for a long time. Finally Amma spoke, her voice hoarse. "Ashish is in love with you?"

"He is. And I'm in love with him."

"And he asked you to the prom?"

"Yes."

"You got a standing ovation . . . at Band Night?"

Sweetie nodded.

Amma sank onto Sweetie's bed, her hands limp in her lap. "You didn't tell me that. Sweetie . . ."

"Yes, Amma?" Sweetie sat too, across from her mother.

When Amma looked at her, tears sparkled in her eyes and she

smiled, blinking them away. "Sweetie . . . you are already doing it," she said wonderingly, shaking her head. "You already have everything I want you to have." She swallowed, and added in a tiny voice, "And I missed everything. Because of my stubbornness, I missed everything."

"You missed *some* pretty big things," Sweetie agreed, scooting closer. "But, Amma, you don't have to miss anything else, not if you don't want to. And you're right, you know. I do already have everything you want me to have. So you don't have to worry about me anymore, Amma. It's not doing anyone any good. You have to stop worrying."

Nodding, Amma closed her eyes as a tear slipped down her cheek. "I have to stop worrying," she said softly. Then, opening her eyes, she pulled Sweetie toward her and tucked her face against her neck. She kissed the top of Sweetie's head and said, "I have to stop worrying because you're okay. You're going to be fine."

"I'm going to be more than fine," Sassy Sweetie said. "Amma, I'm going to live my best life."

They walked downstairs together, and Amma walked right to the Patels (who were now in the dining room with Achchan, Anjali Chechi, and Jason Chettan, looking rather glum) and said, "Sunita, Kartik, Ashish, I apologize. I behaved badly, and you have been gracious. Will you please forgive me?"

Sunita auntie gave Amma her warmest smile. "As long as you forgive us, too."

Amma turned to Ashish. "You. You have been very good to my daughter."

"I've tried," Ashish said, looking at Sweetie in complete shock. She shrugged back and grinned. "But it's nothing more than she deserves."

Amma smiled. "Correct answer. Good."

"And, Auntie, Uncle," Ashish said, looking at Amma and Achchan in turn. "I want to apologize, too. For dating Sweetie behind your backs. It won't happen again."

Achchan grinned and clasped Ashish on the back.

Amma let out a deep breath and grabbed one of Ashish's hands and one of Sweetie's. "Now everything is settled. Why don't we all have some lunch? We have Sweetie's favorite dessert—*pal payasam*. And after that, my daughter needs to get ready for prom!"

Sunita auntie laughed. "That sounds like the perfect way to celebrate."

"Wait." Achchan stood. "I have something to say." He walked forward, took Sweetie by the shoulders, and led her a few feet away, to a quiet corner. Then, taking a deep breath, he shook his head. "Sweetie . . . you are a piece of my heart. I never knew how much pain you were in. I should've said something. I should've told you that I . . . I disagreed with your mother a lot. I think you are perfect as you are. As long as you're happy, I'm happy. I'm sorry, *mol*, for not being stronger for you."

Sweetie hugged her father, her throat painfully tight. "It's okay, Achcha," she said hoarsely. "It's okay."

As they trooped outside to lunch, the girls came running up, their faces anxious. It was clear they'd been watching the back door like hawks. "So?" Kayla asked. "How'd it go? You need us to drive your getaway mobile?"

Sweetie laughed as her family passed her on the way to the food table. Ashish was hanging back, a few paces away, trying to give her her privacy. "No. It went well. Really, really well."

Her friends, her girls, grinned at her. And then they were all hugging and laughing. "Yo, Ass-sheesh!" Izzy called. "You're one of us now. Okay?"

"Does that mean your shoes are staying on?" he called back dryly.

"My mom ordered a *lot* of food, you guys," Sweetie said, laughing. "Please eat or she'll be foisiting heaping plates on you before long."

"You don't have to tell me twice," Suki said, and she led the charge to the buffet table.

Once they were gone, Sweetie turned to Ashish, a shy smile on her face. "You know, you're not so bad at laying it on thick. That speech you gave in the study? Impressive."

"And I didn't even have to play my 'cute butt' trump card." Ashish took her hand. "Seriously though, I wasn't laying it on thick. Everything I said, I meant. One hundred percent. I'm the luckiest guy on the planet, Sweetie. Actually, scratch that. I'm the luckiest guy in the multiverse."

Sweetie felt the heat rush to her cheeks. Forget Ashish. How on earth had *she* gotten so lucky?

They decided to leave for prom directly from the birthday party. By the time the last guests had cleared out and Sweetie had opened all the presents (Ashish had given her a simple silver chain, no pendant, which, while beautiful, left her a little disappointed at its genericness), Amma was totally on board with the prom plan.

"I cannot believe he asked you using parrots!" she said as she helped Sweetie do up her hair. Anjali Chechi was redoing her makeup.

Ashish and his parents were out at their car, conferring about something, while Jason Chettan and Achchan were downstairs talking.

Sweetie snorted and adjusted Ashish's silver chain around her throat. "Yeah, it was sort of a disaster. But aren't you glad I'm going to prom?"

"I'm very glad." Amma finished up and stood back to admire her handiwork. "But you're not going with Sheena in her limo?"

Sweetie pulled a face as Anjali Chechi finished putting on the blush and then snapped the case closed. "No. I think we're just taking Ashish's Jeep."

"Sweetie!" Achchan called from downstairs. His voice held a barely suppressed glee. "Come down!"

Amma, Anjali Chechi, and she exchanged curious glances. "Let's go see what's going on," Amma said, shaking her head.

When they got outside, Ashish was standing beside a bright-pink limo, dressed in a tux. He grinned a little nervously as Sweetie stepped down and walked up to him. "What on earth?" she said. "Ashish, you know we could've just taken your Jeep!"

"Ah, it was sort of Ma and Pappa's present," he said, gesturing to where they stood, beaming happily. "As was the tux, which came in the limo, and . . . this." He reached through the open window and pulled out a corsage.

"Pink peonies," Sweetie said, smiling. "My favorite."

Amma's voice stilled Ashish's hands, which were taking the corsage out of the container. "Wait, wait!" Amma, Achchan, Anjali

Chechi, and Jason Chettan came hurrying down the walk. "We have to take photos, Sweetie!"

Sweetie muffled a laugh. "Of course."

"Oh, us too!" Sunita auntie said, hurrying over with Kartik uncle in tow, his phone at the ready.

"Oh God," Ashish whispered to Sweetie, and she said, from behind her smile, "Be nice. It'll be over soon."

And it was. Once the parental units had taken pictures of (a) Ashish putting the corsage on Sweetie's wrist, (b) Sweetie adjusting the corsage, (c) Sweetie *admiring* the corsage, (d) Sweetie and Ashish smiling totally fakely, and (e) Ashish helping Sweetie into the limo, they were alone.

Sweetie sank against the back of the seat and closed her eyes. "Oh. Em. Gee. I feel like I could sleep for a decade."

Ashish said, "And I could look at you for a decade."

She opened her eyes and smiled shyly at him in the dark interior of the car. "It's over," she said, noting the tone of disbelief in her own voice. "They're all on board with us dating. It's official. No more hiding."

Ashish grinned. "No more hiding. So I can do this without worrying who might see." He reached over and took her hand.

"And I can do this without worrying who might see," she said, smiling and putting her head on his shoulder.

"And I can do one more thing," Ashish said, making her lift her head at his mysterious tone. "But I won't let anyone see."

As he took her in his arms, holding her so tight it was like he was reassuring himself that she was really there, like they were really in this moment, Sweetie couldn't stop smiling. And when their lips met, she knew what happiness tasted like.

CHAPTER 34

Ashish

Ashish was nervous now. He'd been building up so much for this afternoon that he hadn't given much thought to after. He hadn't *wanted* to give much thought to after, to be honest, because what if it didn't work out? What if he'd had to go home and chill with Netflix and a bucket of cheese popcorn?

But now here he was, with the most beautiful girl in the world next to him, dancing to the cheesiest songs a DJ could possibly have picked. "Dancing Queen"? Come on.

Sweetie waved a hand in his face. "Hey. Where are you?"

He looked back down at her and his heart constricted. Oh God. He was seriously going to have a heart attack. Ashish Patel was going to have a heart attack because he was nervous around a girl. It was hilarious. Ashish was the king of romantic gestures. Elijah always asked his advice on what to do for Oliver when important dates rolled around (Valentine's Day, Oliver's birthday, National Pancake Day; the last was sort of their thing—long story). Ashish forced a smile. "Ah, here?" He cleared his throat. "Hey, are you, um, enjoying the music?"

Sweetie smiled. Oof. That dimple. "It's not bad." Then she studied his face. "But we can leave if you want to?"

"Ah, actually, I was thinking we could take a walk," Ashish said.

"A walk." Sweetie pulled back to look at him, a small smile on her face. "Where?"

"Just . . . around." He adjusted his bow tie. Oh God. He really was going to pass out. Why had he enlisted *Pinky* in this? What had he been thinking? This was going to be a total disaster. Sweetie was going to dump him on the spot.

"Ashish Patel, what are you up to?"

He looked into Sweetie's eyes and the panic came on like a tsunami. "You know w-what? Actually, let's just, uh, let's stay here. I don't really feel like a walk."

Sweetie put one hand on her hip and, after a pause, pulled him off the dance floor over to the punch bowl. "You're up to something and now you're chickening out. I can tell."

He poured himself a cup of punch and downed it in two gulps. "Okay," he said. "You're right. I . . . There's this . . . I don't know if you'll hate it."

Sweetie looked at him seriously. "Ashish, whatever it is, I promise you I won't hate it. Now, take me there before I hit you."

He held up his hands. "There's no need for violence, Miss Nair."

She put her hand in the crook of his arm and allowed him to lead her outside.

They walked around the side of the building, their shoes crunching in the gravel. Ashish glanced down at her pretty red toes. "Are you sure you can walk in those heels?"

"Yeah." Sweetie waved him off with her free hand. "Years of experience."

They were silent as the sound of the dance petered out, whisked off in the gentle breeze. The hazy moon winked at them.

"So, I want you to know . . . ," Ashish began as the Piedmont track loomed up in front of them. "We've only been dating for a month, which to a lot of people is hardly any time at all, but . . . I feel really strongly about you."

Sweetie laid her head on his arm. "Me too."

"I think you're one of those people who's going to do amazing things with their life." He licked his lips, feeling ridiculously nervous as they neared the opening in the chain-link fence. "And I'm so grateful you're letting me be part of it, Sweetie."

"I'm glad you're part of it," she answered, her voice serious and completely sincere. Ashish's heart thumped with painful, stupid love. She paused as they walked through the opening and passed the bleachers on the way to the track. "Oh, we're at the track—what's that?"

His pulse pounding, Ashish led her closer. He turned to her and took her hands, walking backward as she walked forward, her eyes shining. "This is where we first met. When you challenged me to a duel and slew my heart."

Sweetie tinkled a laugh that was all silver and music. "It wasn't a *duel*," she said, rolling her eyes, though she was still grinning. Then she looked down, under their feet. "Are these flower petals?"

"Yes," Ashish said, and then added quickly as she bent down, "But don't examine them too closely. Pinky being Pinky, she wouldn't let me use fresh flower petals. So we went to some florist after hours and took all their old, janky flowers they didn't sell. . . ." It occurred to him that that wasn't the most *romantic* story he could've told. "Uh, anyway." He helped her back up. Putting his hands on the sides of her face, he gazed deep into those bottomless hazel eyes. "Sweetie, I love you. I thank the universe or the fates or whoever's in charge every day for bringing you to me."

"Ashish." She sighed, her sweet breath blowing over his chin, leaving him slightly dazed. "Me too. I'm so glad your dad made us sign those contracts."

He laughed and reached into the pocket of his tux. "I have something for you. It's sort of the second part of your birthday present, but I didn't want to give it to you in front of everyone else." He brought out the square deep-blue velvet box and opened it.

Her eyes went satisfyingly wide, and her lips parted in a small O.

Ashish's heart thrilled at the thought that she already liked it. She hadn't even seen the best part yet.

Sweetie

Sweetie gazed at the cameo pendant, nestled in inky-black silk. It was stunning, with a pale-turquoise background and a white figure on top. Sweetie frowned. There was something . . . Leaning forward, she reached out and carefully picked it up. The figure wasn't a woman's profile in silhouette, as they usually were on cameo pendants. This one featured a curvaceous fat woman standing triumphantly with her hands on her rounded hips, her feet apart, hair blowing in the wind. Sweetie grinned, delighted. "Oh! She's so badass!"

Ashish smiled. "Turn it over."

Sweetie did. On the back, inscribed there on the silver, were the words:

sassy sweetie
to know her is to love her

Sweetie traced the words over with trembling fingers, watching as tears splashed onto them. She looked up at Ashish.

He took a step forward, his face worried, those honey eyes searching. "Hey, it's okay. If you don't like it—"

She put a hand on his cheek, smiling through her tears. "I *love* it. Ashish, this is . . . this is everything. You get me. You get *all* of me."

His face relaxing into a smile, Ashish cupped the back of her neck with a big, warm hand and drew her gently to him. "Obviously."

Sweetie laughed, a hiccuping, giddy thing. "Obviously."

They kissed, the smell of roses floating around them, encasing them in here, in now, in forever.

Sweetie

Sweetie ran across the finish line, her hands in the air. The crowd cheered; her entire body lit up with that intoxicating soup of endorphins and adrenaline. She'd done it. She faced the crowd, her hands still in the air, her grin as big and bright as it would go, enough to power the stadium, she was sure.

She'd beaten her best time. The scout from UCLA was there, and Sweetie wasn't even nervous. They'd want her. How could they not?

Her eyes raked the audience in the bleachers, lighting on Amma's and Achchan's proud faces and then on Ashish's. He was grinning and waving like mad, his hooting and hollering reaching her like he was standing right beside her. She laughed at the way the other parents were looking at him, this enthusiastic Piedmont track fan in his Richmond basketball uniform. They were headed to Richmond right after this; of course his game had to be on the same night as her race. But he'd come anyway.

"I wouldn't miss it for anything," he'd said simply when she'd asked if he was sure.

And after his game . . . the ultimate test. Sweetie swallowed. The scout didn't make her nervous, but *that* did.

Ashish

This was it.

It was the last game of the regular season, with only one basket between Ashish and state.

Eleven seconds left. Oliver caught the rebound and looked to Ash for direction. With one eye on the clock, Ashish called the play and moved his team toward the basket.

Nine seconds. Sharing a grin with Ash, Oliver turned and over-undered the ball to Elijah.

Seven seconds. The defenders closed in on Elijah as Ash dodged into the open, calling for the ball.

Four seconds. Elijah bounced to Ashish, relief all over his face.

Two seconds. Ashish sprinted across the three-point line. The final basket. It was up to him.

As Ashish ran, the sounds of the chanting crowd faded into an incoherent whooshing. There was only him and the ball. He had finally found it again—Balltopia. His blood buzzed with effervescent energy; once again Ashish felt completely in his element. The basketball court was his throne; in here, he was king. He'd reclaimed his place.

Ashish threw the ball up into the air. A moment after it left his fingertips, the buzzer sounded, signaling time. The ball whirled through the air . . . and whooshed through the basket. Nothing but net.

Ashish sank to his knees, his arms in the air, just as his teammates jumped on him, Oliver slapping his back and Elijah cheering so loudly, his ears were actually ringing. Through a break in the wall of bodies, he caught sight of Sweetie. She was crying and laughing at the same time, waving around a big foam finger. Ashish laughed and closed his eyes, relief and love and exhilaration washing through him.

When he had a break from all the congratulating and screaming, he began to jog over to his family, but a brown-skinned woman in her midthirties stepped in front of him. She held out a hand. He shook it; her grip was firm.

"Congrats on a game well played," she said, smiling. "I'm Liesa Lopez, scouting for USC. Here's my card. Call me and we'll talk."

Ashish took the card and grinned. "Sounds great."

She nodded at him and slipped away.

Laughing, Ashish ran over to his family.

Ma grabbed him in a hug, saying "*Shabash! Shabash, beta!*" over and over again. Pappa patted him on the back and looked like he'd burst. Sweetie hugged him, whispering "Congrats, baby" in his ear. It sent a shiver up his spine in the best way.

Then he turned to Rishi. And Dimple. His big brother stared at him, his eyes wide with wonder. "Dude," he said finally. "Oh my gods. You're, like, *epic*."

Ashish laughed, pleased. "*Bhaiyya*, Dimple, thank you for coming. Have you met Sweetie?"

Rishi grinned at him. "We have." Then, looking at Sweetie, he said, "You sure about this guy, though?"

Ashish slapped him on the chest, and Rishi made a big show of almost keeling over.

"You need to lay off the workouts, man," he said, gasping theatrically.

Behind her glasses, Dimple rolled her eyes. Turning to Sweetie, she said solemnly, "Welcome to dating a Patel brother. You are seriously in the best kind of trouble."

Sweetie laughed. "I'm getting that feeling."

Ashish bounced on the balls of his feet, still feeling the adrenaline from his win and this whole situation here. He didn't want to admit how much this meant to him. "So, *bhaiyya*," he said, trying not to sound as desperate as he felt, "do we, um, do we have your *aashirvad*?"

Rishi's face got serious. Dimple looked from him to Ashish, a small smile on her face. Putting his hands on Ashish's shoulders, Rishi said, "You and Sweetie have my utter and complete blessing, Ashish."

They hugged, Ashish patting Rishi on the back, hard, to keep from tearing up.

When they broke apart, Dimple had linked her arm with Sweetie's. "So," she said, "what do you guys think of a double date?"

Sweetie grinned. "Let's do it."

As Ashish looked around at his family—and he didn't care if it was silly, he totally included Sweetie under that umbrella—he thought, *Life can't get any more perfect than this.*

But they were young, and it did.

Acknowledgments

Writing the first book in the Dimple universe felt like a dream come true. Getting to write the second book, featuring two of my most favorite characters I've *ever* written, felt like basking in the glow of a thousand silver stars while eating the sun. In other words, it made me happy.

A big thank-you to the extraordinary team at Simon Pulse for being the warm and cozy home to my third young adult novel! Every writer should be so lucky to have a publishing house that feels like family. An especially big hug to Jen Ung, my editor, who helped me shape this book into what it is today and who totally *got* Sweetie from the beginning.

Thank you also to my agent, Thao Le, for being the best and feistiest champion any writer could ever ask for. Having a sounding board you can trust in this business is nothing short of a lifeline.

A huge shout-out to the splendiferous indies and booksellers out there, including my favorite fairy-god-book-people at: Anderson's Bookshop; B&N San Mateo; Book Bar Denver; Books, Inc.; Books of Wonder; Brookline Booksmith; Changing Hands; Elliot Bay Book Co.; Hicklebee's; Joseph-Beth; Kepler's; Old Firehouse Books; Once Upon a Time; Parnassus Books; Porter Square; Red Balloon

Bookshop; Ripped Bodice; Tattered Cover; Third Place Books; University Bookstore; and so many, many more!

Also, a big thank-you to the bookish community at large, including my lovely, steadfast readers who tweet at me about all my corny jokes and pop culture references and send me the most uplifting, flattering, and motivational emails ever! Thank you to librarians and teachers who reach out to say they're purchasing my books for the libraries and classrooms, who care so much about the youth they teach and encourage every day. You are truly an inspiration to me.

A big thank-you smooch to my loving family (even though I know you all laugh behind your hands when I trail off, midsentence, into a daydream about my characters). Without you, this would all be meaningless.

Last, but most important, I want to say to all my fat readers who've been told "fat" is a dirty, shameful word: They're wrong. You're enough. You always have been.

Don't miss the next hilarious, swoony romance from Sandhya Menon:

Turn the page for a sneak peek!

Pinky

The dead body was an especially nice touch.

Pinky Kumar grinned at her friend Ashish's prone figure.

"This is amazing," she said, touching Ash's face. It looked waxy and pale, and his lips were the exact right color of death. Well, what death *probably* looked like, anyway. "You said Sweetie did this?"

"Yeah, she took a stage-makeup class last year," Ash said, cracking open one translucent eyelid. "Does the hair look okay, though? I did that myself."

"The hair's poppin'," Pinky said, lifting up a few strands of the purple wig he wore, the thick locks falling past his shoulders. "You look like you could start shredding on a guitar any minute."

They were in Pinky's living room, where they'd lit a dozen LED candles all over the furniture and floor and drawn the shades for extra ambience. Ashish was lying on the couch, his arms crossed on his chest, barely breathing. Of their friend group, he was the only one who'd been able to help her out on short notice; everyone else had already flitted off to various holiday destinations. Ash himself was leaving for Hawaii later today.

"Okay, do you have what you need now?" Ash said, shifting a bit on the couch. "This wig's pretty itchy."

"Almost." Pinky stepped back and took a couple of pictures with her phone. "Let me get a wider angle. . . ."

"What charity's this for, again?" Ash asked, peeking at her through the fringe of his wig.

"Don't you ever listen when I talk?" Pinky asked, huffing a bit.

Ash laughed. "Seriously? This is, what, like, charity number thirty-two you're helping this week?"

He had a point. "Fine, fine. It's for the GoFundMe page of that nonprofit Super Metal Death," Pinky said, taking another picture. "They used to be just Metal Death, but they really amped up their community-outreach efforts last year."

Ash raised a thick eyebrow but kept his eyes closed. "Right, of course, Super Metal De—"

Pinky peeked out the big bay window. "Oh, crap."

A white Porsche Cayenne had just pulled up, and a moment later, her mother stepped out, eyes hidden by her sunglasses, Hermès pantsuit still perfect after an eleven-hour workday. She speed walked to the house, her thin face wearing that same harried, pinched expression it always did.

For just a moment, Pinky felt a surge of panic. Her mom was, at the best of times, an extremely formidable adversary. But when she'd had a busy day at work and just wanted to unwind with her Sudoku book and was instead confronted by yet another one of Pinky's special projects? Picture that girl from *The Exorcist*, with her head spinning, only instead of green vomit, Pinky's mom wore pantsuits and spewed straight-up acid.

"What?" Ash said, cracking open one eyelid. He itched his scalp, and his fingers moved his wig so it was now half covering his face. "What's wrong?"

But before Pinky could answer, her mom had opened the front door and was clip-clopping her way to the living room. Pinky stood there, frozen in indecision, and then it was too late. Her mom's shadow came first, and then her mom herself emerged into the living room, her sunglasses pushed up on the top of her head.

As she took in the transformation her once-perfect living room had gone through, her face went from pinched to blank to confused to—

"Priyanka! What the hell!" Her mother rushed to the couch, frowning. "Is that a doll?"

Pinky opened her mouth to tell her the truth, but then a tiny pinprick of gleeful defiance bloomed in her chest. Why did her mom insist on calling her "Priyanka" when she was mad, when she knew perfectly well Pinky despised her full name? Also, why was her mom so quick to judge all the time? Why couldn't she approach this situation with a joyful curiosity instead of freaking out? "No, it's not a doll. It's . . . a dead body."

Her mother stopped short, her face going sallow. "No, it's not," she said, but there was a thread of uncertainty in her voice as she took in the candles and the dark room and thought about all the things she likely did not know about her delinquent daughter.

Pinky stared at her mom without smiling—and then grinned. "You totally believed me, didn't you?"

Ash sat up, grinning too, and Pinky's mother shrieked and jumped backward.

"It's just Ashish, Mom," Pinky said, giving him a fist bump. "Pretty sick beat face, right?"

"Pretty what?" her mother said, blinking at the big dude on her couch. "*Ashish?* Is that really you?"

"Hey, Ms. K," Ash said, waving and pulling off his wig.

Her mom looked at the wig for a long moment and then back at Ashish. "Why are you . . . corpsing . . . on my couch?"

"It's for Super Metal Death," Pinky explained. "I'm raising money for them. They're crowdfunding to bring hot meals to band members from defunct bands. Did you know that eighty-two percent of formerly famous band members now live in homeless shelters?" She took a seat beside Ashish, her fishnets digging into her thigh a bit.

Her mother frowned. "There's no way that statistic is right."

Adjusting her position, Pinky swung her black military-style boots onto the couch. "Sure it is. People don't realize how brutal the music industry can be."

But her mother was glaring at her, no longer listening. "Get your shoes off the couch."

"What's the big deal?" Pinky said. "We're going to get them cleaned soon anyway."

There was a tense silence, and then her mother smiled a little at Ashish. "It was very nice seeing you, Ashish," she said. "Please tell your parents I send my regards." Turning to her own flesh-and-blood daughter, she added in a barely controlled voice, "Can I please speak with you . . . alone?"

Ash stood, looking nervous under the cadaverous makeup. "Ah, I better be going. See ya, P. Have a good summer vacay, Ms. Kumar."

"You too, Ashish." Her mother was doing one of those scary, plasticky smiles that made her look like a mannequin. Actually, *she'd* make a pretty good corpse.

Pinky flipped Ashish the peace sign even though her nerves were jangling at the prospect of the argument she knew was coming. "See you when I get back, Ash. Have fun in Hawaii. And tell Sweetie I said thanks for lending her makeup skills to a great cause."

Once the front door had closed behind him, Pinky leaned back against the couch, her arms crossed. The clock on the wall ticked. The air hummed.

Her mom said, in a super-calm voice, "Where's your father?"

Pinky shrugged. "I guess he's still at that meeting in Menlo Park."

"So you invited a boy here when you're home alone. That's against the rules, as you well know. Four days into summer break and you're already—" Her mom broke off and rubbed a hand over her forehead.

"Already what?" Pinky said, her heart starting to trot. When her mom remained silent, she changed tack. "Anyway, it wasn't a *boy*. It was just Ashish."

Pinky's mother pinched the bridge of her nose for a long moment, then walked to the entertainment unit to get the LED candle remote. She turned off all the candles and grabbed another remote to open the motorized blinds covering the big windows.

Turning back to Pinky in the suddenly bright room, she said, "Have you even started packing for the trip yet?"

"We're not leaving till tomorrow afternoon. I've got plenty of time."

Pinky's mom's stare turned icy. "No, you've *had* plenty of time. Pinky, come on. I just want you to be a bit more responsible. Stop spending your time on these ridiculous ventures that don't mean anything—"

Pinky held her breath for a moment. "They mean something to *me*," she said finally, quietly, bunching her fists up on her fishnet-covered thighs. "Why is that so hard for you to understand?"

"And I just want you to make better decisions," her mom said, looking down at her from her vantage, making Pinky feel even more like a little kid. "Why is that so hard for *you* to understand?"

They stared at each other, at one of their many, many impasses. Finally, her mother exhaled, broke eye contact, and unbuttoned her suit jacket. Taking it off, she hung it carefully over one arm.

"One day, Pinky." She shook her head, beginning to turn away. "One day you'll understand that I'm not your enemy. And one day you'll see why it hurts my heart when you insist on making these weak choices."

Pinky threw her hands up in the air, her ankh pendant swinging with the force of her movement. "I didn't make a weak choice! I'm helping charity! Name *one* weak choice I've made lately!"

"Aside from this one? All right," her mother said, turning slowly to face her again. "Preston."

Pinky felt her face close off. Crap. She'd completely forgotten about freaking Preston, her last boyfriend.

"Yeah?" she said, as if she didn't know where her mom was going with this. As if it wasn't the exact same place she'd gone with it ever since Pinky had brought Preston home (well, not exactly "brought him home" in the traditional sense. She'd sneaked him in her window and her parents had caught them).

Her mom gave her a *you know exactly what I'm talking about* look. "He got mandatory community service for something you still haven't disclosed to us."

Pinky groaned. "What's your point, Mom?"

"My point is that maybe this summer, if you happen to get a new boyfriend, as you usually do every month or so, you could find a *real* boyfriend. Someone who isn't prone to finding themselves on the wrong side of a jail cell."

As her mom walked off to the kitchen, Pinky narrowed her eyes. A "real" boyfriend? What'd her mom think Preston was, a ghoul? Besides, Pinky thought, slipping her phone out of her pocket to post her pictures to the Super Metal Death GoFundMe page, "real" boyfriends didn't exist in her world. Though, thanks to the little conversation they'd just had, that wouldn't stop her mom from micromanaging every cute guy Pinky hung out with this summer at their lake house. It would probably become her summer project or something.

One thing was certain: This summer vacation was going to majorly, definitely, monumentally suck.

A brand-new series from Sandhya Menon:

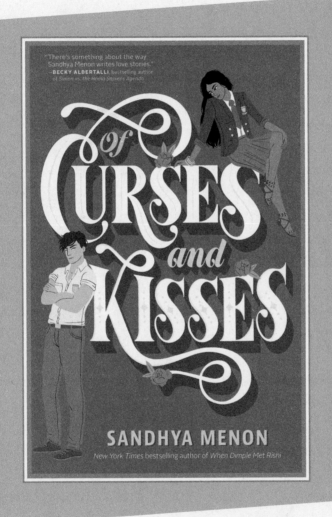

Turn the page for a sneak peek!

Jaya

Being a princess wasn't as glamorous as the media might have you believe. If the courtiers introduced her, say, in this fashion: "Her Royal Highness, Princess Jaya Rao of the Imperial House of Mysuru," most people would immediately picture Jaya cooing to birds and shaking hands with friendly mice, tiara glimmering in the summer sun. The entire Disney enterprise had a lot to answer for, in her opinion.

Jaya's reality was actually quite different. It was always, "Jaya, the townspeople want you to feed their lucky elephant so it'll win in the races tomorrow. Oh, and by the way, the elephant is in musth, so watch your dress" or "Jaya, the Prime Minister of Oppenheim is morally opposed to butter, so you cannot have any at breakfast either."

But it was all right. She was the heiress to the "throne" of Mysuru. (Technically, India was a democracy now, not a monarchy, but Jaya's family used to be the monarchy in this region and still carried the title.) Jaya understood that she would, at some point, have to grasp the reins. She'd have to take care of the city she lived in, just as her father had for years and her grandfather did before him. India wasn't supposed to have royal families—except the open secret was that they were still there, and people still looked to them to be benevolent, firm, and fair. Non-royals depended on them for jobs, for charity, and for a million other reasons Jaya was still learning. Maybe because of this, the Raos were placed upon a pedestal. They were, fairly or unfairly, expected to be perfect in every way; the common citizens needed them to be. The Raos family name and the royal traditions that bound them were everything.

And that was precisely why she had to do what she was about to do. She might be a princess, her parents' firstborn child and the heiress ascendant to the throne, but that wasn't all of her story.

They stood in the grand marble entrance with their small bags. Jaya tipped her head back to look at the enormous crystal chandelier suspended like a dewdrop above her head. The rose pendant hung heavy from her neck, eighteen rubies glinting like watchful eyes, reminding her why she was there.

Isha whistled, low and long, and Jaya glared at her. She cut off mid-whistle, looking only slightly abashed. "Nice setup," she whispered, but her words echoed anyway. "Nicer than our last boarding school in Benenden, even. And the English *really* know boarding schools."

The wall before them was adorned with flags of more than three dozen countries. A gold-plated sign above them boasted "Our students come from around the world!" Jaya's gaze was drawn automatically toward the flags she knew very well—India, of course, along with the US, UK, UAE, China, Japan, Mauritius, and Switzerland. She'd spent summer holidays in all these places and lived in most of them, reading in cafés and parks while Isha foraged through thrift stores, searching for gears or batteries for whatever contraption she was working on.

The floor was drenched in sea-green tiles inlaid with gold, a splash of oceanic beauty here in the mountains. Jaya had heard it rumored that these were a gift from the Moroccan king half a century ago, when his son had been exiled here after an embarrassment of some kind. She hadn't ever unearthed what that scandal was—St. Rosetta's was *very* good at burying what they didn't want found—though she felt a kinship with the king. He wasn't the only one who'd shouldered the responsibility of protecting a wayward family member. Jaya's eyes fluttered to Isha unwittingly, and she forced them away.

Isha gripped her arm, pointing to the wall on their right. "Look!" she whispered. "Is that . . . ?"

They ogled a cluster of colorful paintings, large and small, that contrasted with the Moroccan tiles, depicting smooth desert landscapes that lifted off the page and caressed the eye. "I think so," Jaya whispered back, thrilled. She wasn't sure exactly *why* they were whispering. Maybe because they were in the presence of greatness? It was probably why people felt compelled to whisper in libraries, too. "Georgia O'Keeffe spent a semester here as a teen, and later donated paintings to the school as a thank-you."

Before Isha could respond, thunderous footfalls came rushing down the opulent marble stairs that faced away from them. Without even turning to look, Jaya could guess from the boisterous, deep laughter that it was a couple of boys, though the sheer amount of noise could also indicate a herd of buffalo.

"Come on," her sister said, tugging her forward.

Jaya grasped her wrist and shook her head. "Isha."

"What?" Isha said, her brown eyes wide. "I just want to get to know our schoolmates. We have to spend the next year or two here with them anyway."

As if Jaya trusted those innocent doe eyes. Isha thought she was much more naive than she really was. Lowering her voice, Jaya said, "And boys have gotten you in trouble in the past."

"That is so typical," Isha hissed. "You treat me like such a baby sometimes. It wasn't *boys* that got me in trouble. It was the stupid rules."

Jaya opened her mouth to respond—something scathing about the virtues of rules; she hadn't worked out the details yet—but a jovial voice interrupted.

"*Bonjour!* Are you beautiful ladies new?"

Jaya turned toward the rich French-accented voice. Two boys had rounded the corner and now stood before them. The tall, broad one who had just spoken smiled warmly, like he was greeting old friends. His skin was a golden brown and his straight dark hair hung to his shoulders. Jaya was fairly good at guessing ethnicities, and she thought he was likely a blend of Southeast Asian and Western European.

Isha set her bag down and stepped forward before Jaya could stop her, proffering a hand. "Isha Rao. This is my sister, Jaya. I'm a sophomore, and she's a senior." They shook, and Jaya managed not to wince at Isha's firm handshake, a reminder of her sister's . . . indomitable spirit.